Scattered

John Harvey

SCATTERED

Published 2025 by On-site Creative
OnsiteCreative.ca

ISBN: 9781777720063

FOR MICHELLE.

Prologue

Danny Kou was drowning.

He'd dived into the flooded chamber not knowing whether Pieter had opened the portal. And even if he had, there was no guarantee he'd left it open. After all, Danny had betrayed him.

A stream of bubbles swirled past as he descended; the portal was still open. He followed the trail to a three-foot diameter ring at floor level, then thrust his left hand through the opening. Instantly, a gauntlet of pain seized his arm. *Too fast*, he thought. The wormhole was unstable. He'd have to move slowly to avoid a collapse.

Fighting the instinct to draw a breath, he drifted through the ring at an agonizing pace. The shredding sensation at the wormhole's threshold faded to an annoying prickle, and his left hand had gone entirely numb, but at least it was still attached to his arm.

Finally, he drew his legs through. A circle of light in the ceiling pointed to the room's only safe exit, and he knew exactly where he was now. He was back on Earth, in Detroit. And in mortal danger.

Swimming upwards, he glided into the same narrow tube he'd climbed less than a week ago. The passage had been dry then, and he'd been placing explosives at key points throughout the factory. Those bombs were timed to go off at midnight, only a minute from now.

Danny broke the surface and rolled onto the floor of a tall, slender compartment. The space was lit by the glare of streetlights through a gaping hole in its exterior wall: a victim of Pieter's rage. There was no sign of his former employer, so he staggered to his feet and raced through a doorway underneath a red emergency light. He sped for the nearest stairwell and burst into an empty lobby, where gleaming metal lettering on the wall behind the reception desk welcomed him to Armenau Industries.

He sprinted for the door. In the parking lot, security guards were marshaling graveyard shift employees through the front gate. Danny turned the other way and ran for the fence.

In seconds, Cirrus—the world-sized space station he'd just fled—would be isolated from Earth, possibly forever. And if he had his way, he alone would control who could return.

He lunged for the fence's top rail as twenty-eight bombs exploded simultaneously.

Chapter 1

Jack Scatter waited in the cramped hollow formed by a trio of pine trees. He was nearly invisible in his jeans and blue hoodie, on which he'd blacked out the stenciled lettering. When the moonlight returned, he crept forward again, concentrating on the spell that guided his feet to where they would make the least noise. His opponents, unseen but nearby, were skilled and potentially lethal. One was a martial artist armed with a magical bo staff, and the other could predict the future and had a penchant for throwing fireballs.

He stepped over a fallen branch, and his foot was only inches above the ground when a ghostly footprint appeared two inches to the left. The spell wasn't perfect, but it was only giving him one choice, so he shifted his weight to land directly on the pale mark and sank into a carpet of birch leaves without a sound.

Forty yards, he thought. He could see the cache now in the moonlight: a camouflaged tarp strung between two trees. He eased the other foot over but no marker appeared. *They're close. Time for another spell.*

Crouching to hide in the dense undergrowth, he twirled his wand in a circle near his ear, and the music of distant crickets became a thunderous orchestra. *Filter.* The insects faded and were replaced by a chorus of tree frogs. *Filter.* He silently repeated the command until the only sound was of grass stirred by the cool evening breeze. *Of course, that's exactly what someone approaching using a stealth spell would sound like.*

Returning to the first spell, Jack willed the forest floor to show a safe path, and a pair of footprints appeared at the same moment light flickered in his peripheral vision. He glanced around but saw nothing moving, and when he looked down again, he had a dozen prints to choose from. *Too many possible futures.* Then they started dancing. *It's a trick.*

He'd opened his mind to the AI, and a foe had slipped in an illusion. That was the downside of ongoing spells. They left the caster vulnerable. He guarded his thoughts and the prints vanished. But had he been seen? Or heard? One thing was certain; he couldn't stand there forever. He lowered his foot gently, snapping a twig under his shoe.

The response was immediate. Intense light illuminated the forest as a ball of blue plasma sped through the trees. Jack created a shield and crouched low before the caged lightning splashed against his invisible barrier. Even so, he felt its heat and smelled ozone.

He dove and rolled behind a tree. Hugging the trunk, he pointed his wand and cast a whirlwind. An expanding cone of leaves, bark, and soil hurtled through the forest. It had almost reached his attacker's likely hiding spot when another plasma ball erupted from his left, so close he had to neglect his own attack and raise a new shield. But instead of scattering, the glowing ball passed through his defense without slowing. He threw himself backwards, narrowly avoiding a serious burn.

No, wait. The plasma attack had carried no heat, no ozone. *Another illusion.* "That does it," he bellowed.

More angry at himself than his assailant, Jack abandoned guided attacks and hijacked the portal of a snowmaking machine. Instead of glazing the slopes of a luxury resort on Earth, its ice crystals were diverted to his wand, where he used the wormhole's energy field to compress them into solid pellets, and sprayed them in a ruthless hail without aiming as he ran. The pellets wouldn't seriously harm anyone, but they'd keep his attacker busy. More importantly, he didn't have to focus on the task or risk another intrusion into his thoughts.

The cache was only steps away. He charged through a patch of ferns, hurdled a stump, and threw the tarp aside, eager to capture his prize.

"What the ...?" The only object in the shelter was a twenty-pound quivering mass of lime gelatin in the shape of a flag. He shouted, "That's cheating, Ethan. I can't carry that."

Jack's cousin, Ethan Marke, laughed and stepped out of the gloom. He was also dressed entirely in dark clothing, and his shoulder-length black hair stood in for a hoodie. He poked the wobbly flag with his staff. "Sure you can. You could freeze it, or—"

"The whole point of three-way capture the flag is to get *both* of our opponents' flags. We should be able to carry them, not have to use another spell to deal with them."

Ethan shrugged. "The only rule was that we hide a flag. What's yours made of?"

Jack crossed his arms. "It's an actual flag made from cloth."

"What about the pole?"

"Real wood."

Ethan narrowed his eyes. "How long?"

Jack couldn't pretend anymore, and snickered. "About sixteen feet."

Ethan threw up his hands. "How is that any better?"

Curbing his laughter, Jack asked. "Where'd you get the gelatin from?"

"Sarah helped me find it. She thinks it's from a hospital cafeteria. They'll never miss it." He shuffled his feet, mimicking a popular dance move. "What did you think of the extra footprints?"

Jack frowned. "I should have noticed how big and clumsy they were." He looked toward the lake. "I wonder if I can still get past Sarah?"

She stepped out suddenly from behind a tree. "I doubt it."

"*Gah.*" Jack stumbled as he spun away from her.

"I'm sorry." Sarah stifled a laugh as she flipped back her hood. Like Jack, she had covered the name of their high school to create her stealthy attire. "I couldn't help it. I tried to ignore my intuition, but I still remembered what path you took."

In the seven months since they'd been cut off from Earth and discovered the technology they now called *magic*, Sarah Rogers had mastered a range of skills. Like Jack, she could tap distant portals for their resources, but the *Traveller Effect* also supplied glimpses of her future in a form indistinguishable from her own memories.

Ethan stretched out an arm to help Jack stand. "You know, we'll never be able to do this fairly. Sarah will always know weeks ahead of time what path either of us will take, and you can come up with new spells on demand. Or just sense our crystals unless we're constantly shielded."

"Your two-second warning will eventually be better than my two weeks," Sarah said. "The more often we practice, the more paths I have to remember."

Jack brushed himself off. "You're right. The next time we do this, we'll—" A snapping noise interrupted. Something had fallen through nearby branches, too loud and fast to be natural.

The large crystal mounted at the center of Ethan's staff brightened. "What was that?" He shifted into a defensive posture. At six-feet tall, and with twenty pounds more muscle than Jack, he could be an intimidating figure even when unarmed.

"It's a portal crystal, for sure." Jack pointed his wand. "That way."

Sarah summoned a fireball, which lit the forest with an orange glow as she held it ready to launch from the tip of her own wand. Jack kept his wand up, and his portal-sense led them directly to the fallen object: a gold-plated disc with a shiny central gem.

Picking it up, Ethan spelled a light from one of the four gemstones on his ring, then flipped it over to expose a tracery of delicate lines that looked more like geometric art than circuitry. Disc-mounted portal crystals had been used for decades in everything from power cells to phones, but this one was different. "It's one of Pieter's *Third-Eye* coins."

"How long do you think they'll be falling for?" Sarah asked. She knew what they were because she'd helped disrupt Pieter's plan for using the coins to monitor and control high-level government officials.

"Years, probably." Jack winced at the memory. He'd been there when Pieter's chief engineer destroyed his own shuttle and launched the coins into orbit around Cirrus. "There were five million on Simon's ship when it disintegrated."

"Should we keep it?" Ethan asked.

"*Are you serious?* Dragons can sense these farther than I can. There's nowhere in the village they won't find it."

He scoffed. "How often is a dragon going to come near Icarus?"

"They're obsessed with those coins. I sensed one circling the village last week."

Ethan paled. "*And you didn't tell us?*"

"I would have liked to meet another dragon," Sarah said.

Jack gestured towards the lake. "They swam over to the island. I think they're living there."

Ethan shivered. He didn't even like snakes. "Actually, I'm glad you didn't tell us. I wouldn't be able to sleep knowing it was near."

"*They,*" Sarah corrected, "not *it*. Dragons are intelligent, and they're grown, not bred, so they don't have gender."

"Fine." Ethan rolled his eyes. "I'm not a fan of *them*."

"They won't bother us as long as we don't bother them," Jack said.

"Says the only person who can talk to them. Is that why Dusty was so anxious the other day? Did she know they were around?"

"I'm sure she knew before they showed up."

Dusty, Ethan's golden retriever, was psychic. At least that's how Jack liked to think of it. She was, in fact, the canine version of a *Traveller*—someone who could *remember* their own future through a portal-enabled interaction with an artificial intelligence. But unlike humans, Dusty used her AI memories to sneak up on squirrels.

"What should we do with the coin?" Sarah asked.

Jack levitated it with his wand. "I'll get rid of it."

He flew it at eye level to the limit of his range, about sixty feet, then lined up with a break in the trees and swung his arm over his head in a smooth arc. The coin—at the end of an invisible tether—followed his movement, and by the time he released it, the golden disc was moving at supersonic speed. A whip-like crack signaled the start of a miles-long flight away from the village.

"Should we play again tomorrow night?" Ethan turned to Sarah as they resumed walking. "What's the weather going to be like?"

"I'm not your personal weather forecaster. And we can't tomorrow because of Priya, remember?" She registered his surprise. "Oh, sorry—Traveller-memory." Then she said brightly, "Priya's going to call."

Jack didn't doubt that Sarah was right. Even if she only recalled fragments, she always knew when the event would happen. "What about?"

"I don't know." A worried look crossed her face. "I don't think even *she* knows yet. But it'll be important."

Chapter 2

Seattle stinks, Priya thought.

Of course, if she were still in Olympia, she'd be thinking the same thing about her hometown.

Regardless, she couldn't ignore the smell as she scouted the city's industrial section. Once a model of environmental management, it now choked under the exhaust of massive generators burning the world's remaining reserves of bunker fuel, and foul, ochre streams flowed into the gutters from trash piled in streets once maintained by an army of sweeper bots.

She'd followed a tip to the city's high-tech core, where skeletons of empty warehouses rusted behind shattered glass panels. After two days of searching, she was certain that Angel was hiding in the office building across the street. And if anyone could lead her to Pieter Reynard, it was Angel.

Like its neighbors, the four-story structure had been looted, but the garbage bags piled in front of the doors only made sense if someone wanted to discourage vandals from entering. She raised her binoculars to study the boarded-up, ground-floor windows again. A jungle of overlapping graffiti proclaimed messages of hope, despair, hate, love, or just the artist's tag, and a stylized 'S' caught her attention, not because of its bold color, but because of a break in its swooping curve.

Got you. A small rectangle had been cut at eye-level from one edge of the plywood sheet.

Backtracking from her hideout, Priya turned her jacket inside-out to hide the word POLICE written in large white letters on its back. Without streetlights she'd be nearly invisible to anyone watching, though not entirely safe: Pieter could predict the future and would have warned Angel of her arrival.

Despite the relative handicap of being confined to the present, she wasn't without extrasensory weapons. She drew her phone as she entered the alley behind the office building, pressed a faded lightbulb icon, and the dimly lit passage brightened for her eyes only.

While not as effective as it was for Jack and his friends, the spell processed invisible energy streaming from the phone's tiny wormhole and fed it to Priya as a memory: a lesser form of the Traveller Effect. So, she wasn't exactly *seeing* the back door. She was *remembering* it in real time with enough detail to read the painted sign: employees only.

Vaulting onto the loading deck, she slipped her hand into the two-inch gap below the roll shutter, which rattled when she applied pressure. *That'll make as much noise as any alarm.* Then she tried the handle of the adjacent door. *Locked, but not a problem.*

One of Jack's programmed spells was a burglar's fantasy: a forcefield-pick that worked on any lock. She placed the phone against the door, tapped its icon, and heard several soft clicks. Cautiously, she swung the door open.

The corridor was windowless, so Priya raised her phone and activated the light spell again. Under its false glow, every door was open except for the one at the end of the hall. But a bundle of aluminum ducts blocked the path, and her intuition bristled. The tubes were not only out of place in a building completed decades ago, they were balanced on their ends instead of stacked horizontally. She knelt on the grubby tiles and ran her phone along their base.

Trip wire. Without the memory-light, she'd have caught the nearly invisible ankle-height thread for sure. That would have pulled the tubes down, alerting anyone in this half of the building.

She drew her weapon, stepped over the taut string, and crept the final steps to the steel fire door. Slowly, she turned the knob, but the door didn't open. The problem wasn't the lock. It was the deadbolt six inches above.

Priya let out the breath she hadn't realized she'd been holding. This was good news. A deadbolt could be released from the inside without a key, and her spell could do that silently. She held the phone by the lock and tapped the icon again. The bolt glided home. Then she crouched and eased the door open.

Duck.

Something whooshed over her head, snagging stray hairs before shattering against the metal doorjamb, and wooden shards bounced off her jacket.

At five-three, Priya's height and intuition had saved her from serious injury; the man in the room stood six-four and had swung the 2x4 like a bat. She lunged and drove her head into his abdomen, producing a satisfying 'woof' as she forced the air from his lungs. The move wouldn't have won respect at her dojo, but it was as effective as any of the traditional strikes she'd employed while earning her third-level black belt.

Angel tried to swing again but Priya was quicker. She dropped low and swept her foot into his. Already off balance, he went down hard, and Priya leaped onto his back and wrapped her arms around his neck. He struggled briefly—too briefly—before passing out.

Panicking, she flipped him over and checked for a pulse; capturing Pieter's personal bodyguard shouldn't have been so easy. Under her hands, his gaunt shoulders felt at odds with his broad frame, and a scruffy beard faded into his collar, covering his neck tattoo. Luckily, he was still alive.

Moonlight shining through the notch in the plywood illuminated an unexpected squalor. Apparently, Angel had been *living* in the abandoned office, and from the looks of it, not very well. Other than a thin mattress on the floor, the only furniture was a chair by the window. Priya stepped over him and peered through the opening. *Naef Dynamics.*

It hadn't occurred to her that she'd be able to see the entrance to Holden Marke's former laboratory from here, but the buildings in between were set far enough back from the street to frame Naef's glass doors in the notch. Angel had chosen the ideal spot to watch from without being seen.

She aimed her binoculars through the window. Someone,

probably Angel, had blocked one door with garbage and propped a painted steel bar across the other, bisecting the door into two triangles. Even without binoculars, Angel would know at a glance that someone had entered Naef.

Why watch from a distance? And why had he been doing it for so long? She focused again on Naef, and the fragmented glass that had once hidden three stories of windowless concrete walls: shielding for the many portals within. If Angel had been willing to commit months to watching the building, that's where she'd find an answer. And, hopefully, Pieter.

• • • •

Priya woke Angel by dumping cold water over his head. He swore loudly and lunged at her before realizing he was tied to his chair.

"Morning, tough guy." She swirled the remaining water in the plastic bucket. "Where's your boss?"

Angel struggled briefly with the ropes binding his wrists and ankles. "Aren't you out of your jurisdiction?"

She threw the rest of the bucket at him.

He laughed and shook the water from his hair. "Is that supposed to upset me?"

"No." She tossed the bucket through the open door, where it rolled into a stream of effluent flowing from the overloaded sewer. "But I've run out of clean water."

Angel winced but held his tongue.

Dragging a wooden crate over to sit on, she faced him solemnly. "Why are you protecting him? You're here, so obviously Pieter didn't think enough of you to take you back to Cirrus." A slight furrowing of his brow told Priya she was on the right track, but Angel wouldn't be swayed by a simple play on his emotions.

"You didn't put up much of a fight, did you? And you've lost a lot of weight since I last saw you. It can't be easy for a vegan to get enough protein these days. How long have you been waiting anyway?" She gestured at the blankets piled at the foot of his mattress, which were far too heavy for late-March. "A month? Two?"

Angel remained stubbornly silent while his body language betrayed him. He'd been having doubts.

"I visited Marke's lab while you were sleeping. There's been no one there for months, the same as Pieter's office downtown. The portal frames are damaged, and their crystals are missing. Pieter's not coming back for you." She stood and made to leave.

"Wait." Angel's voice was plaintive. "I can help you."

"How? Wherever he is, you're no longer part of his plans."

"Not Pieter. I can lead you to Danny Kou."

Now it was Priya's turn to be silent. Until now she'd thought that Danny, Pieter's former head of security, had drowned in a sealed water tank on Cirrus. She crossed her arms, letting Angel know he'd have to give her more.

"Pieter sent me back to Earth to find Danny. He wanted revenge." Angel then painted a picture of a man tormented. He was irrational, quick to anger, and suffering from insomnia: symptoms Priya recognized as the mental decay associated with too much portal travel. "And not just with Danny. He was obsessed with that kid, Jack, and *magic*." He said the word like it tasted foul. "I haven't seen Danny, but I know how to find him."

Priya let him wait in silence while she deliberated. Danny's plans for Cirrus were even more dire than Pieter's. "Tell me."

"I want something in exchange."

"What?"

"A letter of recommendation."

"You're applying for a job?"

"No, I want to go to Dawn, but … I've got a record."

"Seriously? You're a henchman for the worst corporate villain in history. The man who engineered *Newton.* The man who destroyed a billion portals."

"Was. You said yourself, Pieter's not coming back."

Priya turned and started to walk away. "You need a lawyer. I can't help you."

"Actually, you can. I've never committed a felony. All I did—"

She rounded on him. "*Never committed a felony?* I could recommend you for a dozen firearms offences."

"Okay, I've never been convicted. All I did for Pieter was act a part. I've only ever been charged with a misdemeanor; I borrowed my old man's car when I left home at fifteen. A juvenile offence doesn't bar me from emigrating, but I need an official letter just to submit an application."

Priya didn't want to argue with Angel, who seemed to think that not getting caught was the same as not guilty. "Why do you want to go to Dawn?"

"Why wouldn't I? Clean air. Clean water. Plenty of food. A fresh start. A chance to have a real life. Earth is *done*. Cirrus is *done*." Angel met her eyes with a determined gaze. "Why aren't *you* going?"

Priya didn't answer right away. She couldn't deny the appeal of a pristine world whose infrastructure had been prepared over twenty years by armies of self-replicating robots. In fact, after enduring seven months of blackouts and water shortages while searching in vain for Pieter, she'd been asking herself that same question. "Tell me where Danny is."

"There's a notebook in the bag beside my bed. It was Simon's before ..." Angel paused, looking genuinely remorseful. "I made sure he got on that shuttle, even though I thought he'd had some sort of breakdown. I told myself I was just following orders ... I should have stopped him."

Priya knew exactly what state Simon's mind was in, and let Angel wallow in guilt. Simon had been virtually enslaved by Pieter's mind-control technology. But in the end, he'd found a way to defeat Pieter while still following orders. She retrieved the notebook, wondering what else Pieter's chief engineer had discovered before sacrificing his life.

Angel continued as she examined the writing. "It's all math and strange symbols except for the addresses he wrote on the last page. One of those is where Danny's portal is. He's been moving gear to Cirrus for months."

"You're sure?"

"The dude who gave it to me has been doing small jobs for him."

"Who was that?"

"Don't know his name. Native American. Slim build."

Paul. Priya unfolded a mugshot she'd been carrying in her pocket. "Is this him?"

"Yeah. Who is he?"

She tucked the page away. "The same guy who told me where to find *you.*"

Chapter 3

Jada leaned her rake against Sarah's outdoor worktable behind the barn. "Don't overthink it."

"Huh?" Sarah hadn't heard her friend approaching over the bleating of the goats in a nearby pen. "How did you know what I was thinking?"

"Because you always get that faraway look, and you always say it's because you're confused about a Traveller-memory, and you *always* remind yourself that you shouldn't overthink it. Take a walk; you'll feel better."

Sarah set her tools down. "You're right. I need a break." She arched her back and touched her chin to her shoulders to stretch her muscles. "This wooden bench isn't the most comfortable seat, either. But it's safer than working indoors."

She idly brushed the scorch mark that covered half the table. Last week, instead of waiting for Jack, she'd tried sourcing argon gas for a welding spell and ended up streaming propane from her wand. He was much better at identifying wormholes and had once been able to divert French fries from what they assumed was a restaurant chain's central factory. They had no idea where on Earth that portal was, but a three-second burst from it would fill a bucket with steaming-hot fries. There was little chance anyone would notice such a small amount of their product missing, and they'd only stopped using it because the restaurant had switched to yam fries.

"What's troubling you this time?" Jada asked.

"Priya hasn't called in weeks. I was already having horrible thoughts when I had the Traveller-memory, and now that's all I can think of."

"But you know she's going to call, so she must be okay. Right?"

"I guess." Sarah flipped over the hexagonal plate she was assembling to check the crystal. Its pearlescent surface reflected the mid-morning sun. "I just want good news for once."

Jada noticed the stack of hexes Sarah had assembled. "Are those new? Can I try one?"

"Sure, they're—*wait*."

Before Sarah could explain, Jada grabbed the hex and backhanded it at Marten, who was walking past the village's tractor at a distance of fifteen yards. The wafer-thin disc struck the ground near his feet and shattered. Marten, completely unaware of the attack, stumbled and fell on the gravel path, even though he hadn't been hit.

Jada's face lit up. "*Cool.*"

"*You're not supposed to throw a hex if you don't know what it does!*" Sarah jumped and ran to help Marten.

"Relax." Jada waved dismissively. "I knew you'd stop me if it was *really* dangerous."

Marten was trying to stand on wobbly legs. "*What was that?*"

"A forced-memory hex." Sarah braced his arm as he swayed towards a split-rail fence. "Are you okay?"

"Yeah." He was steadier now, a good thing because he towered over Sarah at six-foot-five. "I just got clumsy for a second. And your voice is echoing."

"That's because the spell replays the last second of your memory. You might think you know where you're stepping, but your foot is already one move ahead." She kicked aside the crystal shards, which were disintegrating into the soil. "It should stop soon."

Marten poked his shoe at the still-solid fragments of ceramic, which had held the hexagonal crystal rigid as it flew. "I feel like we've done this already. Is that the déjà vu Travellers talk about?" He seemed more stable as the last bits of crystal disappeared.

"That only happens when you pass *through* a portal. This probably seems familiar because Jada's thrown hexes at you before." She glanced back at her best friend before asking, "Are you two fighting again?"

"I thought we were finally getting along." He smiled weakly

and waved at Jada, who was writing on Sarah's hexes. "Thanks for experimenting on me. Really appreciate it."

Jada said something in Hindi that Sarah didn't recognize. It sounded almost playful.

"Actually," Sarah said quietly, "I think this might be how Jada makes friends." She suspected that Jada had a crush on Marten, who, at nineteen, was two years older than them.

"Great. Just don't give her any more of those electric-shock hexes until she's made up her mind." Marten lumbered away to finish his chores.

When Sarah returned to the table, Jada had written 'Fumble' on the gray ceramic side of the new hexes. That thin slice of pottery provided not only a solid backing, but also the weight necessary for a good throw, and metal clasps at each of its six corners held the crystal in place.

"You're very organized today," she said as Jada placed hexes into a leather case with two silver latches. "Where did you get that from?"

"The case? From Terrance. Why?"

"It's just really familiar. It looks like it should hold something important."

"Nah. He used it for cards and poker chips. See, they're a perfect fit."

Except for their shape, the hexes were the same size as poker chips, and Jada had grouped them by color. Red hexes involved fire or heat, blue ones were related to water, and green indicated gasses. The white group was Sarah's specialty: they manipulated a person's memory through the AI's emotion detectors and motivators.

"I needed something secure to store them in for our trip." Jada added an emerald hex—which would emit a stinky cloud of the sulfur added to natural gas—to her collection. "Can you imagine if they broke and released every spell at once?" She mimed an explosion, then laughed.

"What trip?"

"Daddy found a new hamlet south of Aetherton, and Marten and I volunteered to bring them a set of solar panels."

"Marten volunteered?"

"Well, maybe I volunteered him. But it'll be good for him; he hasn't left the village in a month."

Since Newton, people had been leaving the cities to found homesteads near abandoned mills or transfer stations. But all those new settlements lacked one thing: power. Suresh, Jada's father, had convinced the village council to restart Icarus' solar panel factory and share the tech with others. Making a delivery run was about the only way any of them got a break from a day of work on the farm.

"I understand the solar panels," Sarah said, "but why are you taking hexes? We should encourage trade with other communities, not scare them half to death."

"You and Jack take your wands wherever you go. What's the difference? Anyway, I don't plan on using them. They're just a precaution. Somebody has to keep Marten safe." She bit her lower lip and mimed flinging another hex.

"Sure, but who'll keep Marten safe from *you*?"

Jada laughed. Though only five-two, she was a natural fighter and had been the first to experiment with throwing hexes, and was deadly accurate up to twenty yards. Months of farm work had changed her physique as well. Last year, colorful tattoos were her most notable feature. Now, her biceps and shoulders reminded Sarah of a professional wrestler.

"When do you leave?"

"Daddy wants us on the road before noon, so we reach the hamlet in daylight."

• • • •

After lunch, Jack went to his grandfather's place to find Sarah and Ethan. That's where the radio was kept, and Sarah would be waiting for Priya's call. Like the rest of the village, Holden's cabin had been 3D-printed from low-density concrete, sculpted and textured to resemble logs, but he'd converted his second bedroom into a workshop and become the keeper of all things electronic.

Ethan was there raiding the fridge, and Sarah was idly thumbing through one of the many technical manuals Holden had brought from Earth. Jack flopped onto the sofa beside her and nudged her with his shoulder. "You don't look like you're interested in that. What's wrong?"

She set the book on the coffee table beside a stack of cast-off crystals from Holden's experiments. "Do you ever think we should tell people about your grandfather's portal?"

"You know I do. You should have seen the dirty looks I got welding a bracket for Ethan's staff onto Terrance's bike. If they knew where *magic*"—he made air quotes around the word—"comes from, they wouldn't be bothered by it."

"Not just the villagers. Everyone."

"Oh, that's different." Jack stared at the floor while he thought. "I'm not sure, then. They might not use it safely."

"Or they might be responsible with it."

"Yeah, maybe. After all, they can't be much worse than Ethan."

Ethan, sitting at the dining table, aimed a forced smile at Jack.

"Jada wants a hex to turn herself invisible," Sarah said. "I told her that's not possible."

"Well …" Jack reclined and focused on the ceiling. His grandfather's cabin was full of tools and gadgets, and a great place for him to slip into a creative frame of mind. "It wouldn't be too different from a standard illusion. If the person you wanted to hide from had a strong bond with their crystal—"

Ethan interrupted with an exaggerated imitation of Jack. "You could connect the modulator and get a squirrel to run the treadmill"—he slid a finger up the bridge of his nose to reseat an imaginary pair of glasses—"and combine the frequencies—"

"*I don't talk like that,*" Jack snapped. "And I don't wear glasses, either. I'm just saying it's possible with the right combination of spells. An illusion is essentially a memory that you—"

Sarah laughed as he proved Ethan's point. "Sorry, but you do talk like that. And it's adorable, though it's not actually helping."

"Hey, I like solving problems. I didn't say I'd build one for her."

"You should," Ethan said.

"Yeah, right. I don't think that would make people more tolerant."

"See, that's your problem. I never think about anything; I just do it." He tossed a cherry tomato into the air and caught it in his mouth with his eyes closed.

"Good thing you've got a two-second warning, then," Jack said. "I have to consider how the spells I store in a hex crystal will work in *real* time. Besides, I'm not very good at illusions."

"Sarah could do it."

"That's not the point." He and Sarah had very different strengths. Whereas he could create a spell that would juggle six balls while painting a shed; she could craft one that made you think everything tasted of cinnamon. "The point *is*, we're protecting our future. If it hadn't been for Newton, we would all be graduating in a few months. You guys would be in college and I'd be running my drone repair business. Instead, we're playing wargames and experimenting with new spells so we can defend ourselves against Pieter. He'll never stop looking for Grandpa's portal."

"Which is why we should let someone else use it," Sarah said. "If they understood *why* we're practicing magic; they wouldn't be scared of it."

"Okay, but remember that *using it* means traveling to Earth." Jack knew that, despite Ethan's flippant remarks, his cousin wasn't the type of person they had to worry about. "Who would you let go through? Jada? What if that gave her the ability to devise her own spells?"

"Well ..." Sarah considered the pile of crystals they'd eventually convert to hexes. "Maybe not Jada."

"I'm happy with the way things are." Ethan stood and headed for the door. "I'll see you guys later."

Holden's radio emitted a soft beep and Priya's voice sounded from the speaker. "Holden? Are you there?"

Sarah dove for the handheld radio resting in a charging cradle on the kitchen counter. "It's Sarah. Is everything all right? I was worried."

"I'm fine. I got caught up with work."

"We can pick you up in three hours."

"Not tonight. I'm taking a room at the inn. Come over in the morning."

"You want us to come to Earth?" Sarah glanced uneasily at Jack; Priya *never* wanted them to visit. "What's wrong?"

"Nothing. There's an event I want you to observe at the Capitol tomorrow. It might run late. Tell your parents you'll be staying the night."

"We can come up now." She looked to Jack for confirmation.

Priya's voice was firm. "It can wait until morning."

"Then we'll be driving in the dark." Sarah's argument was pointless. Though Holden's portal frame—the only one in existence that could transport radioactive materials—was hidden in a cave high in the Spine, her night vision spells were better than headlights. Jack knew that Priya knew this, but Sarah didn't give up. "There's still time today."

"Fine," Priya said, "but wait for me. I'll be back at the inn by nine." She disconnected.

"Let's go." Sarah leaped for the door. "I'll grab my coat."

"We have time." Jack still had his feet on the coffee table. "Priya says she won't be there right away, anyway."

"I know, but … Let's just go." Her voice faded as she ran to the cabin she shared with her mother.

Jack sighed and pushed himself off the couch, then said to no one, "I guess we're going *now*."

Chapter 4

Danny hated tea. In his youth, his parents had made him attend traditional tea ceremonies. His father thought it would encourage patience and respect in the young man who'd been in constant trouble at school.

While his behavior had not improved, *Appa* had been right about patience. Danny had been waiting silently for Mentor for ninety minutes, despite the antechamber's oppressive heat and hazy layers of incense hanging in the stagnant air. He could manage hours if he had to. So could the guards on either side of the elaborately carved arch.

Not guards, Danny thought, *acolytes*. The men, the only two in the entire organization he could not command, answered only to Mentor. He'd been studying them since one had placed a cup of tea on the low table before him, and decided they were more like disciples than protectors. *But not entirely defenseless*. He was certain they wore body armor under their loose robes.

Almost as much as tea, Danny despised the pomp and ceremony Mentor reveled in. They had styled this room as an ancient Greek temple, situating themselves as its oracle. If their rate of accurate predictions had not greatly surpassed Pythia's, he would not have tolerated such folly.

He was not unfamiliar with the lavish lifestyle Mentor preferred. His family—*his entire country, even*—had suffered generations of rule under brutal and extravagant despots, whose repressive governance had isolated North Korea, leaving it one of the few nations that did not have immigration privileges for Cirrus.

That will change soon. Serving Mentor had always been a means to an end, and Danny's people would eventually have a new homeland: Cirrus itself. He would naturally assume the mantle of leadership during the resettling process, and retain control for as many years as it took to build a strong and independent nation, free of tyranny, free even of Mentor.

Finally, he saw Mentor's indistinct profile moving behind the painted screen they used to hide their identity from visitors. Even the guards only ever referred to the silhouetted figure as *Murshid* or *Shifu*, both of which translated loosely to mentor and did not indicate gender.

"Did you bring coins?" Mentor's watery voice leaked through holes in the screen.

The words bubbled in Danny's mind as if rising through a bottomless pool. He knew this was an effect of the tea and the incense, both of which were mildly hallucinogenic. "I've located another twenty." He opened a cloth bag and let them spill onto the table next to his empty cup. Their central gems reflected flickering light from the incense burners.

Mentor made a tittering sound that wasn't quite a laugh, and Danny wondered why they took such pleasure in the coins. He understood that their crystals were entangled with a set on Earth, and could intercept voice and data signals, but Mentor had acquired thousands of them and—as far as Danny knew—had not employed more than a few hundred.

"The compounds are nearly complete," Danny said. "The rest of the workers will be here by the end of the month." He wanted to be angry but the tea calmed him. "These are not the people you promised to bring to Cirrus."

"They will still come. You will have your reward."

Danny loathed Mentor's overly formal manner of speech. It was as pretentious as the temple's façade. "How?"

"We will empty the cities."

"We tried that already." Danny relived that failure daily: they'd upset Pieter's plans but missed their own goals. Cirrus should have been emptied, a vacant stage on which to enact their scheme.

"This time," Mentor said, "they will leave willingly. They will go to Dawn."

"Dawn?" Danny wasn't sure he'd heard correctly. *Impossible.* "That's …" He struggled for clarity against the tea's soporific.

"Not impossible. Before Pieter crippled the portal network, he planned another route to Dawn. Those who could not travel from Earth through authorized means need only come to Cirrus and pay his price for alternate passage."

Of course. The Armenau corporation would have sent portal crystals to Dawn along with every other major player of that era. That meant … "Paired crystals. Where are they?"

"I've dispatched someone to retrieve them." The word *someone* blurred, coated in ambiguity.

Blasted tea. "I should be the one to secure those crystals."

"*No.*" Mentor abruptly leaned close to the screen. "You will return to Earth to prevent anyone from coming here through more conventional means."

A crystal that could open a passage to Dawn was a major prize, but Danny knew it was already too late. "I'm keeping everyone distracted." Prior to Newton, all it had taken was a well-placed rumor and a minor sabotage to ground every ship capable of flying across the solar system. Since then, he'd had to be more direct.

"Good. I have another task for you. The key has been *used.*"

Used? Danny heard the emphasis, but didn't understand the meaning. "What *is* the key?"

"A weapon."

Danny didn't respond immediately. He hadn't expected such a frank response from Mentor. They'd had this conversation before and Mentor had been typically vague, saying only that Danny would learn more when the time was right. "Where is it?"

"That is not yet clear. I have foreseen only that it will be carried by one of those whom Pieter hunted."

Jack. Or possibly the girl. Hoping for another straightforward answer, he asked, "Then where is Pieter?"

"He is beyond my sight. Not so the woman who seeks him."

"Detective Singh?"

"I have drawn her out. Look for her at the press conference in Olympia tomorrow. Find *her*, and you find the others."

Danny knew Mentor's spy network on Earth surpassed his own, but wondered if they were working from that or their Traveller memories. Sensing the meeting was at an end, he stood and bowed, then stepped outside into bright sunshine at the northern edge of a mile-wide basin surrounded by hills on three sides.

From above, the forested hills resembled a horseshoe, and belts of trees divided its basin into three sections. The administrative hub, covering barely ten acres, was where Danny and those closest to the leadership lived and worked in permanent wooden or steel buildings. The centrally located manufacturing zone—drab, printed-concrete cubes—was four times that size, and canvas tents and prefab barracks covered hundreds of acres in the southern half.

Danny strode to the air-conditioned command center adjacent to Mentor's temple. He didn't intend to be there long enough to enjoy the cool air, even though it cleared his mind of the tea's sedative, and barked orders as he headed to the shielded chamber at the back of the warehouse. "Set the portal for Olympia."

"Olympia is down, sir," a technician answered. "Until noon. There's a brownout affecting—"

Danny cut the woman off. "Seattle, then." He didn't need to find Priya himself; he had people for that. And once he'd tracked the detective, he'd find Holden's undetectable portal, which she was using to travel between Earth and Cirrus. That would lead him to Jack, and then the key.

While waiting for the technician to change the portal's address cartridge, Danny saw movement in his peripheral vision, and turned in time to see a scaly tail disappear behind a stack of bulletproof windshields.

"I know you're there. Don't make me chase you." The dragons, essential to Mentor's plan, were not supposed to be in the warehouse.

A few seconds of silence passed before he heard claws tapping on the concrete floor. Then, a small dragon crept through the gap between a pair of diesel engines that had recently arrived from Earth. Its hide was brown and tan, and it stood only nine inches at the shoulder and wore the black cowl that marked it as one of those loyal to Mentor. Below the cowl, a coin crystal was mounted in a gorget that protected the beast's neck.

"What are you doing here?" Danny knew the dragons could understand him because their crystals connected to an AI that interpreted his words.

The dragon dropped to its belly and flattened itself against the cold floor: a submissive posture.

Danny signaled a warehouse worker. "Get this animal out of here."

What kind of weapon is the key? he wondered as the man escorted the dragon outside. *And who is it to be used against?* His plans for Cirrus would run parallel to Mentor's for only so long, and he wouldn't give up any advantage. When the time came, he would have to arrange an opportunity to either duplicate it or learn to defend against it.

He turned back to the portal. Though its frame had a dedicated power plant, it needed a minute to charge, and Danny took that time to replay the morning's events, to fix them in his memory.

Swift recall was a crucial skill for a *Hopper*. Like Mentor, Danny benefited from the Traveller Effect. His future-memory—limited to just one half-second—was flawless, and the ability to access it quickly had saved his life many times. His regular memory was almost as good, and he'd seen the trespassing dragon before, in places it should not have been. But that was a matter for another time; the wormhole was open. He stepped through, traveling one-hundred-eighty-six million miles in a single movement.

Chapter 5

Jack had already said goodbye to his parents, so he was ready to leave when Sarah met him and Ethan at the parking garage. They'd be taking DAVe, the Scatter's formerly autonomous service truck. Short for Drone Assist Vehicle, DAVe once had a direct link to an AI on the server at the family's workshop. Now, its personality was trapped on a hard drive in Fairview, and DAVe was just another of the community's battered but reliable all-terrain vehicles.

Sarah pulled aside the canvas covering DAVe's cargo area and tossed her bag behind the seats. "Aren't you coming, Ethan?"

"No, I finally convinced Mom to let me ride Terrance's motorcycle." He was gently washing the high-powered bike with a bucket of soapy water. "That's gonna be way more fun than going back to Earth."

"Well, I guess you *did* grow up there," Jack said. "It's still a novelty for us."

"And it would be a shame for it to sit idle now that Terrance can no longer use it." Ethan stepped away from the bike and asked tentatively, "Do you want to check it out?" He wasn't asking if Jack wanted to *ride* the bike. He wanted to know if its power cell was safe.

"Yeah, I should." Jack used his talent to reach into the crystal matrix and check for new connections. Like tendrils of a fungus, the wormhole fabric weaved new threads between portal crystals and strengthened old ones. That meant Pieter—who'd used his mind-control technology on Terrance last year—could find him again through any crystal if he used it long enough.

"It's good." Jack lowered his wand. "There's only the one connection to the main power bank."

"Thanks." Ethan relaxed. "No sense taking chances with Pieter."

"You don't have to worry. He only got into your head for a few seconds. He had Terrance for weeks."

"Where's the case?" Sarah pointed to the back of the bike.

Ethan looked at her strangely. "What case?"

"The one you built the cargo rack for."

"That's for hanging panniers from. There's no case."

"Oh." She shook off her confusion. "I must have been thinking of something else."

Jack shrugged as she headed for DAVe's passenger seat, and Ethan returned to cleaning the bike.

"You should ask one of the ravens to go first," Sarah said when he took the driver's seat. She was looking through the windshield at a pair of three-mile-tall peaks: the Vault and the Mirror.

"Why?" Jack asked as he steered DAVe out of the garage.

"I just think we should know if anyone's there."

"Blue should be." He held Sarah's hand. "Are you worried? I thought you wanted to meet a dragon again."

"I do, but … what if they don't want to see me?"

"You've met Blue already. It'll be fine."

Sarah didn't seem convinced, so Jack parked DAVe and reached out to a raven he'd befriended last year. He still didn't like the idea of commanding it, so he pushed only a memory of the pass through the crystal on its leg band, along with the thought that it could be interesting.

"Okay." He tucked his wand into a pocket. "Hugo's curious now. He should get there before we do."

They encountered snow as they climbed the Vault's rugged trails. DAVe's tires, designed for rough terrain, had no problem crossing the muddy ground, and Jack parked in a familiar spot next to a frozen creek as the sun dipped to the horizon.

Sarah looked around but didn't get out of the ATV. "Where's Hugo?"

"Good question." Jack had also expected the raven to meet them, and scanned the forest. Though they were in shadow on the west side of the pass, the clouds were lifting and sunlight reflecting from the face of the Mirror illuminated the woods. "He'll be here somewhere. C'mon."

They began their hike to the top of a hanging valley alongside a creek. At two miles elevation, it was often frozen, and today there was only a trickle under a thin crust of ice. And only a few small mammal tracks marred the snow-covered meadow below the Vault's portal zone, a region of ultimate access to the AI from which all magic sprang.

Sarah stopped before the huge split boulder that marked the zone's threshold. "Are they here?"

Jack knew she was referring to Blue. Stepping into the zone, he immediately sensed another mind that was alien and familiar at the same time. "Blue is, but don't expect to see them. Every time I've been up to work on the doorway, they've kept out of sight. I think they prefer to be alone."

"What about Hugo?"

"He should have been here." Jack tugged his collar to cover his neck. "Let's go up to the cave. It'll be easier for me to search when we're out of the wind."

"All right," Sarah said, "but … you know … be ready."

"Ready for what? I don't under—" He halted mid-step the moment she crossed the threshold. The calm vibe that normally permeated the zone had shifted, and he would have described it as alert, not threatening. Regardless, he drew his wand. "Put up your—" A piercing screech echoed through the trees.

"*Shield.*" With a word, Sarah abruptly enclosed herself in a shimmering sphere. She had a wand of her own, but her diamond stud earrings—entangled portal crystals—were quicker.

The zone's mood transformed at once. From the cave, still unseen above a tarn, Blue screeched again. The sound was like an eagle's peal, but deeper, and with many notes joined into a single, ratcheting cry. Seconds later, the blue-scaled dragon appeared on the dam. They leaped, more than ten yards, into a tree, sprang from it and landed in another while keeping their eyes on Sarah.

"*Blue,*" Jack yelled, as the dragon prepared for another leap.

"Stop." He instinctively jumped in their path, not thinking for a moment about how much they'd grown over the winter. They now weighed as much as a large wolf.

Blue completed their leap but didn't move closer. Instead, they lowered their head and growled at Sarah with their fangs bared and their three-inch claws gouging the earth. Their tail thrashed, cat-like, shattering bark and knocking snow from a birch tree. The snow that didn't immediately slide from their armored hide quickly melted into glistening beads on iridescent scales.

"Jack." Sarah's voice trembled. *"Do something."*

Jack kept his body in the way as Blue shuffled to keep Sarah in sight. "Why are you acting like this? You've met Sarah before."

[…] Blue's vocalizations were only deep rumbles, but the emotions conveyed by the AI were so clear they may as well have been words. [Trespasser]

"What? No, we're not …" He glanced at Sarah. "They say we're—"

"Trespassing." Her voice held a note of awe. "I actually understood them this time. But it's not *us*. It's *me* they don't trust."

"*Blue*, you *know* Sarah. She saved you from Pieter."

"I only helped, and that's not it, anyway. See how they're herding me? They're protecting the zone. For *you*." She backstepped through the threshold and the zone's mood changed from hostile to cautious.

Jack was still trying to understand what was happening when Hugo called from a tree just outside the zone.

"See." Sarah indicated the raven. "Hugo won't cross either. Blue must think this place belongs to *you*. You have to give us permission to enter."

"Permission? How do I do that?"

Sarah took a deep breath and offered her hand to Jack. "Let the AI handle it. Just invite me in."

"When did you drop your shield?"

She only just seemed to notice it was missing. "I must have done it without thinking. But it's probably better that way, to prove I'm not a threat."

Jack was anxious about her being defenseless, but she was determined, and he guided her back over the threshold while facing Blue. "This is Sarah. She's our friend." And though it felt strange, he added, "She has my permission to be here. So does Hugo."

Blue watched without aggression as Sarah entered, followed a moment later by Hugo, and Jack felt the tension leave his shoulders when the dragon's posture loosened. He chuckled nervously. "That was intense."

Sarah relaxed too. "Thank you, Blue."

The dragon bobbed their head.

"What triggered that?" Jack wondered as they resumed their trek. "Priya's been here many times. So have Suresh, Terrance, and Anders. No one's ever reported a problem."

"None of them can use magic."

"Oh." Could it be that simple? He turned back to Blue, who was still watching them. "Sarah is allowed to use magic here. Okay?"

[...] Blue snorted, raising twin clouds of steam from their nostrils, before turning and galloping into the forest.

"I think that was a *yes*," Sarah said hopefully.

As they scaled the stony dam, Jack asked, "Why would Blue think this zone belongs to me?"

"You invited *them*, remember? You suggested they'd be safe here."

He recalled pushing a memory of the Vault to the dragons after they'd defeated Pieter. "Yeah, but that doesn't make it mine."

Sarah scrambled over the final rocks to reach the top of the dam. "You found this zone. And you were the first to use magic here."

"Actually, Uncle Carl found it years ago. He called it a ley line."

"And you used it to commune with *him*. If anyone *owns* it, it's you."

Jack considered this. It was true that crystal-to-AI connections grew stronger with use—Terrance was living proof of that—but there was a positive side: that familiarity allowed him to quickly spell matter or energy through a portal when needed. "Does that mean whoever uses magic in a zone first owns it? Uncle Carl said there are hundreds."

"You could ask. We have time."

Jack stepped past the large slab of rock that sheltered the cave's opening and rounded a corner to stand before a small lake. He sensed the tangled line of artificial-gravity crystals—tiny wormholes—deep under the ice, felt the energy field radiating from them, and their multitude of AI connections. If he chose, he could use them to speak with his uncle in a variation of Traveller-memories.

"Not tonight," he said. "Links across time are unpredictable. He could be even younger than the last time we met."

Sarah joined him at the shore. "Okay. We have a couple of hours before Priya gets to the inn." She tested the ice with her foot. "Want to skate?"

Jack sensed that the ice was thick enough to support their weight, and the wind had blown it clear, leaving it mirror-smooth. "How?"

She willed a blade of portal energy to create a lifting force under her shoes, then stepped onto the ice as if balanced on skates. Jack smiled as Sarah, tall and graceful, glided to the center of the hundred-foot rink. Normally, she tied back her chestnut hair when she went for her daily jog, but tonight it flowed freely. He copied her spell, lurched away from the rocks, and promptly fell on his butt.

"*Ow*. How are you so good at this?"

Sarah swooped over and helped him stand. "I'm cheating, obviously." She lifted a foot and made the supporting band of energy around her ankle more opaque.

Jack grinned. "Got it." Then he refined his spell to brace his ankles, and together they slid and spun, laughed and hollered under the moonlight. And though he fell several more times, he felt the evening counted as one of their more enjoyable dates; there were few shareable activities in their small village. But even if they were living in a larger community, Cirrus no longer supported social events they might have enjoyed prior to Newton: music, dancing, festivals, arcades, even restaurants wouldn't return until someone figured out how to restore reliable power.

Nearly an hour later, tired and thirsty, they threw their jackets onto the cold rocks and lay back to gaze at the Milky Way wheeling overhead. With only four miles of atmosphere between them and Cirrus' transparent roof, the only better place for stargazing would be outside of the station.

Jack planted his wand in the snow and sparked a warming flame from it while Sarah spelled an invisible half-dome around them to retain its heat. He took her hand, which was surprisingly warm. "We should come up here more often."

"Yeah, this is nice." Then she added, "I wish Priya would visit more, too."

"Hmph. You'd drive up in a blizzard if she asked you to."

Sarah feigned a look of shock. "Are you jealous?"

She was still holding his hand, so his answer was obvious. "Not at all."

"Good." She hooked a leg over his and wriggled closer to share his body heat.

Priya and Sarah were a dozen years apart, but Jack knew the detective was like a big sister to her, or maybe a favorite aunt. Sarah's father had walked out when she was five, so it was possible that Priya filled the niche of a second parent. She was certainly stern enough.

The second hour passed too swiftly under the stars, and Jack wasn't aware of the time until Sarah sat up abruptly. "*We have to go.* Priya will be waiting for *us* if we don't get moving."

They'd had to crouch to enter the cave, but then it was tall enough to stand in, and she cast a light from her wand as they navigated its meandering tunnel. The cold rock seemed to deaden all sound, even their footsteps, as they walked the sixty paces to the steel door that was mortared into the cave wall.

Jack turned the handle, pushed, and the rubber seals around the door stretched and creaked before giving way to an antechamber the size of a hotel elevator. On the opposite wall was his grandfather's portal: a square, silver mirror set in a black metal frame.

Sarah checked the power indicators on the frame as Jack sealed the door. "It's charged." She doused her wand and pressed a switch to open the wormhole.

The chamber lit up with artificial light from Fairweather Castle's Hall of Mirrors, and warm air vented through outlets spaced around the frame. As the pressure equalized, the aroma of the ancient inn filled the air: mahogany, roses, furniture polish.

A huge grin spread across Sarah's face when she saw Priya standing in the hallway. She started to reach for the one-way glass pane that still sealed the portal, then paused. "Priya's holding her phone in her left hand. It's not safe yet."

Jack noted the phone. "That's fine. We still have to stash our crystals, anyway."

He set his wand on a shelf near the portal, and Sarah did the same. She removed her earrings too; they couldn't take their crystals through another wormhole without breaking the entanglement. Then they waited for Priya to shift the phone to her right hand, the signal that it was safe to cross.

They'd taken many steps to keep the portal hidden in plain sight: the rubber seals prevented air from rushing into the high-elevation mountain cave; the metal door itself blocked questing radio waves; and a thick, half-silvered pane of glass lay behind the Earth-side portal crystal. Even when open, a person standing in front of the wormhole would see only their own reflection, no different from any of the dozens of true mirrors lining the corridor.

Finally, Priya swapped the phone to her other hand, and Sarah swung the glass panel aside, then crawled through the frame. At only two feet across, it was a tight fit, but they'd also mounted it just two feet off the carpeted floor, so she was able to move silently.

The spring-loaded glass swung back into place after Jack crossed, and he tapped a hidden switch on the Earth-side art déco frame to close the wormhole. Once inside Priya's suite, Sarah seized the detective in a fierce hug.

"Yes, yes," Priya said. "I'm happy to see you, too."

"It's been weeks. I was worried."

"I've been busy. Not only do I have a regular job, I've been tracking Pieter on my own time."

"Is that what you wanted to talk to us about?"

"Yes, but I also wanted you to see this." Priya pointed a remote control at a wall-mounted television.

A staticky image appeared on the screen, and Priya began fiddling with an antenna resting next to it on an antique sideboard. While she worked to clear the picture, Jack surveyed the room.

Imported from England and rebuilt in Washington, the late-Tudor castle was now a luxury inn, and its rooms rented for more than a police officer could afford. But Priya was friends with the owners, and the inn was mostly empty these days, so they allowed her to use their smallest room on her infrequent visits.

Besides a television of limited function, only one of the wall sconces bordering the four-poster bed was working. There was an old-fashioned writing desk next to a fireplace, and leaded stained-glass windows, framed by brocaded curtains, opened to the rear lawn, which bordered a forest.

Jack recognized the building on the glossy cover of an architecture magazine on the desk: Pieter's office tower on Cirrus. Next to that, he spotted a mugshot Priya had shown them months ago. She'd drawn a line through the name 'John Doe' and written 'Paul ?'. He flipped open one of Priya's file folders, wondering if she had learned more about the man suspected of robbing his grandfather, but the documents within related entirely to Priya herself.

"*Hey*," Sarah hissed at him, giving him a cross look. He dropped the folder and returned to her side after taking the two phones Priya had brought for them.

"Got it." Priya stepped back when an image of a newscaster appeared. His lips were moving but there was no sound, and a banner at the bottom of the screen declared: Cirrus Destroyed.

"What does that mean?" Jack asked.

"They're saying Cirrus broke apart shortly after Newton. That it was sabotaged and its gravity generators failed."

"That's impossible." He pointed at the stock image of Cirrus behind the newscaster. "The ring is made up of literally *billions* of independent lines. You could punch right through the station with an asteroid and ninety percent of them would work right to the edge of the hole—which would then fill in with ice from the inner surface."

"It may be impossible, but so was destroying every mass-produced portal crystal in one night. The rumors have been circulating for months."

"Is that why no one has tried to get to Cirrus yet?" Sarah asked.

"That's more to do with the fact that it takes six months to grow crystals, and the top priorities are food and water, not spacecraft."

"Why would anyone claim that Cirrus was destroyed? What could they stand to gain?"

"I think it has something to do with *this*." Priya changed the channel. Again, the sound quality was poor, but the headline told Jack everything he needed to know: First Portal Crystals Arrive at Dawn.

"That's good news," Sarah said, "isn't it? If Earth's factories are delivering new crystals, things will get back to normal soon."

"They don't mean dawn tomorrow," Jack said. "They're talking about the *planet* Dawn."

Priya changed to the only other working channel, which was running the same story, except with an orbital image of a blue world with a single ocean straddling its equator. "Apparently, hundreds of crystals reached Dawn last month, but the news only became public this week."

"That's incredible," he said. "No one expected more than a handful."

"Why's that?" Sarah asked.

"They've had thirty years to go off track," Priya said. Smaller than grains of rice, tens of thousands of portal-powered thrusters had been launched and accelerated to near-light speed. "Some of the corporations that sent them have since gone out of business."

"And they didn't even have a plan for catching them back then," Jack said. "Recovering one percent is a great result."

"Okay." Sarah shrugged a shoulder. "So they can build portals and anyone can travel to Dawn now. How does that change anything?"

Priya sat in an antique chair by the fireplace. "Take a seat." She waited until they both sat on the bed. "There's no sign of Pieter on Earth. I've followed dozens of leads, interviewed hundreds of witnesses, and the feds have checked every corporation he ever had ties to. Most likely, he died of infection after the dragons burned him."

"You can't give up." A note of alarm sharpened Sarah's words. "He might have survived."

"I don't think so. And I don't have a choice, anyway. The UN is reestablishing off-world policing." Priya hesitated. "They've offered me a new position and a promotion."

"Where?"

Priya spoke quickly, as if to get through her explanation without interruption. "The corporations have been planning for those crystals for decades. There's already infrastructure for hundreds of cities, and the robots can build housing as fast as people can immigrate. By the end of the month, there will be enough portals to transport a million people a day."

Oh no, Jack thought. Sarah was waiting quietly for Priya to continue. *How can she not see what's coming?* In fact, he was certain that she must know, and that she was denying something she'd already foreseen.

Priya leaned forward and took Sarah's hands. "They've offered me a job on Dawn."

"For how long?" she asked.

"It's a one-way trip."

Chapter 6

Jack didn't know what to say to Sarah as he walked several paces behind her, and decided it was best to wait until she was ready to talk.

Last night, after Priya announced her plans for leaving, possibly forever, she and Sarah argued. The quarrel had resolved nothing, and Priya left the inn soon after, then returned quietly before dawn to leave detailed written instructions for the event at the Capitol.

Sarah had read the note, which had been slipped under the door, then marched out without a word. And she hadn't spoken in the hour they'd been walking, despite the fact they were moving through an area of the city neither of them had seen before.

Of course, the scenery wasn't as noteworthy as it had been. A year ago the neighborhood might have graced the homepage of a website dedicated to fine living. Today it looked like a slum: trash clogged its gutters, lawns once manicured by armies of landscaping robots had gone to seed, and flower beds had withered. Not only had Newton deprived maintenance machines of power, but fresh water was also in short supply.

Sarah stopped unexpectedly and rounded on Jack. "How stupid can people be?"

That wasn't the direction he expected her to go. "I assume you're talking about people in general, not Priya."

"I'm not mad at her. Well, maybe I am. But how dumb is it to abandon Earth and poison another world?"

"I don't think our parents *abandoned* Earth when they moved to Cirrus. You once said yourself that the planet needs time to recover, and taking a few billion people off for a generation can only help."

"But that's not what'll happen." Sarah resumed walking.

"Look who's going first. Only those who own property they can trade for a place on Dawn, or those with high-paying jobs. That means all of Earth's resources will eventually go there. It would take hundreds of years to fix Earth's environment if people were actively working on cleaning it up. It'll take *thousands* on its own."

Jack decided not to argue. He'd just be repeating the same debate they'd heard on Priya's television, and regardless of which side they were on, the experts estimated there would be two billion people left on Earth. "Still, it's a good career move. If she goes now, she'll end up at the head of her department."

"If people knew they could get to Cirrus," Sarah said hopefully, "she could stay."

Jack dropped his gaze. He'd thought the same thing. "How can we do that without revealing Grandpa's portal?" In the wrong hands, Holden's invention would be a nightmare, able to deliver a nuclear bomb anywhere without detection. "The government would seize it, figure out how it works, and weaponize it."

"We don't have to reveal anything. All we have to do is prove that Cirrus is still there."

"How? Kidnap someone? Blindfold them and take them through?"

Sarah crossed the street before answering. "We could bring something back that could only be from Cirrus."

Jack considered for a moment. "That might work. It would have to belong to somebody who's travelled back and forth, would recognize the object, and is important enough that people would listen to them."

"There you go. All we have to do is break into a celebrity's place on Cirrus, track them down on Earth, and deliver their property."

"You sound like Ethan," he said.

"It was *your* idea. Do you have a better suggestion?"

"Not right now." Jack sighed. "But we should be able to think of something that doesn't land us in jail."

Sarah turned at the corner toward Friendship Bridge, where an oily gray cloud drifted over Budd Inlet from a battery of generators on the deck of a tanker anchored there. "Why does it have to be a one-way trip, anyway? People have been traveling to and from Dawn for decades."

Priya had already explained this to Sarah. A spaceship could travel there through a temporary, dynamic wormhole in about a month, but the energy, and therefore the cost, was phenomenal, even if it didn't have to be expended all at once. Jack didn't want to point out that no agency was going to shell out that much for a police officer, so he just said, "Not by portal, they haven't."

"They can now."

"True, but it'll only be the rich and famous. Dawn is deeper into the galaxy's gravity well, and it takes a hundred times less energy to get there than to return. There'll be so much traffic going that direction there won't *be* regular travel back to Earth."

Sarah looked like she was thinking of a counterargument, so he added, "There's something else. I saw a doctor's report on Priya's desk."

Sarah stopped abruptly. "*She's sick?* What did it say?"

"I didn't really understand it. There was stuff about increased aggression."

"She's under a lot of pressure."

"Maybe. But haven't you noticed she's been short-tempered lately?"

"That's not new. She's always been strict." Sarah started walking again. "If you were the only one who knew that Pieter survived Newton, and had to track him down in your spare time, you'd be stressed, too."

"Or it could be that she's taken too many trips through portals." That was something they both worried about. Except for Holden's one-of-a-kind device, portals were dangerous. You could feel a wormhole's interface drag across your skin. *Under* your skin. You could even *taste* it. "If that's the case, they'll cut her off. Portal travel may have been what caused Pieter to turn homicidal." He whispered the last part as they were only a block from the campus and the streets were now crowded with

Monday-morning commuters.

This was the event Priya had called them about. The governor was scheduled to address the public, and Priya wanted Jack to scout for Third-Eye crystals while she conducted her own investigation. She'd learned of a possible sale of crystals from Pieter's office. If it were true, there might be a way to open another wormhole to Cirrus, one they didn't have to hide.

As they walked beside the State Patrol building, Sarah said, "I'm guessing you can sense phone crystals there."

"A few." Pre-Newton, Jack would have sensed hundreds through the walls. "Oops, I forgot to give you this." He moved closer to hide their hands, then passed her one of the phones he'd taken from Priya's suite. Their crystals, paper-thin and less than a quarter-inch in diameter, would give them both access to wormhole energy and its governing AI.

They continued past the six-story building, which also housed an office of the UN's Off-world Police Force: Priya's former employer. The press conference would take place on the Capitol steps, but Jack turned towards the East Plaza, where hundreds of people queued before banks of public telephones under a large tent.

"I'll be right back." He walked to within fifty feet of the temporary structure, paused, then returned. "There are smaller crystals running the booths we saw the last time, but there's just one of Pieter's in a cabinet near the new booths. I think they've set it up as a sort of mini-exchange."

"Which means no one is close enough to it to be controlled, right?"

"Yeah, it would have to be a personal phone. Do you have any memories of where they are?"

"No, but Priya wanted us to check the whole area." She led Jack onto a footpath where two uniformed state troopers stood near an intersection. "Anything?" she asked after they passed.

"Regular crystals," he murmured. "Not like the woman in the suit walking towards us." The woman was tall, fit, and very attentive as she strode the center of the path. Jack noticed a thin, coiled wire between her ear and collar as she passed. "Must be private security."

The same pattern repeated many times as they circled and crisscrossed the campus. Every police officer carried a crystal-equipped radio or phone, and they were all unique, as if scavenged from different sources. Only the private security personnel had Pieter's crystals. Finally, they came to the crowd arrayed in front of the steps.

"How are you feeling?" Sarah asked. They'd stopped well back from the main body of spectators, where they could speak freely.

"I'm fine." He knew she was referring to his demophobia. "There are definitely emo-detectors in some of those old phones, but they're not working the way they used to."

Strictly speaking, Jack did not have an actual phobia. Pre-Newton, phones linked to an AI to automatically select emoji during chats, and he was vulnerable to the feedback from that system. He wasn't *afraid* of crowds. He just couldn't handle the flood of other people's emotions whenever there were too many phones around—which used to be most of the time.

But he didn't need an emotion detector to understand the mob's current mood. At least a dozen groups shouted and waved placards protesting corruption, food and power shortages, or poor sanitation and public health. He noticed Sarah's expression as a group of government officials took their places near the podium. "What's wrong?"

"Someone up there is being controlled through a Third-Eye coin, the same way Terrance was. There's going to be a fight involving the governor, but not here. After she leaves. She doesn't get hurt. Someone else does."

"That's ... that's a lot of detail. Are you sure?"

"They're just fragments, but it's what I remember. Can you detect crystals?"

"We're too far from the podium." He spun his gaze to the right. "Wait."

"You found it?"

"No, it's one of Grandpa's." To Jack, every portal crystal had a signature, like an individual voice in a choir. He normally had to pay attention to tell them apart, but the one he'd just sensed was like an off-key singer. "It's the orb that was stolen from his safe."

"Here? How?"

"I don't know."

"Jack, come back." Sarah tried to grab his arm as he darted toward the crowd. "Priya needs us to—"

"This could be more important." He tried pushing his way into the spectators but received so many dirty looks that he felt an anxiety attack coming on. He apologized and backed off. "It's no good. I lost them. But they might have been heading for the steps."

"We need to be on the south side." Sarah started walking. "That's where the governor will leave after her speech."

"Yeah, in a minute." Priya's main concern was whether the governor herself was being controlled, but Jack's priorities had shifted.

He stood on a bench and scanned the audience as ceremonial music played from speakers around the stage. The governor, a charismatic woman in her fifties, reached the podium amid loud cheers. She began her speech traditionally, recognizing supporters and constituents, but Jack was only dimly aware of her words.

How did Grandpa's diffusion sphere end up here? He'd last sensed it when he and Ethan were running from Pieter's men. Then, it had been in a bag carried by the man in Priya's mugshot. *Paul?*

Unable to sense the crystal again, he noticed a shift in the crowd's mood; the governor had handed the podium over to an advisor named Fletcher. A stock image of Cirrus, the world-sized space station, filled a giant screen behind the stage, peaceful against a starry background.

"It's my sad duty to confirm the rumors." Fletcher's voice was professionally grim, and the image changed to a looping series of grainy black and white stills. "NASA briefly restored contact with its solar observatory. This video was obtained a week ago."

The solar disk at the center of the image was blacked out, allowing the camera to capture ghostly coronal mass ejections against a backdrop of stars. Earth was a bright circle on the left, and Cirrus should have been exactly the same distance from the Sun on the right, a narrow ellipse tilted at twenty-three and a half degrees. But instead of surrounding a dark center, the ring was broken, and its segments did not align.

Jack couldn't focus on anything Fletcher said as he zoomed the image. This was his *home*, where his family and friends lived, split into three large crescents and hundreds of smaller chunks, tumbling in space. Tears welled in his eyes.

"It's not real." Sarah squeezed his hand. "He said this image was taken last week."

Jack wiped his eyes. "I know, I know. But it's still … it's horrifying."

Fletcher concluded his speech with a description of Cirrus' fate: a year-long tumble into the Sun, leaving no trace of one of humankind's greatest achievements.

Jack stepped down from the bench. "Why is he saying that? Does he know it's fake? Is he the one being controlled?"

"It can't be just him. He said the pictures came from NASA. This has to be Pieter's doing."

"Why? What could he gain from this? He intended to make billions rebuilding the station's portal network."

"Until he was betrayed by Danny."

Jack shook his head. "Danny wanted to make even more by reselling Cirrus. This story doesn't work for either of them."

"It must. We just can't see it yet. And the timing with portals on Dawn can't be coincidental. One of them planned this."

"Then it has to be Danny." Jack didn't want to upset Sarah, but he agreed with Priya. "Pieter's gone."

The governor retook the stage to add her closing comments. "As you've heard, Cirrus will eventually fall into the Sun. We can do nothing for them, but we can give them dignity. The governments of this world have declared the station's remains to be consecrated ground, the final resting place of ten million brave settlers. No salvage will be permitted, and no ships may visit or record images." She then expressed heartfelt condolences to the families of those lost on Cirrus. Even though Jack knew they were safe, he was still shaken. Worse though, were the opinions of the crowd.

"It's awful," a middle-aged woman said. "And I shouldn't say this, but we don't need Cirrus anymore. We get enough grain from overseas to meet our needs."

"That's because Cirrus never existed in the first place," said a man wearing a baseball cap. "That video was so fake. A revolving space station would have flown apart, not clumped together. The angular velocity—"

"You're forgetting about the artificial gravity," another man interrupted. "It's more like reinforced concrete with the core holding it together under compression. What you saw was—"

Jack walked away. "I've had enough."

Sarah hurried to catch Jack. "Ignore them. They're just science trolls. If the internet was still working there would be a million of them trying to prove they're smarter than everyone else."

"Yeah, but even those who know Cirrus is real only care about its crops. And what did that woman mean about getting enough from overseas? Earth hasn't been able to feed itself for decades."

"No, that doesn't make sense." Sarah noted one of the governor's staff taking the podium to answer questions. "She's leaving now. Let's move."

Jack followed Sarah to the parking lot behind the Capitol, where a low steel barrier created a protected aisle between the building and a fleet of black limousines. He didn't need to get closer than that. Also, if Sarah's recollection about a fight came to pass, he didn't *want* to be near, and they waited quietly behind a gang of reporters until the governor appeared.

It took less than a minute for her entire entourage to load themselves into the cars while reporters lobbed unanswered questions. As the motorcade drove away, Jack gestured for Sarah to follow him to the park.

"Did anyone have one of Pieter's crystals?" she asked.

"Everyone *but* the governor."

"Really? It should be the other way around. Why—?" Jack wasn't listening. "What's wrong?"

"Grandpa's crystal is back." He stood on his toes and glimpsed someone in a gray jacket moving through the thinning crowd.

"Where are you going?"

Jack, already starting to pursue, spun to face Sarah while walking backwards away from her. "I have to follow them."

"It could be dangerous. Wait for—"

"Sorry." He turned and began to run. "I'll find you."

Chapter 7

Sarah would have shouted at Jack for ignoring her, except what she wanted to say would definitely draw attention, and this wasn't the place for it. Now, he was already out of sight, having skirted around the back of the crowd.

Priya's waiting for us, she thought. She looked across the park to the road they'd have to take and saw a bodyguard Jack had identified as carrying a Third-Eye crystal. He had just ended a call and was returning his phone to a jacket pocket next to his knife.

Knife? Sarah couldn't possibly have seen that. Another memory had intruded on her thoughts: *He's the one who was fighting. And the person who got hurt was … Priya!*

Sarah's heart raced as memory fragments abruptly merged into a single, cohesive vision. She knew exactly what happened/would happen because she was/would be there. She hurried away from the Capitol, knowing she couldn't run without drawing suspicion. The police would surely stop her, and she couldn't risk that delay.

The man had a substantial lead, but Sarah knew where they would be. Instead of following him, she turned onto a different street and sprinted to the end of the block, arriving as he entered Union Avenue near where Priya waited beside a shuttered business.

Sarah yelled a warning but she was too far away. She started running and waving her arms, wishing Priya would look her way. The man was close now. He reached into his jacket just as Priya glanced in Sarah's direction.

At one hundred yards, Sarah saw a flash of sunlight on steel as the man swung his knife, and Priya went down.

Sarah screamed, but Priya wasn't out. She swept her leg into her attacker's knee, and he tumbled into a pile of trash bags.

Ignoring everything Priya had ever said about secrecy, Sarah drew her phone. She was preparing a very loud and conspicuous spell when the governor's black limousine raced past, followed by two police motorcycles. And she was still half a block away when the car swerved toward the fighting pair, mounted the sidewalk, and crashed into a bike rack. Then the limo driver leaped from the vehicle and tackled Priya's assailant, sending him flying, and the uniformed officers arrived moments later.

Sarah wanted to rush to Priya to see how badly she was injured, but the detective stood and waved her away. And five police cars were converging on the scene anyway, so Sarah pocketed her phone before anyone noticed it, then crossed the street to join a growing crowd of bystanders.

• • • •

Jack tailed the person carrying his grandfather's crystal into the Historic District north of the Capitol. From a distance, he saw only dark, shoulder-length hair until the stranger turned his head while ducking into an alley.

It is *Paul.* He recognized the thin beard and Native American features. This was the same man who'd watched him and Ethan hide from Pieter's goons the last time they were on Earth. *What's he doing here? And why is he still carrying that crystal?*

Jack rushed to the alley, bobbed his head around the corner, and recoiled. The stench was overwhelming. But he'd lose Paul if he lost sight of him now, so he took a deep breath and looked again.

The alley, dimly lit by reflected sunlight, appeared to be empty, which meant Paul had either run to the opposite end, entered a building, or— *Am I walking into a trap?* Slipping a hand into his pocket to grip the phone, Jack wished he had his more powerful wand. *No choice.* He couldn't sense the crystals Paul was carrying, so it was unlikely the man was lying in wait behind a dumpster. And why would he have chosen the worst-smelling path if he could have gone around?

Taking another deep breath, Jack steeled his nerves and padded briskly into the narrow and cluttered alley. He managed to hold his breath until a rat scurried out from a heap of soggy cardboard boxes, nearly causing him to step into a puddle of dirty water made worse by a glistening oil slick.

Then, halfway along the block, he detected the crystal's energy field streaming from a two-story cinderblock building on his right. There were no ground-level windows into the alley from it or any of its neighbors, and its door bore reminders of past tenants in scratched-out logos on its dimpled surface.

Holding his phone ready to produce a shield, he gently pulled the battered door handle. But instead of a room, the steel door opened to a hallway that ran straight through the building to where pedestrians, visible through a glass door, passed on the opposite street. Jack didn't think for a moment that Paul had escaped that way, because the energy field was emanating from below. *There's a basement.*

Three doors flanked the hall. The single door on the right belonged to an accountant, and one of those on the left to a realtor. Still wielding his phone, Jack turned the knob of the unmarked third door. *Unlocked.* And the space beyond was dimly lit but bright enough to see the stairs.

He crept to the basement and found the light source: a glowing keypad on the wall beside a shiny metal door. The field signature—*no, signatures*—were stronger now. A narrow shelf stuck out from the wall below the keypad, and two objects on it reflected the dim light: a red crystal icosahedron, like a gaming die; and one of Pieter's Third-Eye coins.

Had it been just the coin, Jack would have fled. But he recognized the twenty-sided crystal from Holden's workshop and knew it was unique, and therefore not paired with any other. The coin, though, had to be linked to something, or someone. If it was a trap, it wasn't well thought out. He could use the icosahedron to protect himself from any threat.

Stepping closer, he saw that someone had written the numbers up to twenty on each face with a fine black marker. *It's a game.* Now he knew it wasn't Pieter. *Pieter wouldn't play games. He'd have had his goons waiting here.* That meant Paul—or whoever he was working for—*wanted* him to have both crystals.

But why go to all this trouble? Why bring me here? Jack scanned the door. It was featureless except for a set of massive hinges. And without meaning to, his curiosity drove a tendril of energy into it from the icosahedron. That brief touch not only confirmed the crystal's power, but allowed him to sense the door's mass. *It's like a bank vault.*

Jack almost laughed when he figured it out. *It's a bribe.* The large crystal would be payment for opening the vault. So the question was: who wanted it opened, and why? And was it worth the risk?

The icosahedron was thousands of times larger than a tissue-thin phone crystal, making it incredibly useful. And as much as he wanted it, he also had to know the reason for its being there. *Even if I open the vault, I don't have to leave it open.*

Having convinced himself that he'd be safe, he picked up the coin and opened his mind to its portal.

[Hello, Jack.]

• • • •

Sarah sat some distance away, watching the police clear up the fight scene. As they put the assailant's knife into an evidence bag, she regretted the resentment she'd felt earlier for something so minor compared to the risks Priya faced every day. *I should have supported Priya's decision. It couldn't have been an easy one for her to make.*

The officers took statements from witnesses, and paramedics attended to a cut on the limo driver's hand, but Priya hadn't suffered so much as a scratch in the brief tussle. She declined the offer of a ride from a colleague and walked away, and Sarah waited a while before following on the other side of the street.

"Where's Jack?" Priya asked without turning her head when Sarah finally caught up with her. At the same time, Sarah asked, "Who attacked you?"

Priya stopped short, waiting for an answer.

"He followed someone who had one of his grandfather's

crystals."

"*I warned you to stay—*"

"I know. He wouldn't listen. But I'm sure he's safe. Was the man with the knife the person you were supposed to meet?"

Priya made a noticeable effort to control her voice. "No, they never showed. I'm not even sure now it was real. The whole thing might have been a setup."

"Then who was he?"

Priya shook her head. "It makes no sense. The governor's driver recognized him as a member of her own private security detail."

"Jack sensed a Third-Eye crystal on him before the speech. Could he have been controlled by Pieter?"

"Actually, I got the impression the driver was. He said he thought the bodyguard was up to something but couldn't say why. And he left the motorcade *with the governor in the car*. Those troopers were chasing the governor, not the bodyguard."

"Jack sensed a crystal on the driver, too."

Priya started walking again. "Someone other than Pieter is using his crystals." Her tone was confident; she wasn't speculating.

"Why do you say it's not Pieter?"

"Assuming he's still alive, what would he gain by stopping me? I've been searching for months and haven't found a trace of him. No, this was done by somebody with a different agenda. Maybe they're not *controlling* people the way he did, but they're definitely influencing them."

Sarah stopped at an intersection. "Jack went that way. Um, I think."

"What's the matter? Is he in trouble?"

"No, not at all."

"You're obviously upset."

"It's just … I *remembered* that you got hurt." Tears welled in Sarah's eyes. "But I was there during the attack. And I've always been able to tell the difference between memories of things I experience and things someone tells me later. This wasn't supposed to happen."

"Sorry to disappoint you. I was fighting for my life."

"That's not—" Sarah calmed when she saw Priya was joking. "Pieter planned Newton years ahead. How can I trust my predictions if they're wrong after only a few minutes?"

"*You can't.*" Priya lifted Sarah's chin to force eye contact. "*That's the point.* Pieter didn't rely on just his talent. He may have been driven mad by too many portal trips, but he was a smart and experienced businessman. He had a goal, and he manipulated people towards it for decades. I doubt *everything* went as he planned. It certainly didn't in the end. But he essentially fulfilled his own prophecy through hard work."

Sarah nodded. "You're right."

"So, what happened to change your vision?"

"Actually, my first memory was unclear. I would have missed the fight completely if Jack hadn't run off."

"There you go. You changed the future you saw by trying to warn me."

"And Jack changed *my* future by leaving, and the person with Holden's crystals changed *his* future by being there." Sarah tipped her head back. "It's too complicated."

"Tell me about it. Anyway, where is Jack?"

Chapter 8

Sarah passed a series of nearly identical storefronts, stopped at one, and ran her hand over the doorjamb. A deep scratch revealed layers of paint built up over a hundred years, each a slightly different shade of white. "This is it."

Priya swung the door open, entered the darkened hallway, and headed straight for the basement. "Jack?"

"Down here."

Sarah hesitated before following Priya. There was nothing unusual about the doorway. It was flanked by the same red brick, topped by the same transom, and sheltered by the same faded awning as every other. This one just felt right. But she was troubled by how certain she was of Jack's location. Why was her memory of this rather plain building as strong as the one about Priya, which had turned out to be only partially correct?

They found him downstairs, sitting on a metal stool in the middle of a brightly lit vault filled with dozens of rack-mounted computers. Priya immediately launched into a lecture about the dangers of running off by himself. She was less than impressed when he admitted to knowing that Paul had led him there.

"Sorry," he said when she finished. "But I recognized him. He had a chance to turn me and Ethan over to Pieter's thugs months ago. He didn't do it then, so why would he do it now? And you said Pieter's gone. I knew it was safe."

"You didn't *know*," Priya said. "You *guessed*. That's not a good survival strategy." She blew out an exasperated breath and rubbed her temples. "Did you know Paul worked for Danny?"

Jack's face fell. "He did?"

"Danny hired all the contractors for Pieter's work, meaning Paul actually worked for both of them. And he's the one who told me where to find Angel, so I don't know who he's working for now."

Sarah knew Priya's words were aimed at her, too, and didn't feel any better for it, but Jack would be feeling worse. He'd be beating himself up for a long time over a mistake this big. And Priya didn't seem to be in a forgiving mood, so she decided to change the subject. "Where are we?"

Jack answered by handing her a thin, bound volume of papers. The cover page read: Distributed Artificial Intelligence Global Observation Network (DAIGON 135).

"Is this … Little Brother?" She used the informal name for the ubiquitous network of public cameras.

"Part of it. Apparently, this is hub number one-thirty-five. There are rooms like this all over the world."

Noting the server's display panels, Sarah abruptly forgot about Priya's anger. Two of them were transferring data. Little Brother might not be functioning at its pre-Newton level, but it still existed. "We can use it to prove that Cirrus is still—" But Jack was shaking his head.

"That was the first thing I checked. There's no response from Cirrus' camera network."

"How did you get in here?" Priya asked as she inspected the vault door. Its inner workings were visible behind a pane of tempered glass. "The bolts are in the locked position." Connected to a sturdy gearbox, the six metal cylinders protruding from the sides of the thick door would prevent it from closing.

"It was already open."

"Who opened it?"

Jack shrugged. "I just followed this." He held a multi-sided red crystal between thumb and forefinger. "It's Grandpa's. Paul left it here." Then, before Priya could reprimand him, he mumbled, "It's one of a kind. It can't be controlled …" His voice trailed off.

"Not like that one, then." Sarah tapped the glass panel on the face of an active server. An arc of gold was visible at the top of its coin slot. "That's one of Pieter's. We should remove it."

He shook his head. "We don't have another coin portal to replace it with. Anyone monitoring this network will notice right away." He gestured to the camera mounted over the door. "And then they'd know who did it."

"But if Pieter has a direct link to Little Brother—"

"Jack's right," Priya said. "It's no coincidence one of those crystals ended up here. This was planned."

"Yeah." Sarah looked at each of them in turn, wondering why they couldn't see the obvious. *"By Pieter."* She expected Priya to argue that Pieter was gone, but it was Jack who said, "We don't know that. It might have been put here by someone else, for a different purpose." *He's evading.* Sarah sensed that Jack knew more about the coin than he was letting on.

"I don't think that was Pieter either," Priya said. "He lost control of those coins. And this morning's attack proves that at least one other party is involved. The real question is: why did they lead you here?"

Jack shrugged. "I don't know."

The lie was so obvious that Sarah was surprised Priya didn't jump on it right away, but it turned out she was only thinking aloud and answered herself. "They want to prove they have access to Little Brother."

"Why?" Sarah asked.

"DIAGON was never controlled by the government, or even the corporations. It was run by volunteers and funded by donations, but it was as influential as any of the major social media sites. I think someone is trying to tell us that's changed." She glanced at the camera. "Let's get out of here. We don't need anyone to hear how much we know."

Outside, Priya leaned forward to inspect the keypad. "How do I unlock it?"

"I'll get it." Jack raised the crystal. It took a few moments before the bolts withdrew, longer than Sarah thought it should have. After swinging the door shut, he flicked his wrist and the massive cylinders slid into place, securing the vault again. Then he squinted at the crystal. *"That cheater."*

"What are you talking about?" Sarah asked.

"Look." He held the crystal out for her to see, flipping it one-hundred-eighty degrees. "Two twenties."

"So?"

"Opposite sides should always add up to twenty-one. There's no number one." Faced with blank stares, he added, "It just means he can't be trusted."

Priya looked at him sharply. "You needed numbers to figure that out?"

Sarah also thought that Jack had been too trusting, and even though she understood that he could break any crystal's entanglement, she said, "You can't take it with you."

"I wasn't going to." He crouched by the keypad. "But this could be the biggest portal crystal on Earth, and we may need it someday." He pushed it into a gap under the shelf, and it fell and rattled onto a hidden bracket.

• • • •

To get back to the inn, Priya took Sarah and Jack on a series of buses to a neighborhood two miles away, then hiked into a wooded area with many trails. Priya saw that Jack was alert for any portals that might power a camera, but she was even more confident that no one had learned where she'd been staying. After all, they wouldn't have attacked her on the street if they had known where to find her.

It was fully dark by the time they entered the inn's basement through a back door and crept up a narrow staircase once used by servants. Priya peeked through a slender gap to check that the hallway was clear. "Go." She ushered them into her room and turned on the television.

Unsurprisingly, news of the attack was the lead story. There were photos of the governor's car speeding onto the sidewalk, and there would have been full video except that Little Brother protected its content by distributing individual frames across its network, and few hubs were functional yet. But it was the governor herself who was credited with having directed her driver to save an unnamed woman from being mugged.

"That's not what happened," Sarah said angrily. "Does this mean the media is being controlled, too?"

Priya considered. "Not *controlled*, as such. The attack may have been staged to polarize opinions before the next election. The governor will earn points for her actions, and her rivals will blame her for the growing crime rate. She'll get more support for her plan to cut hydroelectric power to neighboring states, and the opposition gets to advance their own trade plans." She shrugged. "Everyone wins; everyone loses."

"I don't get it," Jack said. "Other than getting people worked up, who benefits?"

"Not Danny," Sarah said. "His goal was to sell Cirrus to the highest bidder. He can't do that if everyone thinks it was destroyed."

"Right," Priya agreed. "He's working for someone else, someone we know nothing about."

"What about Paul?"

Jack shook his head. "Paul worked for Danny, not the other way around."

"No, I mean; what's his involvement?" Sarah glanced nervously at Priya before continuing. "Why is he still carrying your grandfather's orb? Wouldn't that be the most valuable one to sell?"

"Not really," Priya said. She'd caught Sarah's expression and recalled that Jack hadn't mentioned the stolen orb, a minor lapse compared to his other actions. "Before Newton, they were selling online for less than a thousand dollars."

Sarah turned to Jack. "I know you can't track him down through it, but can you get any clues?"

"No, they're made of thousands of crystals mashed together." He intertwined his fingers. "Like a network within a network. And a few of those crystals connect to entirely different orbs, which connect to others, and so on."

"So what good are they?"

"The whole point of diffusion spheres was to spread the

atmosphere evenly around Cirrus. They were designed so air and water would filter through, and they can also pass energy. Pieter connected cameras and microphones directly to his crystals, but with an orb you could probably just shout at it and be heard on the other side."

That was something Priya hadn't thought of. "So he might be using it to communicate with someone on Cirrus?"

"It's possible," Jack said. "A signal would get weaker with each portal, but it might eventually be picked up by *any* orb."

Priya didn't know if that was good news or bad. An orb wouldn't be a secure form of communication, but it would be untraceable. It could mean that Paul was part of a larger network.

• • • •

Jack had difficulty falling asleep that night, and his dreams were troubled when he finally did.

He was on Cirrus, in a boat on Icarus Lake. Paul, framed within a life-sized mugshot, stretched an arm out from the page and rolled a die. Every face was numbered one. Then the die morphed into an orb, and he heard a voice. "You lose." The orb grew massive, splintered the hull, and plunged through the bottom of the boat to form a whirlpool that spread to the island. The island itself caved in, its trees folding and swirling as it dropped into the core, drawing the sky with it. A colossal tear split Cirrus' roof, and the Spine, the space station's magnificent world-spanning mountain range, crumbled.

Jack woke with a start and quickly sat up to get his bearings. He was on top of a layer of blankets that cushioned the hardwood floor, Sarah was still asleep in the four-poster, and there was no sign of Priya. Also, the curtains were drawn and he didn't know how long he'd slept or what time it was. He slipped his socks on to warm his toes and muffle his footsteps as he crept to the window to gauge the hour.

"You put that coin portal into the DAIGON server, didn't you?"

Jack flipped a corner of the curtain to let some light into the room before he faced Sarah. He'd wanted to tell her everything last night, but not with Priya around. "How did you know?"

"Your phobia. You walked behind us all the way through the city. You haven't done that since before Newton. The emotion detectors are stronger now, aren't they?"

Jack nodded solemnly. "I didn't expect that. The coin was only supposed to open an outside link so the servers could start rebuilding themselves. We'll have Little Brother again. Well … Earth will, anyway."

"So Paul wasn't sending a message about somebody new controlling DAIGON?"

"No." He grinned sheepishly. "I just didn't have time to close the vault."

"And you programmed a vault-opening spell into the die and left it for him."

"Yeah. He's supposed to enable more hubs."

"*Why did you help him?*" Sarah's tone was accusing. "You already knew he was working for Danny."

"*Was.* We don't know if he still is. Anyway, that was part of the deal."

"What deal? With who?"

"I don't know their name." Jack felt genuinely guilty for not having told Sarah the truth earlier, but he still felt he was making the right decision. He reached for his shoes. "They want to meet."

Her suspicion turned to alarm. "You spoke to them through the crystal?"

"It wasn't Pieter." Jack hurried to make his point. "And I could have destroyed that connection in an instant if they tried to influence me."

She clearly had misgivings and took a moment to respond. "Where do they want to meet?"

"They're waiting for us on Icarus Island."

"Us?" She slipped off the bed and wrapped herself in a robe.

"They want you to come, too." He asked apprehensively, "Is that okay?"

"Is it safe?"

He took a deep breath. "Probably better than them coming to the village."

"When?"

"Whenever. It sounds like they're living there."

"So, somebody on Cirrus—*who's been staying on the island*—wants DAIGON restored. And they want direct access to it, and you don't think it's Pieter."

"I *know* it's not," he insisted. "I'd have recognized him."

"Oh, I really hope you know what you're doing."

So do I, he thought. "We'll check in with the village first."

The inn was quiet when they crept to the portal. But the aroma of bacon cooking downstairs wafted into the hall, and Jack regretted they couldn't pretend to be guests. After following Sarah through the wormhole, he retrieved his wand and turned on the radio.

"Vault to Icarus. Anyone there?"

"*Jack*," his mother cried. "Thank God. Come home, *quick*."

"What's wrong?"

"Jada and Marten have gone missing!"

Chapter 9

Priya left the inn well before dawn. Despite her confidence, it was prudent to follow a routine that limited the number of people who might see her in the area, which meant taking an indirect, two-hour route to her old office.

Little had changed in the months she'd been away. The elevators still weren't working—a low-priority task given that half the offices were empty—and the only addition was a gallery at the top of the stairs: photos of officers believed lost on Cirrus. Priya paused by Davis' picture. She was saddened that she couldn't tell his friends the truth; that both he and Cirrus were safe, but the fine layer of dust on the portraits reminded her how important it was to keep Holden's portal a secret: someone had made the decision to hang the memorial photos weeks before the public announcement.

At the end of the hall, Katherine was at the desk they once shared. She waved to Priya, then held a hand over her phone. "I'll be done in a minute. I got you a coffee already. It's not as good as you remember, but that doesn't stop everyone from drinking every last drop on the days it's available."

Priya sat in the office's second chair, the uncomfortable one they used to discourage visitors from lingering. She spotted a security briefing about North Korea on the desk and started reading. With Danny Kou having resurfaced, she was keen to follow any news about the reclusive nation.

Apparently, the North Koreans had built hundreds of new portal frames last month, fueling rumors that they'd sent as many crystals to Dawn and were planning an invasion. Calmer heads reminded the world that less than ten percent of all crystals had survived the trip. Also, a single interstellar portal required as much power as a small city, and the report concluded that the frames were most likely fake; another attempt to force the UN to grant them immigration rights.

The report was troubling, but not what bothered Priya as her friend put down the phone. "Were you expecting me?"

Katherine looked confused. "Didn't we say nine-thirty? Sorry, I've been so scattered lately. I transfer in a week, and I'm going crazy tying up loose ends here. Have you made up your mind yet?"

Priya considered the coffee. *No, we didn't say nine-thirty.* In fact, they hadn't spoken since January, when the UN recalled Katherine to her former position. In hindsight, that meant someone in the upper ranks had anticipated the mass arrival of portals on Dawn. Regardless, she knew what decision Katherine was referring to. "No, I haven't decided about Dawn."

"You should come. You really should. It's so crazy here, I can't keep up."

"You don't think it will be worse there, where everything is new?"

"That's just it. I don't know what to expect. Here, things are predictable. There are endless meetings, but we only resolve exactly what I expect. I want to get back to the old days, when we were properly investigating crimes. All I've been doing for the past month is following up on people we already know. Don't get me wrong, my clearance rate is phenomenal, but I'm just rounding up the usual suspects. Whenever anything happens, I already know who did it. It's … boring."

Priya nodded but didn't voice her suspicions. "Hey, do you remember the last guy you escorted off Cirrus?"

"Yeah. What's your interest?"

"Just following a lead. He called me last week with a tip. Did he leave any personal effects behind?"

Katherine shook her head. "He bolted the moment the lights went out. Whatever he had will still be in lockup."

Priya followed Katherine to the lockup next to the immigration chamber. That section did not have a working computer terminal, so Katherine consulted a logbook and found the entry for John Doe from that night, then led Priya to a box on a shelf in a locked room.

This wasn't a typical lockup for Priya. In Seattle, most of the storage space was filled with firearms and drugs. Here, the few items that hadn't been claimed by their owners, or sent to another jurisdiction for trial, were banal: clothing, shoes, keys. The container marked with Paul's case number held only a slip of paper with a series of numbers scrawled on it.

"That's all?"

Katherine checked the file. "He was also carrying one of those diffusion spheres that collectors go mad over. It says here that it was left on Cirrus."

Priya picked up the list and scanned the numbers. "Do you know—" She stalled in surprise when she read the first sequence. *That's the guest code for Holden's house.* She'd used it herself several times before moving his portal to a safer location. So how had Paul come by the number? And what did he need it for? She also recognized the handwriting: *Simon.*

"Do I know what?"

"Nothing." Priya waved the slip. "Can I take a copy of this?"

"I don't see why not. We never did learn his surname. No one's going to follow up after I'm gone if you don't."

Priya wrote the remaining numbers on her own notepad. It was faster than searching out the building's only working copy machine on the second floor.

"I really hope you'll come to Dawn," Katherine said later as she walked across the lobby to see Priya out. "It would be good for you. A new beginning."

"I haven't ruled it out," Priya admitted.

For Katherine, Dawn represented a fresh start on a world with clean air and unlimited opportunity. She'd already put her life in order and cleaned up her outstanding caseload. Priya, on the other hand, still hadn't achieved closure regarding Pieter. He'd caused suffering and devastation around the world, murdered a man on Cirrus, and never faced justice. As long as she still had a chance to fix that, Priya couldn't walk away.

• • • •

Her next stop was only a short distance from Katherine's office, where she could test a theory about Paul's list of numbers. Twenty minutes later, she stood in front of an unmarked steel door. In the dim red light, it resembled a bank vault even more than before.

Besides Holden's code, there were three nine-digit sequences on her list. Which should she try? Logically, if she entered the wrong one, the door would seal itself and notify someone of an intruder. She glanced at the camera lens built into the keypad.

Each sequence comprised at least five digits. The first had three ones, which might have been useful if the pad had a soft cover that showed wear, and the third combination was the only one of the three to use an eight. She leaned over and breathed against the keypad to fog its surface. Smudges appeared. *No eight.* The remaining marks were too hazy to be definite.

With only her intuition and fifty-fifty odds, she typed the second code. The keypad beeped, a motor whirred, and the lock icon turned green. She pulled the heavy door open for confirmation, closed it again, and stormed up the stairs. *Jack lied.*

Her first instinct was to return to the inn to confront him, and she was already halfway to the bus stop before her temper cooled enough to let her think rationally. Yes, he'd lied, but then she hadn't been honest with him either. She'd already known Paul was involved because she'd been to the basement under the realtor's office days ago. It was one of the addresses in Simon's notebook.

She slowed her pace and assessed her feelings. Her anger wasn't justified, and she'd been letting her emotions run unchecked again. What she really needed was to assemble the puzzle from the pieces she'd already collected.

Taking a deep breath, she silently listed the facts. *Paul was arrested on the eve of Newton with an orb from Holden's apartment. CorpSec confiscated it and handed him over for extradition. But some of Caerton's corporate security officers were working for Pieter, so the arrest may have been part of a plan to return him to Earth where he would complete his assignment. That would explain why he was a John Doe at the time.*

What happened next was speculation, and Priya assumed that his list of codes would have been returned had he not fled during the worldwide power failure. Without the codes, he'd been forced to find another way to access the vault, and lured Jack to DAIGON with a second orb from Holden's house in Newcastle.

That made sense, and Priya was feeling better until she realized that Jack had opened the door willingly. And that meant—*The gaming crystal. He'd have needed it to open the vault. And then*— She swore loudly, startling nearby pedestrians as she figured out what Jack had done. *He programmed a spell into it and left it for Paul.* She started for the realtor's office but quickly realized it was pointless. Paul would certainly have retrieved it by now.

So, she was back to the original problem. She didn't know why someone wanted access to DAIGON, but Paul had the access codes for two more hubs, and *she* had their addresses.

Chapter 10

Jack asked Sarah to drive down the mountain, not just because her talent could recall dangers on the treacherous path, but so he could scan for Jada and Marten.

"Anything?" Sarah sounded as anxious as he felt.

He roused from his meditative state and set his wand aside. "I can't sense their radio portal or the car's power crystal."

"Could they have had an accident?"

"The power cell is in a hard shell, inside a fuse box. And the radio's coin slot is strong, too. It would be impossible to shatter them both in a crash. This is …" He tapped his wand anxiously against his leg as he searched for a logical explanation. "This is something different."

Dusty was waiting on the riverside road that led to their hidden village. With her tail held high, she raced alongside DAVe for the final mile to the rocky beach, where a light rain was falling on the villagers gathered in front of the lodge. Jack's father, Victor, was helping Marten's grandfather, Anders, to load vehicles with ropes, blankets, tools, jugs of water—anything that might be useful on a rescue mission.

Emily, Jack's mother, ran to the road and embraced him the moment he stepped from the car. "I've been so worried. Marten and Jada have been missing since four o'clock on Sunday."

Jack couldn't see Jada's parents in the crowd. "Where are Suresh and Hélène?"

"They're searching near Aetherton." She turned to Sarah. "Your mother went with them."

"Have you heard from Ethan yet?" Sarah asked.

"I spoke to him fifteen minutes ago. He and Nathan are on their way home."

Ethan and his father had been on a two-day foraging run to an orchard south of Caerton. Jack had already sensed vibration from the power crystals in Nathan's car and Terrance's bike, but that only told him they were moving, not who was driving or where.

"We'll go with the next group." Jack started to walk to the cabins. "I'll grab a change of clothes."

"You're not going anywhere," Emily said sharply. "There's nothing you can do out there."

"But, Mrs. Scatter," Sarah pleaded, "we can … I'm not sure. But we have to help."

"Sorry, it's just not safe." Her tone was softer with Sarah than it had been with Jack. "Your mother would never allow it."

Sarah started to follow as Emily walked away, but Jack grabbed her hand and gestured for her to walk with him.

Jerking her hand back, she said, "We can't give up that easily. They need us."

He lowered his voice. "I agree, but we have a meeting."

It was obvious that Sarah still wanted to join the searchers, but realized that wasn't going to happen. "Do you think whoever contacted you has something to do with Jada and Marten?"

"Not directly," Jack said. "But I don't like coincidences."

They headed for the dock and selected a canoe from the dozen boats moored there. Instead of picking up a paddle, Sarah pointed her wand and willed the boat towards the island while Jack smoothed turbulence under its thin hull. Soon, their small craft was silently cutting across the lake faster than any racing scull could.

"Where are we going?" Sarah asked.

"They gave me directions to a spot on the south side of the island," Jack said as he prepared to cross into the island's portal zone.

Much larger than the one on the Vault, the island's zone comprised billions of microscopic wormholes: fragments of Cirrus' artificial gravity belt that had been dragged to the surface by an asteroid impact. And like the Vault, Icarus Island had its own vibe. Also like the Vault, Sarah was sensitive to it.

"*It's a dragon.*" Sarah gasped as they crossed the threshold.

"That's who you spoke to. That's who has the third coin in the set you connected to the DAIGON server."

"I wanted to tell you, but after what happened with Blue, I was worried you might say no."

"They're the same one we met in the mill last year, aren't they?"

"Yeah." That dragon was even larger than Blue, and Jack half expected Sarah to slow the canoe. But if anything, she pushed it harder.

Neither of them spoke as they passed the charred remains of Niels' cabin, and Jack wondered if the man had known about or even encountered dragons. As the island's only former resident, he'd drawn upon the connections of its massive portal zone to become the most gifted Traveller ever. But even his foresight wasn't perfect, and it hadn't saved him from Pieter's deadly wrath.

The southern tip of the four-mile diameter island was inhospitable, and little more than fractured rock with scattered forest. It was where he and Sarah often rowed to when they wanted to practice their more energetic spells, ones the villagers would certainly disapprove of, and the near-vertical wall overlooking the lake was pitted and scorched from their experiments with fireballs and plasma missiles.

Jack pointed to an isolated group of pines on the shore as the sun emerged from the clouds. "They said to look behind those trees." He steered the canoe to a rocky shelf and wrapped its rope around a sturdy trunk.

Sarah didn't hesitate while he tied up the boat. She skipped across the tops of boulders and landed on a slope of gray talus fallen from the crest of the hundred-foot bluff. "There's a cleft back here."

Jack joined her in the cool draft flowing from the towering split in the rock. Though the channel was open to the sky, many large boulders had spalled from the upper wall and jammed at lower elevations, forming sheltered wells between stretches of ankle-breaking rubble. An unpleasant odor of decay developed as they hiked deeper into the dim light, stepping over the bones of deer and smaller animals.

Sixty yards from the opening, the channel widened and its floor climbed. They were now less than forty feet from the surface, but the rim above was lined with spruce and fir trees, and little direct light reached them. Deep shadows hid voids where the walls angled apart at their base, and Jack's portal-sense told him of crystals heaped within.

"There are thousands of crystals here, and a lot of them are Pieter's. And—" One of them was moving. Jack faced a darkened hollow and called, "What do you want?"

Knowing it was a dragon, he expected an AI-moderated reply, an ethereal voice inside his own mind. But the response was as clear as if they had spoken aloud.

'A favor.'

Jack was momentarily stunned. He'd communicated through the AI with other dragons and people, even Sarah, but those exchanges had been gist and emotion, where the meaning was subject to interpretation. These were actual clear-cut words.

"What sort of favor?" Sarah asked.

"You …" Jack wasn't expecting that. "You heard them, too?"

Sarah nodded. 'Yes, and they can hear us.' She smiled at his startled reaction.

How—? Jack couldn't voice the question. He'd understood Sarah clearly, though she hadn't spoken aloud. He could think of only one way that might be possible, and extended his portal-sense into the largest recess to comb through the crystals there. *It's Ethan's lucky coin.*

'It is safe here.' The dragon lumbered out of the darkness, their head swaying at the end of a muscular neck. Thick scales rasped against stones as their six-foot-long tail curled into view.

Jack was more alarmed by the dragon's words than by how much they'd grown since last year. *Can they read my mind?*

'Do not be concerned,' the dragon said. 'Your thoughts are so guarded that I sense only the emotions another human would see on your face.'

He wasn't entirely reassured. *What do they mean by* safe? His eyes had adjusted to the dim light, and he leaned aside to focus on the pile behind the dragon. They may have kept Ethan's coin portal from Pieter, who intended to use it to control Sarah and Ethan, but someone was influencing people on Earth. And something strange had happened to his friends. He directed his thoughts to the dragon. 'Where are Jada and Marten?'

'They are hidden from me.'

'What does that mean?'

'There are places on this world we may not go.'

That made no sense, but Jack had other concerns. 'Why did you ask me to bring Sarah?'

'She may convince you to help us.'

Jack glanced at Sarah, who was silently following their soundless conversation. He asked, 'Help you with what?'

'War is coming. To both your homeworld and this one. *Danny Kou* is growing stronger.'

Jack had so many questions. The dragon had said '*us*', and '*war*', but he focused on their last statement. 'What does Danny have to do with this?' At least, he thought they'd said Danny. The words streaming into his consciousness had faltered then.

'He will spread conflict among my people. You can stop him.'

'How do you even know about Danny?'

'Many of my kind have joined his forces. One is an ally.'

'You've got a spy? And you want me to go up against Danny as a *favor*?'

'You will not be alone.' The dragon uttered a quivering growl that was out of sync with their words as their tail flicked from side to side like an annoyed cat's. 'Call on me and I will send aid.'

Jack had never had greater doubts. A dragon weighing four or five hundred pounds was asking him to take on a hired killer and stop a war. 'I … I don't know. If I agree to this, how am I supposed to stop him?'

The dragon lowered their scaly snout onto a large stone. 'Come closer.'

• • • •

Sarah was just as surprised as Jack after he asked, "What do you want?" She *heard* the dragon's response, though they had made no sound.

"What sort of favor?" she asked.

"You …" He stammered. "You heard them, too?"

Without really knowing why, Sarah decided not to speak. Instead, she thought, 'Yes, and they can hear us', but with the intent that Jack would somehow understand. She almost laughed at his shocked expression, but she had questions for the dragon. And since it seemed they preferred to communicate silently, she continued that way. 'What's your name?'

'My kind have no need of names.' The dragon's projected voice was a deep rumble. 'If you direct your thoughts to me, I will hear.'

'Okay, um, how about I call you Asterion?'

'Am I a monster?' the dragon asked as they swaggered into the light.

'*No.*' She fought a rising dread. Excluding their tail, which was as long as their body, the armored beast was the size of a bear. 'But … the island is called Icarus.' She glanced into the unlit recesses that surrounded them. 'And this place is kind of a maze, so—' Sarah's labyrinth explanation was cut off by her realization. 'You know ancient Greek mythology? How—' *The coin portal Jack installed in the server.* 'You can access the internet now, can't you?'

'We have always had that. The three-way link merely brings it closer and enhances our speech.'

Three-way link? Asterion was using terms not known to the public or the internet. Then she realized the words were not theirs, only an AI interpretation for her benefit. *What else can the AI do?* 'Can you also see the future? Like a Traveller?'

'We have enough memories to occupy ourselves.'

Memories? Sarah saw Jack focusing on the cache of crystals behind the dragon. They both knew Asterion had claimed Ethan's coin. 'You can access human memories?'

'Do not worry. We do not trade them lightly.'

Worrying was exactly what Sarah was doing: Asterion had just admitted to trading in memories. 'Whose memories can you retrieve?'

'Retrieve is the wrong word. Through portals we sense your thoughts, but humans dwell in the past as much as they live in the present. You needlessly regret bygone decisions and boast of ancient triumphs.'

'So it's only those memories we *choose* to recall. And you trade those? Why?'

'Why do humans read? Why do you watch videos?'

'Our memories are entertainment for you?' Sarah realized as soon as she said it how limited that assumption was. Passwords, secrets, cover-ups. Almost anything unspoken would be of greater value.

'It is humans who roam the network freely, and intrude on the thoughts of others.'

'I only access my own memories.'

'Are you certain? There is another mind linked to the crystal through which we are joined.'

Asterion was right. She and Ethan had not only touched each other's thoughts through his coin, they'd attempted to control each other. And Jack could sense the emotions of any animal that was near a crystal. 'We gave each other permission. What you're doing is nothing like that.'

'You use the beasts of this world for your own purposes. Even now you contemplate sending them to do your bidding.'

Did Jack ask the ravens to search for Jada? 'We're trying to help our friends.'

'Are we so different?'

Asterion had a point. The line between asking and compelling was thin. 'You said you trade memories. What will you take in exchange for Ethan's coin?'

A fluttering growl that could only be laughter accompanied

their answer. 'You ask for much. Through that coin I learn more about your kind than through the others combined.' Their tail flicked cat-like, from side to side.

'As long as that coin exists, my friends and I are at risk.'

'Very well.' Asterion reached their decision in no time. 'If you bring me the key, I will return the coin.'

'What key?'

Asterion dipped their head. Sarah didn't understand the meaning of the gesture until Jack stepped forward with his arm outstretched. He hesitated with his hand hovering over their head, then cautiously felt along a bony ridge to the base of their skull.

"You have a crystal embedded here." Jack's wavering voice was almost a question, as if he couldn't believe what he was sensing. "And there's a tattoo—"

Asterion abruptly whirled and lashed their tail, causing Jack to stagger as they plunged into the narrow end of the channel. They disappeared briefly in the darkness before thundering up the wall. A clatter of falling stones marked their passage, followed by a flash of green when a stray beam of sunlight reflected from their scales.

"*Jack,*" Sarah cried. She ran to help him as he stumbled into the rock wall.

"I'm okay." He'd regained his balance but was trembling. "Let's get out of here."

• • • •

As the canoe drifted into the lake, Jack steadied his breathing. Sarah was waiting for an explanation.

"I was about to have an anxiety attack. There were so many emotions. They weren't directed at me but—" He shivered.

"What emotions?"

"Fear. Shame. Rage."

"*Shame?* How bad was the tattoo?"

"It was just a few characters. I didn't have time to read it."

"Why did you place your hand on their head?"

He stretched out his hand, recalling the rough texture of the dragon's scales, and their surprising warmth. "I sensed a crystal under their skin."

"A tracking tag?"

"I don't think so. This was deep. I think it was in their skull."

She grimaced. "That's disgusting."

"What? How?"

"Don't you see? It's not for tracking. It's a direct port to their brain. Whoever engineered dragons wanted the ability to kill them."

Jack didn't see, but Sarah had interned at the aviary in Caerton and probably had a good reason to think so. "Why?"

Before answering, Sarah spelled the canoe forward, but only slowly so the wind wouldn't make it hard to talk. "They're apex predators. We know they hunt only designated prey, but what if that conditioning failed? What if they started hunting livestock instead?"

"I don't understand, then. I could have broken the connection. They asked me to help but left before I could do anything."

"Could you still find the other half of the pair if you broke the link?"

"Well, no. Why would I want to?"

"Breaking one connection would only help Asterion. I think the key they're looking for works for all dragons. If we find it, they'll give us Ethan's coin."

"Huh? What key? Who is Asterion?"

Sarah repeated what she'd heard, creating a lot of confusion, and Jack told her what *he'd* heard, adding even more. "It's incredible," he said. "They were having two completely different conversations at the same time."

"They also said we use animals for our own purposes. Did you send the ravens to look for Jada?"

"No, but that's a great idea."

"Asterion thinks we already did, which means dragons *can* remember future events, although it sounds like they perceive them as current. *That's* confusing."

"Nobody really understands consciousness," Jack said as he guided the canoe around the island. "We've always assumed the AI works across time, but maybe it's a natural function for dragons."

He beached the canoe in the cove near Niels' cabin, where it would be easier to convey a message to the ravens without the motion of the waves distracting him. They climbed the stairs cut into the rock and sat on a wooden bench next to a grassy mound that was sheltered from the wind by a semicircle of trees, but far enough away to be always in the sun. According to his friends, this had been one of Niels' favorite spots, and they decided it was the best place for his grave.

While Jack was in the meditative state he used to commune with the ravens, Sarah noticed engravings on the bench's lacquered surface: numbers, in combinations of six digits from one to forty-nine.

Jack stirred. "Hugo is on his way to Aetherton, and I've asked Arven to look in the Spine."

"Isn't Arven younger? Shouldn't *he* be the one to go to Aetherton?"

"He has the better memory, but he doesn't have Hugo's experience. They both know what Jada looks like because she's been feeding them, and Arven thinks of Marten as some type of giant, but he can't understand the difference between a car and a tractor. I'd have to review everything he saw on four wheels."

Sarah ran her fingers over the engravings. "Did you notice these before?"

Jack leaned closer. "Huh? Lottery numbers."

"That's what I thought, too."

"Like a trophy, maybe?" In his experience, Niels was far too humble to brag though he had predicted dozens of winning numbers decades ago, which led to him buying the land around Icarus and crashing an asteroid into it, which—paradoxically—created the giant portal zone that helped him pick the right numbers in the first place. "That doesn't seem like Niels."

"No, that's not it at all." Sarah seemed puzzled. "How many times have you heard Ethan tell the story of the time he was shot?"

Jack chuckled. "Too many."

"And does he ever change the facts about his part?"

"He exaggerates. And the last time I heard it, he said I was hiding under Priya's bed. But no, he always describes his *own* actions correctly."

Sarah stared across the lake as she explained how she'd got the details wrong about the attack on Priya. "Everything happened so fast, and I was angry at you for running off. I can't entirely remember what I did, even now." She turned sideways on the bench, her whole body facing Jack. "What if this is how Traveller-memories work? Asterion talked about people *choosing* to relive certain memories. What if Niels had to constantly study the numbers the way Ethan retells stories? As I understand it, he spent a lot of time here."

"I don't know." Jack had heard Niels ponder the Traveller Effect without ever fully understanding its nature. "I don't know if *anyone* knows. But I *do know* we have to find Ethan."

"Why?"

"Because Asterion asked you for a key, and you asked Ethan about a case. I think the two are related. Besides, he has to cover for us."

"What do you mean; *cover for us*?"

"We're going to find Jada and Marten."

Chapter 11

Danny had a good reason to be upset when he returned to Cirrus: his agent had failed to track Priya to Holden's portal, meaning he was now behind on that aspect of his long-term plan.

Typically, a failure like that would result in extreme sanctions, and the best Paul could hope for was to lose future contracts instead of body parts. However, it wasn't entirely his fault. The detective had been attacked on the street, making it too risky to follow her.

It wasn't just the delay that troubled Danny, or that the attack had been carried out in public, or even that bits of it were captured on video and streamed through Little Brother. No, the worst was that he recognized the attacker as someone he'd once contracted for similar work. That meant someone in his own circle was responsible.

Danny retrieved his phone from a locker, then strode from the portal chamber with the intent of speaking to Mentor. He'd only crossed half the warehouse when he spotted the same brown dragon that had been hiding there when he left for Seattle.

"You," he snarled.

The dragon dashed across the floor and Danny raced after it, weaving between stacks of crates and half-built frames of armored cars. He sprinted into the wide aisle that led to a side exit, and the dragon was already there, too small to trigger the automatic door.

Trapped.

The dragon raised itself on its hind legs and flicked its head back. An orange flame spat from the crystal in its gorget, and the door swung open.

Clever beast, he thought as it slipped through the widening gap. He knew they could produce shields and call fire from their crystals, but this one had learned to waft the heat from its meager flame to trick the door's sensor into thinking a human stood there.

The little dragon could run much faster than Danny, and he expected to find the alley empty. Instead, it was waiting for him at the corner of the next building. If he'd had a weapon, he might have blasted the creature before noticing how it held its head low to the ground. He had seen enough fights between dragons to recognize the awkward pose as a submissive gesture.

He walked calmly to the corner, and the dragon waited until he'd come half the distance before spinning around and slinking away. When he reached the lane, it was at the screened opening to the building's crawlspace. It let him take a few steps before pushing aside the hinged panel and slithering out of sight.

The dragon clearly meant for Danny to follow, but it wasn't the too-small vent that deterred him. This was Mentor's home.

Of course, Danny could enter the temple freely through the main entrance, and there were places within where he wouldn't attract the attention of Mentor's guards, human or dragon. The mystery, though, was why the creature wanted him to follow. And why had it been watching him before?

He wanted very much to return to the problem of the unexpected attack on Detective Singh, but the meddlesome brown dragon was a matter he could deal with quickly, and he circled around to the portico. If the dragon had gone into an office on the outer wall, he could explore without interference. And it seemed he had no choice, anyway.

As he entered the hallway that ringed the inner sanctum, he saw a dragon with a red cowl: a member of Mentor's personal guard. Like the acolytes, each of the puma-sized dragons—there were four of them—answered only to Mentor, and the one patrolling the inner vestibule watched him closely as he turned to follow the outer corridor.

The building's thick whitewashed walls shielded it from the stifling heat of the midday sun, and its twenty-foot ceilings kept the hallway cool. Danny ignored the many statues, amphoras, and other reproductions of ancient Greek culture as he hunted towards the back of the temple. To him, these things were foolish and a waste of not only money, but his time. Finding only a single door ajar, he pushed it open and spotted the brown dragon perched on a desk in the center of the room.

'Welcome back,' the beast said in flawless Korean.

A Hopper's world held few surprises. This was one of them. *"I can hear you."* Not only had the dragon spoken Danny's native language, it was using his own dialect.

'Soon you'll be able to hear all of us.' Its voice was upbeat and lilting, totally unsuitable for the unsightly creature it came from.

Whenever he faced a new or challenging situation, Danny relied on his talent for a half-second of clear thinking. There was no attack coming, so he swiftly assessed the room and everything in it. Foremost, the dragon's posture was no longer meek, and its voice was … not a voice. It seemed to bypass his hearing and speak directly to his mind. The doorway he stood in was the only entrance—or exit—and the orb on the desk was one he'd arranged to be stolen from Holden's safe months ago. The only thing he didn't grasp at once was the meaning of the dragon's words.

"Explain."

'Mentor's reach grows with every crystal,' it said cheerfully.

"I'm in no mood for riddles."

As the dragon shuffled across the desk, sunlight streaming from a window set high in the north wall reflected from its neck-mounted crystal, and Danny recognized it as one of Pieter's coins. 'Mentor sees all,' the dragon said.

DAIGON? Danny knew the network of cameras was Mentor's main source of information, and in addition to tracking the detective, he'd tasked Paul with finding crystal pairs for expanding its coverage. *He* didn't care what crystals they used; it was Mentor who specified they should be Pieter's. "What does that have to do with why I can understand you now?"

The dragon attempted to explain the fusion of machines and minds, and Danny learned as much through distortion as he did through detail. Clearly, the creature did not speak Korean, or even the English that was spoken by many of those in Mentor's enclave.

Instead, DAIGON's AI passed meaning and context to the listener in real-time. Not only that, it interpreted phone conversations heard by dragons through three-way coin links, and allowed them to perceive what its cameras saw. The system wasn't perfect, though, and the little dragon had trouble with people's names.

"The dragons are Mentor's spies?" Danny's question was rhetorical. If this creature had one of the linked coins, then so did the rest. "They report what they hear in phone calls?"

'The link goes both ways.'

Both ways? Pieter manipulated people through subliminal suggestions and false memories. If Mentor had learned the same trick, that would mean— "Mentor ordered the attack on Singh?"

The dragon tilted its head, a gesture that seemed to mean *yes*.

Danny suddenly understood that Mentor, with hundreds of coins, was more than one step ahead of him. "Why tell me now?"

'Mentor will soon have the key. Dragons everywhere will suffer.' And still its voice was at odds with its words, almost cartoonish.

Everywhere? "The key is some sort of remote control?"

The dragon cocked its head again.

Danny smiled. He'd heard enough. While dragons were essential to their plans, he would soon need a way to restrain the four that protected Mentor. "If you want me to help, you will do something for me."

● ● ● ●

Danny ordered the warehouse tech to set the portal address to Olympia. It was far too late to catch up to the detective, but there was other work to be done.

He would keep blocking attempts to reach Cirrus from Earth. That would satisfy Mentor, and the job would be easier now that he knew Mentor was playing both sides. He'd also have more time to pursue his own nation-building goals there. Meanwhile, his new accomplice would acquire information vital to his plans for Cirrus.

Chapter 12

Ethan had hoped to boast of riding Terrance's motorbike on his recent trip, but the mood was sober when he joined Jack at Sarah's cabin. He already knew his cousin had failed to get permission to join the search.

"I tried convincing my parents to let me go, too." Ethan shook his head. "No luck."

"My mother went with Suresh before Jack and I got back," Sarah said. "I never had the chance to ask."

"Then she never said no, did she?"

Sarah shot him a dirty look even though he was only trying to lighten the mood. He knew that Mrs. Rogers, a former CorpSec officer, was very strict. He flopped into a chair. "What did I miss on Earth?"

Jack and Sarah recapped the past two days for him: Paul, the attack on Priya, the orbs, the governor, Asterion, and Priya's opinion that Pieter was either dead or so damaged from portal use that he may as well be. They had no idea what the key was, but it seemed connected to Danny, Jada and Marten, and possibly a war.

"War?" Ethan asked. "With who? You said everyone on Earth thinks Cirrus is gone. Unless Asterion is lying. Did you consider that?" From the looks on his friends' faces, it was apparent they had not. "You know cynicism is a *good* thing, right?"

Sarah glared at him. "*I* believe them."

"It doesn't matter anyway," Jack said. "I never agreed to help. We're only interested in finding Jada and Marten."

"Okay," Ethan said, "but there's something else I don't understand. We know Pieter originally intended his Third-Eye coins for spying through phones and networks, and that he only learned he could use them for mind control later. But he was just controlling Terrance, James, and Priya's boss. If Earth's politicians and media are being manipulated the way you say they are, who's doing it? Even if one person could handle a hundred others, you'd still need hundreds of controllers working together."

That was a factor neither of his friends seemed to have considered. Sarah had to think for a moment before she added, "And they'd have to be on Cirrus, too."

"There's got to be an aspect of mind-control we don't understand yet," Jack said. "Simon couldn't resist Pieter even when we blocked the connection between them, so the AI must keep the effect going. Like the way our spells run after we cast them, or how Asterion heard both of us at the same time."

"There was something else," Sarah said. "I understood Asterion perfectly, except for when they mentioned Pieter. I *knew* they were talking about him, but it was like they couldn't say his name."

"Yeah, I noticed the same thing. Even when they referred to you. What's their problem with names?"

She shrugged and turned to Ethan. "Anyway, Jack and I are going to the coast as soon as we can sneak out. The ravens are already looking, but they have no way of telling him where they are if they find something. If we're nearby, they can just lead us there."

Jack nodded. "It's the fastest way to get results."

"I'm not arguing," Ethan argued, "but I should go, too."

"If we all leave; Dad will cut DAVe's power. One of us has to stay."

Ethan looked at Sarah, and she warned him off with a glare. "*Fine*, I'll say you're still on the island. But that won't work for long."

"We'll be at the crossroads in four hours," she said. "From there we'll catch up with Suresh or Anders. Mom will be happy knowing I'm safe, and no one here will have anything to worry about."

"How are you getting DAVe out of the village without anyone seeing?"

Jack dug his wand out of his pocket. "You can help me take the back wall off the garage."

That sounded perfectly reasonable to Ethan, so they snuck away from the cabins to the driftwood shelter that served as a parking garage. The front of the structure was in direct view of the lodge, but the rest of it was in the trees to hide it from passing drones.

Jack readied his wand. "I'll keep it from falling apart while you pull the logs off."

The crystals in Ethan's ring were smaller than the one in his staff, but there were four of them. He spread their energy beams across a twelve-foot-long, sun-bleached log that braced a wall of thick planks. The garage shook and groaned as he pulled, while Jack used a bracing force to keep the roof from collapsing. Then Ethan assembled the freed boards into a ramp so DAVe could climb the steep bank into the forest.

Fifteen minutes later, Ethan wasn't surprised to find Dusty waiting for him as he guided DAVe onto the overgrown track on the east side of the lake, though he hadn't himself known where he would exit the forest. Jack and Sarah were close, too. They'd left the village in a canoe, in full view of everyone, apparently headed for the island.

"Good luck." Ethan said as they traded vehicles. "I'll tell your parents you wanted some private time together."

Jack's face turned beet-red and Sarah warned, *"Don't you dare."*

Ethan laughed and started paddling. *"Relax.* I'll tell them you're talking to the ravens. But, you know, at some point, that's gonna be more upsetting to them than anything else you guys might get up to."

• • • •

Thanks to Ethan, the first leg of the journey was awkward, and Jack was glad for the excuse of navigating the rough road in silence. Everyone knew he and Sarah were dating; it was impossible *not to* in a village of a hundred people. But their relationship was … confusing.

They'd known each other since childhood but had only met in-person eight months ago, and within twenty-four hours were engaged in a battle to save the world. There's nothing like a life-or-death conflict to cement a friendship.

When they went their separate ways after only a few days, Jack hoped he wouldn't have to wait until graduation to see Sarah again. He hadn't expected fate—or perhaps, Niels—to bring them together in Icarus just two months later. Since then, they'd hung out constantly, shared a kiss, thwarted a villain—normal stuff for seventeen-year-olds during a technological apocalypse—and become closer than ever. But facing dragons was less stressful than planning for the future, and he worried that she might expect more from him. *Should I be pushing our relationship to another level or waiting for her to make a move?*

"I'll drive," Sarah said.

"Huh?" Jack felt the color returning to his cheeks.

"You should check with the ravens. I'll drive DAVe."

"Oh, right." They'd just reached the highway, and it would be easier for him to concentrate while they were on a paved road. He pulled over and swapped seats with Sarah.

On Icarus Island, communicating with the ravens was relatively simple. Jack had only to imagine talking to them, and the AI handled the rest. With only his wand to work with, he had to envision a virtual landscape of wormhole connections and locate their individual crystals: a leg band for Hugo, a stomach stone for Arven.

"Hugo hasn't reached Aetherton yet, but Arven has seen hundreds of vehicles." Jack imagined seeing them himself, and let the AI coax Arven into recalling his own observations. "He's following the highway west like I asked, and flying high enough to spot anything ten miles to either side."

"Has he seen any homesteads?"

"Quite a few. He's already south of the crossroads."

Arven, naturally curious, checked out settlements on his own, but *his* real focus was food, and Jack's stomach grumbled in response to the bird's interest in gardens and smokehouses. But viewing Arven's memories wasn't like watching a video. The impressions Jack received were hazy but empathic, and he understood that none of the people the raven saw were Jada or Marten.

The highway ran parallel to the Spine all the way to the coast, and after four hours of driving parallel to it, Sarah announced that they'd reached the crossroads. "We'll have to check in soon, or find Suresh and my mother."

"Hold on." Jack was following Arven's memories through the pass, though the raven was already miles beyond. "I think I found something."

"Their car?"

"No, it's strange. Arven has been circling every community looking for food, but there's one he flew over without stopping. At least, I *think* he did. It's like there's a gap in his memory."

"Should you ask him to go back and look more closely?"

"He's about an hour ahead of us now."

"Why would Jada and Marten have gone south?"

"I remember going this way when I was a kid. There's a great view of the Wayward Sea from the summit. Maybe they wanted a look." Jack didn't mention the cliffs he recalled below the viewpoint. "We could be there in twenty minutes."

Sarah agreed and steered DAVe south towards Port Isaac instead of north to Aetherton.

The highway pass between the two cities was the lowest of the three on this side of the sector, but the rising terrain it cut through was still formidable. No barriers separated the winding road from steep drops into rocky, barren chasms as DAVe climbed to a bleak plateau three thousand feet above sea level.

"That'll be it." Jack indicated a flat, windswept area large enough for a bus to turn around on.

Sarah pulled into the turnout. As with the highway, there was no barrier to prevent traffic from going over the precipice, and she parked well back from the margin of thin grasses growing at the perimeter of the gravel lot.

"Look." Jack pointed at the ground beside DAVe. "Tire tracks."

Sarah got out and followed the shallow grooves. "There's a lot of them, but they all go back to the highway." She walked to the cliff's edge and peered over. "That's a long way down."

Jack joined her at the viewpoint. In some places, the Spine was four miles tall and just as narrow as it snaked across the sector. Here, there were no sharp peaks between them and the sea, only a twenty-mile-wide ribbon of rolling hills. Beyond that, the Spine resumed as a meandering chain of islands that continued to the opposite coast.

"I hear dogs," Sarah said.

Jack scanned the surrounding landscape. There wasn't a single tree on the hills to the west, and an endless, deserted plain stretched north and south along the coast. Also, the wind was buffeting around DAVe's door panels, making it hard even to speak at a normal volume. "Are you sure?"

She nodded.

Jack turned into the wind, listening. He couldn't detect anything until he used a spell to enhance his hearing, which meant Sarah had sensed the sound as a Traveller-memory. Though the spell confirmed barking, he couldn't say how far it had carried. But the direction was right.

"It's coming from the foothills." On the other side of the highway, the Spine was much taller, and some of the distant peaks were capped with snow or hidden in the clouds, which matched the impression he had received. "That's where Arven was. Let's check it out."

Sarah looked at the hills nervously. "We should call Suresh."

"If I'm right, that village is only fifteen minutes away. If we call now, they won't let us keep searching."

"If we *don't* find them, Mom will be furious that we left the highway."

"We'll be quick. I remember the roads Arven saw." Jack took the driver's seat and sped onto the highway, which quickly dropped to half the elevation of the plateau. They were surrounded by forest again when he braked hard, leaving patches of rubber on the pavement. "Sorry, I almost missed the turnoff."

The gravel road he then entered widened into a parking lot filled with snowplows and other highway maintenance vehicles. "It's a dead end," Sarah said.

"Arven saw a road." Jack circled the lot. "It should be … There." The gap in the trees behind two plows was hard to spot. "Anders would have missed that if he hadn't known what to look for."

He steered DAVe between the larger vehicles and onto a narrow track, which immediately turned and descended through a forest of conifers. Culverts under the road channeled small streams from the uphill side of the road into a larger creek on the downhill side.

"They've got to be here." Jack's speed matched his enthusiasm, and he noticed Sarah's expression. "Nervous?"

"A bit."

"Why? There's nothing to be afraid of. You could light up this forest with fireballs. Together, we're unstoppable." He grinned and reached for her hand.

"That's not what worries me." She seized DAVe's grab bar.

"Hey, I'm not a bad driver. I—"

"*WATCH THE ROAD.*"

Jack swerved in time to avoid three bounding deer, then fought to recover DAVe from a high-speed skid that tossed gravel in an expanding gray wave. He'd just straightened the car when its dashboard lights blinked out.

"What was that?" Sarah cried.

He stomped the brake pedal and it sank right to the floor. "We've got no brakes."

In seconds, DAVe accelerated to highway speed down the steep hill. Sarah held on to the roll cage with both hands. "*Do something.*"

"*I'm trying.*" Jack went for his wand as DAVe juddered wildly over the washboard surface. A front wheel slammed into a pothole and bounced him into the roll cage's foam padding, driving the air from his lungs and knocking the wand under his seat. He got his hands back on the steering wheel and tried to focus on the road, but his vision was so blurred by vibration he could barely make out the sharp corner ahead. That's when he finally remembered the parking brake.

"Wait," Sarah shouted as he reached for the lever. Too late. Jack jerked the handle, sending DAVe into an uncontrolled spin.

The forest whirled and was soon lost behind a veil of dust. DAVe's tires sunk into loose gravel and checked the spin, but now they were sailing backwards, and branches whipped DAVe's side panels before they finally lurched to a stop. In the sudden silence, a trailing cloud of debris settled on them and the car.

Coughing, Jack saw that they'd coasted a quarter mile and dropped at least five hundred feet.

Sarah spat a gob of tiny stones she'd collected when DAVe spun, then gave him an exasperated look. "You were saying?"

"Okay, I'm not a *great* driver, but"—he spotted a car in his rearview mirror—"Hey, we found them!"

Sarah twisted in her seat. DAVe had stopped inches from the bumper of Jada and Marten's car. She slapped her seatbelt's release button and shook off the harness. "Where are they?"

Jack checked the area around Marten's car. Its wheels had plowed into the same loose soil that finally stopped DAVe. "I see footprints. They walked away."

"I'll call Suresh." Sarah pressed the radio's power button but it didn't light up. She jiggled it, then tapped it on DAVe's hood. "It's not working."

Jack leaned into the other car. "Their radio is gone. And the solar panels they were supposed to deliver are still on the roof." He looked up the hill. "We'd have seen them on the road." He estimated they'd driven ten miles from the highway.

Sarah slapped the dust off her clothes. "Did you feel something when DAVe's brakes quit?"

"Terror."

"No, I think we passed a threshold. Like the one on the Vault."

"Really? I was kind of busy." He shook grit from his hair. "I need to wash the dirt out of my eyes. That creek we saw should be over there."

Jack pushed through branches and discovered a swiftly running stream only a dozen yards away. The water was freezing but relieved his eyes.

"I know where they went," Sarah said.

Jack assumed she'd had another Traveller-memory until he saw the wooden bridge she was pointing at downstream. It spanned only fifteen feet and was constructed from tree trunks at least a foot in diameter. Had DAVe coasted a little farther, they'd have been able to drive across it.

"That's not a temporary structure." He flicked cold water from his hands. "That was built to last decades."

"So they found a settlement, after all. What made them come this way in the first place?"

"I don't know, but I hear music." He drew his wand, holding it loosely at his side. "Let's go see."

When they got closer, Sarah slowed her pace to soften her footsteps. "That sounds like a lute. And—" She faltered when three camouflaged men stepped onto the road. One of them was carrying a rifle.

Jack was initially too surprised to react, and the unarmed men only gaped until the third fumbled with his rifle and Jack instinctively raised his wand. With months of practice, he'd become so confident that he actually stepped forward while summoning the barrier. "*Shield.*"

The men's expressions mirrored Jack's confusion; no shield had formed. He repeated the command. Nothing.

The armed soldier finally got his bearings and fired a shot into the ground at Jack's feet, causing Sarah to yelp as he jumped backwards. Then he shouted and gestured at the wand, and Jack let it fall as the man circled behind while motioning for him and Sarah to follow the others. They didn't know Sarah still had her wand, but it didn't matter—the magic was gone.

Chapter 13

As the soldiers marched him and Sarah along the dusty road, Jack whispered, "Are your earrings working?"

Sarah was clearly alarmed, but not so much that she couldn't concentrate. "I can't sense a connection. Do you think magic has stopped everywhere? Has there been another Newton?"

"No, Marten's car must have lost power the same way DAVe did, and that happened days ago. This is …" Trying to think logically pulled him from the initial shock he'd felt, and let him focus on the men's conversation. "What language is that?"

Sarah listened for a few moments. "I think it's Korean."

Jack couldn't understand a word, but their tone suggested unease. He also noticed how different they were. The armed man looked to be around thirty, but the ones in front were perhaps nineteen or twenty, and their camouflaged fatigues hung loosely on gaunt frames.

They passed through a tall chainlink gate topped with razor wire, and came to a drab building with a metal roof. Its barred windows overlooked the settlement Jack had seen from Arven's point of view, and its entrance was at the top of a short flight of stairs. One of the soldiers made a sweeping motion that was clearly an order to go inside.

"Where is everybody?" As she climbed, Sarah's footsteps rang through the foundation of steel trusses that held the building a foot off the ground, and the hollow sound added to the sense of desolation; they'd seen nobody but the three soldiers.

"And why did Arven fly over without stopping?" Jack wondered aloud. The settlement below was even larger than he expected. At a glance, he estimated that the double-ring of yurts could house two hundred people. Surely the huge kitchen tent should have attracted the raven's attention.

Sarah stopped on the small deck outside the open door and

reached for his hand. Not knowing what he was stepping into, Jack also hesitated, until a soldier shoved him through.

His arrival caused a brief lull in the conversation, followed by a flurry of shouted commands as Sarah joined him. Apparently responding to orders, five soldiers grabbed rifles from a cabinet, rushed outside, and raced off in separate directions. The older man giving the orders was also dressed in fatigues, mostly shades of gray, and had gold bars on his shoulders. He barked something at the soldier who'd brought them inside, and the younger man gestured for them to sit on the floor against the far wall.

As the heated discussion between the officer and soldiers continued, Jack recalled Asterion's words: war is coming. *And it looks like we've stumbled right into it.* But they weren't in immediate danger, so he studied the adjoining rooms.

"We're in some sort of barracks." In addition to a dozen beds, the building had a kitchen and dining hall.

Sarah was scanning the office, which had only one desk for the senior officer. And though she was doing the sensible thing—assessing their situation—Jack could tell by the way she clenched his hand that she was frightened. She tipped her head towards the wall behind the tidy desk and murmured. "Look at the map."

The diagram matched what Jack had observed, except there were two barracks and a second circle of yurts. Assuming they were currently in the building in the top-right corner, the fenced compound continued three hundred yards to the west, where everything was duplicated. The map depicted only one other notable structure—outside the fence. He couldn't tell what it was from its outline, but guessed it had to be important because a road led directly to it from a gate in the southern fence.

The soldiers who'd run out returned individually, gave their reports, and locked up their rifles before leaving. The officer calmed with every update, and Jack assumed he'd sent the men to see if he and Sarah were alone. The last man to return carried the gear from DAVe's cargo box and Jack's radio.

The officer fiddled with the radio, but it was still dead. He searched their bags, then turned his attention to Jack. "Stand up." He spoke English with a Slavic accent.

Jack got up and spread his arms when ordered, and a soldier patted him down. Sarah submitted to the same treatment and the man tossed her wand into a plastic crate with the rest of their belongings.

"Your name?" the officer demanded.

Jack saw no reason to lie. "Jack Scatter."

"And yours?"

"Sarah Rogers."

The man spotted Sarah's diamond earrings. "Give me those." She handed them over and he dropped them in his desk drawer. Then he picked up his own radio and began a conversation in Chinese. After a pause, a new voice joined the exchange, prompting him to switch to Russian. He repeated Jack and Sarah's names, growing increasingly agitated as he listened and argued. Jack couldn't follow any of what was said until the very end when the voice on the radio said, "Priya Singh". The officer abruptly slammed the radio down and reached for a blue phone.

Without turning his head, Jack whispered, "He's calling someone on Earth." In his experience, phones were color-coded to identify their home network. Green phones originated on Cirrus, and blue ones connected through an exchange on Earth. The officer now spoke in Korean, and his tone was very different.

"And they're *not* happy," Sarah replied. From the officer's demeanor, the person on the other end was clearly a superior.

The officer listened without speaking, then put down the phone after the other disconnected. He seemed anxious as he glanced from Jack to Sarah, and ran his hands through his neatly trimmed, thinning hair before speaking to his soldiers. From his gestures, it was clear that he intended to separate them.

Sarah squeezed Jack's hand so hard her nails bit into his skin, and he would have shoved the man approaching them except that a second soldier pulled a chair back from a table in the dining room and beckoned her to sit down.

She released his hand and said, "I'll be fine," though her eyes betrayed her doubts. She went to the table while the first soldier guided Jack to the opposite end of the barracks.

On the way to what turned out to be a supply room, Jack passed a round table on which Jada's hexes were stacked in piles of matching colors, and four hands of cards lay face down in front of each seat. *They've been playing poker with hexes!* At a glance, the prize pot in the center of the table contained a Roman candle, an oil slick, and a spell to make one recall their worst fear in vivid detail.

What followed was hours of interrogation with the same questions repeated and the same answers given. The officer, alternating between him and Sarah, wanted to know who had sent them and why. It was well past midnight before Jack finally got a break, and then only because someone called on the man's radio.

I know that voice, Jack thought.

The officer stepped out and shut the door for the final time, leaving Jack in silence. He slouched on an upturned mop bucket, the only seat in the room, and tried to place the voice. Unfortunately, he couldn't concentrate. Not only was he exhausted, he was worried about Sarah. Scanning the shelves, he found nothing he could use as a weapon, and he couldn't move without alerting the guard outside anyway. Two hours passed before he heard someone approaching.

The new arrival spoke briefly in Korean before the guard walked away, and Jack experienced a wave of dread. *Whatever's happening can't be good.* Then the door swung open and a familiar face looked down at him.

"Pieter was right about one thing," Danny Kou said. "You certainly interfered with his plans."

• • • •

Jack waited in the supply room another hour before Danny returned to ask his own questions, which revealed as much as he learned. He asked about Pieter, confirming Priya's theory that Pieter had nothing to do with current events. He didn't mention

Holden's portal, though, which meant he didn't know Jack had been on Earth. That suggested Paul wasn't currently working for him.

Danny called for the guard, who handed him Jack's radio, now in pieces. He tugged the wires that should have gone to an antenna but ran instead to a coupler circuit and a portal crystal. "You've been talking to Detective Singh."

"Yes." Jack had decided early on to answer any question that didn't reveal his grandfather's portal, and felt confident Sarah would do the same. If Danny assumed the portal radio was paired with another on Earth, and was their only access to Priya, then that was his fault.

"Where is she?"

Jack was dead-tired and losing patience. He was also starving, his mouth was dry, and he had a headache. Glancing at the radio, he said, "I don't know." Then added in a snarky tone, "It's not a camera."

Danny sneered. "Did she send you here?"

"No."

He leaned closer. "Where is the key?"

"I don't know what you're talking about."

"THE KEY," he roared.

That was the last straw for Jack. He stood and swore and would have blasted Danny if he'd had his wand. He shouted, "I don't have a *key*. We're just looking for our friends. I don't give a damn about your billion-dollar schemes, or your war, or Paul. Smuggle as many people as you want to Cirrus, but leave us alone. We—" Jack realized he shouldn't have mentioned Paul.

"Be careful what you ask for." Danny's smile was genuine as he turned and walked away.

Shortly after that, the officer returned and instructed his soldiers to take Jack to a yurt at the bottom of the hill below the barracks. It wasn't a traditional structure built from natural materials, but rigid, insulated panels. And like the barracks, it sat on a raised platform. A guard led Jack up three steps to the wooden door, then pushed it open and shoved him inside.

The yurt was dark except for the dim light from the eastern window; dawn was only an hour away. It was also larger than the family-sized ones Jack had seen in photos: twenty cots ringed its circular wall, and a wood stove was centered below the peak of the fifteen-foot ceiling.

A shadowy figure, easily distinguished by his height, sat up and muttered, "Jack?"

"Marten?"

A gruff voice from another bed mumbled something in Chinese, and Marten apologized, then whispered for Jack to take the empty cot next to his. "You found us," he said, though his tone of disbelief made it more of a question.

"Yeah, I guess we did. You're welcome." Jack wanted to go to the window to look for Sarah, but the bed's foam mattress was covered with a decent wool blanket, and the yurt was warm and quiet, free of soldiers, bright lights, and endless questions. "I just need to close my eyes for a second."

Chapter 14

Driving to Spokane had been a gamble. Portland, the other address on Paul's list, was closer, but Priya's intuition told her he'd been there first and would already be gone. Also, there were reports of protesters on the bridges into Oregon, angry over Washington's power rationing plan.

Her destination, like the hub's location in Olympia, housed a range of businesses. She found an unmarked door in the common hallway on the ground floor, picked its lock, and entered a windowless office. Except for the metal door and keypad behind the reception desk, it could have passed for a dentist's waiting room: plastic plants, coated in fine gray dust, occupied the corners; there were black and white photographs of local scenery on two of its walls; and even outdated magazines on the coffee table.

She rifled through the desk drawers, found a tape dispenser, and covered the camera over the vault door.

"Good luck in there," she said, knowing it would be a killer line if Paul turned out to be inside. And if she'd already missed him, or he had yet to arrive, then only she would know.

But it didn't take long for doubts to creep in. Her biggest concern was that Paul was a Traveller and had known to avoid Spokane. Like Katherine, he'd gone through a portal during Newton, while every portal crystal was in resonance. That was the common factor with all the Travellers she knew, though Katherine seemed oblivious to the foresight that was so obviously guiding her.

To be fair, Priya wasn't sure her own instincts hadn't been sharpened by her passage earlier that night. After all, the best scientific minds in history had failed to unravel the mystery of consciousness, and perhaps it was the Traveller Effect that made her believe Paul would eventually show up.

Eighteen hours wasn't the longest stakeout she'd ever made, but it was the most anticlimactic: the vault opened, Paul stepped out, and dropped into the receptionist's chair.

"So ..." Priya hid her relief. "Not a Traveller, then?"

"I have a few talents. That's not one of them." He eyed her suspiciously. "How about you?"

She shrugged. It was better that he had some doubts. "And you're working alone, otherwise you'd have called someone to clear me out." Paul didn't deny it, leaving her to wonder if he'd tried and been unsuccessful.

He tilted his head toward the restroom door. "Do you mind if I ... It's been a long wait."

Priya shrugged. She'd already checked the room for escape routes and weapons. "I'm not going anywhere."

When he returned, Paul's characteristic swagger came with him. "So, what's the deal?"

She decided not to speak.

"I understand you've been looking for me for a long time, but you haven't arrested me. What do you want?"

"You stole a crystal from Holden's apartment in Caerton. And you stole multiple crystals from his house in Newcastle. Why?"

"A house in Newcastle *and* an apartment in Caerton." He flopped casually into a chair facing her. "Doesn't sound like he's gonna miss them."

Again, Priya waited for him to continue.

"Fine." He leaned forward and rested his elbows on his knees. "I was hired to recover some stolen items and take them to CorpSec headquarters."

Recover? "You got arrested on purpose?"

"That was the agreement. I'd be transported to Earth, the charge would be dropped, and I'd get the rest of the items from his house."

"Who hired you?" she asked abruptly.

"Reynard."

"You worked for Pieter Reynard?"

"Indirectly. His security guy never told me who *he* worked for, but I figured it out."

"So Danny Kou paid you to break into Holden's safe?" Priya knew that couldn't be true. She'd seen Danny on video opening the safe himself.

He hesitated. "Maybe. I got details and addresses through a text—same as always—and CorpSec sent me back to Earth as planned. Then the lights went out, and I had no way of communicating, so I decided to open the second safe and wait for instructions."

"You weren't told where to deliver it?"

"I wasn't even told what would be in the safes." Paul sat back and frowned. "That's not how Danny works. If I don't know the whole plan, there's no way I can tell anyone."

Priya noted his furrowed brows, but there was no anger in his voice. He wasn't upset about not being kept in the loop; he was scared of Danny. She softened her voice to draw him in.

"Why that pair? They're uncommon, but not particularly valuable."

"No idea."

"How did you find Holden's house? That address wasn't in Simon's book."

"Easy. I'd been going to his place for years. He had expensive tastes." Paul's tone suggested he admired Holden's style.

"What does that mean?"

"He'd been asking me to source various luxury goods, which I delivered for a healthy commission: wine, cigars, that sort of thing."

"Describe Holden for me."

"I only ever spoke to him on the phone. I'd say fortyish, Texas accent."

Terrance. "Did it occur to you that those items were being smuggled to Cirrus?"

Paul chuckled. "That's exactly what occurred to me." Then he shrugged. "I was just a courier."

"You didn't go to Cirrus as a courier. How did you get there?"

"Same as everyone else. I filled out the forms and took a liner." When she responded with a skeptical look, he explained. "Okay, I only applied two weeks before I left, but I assume anything's possible with enough money. That's how I knew it had to be Reynard."

Priya had doubts. If Pieter had wanted a set of orbs, he could have bought them from a collector. It had to be someone who wanted *that* pair. *Niels?* He certainly had the money to arrange Paul's impromptu travel. But if *he'd* wanted them, he could have just asked Holden. *Danny? Maybe.* Whoever he was working for would also have the means, but then why hadn't Danny collected the orb from Paul after the job was done?

"So, let's assume Pieter hired you to steal the orb and other crystals. What did—" She caught a fleeting change of expression. "The other crystals weren't part of the deal, were they?"

Paul's arrogance faded, and for the first time, he seemed uncertain. "It's … not easy to explain."

"Try."

He scratched his leg, shuffled his hands, and shrugged his shoulders while looking for an opening. Finally, he reached into his pocket and withdrew the orb. "It … *talks* … to me."

She raised an eyebrow.

"I'm not crazy." He rolled the orb in his fingers. "It's some sort of communication device. It helps me find things."

That's it. She recalled what Jack said about the orbs being used for untraceable communications. *Someone wanted Paul to have* an *orb,* any *orb.* But he didn't seem aware of that, so she wasn't going to tell him. "And that seems normal to you?"

Paul raised his hands beside his head and chopped the air defensively. "*Not crazy.*" Then he slumped and drew a deep breath. "I'm not. But I've always had a talent for finding things. Even as a kid, if someone lost something, I'd dream about where to find it."

Oh, great, Priya thought. *Another oblivious Traveller.* Like Jack,

Paul had used the Traveller Effect long before the event that caused it. A paradox, to be sure, but one for which there was a lot of evidence. "How does the orb figure in this?"

"I actually held one of these when I was a kid." He lifted the orb to eye-level and smiled at the memory. "It was on a school field trip, right after the news broke about a giant space station being built on the other side of the sun."

Priya recalled the event. She'd also been a child when the world learned about Cirrus, already a decade into its construction.

"That was the first portal crystal I'd ever seen," he continued. "And I guess that fascination stuck with me. When I guessed that's what was in the safe in Newcastle …" He juggled the orb to his other hand. "I couldn't resist."

"You said it talks to you."

"It began as a recurring dream. I was back at Holden's, collecting more crystals. I thought my subconscious was telling me I'd miss something important and the dream would stop if I went back. It did, but then I started dreaming about two kids under an overpass in Olympia. I knew they needed my help."

Priya had already heard about the encounter. "Jack and Ethan."

"Right. I spent the morning there. Sure enough, a couple of guys showed up in a black SUV looking for them. One of them was Angel. Reynard's driver. I sent them in another direction."

"And your dream told you to find Jack at the governor's speech, and lead him to the hub. That's a lot of information to convey in a dream."

"By then it wasn't a dream. Hasn't been since Bellevue." Paul's hand drifted to his pocket again. "That's where I got this." He pulled out a shiny disc, gold on one side with a crystal inset on the other: one of Pieter's Third-Eye coins.

For the next ten minutes, Priya kept her eye on the door and her hand near her pistol as Paul described how his dream guided him to *liberate* coins and phones from a mansion on the shore of Lake Washington before they were auctioned on the black market.

She fully expected Pieter's men to burst through at any moment, but nothing happened as he explained how the dream became a voice—a person—after he'd *acquired* them, and how they'd instructed him to install the coins in servers at DAIGON hubs.

She calmed when she remembered that not only hadn't Paul turned Jack and Ethan over to Pieter in October, he could have done the same yesterday if he wanted to. So, even though he carried a coin, it wasn't controlling him. At least *Pieter* wasn't controlling him. In fact, it seemed more likely than ever that Pieter was out of the picture entirely.

"Why did someone on Cirrus want you to swap the crystals?" she asked. For by that time, Paul had worked out that his contact had limited knowledge of events on Earth.

"I think it restored the internet there. As soon as Jack installed that coin, they knew a lot more about what's happening here."

Funny how a global network of cameras will do that. She had a good idea what the phones were for, but asked anyway. "How many phones did you have?"

"A hundred or so."

Priya did some quick math. Paul couldn't possibly be working outside the Pacific Northwest. If there were others like him, that could mean thousands of phones across the country. Of course, that paled against the number of legitimate users—Pieter had grown five million crystals for government, police, military, and critical industries. Still, it had taken only one phone in the hands of a bodyguard to start a chain of events that might affect the next election.

Paul wasn't acting like a person controlled, or even influenced. Did that mean there was more than one party on Cirrus using the coins? Priya didn't have enough information to open that line of inquiry, but she still had unanswered questions. "Why did you rat out Angel?"

All traces of humor faded from his face as he met her eyes. "Because someone has been looking for *you*. And that hasn't worked out so well for others lately."

"For how long?" She should rightly have asked who was searching for her and why, but was more concerned about how many times she'd been to the inn.

"Two weeks."

She'd only used Holden's portal once in that time. Was that once too many? "Who's looking?"

"Not Danny. He'd have gone after Angel by now."

"Did you have anything to do with the bodyguard and the governor?"

Paul flipped the coin through his fingers like a magician doing a trick. "No. But I knew it was coming." He held up a hand to dodge her next question. "And I knew it would fail. According to my contact, the same person who arranged the attack set up the rescue."

"And I'm guessing the bodyguard had one of your phones."

He smiled. "Now you're getting the hang of it."

"So, someone is playing both sides. What's their endgame?"

"I'm not sure. Those were just opening moves. The real action is about to—"

Priya felt a jolt, as if someone had kicked her chair. There was no noise, but Paul reacted as if he'd felt it, too. *Earthquake?* A moment later, a second bump.

Paul dashed to the door, and she hurried outside after him to join a growing crowd on the street. A dark plume was rising in the east near the state line, the kind of oily black that spoke of catastrophe, and it was roiling as if from a great heat below.

"Is there a refinery over there?" She turned to Paul but he had disappeared.

• • • •

Priya was still angry about losing Paul as she drove back to Olympia, though she couldn't have detained him much longer, anyway. He'd never actually been charged with a crime. She was more troubled by today's attack on the railway.

Idiots, she thought. *Can't they see that preventing food from leaving the state blocks it from entering as well?* Washington's borders were now effectively closed to large cargo.

She'd driven across town to aid her colleagues and learned there were no casualties. In fact, there was no damage except to the bridges that had been destroyed by a pair of explosives. During the eighteen hours she'd waited for Paul, the radio waves had been alive with threats by newly formed militias, and all rail traffic in the state had been suspended six hours ago, depriving people of the food-security they were fighting for.

And why can't Sarah and Jack trust that I'm telling them what to do for their own good? Even if Jack had reacted impulsively to Paul's presence at the Capitol, Sarah should have known something was up and confided in her.

No, she decided, *that's unfair. I asked them to come. And Sarah actually tried to stop Jack. I'm the one who's responsible for their actions.*

If she were being honest with herself, none of those things were behind her current mood. She'd barely passed her latest psych evaluation, and that would soon change the course of her life and career.

Portal travel could be dangerous. A wormhole collapse was almost always fatal, and even when everything worked properly the stress on one's brain was like a mini-concussion. Too many trips led to headaches, mood changes, or worse. And Priya had taken hundreds.

The UN didn't take chances with mental health. They screened their people often and shuffled those with early symptoms into jobs that didn't require travel. In her case, they'd approve just one more trip, leaving her the choice of moving to Dawn or continuing a pointless hunt for Pieter. So, even if she found a way to Cirrus without Holden's portal, she wouldn't be able to use it.

Maybe it's best for Cirrus to be on its own, and free of Earth's troubles.

The newsreaders were calling today's events terrorism, but to Priya it felt like manipulation, another threat to ensure as many people as possible, and their money, went to Dawn.

Whoever attacked me must be involved. But how far are they willing to go? Would they actually risk a civil war to prevent people from learning that Cirrus survived?

If that were true, then she should let Danny smuggle those who were willing to pay. After all, she reasoned, how many could that possibly be when Dawn offered an easier and more certain future?

And what would that mean for me? Earth would stagnate while Dawn grew and prospered. She had the opportunity to be in the first wave of immigrants, and help chart the course of law enforcement on a new world.

Angel is right. Professionally, Earth is a dead end. If I want to advance my career, there isn't much choice at all.

Chapter 15

"*Jack.*" Marten shoved him again. "Get up."

"Mmph," Jack mumbled. He'd meant to say something coherent, but his mouth was so dry it felt no different from the wool blanket he was face-down upon. And as his troubled dream faded, he realized that Marten had been shaking him for a while.

"We have to go." Marten pulled him upright. "I already let you sleep through breakfast. You don't want to be caught lying in bed here."

"Where's Sarah?" Jacked staggered to his feet and looked around. Sunlight filtering through the yurt's four windows revealed only empty beds. "Where are *we*?"

Marten, probably the most optimistic and even-tempered person Jack knew, looked downcast. "I was hoping you knew."

As the previous day's events trickled into his mind, Jack shuffled groggily from anxiety to relief to confusion: Marten, missing for several days, was safe but— "You were supposed to be a hundred miles north of here."

"We followed a dragon."

"Dragon?" Jack's first thought was of Asterion. "How did—"

"Well, at first we thought it was a dog. Then it led us to this valley, where we saw smoke and thought it might be a new village."

"And you lost power and crashed at the bottom of the hill."

"How did you know that?"

"That's what happened to us."

"Does Afi know we're here?" Marten used the Icelandic term for his grandfather, Anders.

Before Jack could give him the bad news, gruff voices from outside interrupted. They were speaking Korean again, and he couldn't understand a word.

"C'mon." Marten ushered him to the door as the voices became aggressive. "They're doing the head count."

Outside, sixty or so men had lined up in the round clearing between the circling yurts, while a similar number of women formed ranks by the large dining tent. Jack spotted Sarah standing in the women's group. She didn't look as tired as she must be, and stood defiantly as their captors counted. Jada was there too, and Jack was relieved to see that, like Marten, she was unharmed.

"Who are these people?" he whispered.

Marten didn't answer so he scanned the crowd again. More than half were Chinese or Korean, which struck him as odd. With Cirrus' diverse population, he'd never seen a majority formed by *any* ethnic group. Also, he and Sarah were the only ones wearing regular clothing. Everyone else, Marten and Jada included, wore white cotton work clothes, like loose-fitting pajamas, though Marten's didn't cover his ankles.

Two armed men moved between the yurts, checking for stragglers, while another pair argued in Korean in front of the men's group. Last night, Jack had assumed they were trained soldiers, but now they seemed disorganized and incompetent: their uniforms bore no insignia, and they all wore different boots. *These men are guards, not soldiers, and not professionals, either.*

Finally, a guard faced the men's group and shouted a command. The workers turned and started walking towards the west end of the clearing, and Marten prodded Jack to join them. "Let's go. If we don't work, we don't eat."

Two guards led the group to a gate on the compound's southern border, while four more trailed behind. Somewhere distant, dogs barked, and they didn't sound friendly. And just inside the gate was a pit covered by a mesh of steel rods.

He was shocked to see fingers wrapped around the bars. "*There's—*" He started again in a whisper. "There's somebody in there."

"That's where they put people who break the rules," Marten muttered. "He tried to escape."

While those around him deliberately avoided looking at the

prisoner as they passed, Jack noted that the pit would soon be in direct sunlight, and would remain that way for hours.

They'd hiked through only a quarter-mile of mixed forest before the path widened onto a windowless building: the structure he'd seen on the bottom edge of the map. Its right side, a narrow forty-foot silo, poked through the leafy canopy of aspen and spruce, but its left side resembled a garage, with a set of doors wide enough for a truck to pass through. Inside, bright lights shone on walls covered in a mosaic of gray plates.

"Hey, those are shielding panels," he said. "They have a portal?"

"For the grain." Marten indicated a large open-topped trailer and tractor parked farther down the road. "They've converted a couple of harvesters to run on diesel."

The workers were climbing into the trailer when a guard pointed at Marten and said something Jack couldn't understand. Marten slumped and acknowledged with a nod. "C'mon, Jack. The Ferret wants us to get a wagon." He turned and headed for a group of smaller carts.

"His name is Ferret?" Jack asked after checking that they'd moved out of hearing range.

"Doesn't he kind of look like one?"

Jack agreed that he did, and that he also had the appearance of someone who was trying to appear older than he really was. He wore thin silver stripes on his shoulders that marked him as a junior officer, but he was as gaunt as the others and his fatigues fit just as poorly.

A variety of two and four-wheeled carts stood next to the grain trailer, and Marten tossed his shovel into a smaller wagon with sturdy wheels and metal straps bracing its wooden slats. Then he picked up its T-handle yoke and started pushing.

Jack threw a shovel in with Marten's, then helped steer onto a narrow side road, even though Marten could have easily managed the cart by himself. Ferret followed them while the remaining workers and guards trundled down the main road.

How can a place like this exist? he wondered. Other than Priya and her UN colleagues, Cirrus had never even had an armed police force. Now, there were armed guards who answered to Danny, a known smuggler. *Did Asterion know about this place? And if so, why didn't he warn us?*

After only a few minutes of pushing, they reached the base of a broad escarpment that Jack recognized from maps. It ran parallel to the highway for fifteen miles, then curved around the north side of the compound and merged into the Spine. Here, it was two hundred feet tall and unclimbable because of poor-quality stone that crumbled into sharp gravel. Worse, he spotted an armed guard leading a dog along its crest. There would be no escape in that direction.

Marten guided the cart to the wall and retrieved his shovel, and Ferret hopped onto a large, flat-topped boulder where he could sit in the sun.

"Where are Sarah and Jada?" Jack asked.

"Not now," Marten mumbled. "The Ferret understands English." He began shoveling.

Working in silence, they loaded hundreds of pounds of gravel into the cart. However, as soon as they started pulling, its axles squealed so badly they could speak freely without Ferret hearing.

"They're not big on gender-equality here," Marten said. "The girls will be working in the kitchen or vegetable gardens." He chuckled. "You can guess how Jada feels about *that*." Then he described how they'd been caught and interrogated after finding the compound.

Ferret ordered them to stop after less than a mile, and Marten dumped gravel into a deep rut that was choking the road. Jack helped him stamp it down, and they continued doing that until their cart was empty.

When they got back to the portal chamber, Marten dropped the yoke. "I'm stopping for water." He didn't even glance at The Ferret to see if that was okay, and the guard waited on the road while he and Jack filled cups from jugs on a table beside the silo.

The building's door was closed now, and Jack couldn't spot cameras or movement sensors. "How often do they use the portal?"

"A few times a day, I think. And they take a couple of workers out there at night, around ten o'clock. Why?"

"Somehow, they're disabling wormholes here. But if they have to turn off the block to transport the grain, maybe I can connect to a crystal in Icarus and let them know where we are."

"How?"

"I …" Jack suddenly realized how little he knew. It only just occurred to him that whatever was blocking the wormholes had also interrupted Arven's reconnaissance, and probably thwarted Sarah's Traveller-memories. "I'm working on it."

The Ferret said something in an impatient tone, which Jack understood to mean they were taking too long. Marten glanced at the guard but didn't move until he finished his drink.

"I don't think he appreciates how laid-back you are." Jack knew his friend would follow orders, but someone Marten's size could create a lot of trouble if he wanted to.

"Afi always told me that cowards would hurt my friends if they couldn't hurt me. It's not worth fighting when so many others are at risk."

Jack's thoughts turned to Sarah, and it must have shown because Marten added, "The guards are indifferent to women here. They'll be fine." But his expression betrayed his own doubts.

"You don't sound so sure."

"Well, you know. Jada's impulsive." Marten grinned. "Which is great … sometimes." Then the crease returned to his brow. "But not here. I don't want her to get in trouble." He set his cup down. "Let's get back to work."

And that's how the entire day went. On some trips, they encountered the grain-laden trailer being towed to the silo, but mostly they worked with only their silent observer for company. Finally, as the sun was setting, the fieldworkers returned, singing an unfamiliar tune that had the relaxed cadence of a working song.

Marten dumped the last of the gravel and followed the weary men, and Jack was relieved to see that the mesh was off the now-empty punishment pit.

A fire burning in the clearing cast flickering shadows among the surrounding yurts, but he could have found his way to the dining tent with his eyes closed; he'd never been so hungry. Under the shelter, the women preparing dinner had only a sparse string of electric bulbs hanging over the stoves to work with, and the folding tables and chairs sat on bare earth. It all seemed poorly planned, but also reinforced Jack's opinion that they'd been there for months.

He'd hoped to talk to Sarah, but she was washing pots. So he queued at the counter with the men, then joined Marten at an empty table. Though he couldn't see any guards in the now-gloomy compound, there was an unmistakable tension in the air. Most of the workers ate in silence, and those who spoke to their companions did so furtively, as if they might be overheard.

As they had been the last to be served, it was only a minute before Sarah and Jada sat next to them with their own bowls of watery bean and vegetable stew.

Sarah didn't give Jack a chance to ask if she was all right before telling what she'd learned. "Half these people left the cities to start homesteads and were captured." She indicated an adjacent table occupied by a group speaking what sounded to him like German. "But the Chinese and North Koreans came directly from Earth."

"*What?*" he asked. That explained their numbers but created more questions. "How? And why?"

"They're mostly farmers who think the grain they're harvesting is going back to their villages." She scowled. "I don't think it is. Remember the crystals Danny smuggled to Cirrus?"

"Who's Danny?" Marten asked.

"Oh, right." Jack remembered that they hadn't met Marten until months after Newton. "He worked for Pieter. And until a few days ago, we all thought he drowned. But he was here last night and it looks like he's in charge."

Sarah continued. "Priya originally thought he wanted to sell passage to Cirrus after Newton, but now it looks like he had other plans. There could be hundreds of compounds like this. *This* is where Earth's overseas grain is coming from."

"Okay, so we know how people got here." Jack whispered, "How do *we* escape?"

Marten leaned in. "How far are we from Fairview?"

Jack had grown up there. "About a hundred miles."

Marten looked at Jada and shook his head. "That's farther than I thought. Our only option is the Spine." She nodded in agreement; they'd obviously had this discussion.

"We're only ten miles from the highway," Jack said.

"We thought about that," Jada said, "but they've got dogs and vehicles. We can't beat them wherever there are roads."

"And I was hoping we could leave at night and hide in the fields," Marten said, "but they'd have days to find us."

Sarah, having been quiet while they plotted, shook her head. "We shouldn't try to escape."

"*Are you kidding?*" Jack glanced around but no one had noticed his outburst. He lowered his voice. "We only found this place by accident. *Literally.* Nobody knows it exists."

"I only meant it would be safer to work on sending a message. We don't have food, or proper clothing, or—"

With a sudden whoosh, the fire in the clearing flared, and its glare easily overwhelmed the meager electric lights. Marten, like those closest to the firepit, ducked instinctively.

"What was that?"

"I didn't see anything." Jack had been facing the clearing when the flames leaped ten feet from the pit. "There was no one—"

A woman screamed from the kitchen and then bawled in Spanish. Then, speaking as if the event was completely normal, Jada said, "Oh, yeah. This place is haunted."

Jack, thinking it was not, exclaimed, "*What?*"

"She's saying something about the cookie jar being empty."

"They have cookies?" His stomach growled. "Sorry, I'm still

hungry."

Jada, who had a talent for languages, continued while other women ran to calm the first. "Apparently, strange things have been happening for months. Food goes missing, instruments play themselves when no one is around, and there are places the dogs won't go."

As subdued conversation resumed at the other tables, Jack considered the firepit and the branches hanging high above. *Pine needles would have flared like that.* He didn't believe in ghosts, of course, but it was impossible that enough dry needles had somehow funneled themselves into the pit all at once.

A loud clanging forced his attention back into the tent. At the serving counter, an elderly woman was banging a wooden spoon against a pot for attention. She spoke a few words, and the workers started gathering their bowls.

"What's happening?" Sarah asked over the excited chatter.

"I don't know," Jada said. "Everyone usually just wanders away after dinner. I understood the word *river*, though." She pointed at a gate to the left of the barracks. "There's a bathing area over the hill."

Jack and his friends followed the workers, who spread out along the fence instead of going through the gate. Jada stood on a stump and used Marten's shoulder for balance, while he and Sarah found a spot where they could see over the heads of the front row.

The compound's northern fence, except for a stretch next to the barracks, was topped with coiled razor wire. Beyond that section, a second fence enclosed a hundred-foot length of river that had been dredged to create a thirty-foot-wide pool spanned by a wooden bridge.

The workers obviously knew what was going to happen because they fell silent as four guards marched onto the bridge, which had a rectangular structure underneath: solid walls that formed a narrow channel aligned with the current.

Two guards flipped over hinged metal grates on top of the

channel, then locked them in place to create rigid platforms. The others lifted a floor plate, splitting the bridge deck in two, and Jack saw how they were going to escape.

"It's a portal," he whispered.

"In the river?" Marten asked.

"Water is about the same density as a person. It prevents a sudden change in mass from collapsing the wormhole."

With the grates out of the way, Jack could see perforated panels that slowed the river's current to a crawl. The portal ring itself was completely submerged, and a thick conduit rose from the water into a sealed control box. He traced it to the shore, where a shell of concrete protected it all the way to the barracks.

"What's that high-pitched squeal?" Sarah asked.

Jack tilted his head, trying to locate the sound. It was one of those electric whines that was just at the edge of the audible range and was coming from the generator cage behind the barracks. "Capacitors. They'd need to store a lot of power to run the portal."

He studied the guards as they activated the portal and felt the unmistakable presence of a wormhole when one flipped the last switch. Unfortunately, trapped beyond the fence, he was too far to manipulate its energy field. And he didn't have a plan for what to do with it anyway, so he started counting.

Movement below the water's surface created a swell, and two guards reached down just as a man emerged from the stream. They grabbed him by the arms and guided him to a ladder as a second person appeared, then two more. Each looked around in confusion as they climbed onto the bridge.

Then the guards directed the newcomers to the gate, where they were met by an older Chinese man. Those nearest listened carefully as the group exchanged polite greetings, but then walked away in obvious disappointment.

"What's wrong?" Sarah asked.

"They're not from the same village," Jada said.

The crowd dispersed as two guards escorted the new arrivals into the barracks, but Jack waited until the others finished with the portal before joining Sarah by the firepit. Some of the workers were playing stringed instruments there, but quietly, as if to not attract the attention of the guards who patrolled in the gloom.

"The portal was open for ninety seconds," Jack said. "That's plenty of time for all of us to go through, but we need to charge the capacitors beforehand. We'll need a distraction."

"How long will they take to charge?" Marten asked.

"I'm guessing at least an hour."

"That's gonna have to be a big distraction." A gleam appeared in Jada's eyes. "A fire?" She looked far too eager.

"Wait," Sarah said, "we don't know what's on the other side. It might be rural China. We could end up stuck in a remote area with no communications."

"Well, they're selling the grain," Jack reasoned, "so their operation has to be run from somewhere with transportation."

"Then why not use the grain portal?" Marten asked. "They charge that one every night."

"Too dangerous. We need the water for a mass buffer." Jack waited for anyone to argue, but no one did. "Okay, then we just need a distract the guards."

While the others made suggestions, he hunched over and stared into the fire as the workers began a folk song.

Should we be trying to escape? he wondered. Sarah had a point. No matter how many details they worked out, it would still be dangerous. But the compound had existed for months, and Suresh knew nothing about it. That meant they could be trapped for just as long with no way to warn anyone about Danny or the war Asterion spoke about. And they didn't even have Priya around to save them this time. *No, we got ourselves into this mess. We have to get ourselves out.*

Chapter 16

Ethan slammed his bo staff into the trunk of a maple tree. *"Why?"* he yelled.

He pivoted and swept the bo in an uppercut. As he shifted into a cat stance, he drew energy from the portal crystal mounted at the staff's midpoint, and funneled it into the striking tip. A branch thicker than his arm shattered and flew into the tall grass.

He called the technique *mass-shifting*, because that's what it felt like. At the moment before impact, the last foot of the bo gained a hundred pounds with no loss of momentum. The concentrated energy also reinforced the wood, and it could shatter concrete without taking a scratch.

The tree had lost most of its crown in a windstorm last year, and bore the scars of past practice sessions. Today, it shuddered under Ethan's demands. *Why won't my parents let me go?* Another branch flew off. *Why did Jack and Sarah leave on their own?* A two-foot length of trunk splintered and the tree listed to one side. *Why didn't I stop them?* With a final blow, the tree lurched, groaned, and fell.

Slumping to his knees, he drew breath in great heaves. He'd hoped to feel calmer after venting his anger, and he did, but not enough. His best friends were missing and he was powerless to help.

He'd avoided questions Tuesday afternoon, hoping Jack would check in, but by nightfall he suspected the worst. And when Jack's mother asked where her son went, Ethan caved right away. Now, twenty-four hours after they left, Suresh's party had found no trace of them.

As soon as Ethan's role was revealed, his father removed the power cells from Terrance's bike and the village's remaining vehicles, meaning no one could leave without permission from the council. In fact, they were probably expecting him home by now.

He stood and looked for his dog. "Dusty? Where are you?" She'd been watching him train only a short while ago, but now she'd disappeared. He wasn't too worried, though. How much trouble could a psychic dog get into?

His training ground was a secluded clearing across the river, and the path from the village to the nearest grain road ran alongside the opposite bank, so there was no bridge near the lake. At this time of the year, the water flowed waist high, but Jack had used his greater mastery of wormhole energy to build stepping-stones from large boulders.

Ethan jumped from the shore to the first stone without trouble. The second was shorter and damp from lapping waves, so he aimed for its center, intending to carry his momentum into an immediate leap for the third. But his mind was still preoccupied, and even though he had a two-second warning of the raven's approach, he landed an inch to the side after it buzzed his head mid-jump. With arms flailing, his foot slipped on moss and he tumbled into the river.

When he righted himself, spitting water, the raven was on the far bank, croaking in a rhythm that sounded suspiciously like mocking.

"Laugh it up, birdbrain." Ethan realized after speaking that it wasn't much of an insult to an actual bird. "At least I can swim." He shook the water from his hair and started for shore, using his staff to push himself forward. Then he stopped and looked downstream. "Hey, not only can I swim, I can *paddle*."

Without computers, Cirrus lacked maps. But he'd once made his way from Port Isaac to Caerton, relying on his memory of the route as seen on a GPS screen, and he knew where this river went. It joined a much larger river that flowed from Caerton all the way to the sea. And that's where he needed to go.

The raven was still squawking, but it no longer mattered if it was laughing. Ethan's spirits had lifted, and he had a plan. "I can mass-shift with a paddle. That'll be almost as fast as driving. Thanks, I owe you one ... *Hugo?*"

Hugo quieted and cocked his head.

"Hugo." Ethan splashed to the shore. "Where's Jack?" Of course, he knew he didn't have a talent for communicating with birds, but he'd seen Jack do it so many times it just felt right. He stumbled onto the rocks and knelt in front of the raven. "Can you find Jack?"

Hugo hopped back and forth.

"Does that mean yes?" He scowled when Hugo repeated the move. "No?" Hugo hopped again. "I don't understand; that was the same hop. Do something different." *Damn it, I'm arguing with a bird.* He leaned closer and spoke slowly. "I'm looking for Jack. *Jack.*" He plucked at his shirt. "He looks kind of like me, but shorter and nerdy. Do you need a scrap of clothing? No, wait, that's a dog. Uh, how about … *Arrgh, how does Jack do this?"*

He patted his pockets, wondering if he had anything of Jack's, and Hugo followed his hands, so he was clearly paying attention. Did that mean the bird understood? Ethan picked up a wand-sized stick. "That'll work."

He mimed Jack's wand-handling. "I'm Jack. I move things." He sent a rock tumbling with a narrow beam of energy from his ring. Then he patted himself on the chest and lowered his voice. "I'm Ethan. I'm going to find Jack." He tossed the stick into the river and pretended to paddle after it. Then he pointed at Hugo. "I need *you* to find him for me." He flapped his arms to suggest flying. "Do you understand?"

"I'd say you were crazy," someone behind Ethan said, "but I asked your dog where you were and she led me here."

Ethan spun to find Davis and Dusty standing on the road above the riverbank. Hugo departed with a flap of wings and a loud squawk, and Dusty wagged her tail happily. Not only had she responded to Davis' question, she'd gone back to the village to get him, meaning she knew he was coming.

"Oh, hey." Ethan chuckled to hide his embarrassment. "What are you doing here?"

"Well, right now I'm waiting to see your impersonation of

Sarah. I hope it's better than your Jack."

"*Funny.*" Ethan climbed the bank. "I meant, what are you doing in Icarus?"

"Your parents called me." Davis, Priya's fellow UN Police officer, had a two-channel radio Jack's father built for communicating with the Vault and Icarus. "They're worried you're going to do something stupid. I ..." He shook his head. "I'm not sure what to tell them."

"Jack, Sarah, Marten, and Jada are missing. They—"

"Yeah, I already got that. And you would be too if you went after them on your own."

Ethan twirled his staff with one hand, then planted it in the rocks. "I can take care of myself."

Davis, a stocky man with large hands, crossed his arms. "I've seen Jack knock down a wall with a stick, and *he's* still missing."

"Are you here to search for them? Because I'm going with you."

"No, Suresh and Anders have enough help. But you *are* coming with me. Tomorrow morning. I've already talked to your parents."

"Where are we going?"

"There's something strange happening in Caerton." Davis ran a hand across the stubble on top of his head. He hadn't shaved in weeks. "I think it falls under the category of your"—he flicked his hand as if holding a wand—"hocus-pocus thing."

Chapter 17

Sarah's second day began much the same as her first: she worked in the kitchen during breakfast, cleaned up afterwards, then followed a group of women to the terraced gardens that provided most of the compound's food.

She barely noticed the hours passing as she weeded rows of vegetables. Cool air descending from glaciers in the Spine kept her comfortable despite the sun on her back, and the work was easy once she got into a routine. Working with her best friend nearby, she could almost forget they were being held against their will.

"We could just leave, you know," Jada said.

"Huh?" Sarah looked up from her weeding, only now noticing they were alone.

"The guards have so little respect for women that they don't even bother watching us."

Sarah stood and surveyed the garden. She and Jada had drifted uphill from the other women as they worked their row, and there wasn't a guard in sight. "Then why didn't you leave on the first day?"

"I did, but the others called me back. They were worried the guards would punish Marten."

"So they control the women by threatening the men?"

"Yeah, they'd probably have tortured him." Jada tried to feign a mischievous grin, but her heart clearly wasn't in it.

"Aww," —Sarah tilted her head—"you *do* have a soft spot for Marten."

"He's my ride home."

"You know how to drive."

"Whatever."

Sarah chuckled. Jada might be fooling herself about Marten, but she was right about the guards. "Stay here." She hunched low and slipped away between the rows of tomatoes.

"Where are you going?"

"I'm not leaving. I just want to check how far the wormhole block extends. If we can get outside it with a crystal, we can call for help and not have to worry about getting caught escaping."

Jada moved to a spot where she could watch the lower half of the garden. "I'll whistle if I see a guard."

Sarah hurried away, following a winding road to the east. There were several sets of tire tracks on it, which proved only that the guards patrolled this far, not how often they did.

When she was certain she was out of sight, Sarah began to jog. Although it had only been a few days, she longed for that part of her daily routine. She and a few other villagers had already worn in a decent running track through the forest around Icarus' solar farm. Fortunately, though the guards had confiscated her regular clothes, they'd let her keep her shoes.

The threshold was only half a mile away, and she nearly missed it because it passed over her like the lightness that came when she was properly warmed up and hitting her stride.

It's a portal zone.

Jack thought there was some sort of technology blocking wormholes in the compound, and maybe he was right, but the transition had felt the same as in the zones on the Vault and around Icarus Island.

Well, not exactly the same. As she moved back into the zone, she sensed a distinct change of mood: *defiance.* She hadn't noticed the pervasive aura before because she'd been living in it for two days. But now, paying attention, the vibe was obvious. She backed over the threshold again to consider.

Why defiant? On the Vault, she'd felt Blue's mindset, so it made sense that this zone's mood echoed the workers' attitudes. But though they would leave given the chance, they were obviously intimidated by the guards and were following every order. *Does the zone reflect just one mind? Does someone here know what's coming? If Asterion is right, Danny's war plans must surely include this place.*

Sarah turned slowly, surveying what she could through gaps

in the trees. Dark clouds were building on the horizon beyond the fields, and there were no settlements out there. They were truly isolated. *What did Jack say about Asterion? They would come to his aid if he called?*

"That's great, Asterion," she said to the sky. "We need your help, but how can he call you?" She sighed. *I have to find a—I hear music.*

A simple tune, playing on a string instrument, was coming from the forest inside the zone. It was the same one she'd heard the night they'd arrived, just before—

Guards!

Whether she'd finally had another Traveller-memory, or subconsciously registered the noise of a vehicle, Sarah knew they were coming. She dashed into the zone, leaped into the forest, and struggled towards the music. She couldn't know if the person playing it was friendly, but they had to have a shelter where she could hide.

The music stopped as she scrambled upslope to an impassable hedge of blackberries, and that's when she heard an ATV approaching. She ducked, hoping to hide in the weeds, and noticed an arch formed by intertwined branches. With no other options, she crawled into the shadowy brambles, snagging her clothes on thorns. It was a tight fit, and the passage didn't lead to the other side. Instead, she found herself in something like a leafy igloo, which was empty except for a three-stringed lute lying on the ground.

Her heart was racing as the ATV rolled past, and she only relaxed and released the breath she'd been holding when she could no longer hear its tires crunching gravel.

Where am I? The shelter was not a natural formation. That was obvious from the way its branches had been woven into a dome. A second archway opened on the uphill side of the brambles, and was just as small as the one she'd entered through. Gouges in the dirt suggested someone had used it recently. "Hello?"

Nobody answered, so Sarah picked up the lute and plucked a

string experimentally. The tone was pleasant, though the instrument itself was shabby and had the appearance of being homemade. Setting it down, she peered through the brambles. The road was clear and the ATV hadn't been travelling very fast, so if what Jada said was true, it was likely the guards didn't know she was missing.

An unexpected string of notes startled her. She tried to spin around but caught her hair on thorns, and ended up staring at the sky with her neck bent backwards. *"Who's there?"* No reply. The lute sounded its familiar tune as Sarah fought to release herself. Then it stopped and she heard the ATV again. She froze, still unable to turn her head.

The guards were laughing as they drove past, and Sarah breathed a sigh of relief. They weren't looking for her. "Can you help? I'm stuck." No answer. "Okaaay, I'm officially freaked out now." She tore at the branches binding her and managed to tilt her head. There was no one there, and the lute was on the ground exactly where it had always been.

It took Sarah five minutes to free herself from the brambles, but only half that to sprint back to the garden. She was driven partly by panic, but also scared of what the guards might do to Jack if they found her out of bounds.

"You look like you've seen a ghost," Jada said as Sarah collapsed beside her.

Catching her breath, Sarah puffed, "I think I did."

• • • •

Jack was still fixing the road with Marten, and was also wearing the same shapeless white work clothes as everyone else. He paused to stretch out the kink forming in his back and surveyed the fields below.

Ferret had led them to a spot above the fields where a cluster of potholes had merged to become a treacherous obstacle. Jack already knew the cropland stretched all the way to Fairview, so he wasn't surprised at the endless expanse. He felt both nostalgic and intimidated: his hometown was just on the other side, but the other side was a long way away. Also, the rifle-toting guard in the nearby thirty-foot-tall tower had an excellent view of them and the road.

A dust plume rose from the base of a second tower a few miles away, and Jack puzzled over it for a minute before realizing it was being dragged by the tractor. He slumped a little as he turned away. *How can we plan an escape route if we don't even know where the towers will be?*

With fewer trees around, he had a better view of the Spine, too. The mountains directly north were over a mile tall, and the roads running east and west weren't an option. Even now, he could hear the dogs on their patrols.

When the pothole was filled, Ferret directed them back to the upper road. He'd given up trying to eavesdrop and instead found a comfortable spot to sit where he didn't have to move as they slowly advanced the cart. He was thirty yards away when Jack heard a familiar croaking.

"Is that one of yours?" Marten asked.

Perched on the cart, a large black bird was watching Jack. It looked like any other raven, solid black with a hint of brown on its chest, and Marten might have been jumping to conclusions except that this one had landed within arm's reach.

"*Hugo,*" Jack exclaimed. He didn't think of the ravens as *his,* but this was definitely one of those he knew well.

"Hugo?"

"It's from Norse mythology. Odin had a raven—"

Marten, whose grandfather was even taller than him and somewhat Viking-like, interrupted, "I'm familiar with the story. But Odin's raven was *Hugin.*"

Jack bobbled his head. "I thought that sounded pretentious."

"So, the other one isn't Munin, then?"

"Arven, actually."

Marten raised an eyebrow. "Arven the Raven?"

Jack shrugged. "I'm not good with names." Hugo flapped his wings and made a clacking noise at Marten, then dropped to the ground where Ferret couldn't see him. Jack crouched. "Can you understand me?"

Hugo cocked his head to the side.

"Was that a yes?" Marten asked.

"I think he's confused. We normally communicate through the AI, but I need my wand for that."

"Uh, Jack," Marten mumbled.

"They don't understand our words, just our emotions. Hopefully, that's what'll come through." Jack leaned closer and spoke earnestly. "I need you to lead someone here." He stood with his shovel and spun it in a poor imitation of Ethan with a bo staff. "Ethan. Bring Ethan." With that, he fumbled the shovel and startled Hugo into flight.

"*Ja-ack.*" Marten's tone was insistent. "I think we're in trouble."

Jack looked over his shoulder. A cohort of men returning from the fields was standing on the road, and had seen his interaction with Hugo. A hushed conversation spread among them as he stepped forward, raising open hands in the universal *I can explain* gesture. But before he could speak, one of them tore away from the group and sprinted towards the compound.

"Oh, crap." Marten threw his shovel into the cart. "He's going to alert the guards."

"Wait," Jack said as the workers scattered, keeping a wide berth from him while they joined the rush to the compound. Fifty yards back, two guards hurried to catch up. They'd missed Hugo entirely. After they had all passed, he turned back to Marten. "Did I just break a taboo?"

"*You were having a conversation with a bird.* That's weird in any culture. Grab the cart." Marten pulled on the yoke, and they were soon moving at a slow jog. Ferret jumped to his feet, surprised at their sudden burst of speed.

Together, though widely separated, the workers and their guards, Jack and Marten, and Ferret hustled to the compound. Marten stopped to park their cart while the others raced ahead.

By the time Jack arrived in the clearing, whatever concern the men had about him was spreading through the kitchen. The women were huddling in small clusters, whispering among themselves, and Jada was trying to listen to several groups at once while Sarah—too far away for him to speak with—looked at him questioningly.

"I don't know," he mouthed, lifting upturned palms.

An elderly Chinese woman, probably the oldest person in the compound, approached him from a gap between the two rings of yurts. She said something and beckoned him to follow. Without waiting to see if he was, she tottered away.

"What do I do?" he asked Marten, who'd finally caught up.

"No idea." Marten ran his hands through his hair, looking lost. "But an old woman is safer than a group of angry men. Go with her. I'll tell Jada and Sarah what happened."

Marten hurried away, leaving Jack to catch up to the woman, which didn't take long as she moved with more of a shuffle than a walk. She led him to a yurt that was separated from the outer ring by its own small clearing, and was sheltered under the branches of a tall yew.

He wanted to grab the woman's arm to steady her as she mounted the three steps, but worried he might break another rule. She climbed with slow, deliberate movements, and eventually reached the door, then waved her hand at it.

"You want me to go in?" he asked, and she nodded. With no better idea of what to do, Jack stepped inside.

The room was dimly lit by a lantern hanging from a cord. Its warm yellow glow revealed two occupants: a young girl, possibly eleven or twelve; and a younger boy, maybe six years old. The boy was hunched over a low table and seemed to be studying a scroll. The girl stood and hurried to meet Jack. She bowed respectfully, then held out her hands, offering the wand he'd dropped on the road two days ago.

"Hello," she said in accented English. "I am Mai. You will teach me magic."

Chapter 18

Ethan stood at the base of a needle-like tower, where the surrounding street was filled with broken glass and shattered office furniture.

"You ready?" Davis asked. He was wearing his blue jacket with the word POLICE written on the back, and the UN logo on the front.

"Absolutely." Ethan tightened the straps on his backpack, which held the bottles of water he would need for the climb. Although he'd prefer to be searching for his friends, this was *Pieter's* office tower. And though he agreed that Pieter was gone, he was certain the man's legacy of greed and manipulation was somehow involved in their disappearance. He examined the broken windows above. "It looks like the vandals have only hit the first forty floors."

"I'm not worried about vandals. They're lazy. But whoever climbed right to the top and trashed the place had a serious grudge."

As they passed through the lobby, Ethan unrolled the magazine Priya had asked Jack to deliver to Davis. She'd circled a paragraph in the article about Pieter's penthouse. "There's supposed to be a waterfall up there identical to the one in his Seattle office."

"I remember seeing it."

"According to this, the water came to Earth directly from his ice mines in the Oort cloud, and then to Cirrus through a set of portals." Ethan flipped the page. "Then it talks about how that symbolizes progress and Pieter's dedication to providing clean water for drinking and irrigation, blah blah blah." He scoffed. "Anyway, Priya was tracking someone who claimed to be selling the crystals from the waterfall in Seattle."

"That doesn't seem like something he'd have left behind. And even if it wasn't just a ruse to get to Priya, chances are somebody read the same article and was running a scam."

"She wants to be sure."

"I get that. I'll be the first to go back if we can open another portal."

Ethan felt a twinge of guilt as he followed Davis through the wreckage in the lower stairwell. After all, he'd been to Earth since Newton and could have gone again recently with Jack and Sarah. He tossed the glossy magazine on the floor with the rest of the garbage, knowing that it was Priya and her colleagues who embodied dedication, not Pieter.

The steps were clear of debris above the fortieth floor, though graffiti still lined the walls. At the sixtieth, Davis left the stairwell and flopped into a comfortable office chair beside a floor-to-ceiling window. He wiped sweat from his brow, drank deeply from his water bottle, then craned his neck toward the sky. "Not much of a view yet." Pieter's tower was in the center of the city, and all the surrounding buildings were at least a hundred stories tall.

"You still haven't told me why you wanted me to come along," Ethan said.

"Mostly, you're here because your parents want me to keep an eye on you." Davis capped his bottle. "But I didn't want to scare you with the other reason."

Ethan raised an eyebrow.

Davis grinned. "There are rumors going around about monsters roaming the streets at night."

"What kind of monsters?" Ethan frowned, though he already knew the answer.

"Dragons." Davis watched him for a reaction. "Would you have come if I had told you?"

Ethan suppressed a shiver. "Yeah, no problem." He knew Davis had seen dragons last year in the battle against Pieter, and hadn't run away like others had.

"They may have been here, too." Davis pointed upstairs. "I

want your take on some scratches I found in Pieter's office."

Ethan sighed. He really didn't want another encounter with a dragon. "I'm not exactly an expert."

"You know more than I do."

Ethan wondered if he should say that Jack had not only spoken to one, but suspected *anyone* could speak to dragons now. Unfortunately, that might lead to revealing what he knew about Asterion, and he doubted those in Icarus would take well to knowing a dragon was living near their village. "Fine." He checked that his staff was securely strapped to his backpack and slung it onto his shoulders again. "I'll lead."

After another twenty flights, Davis muttered something about disrespectful youth. Ethan noted that at least two different artists had tagged every landing, but he slowed his pace in case Davis was talking about him.

The graffiti continued all the way to the penthouse, where the door was missing entirely, and probably lying in the street two hundred and fifty floors below. Ethan poked his head into the foyer and felt a cold draft. There wasn't a single window remaining on the entire floor. Then he moved cautiously through the room, listening for unusual sounds.

Davis nudged his toe into fragments of a once-priceless vase scattered across the pitted hardwood floor. "Whoever or whatever was here is long gone." He hadn't even unzipped his jacket to expose his shoulder holster.

"Well, something's been trying to get into the portal chamber." *Scratches* didn't begin to describe the marks Ethan was seeing. The wood veneer covering the hidden panel was shredded, and the gouges continued into the underlying steel, which held only because it was an inch thick. "I've seen a grizzly bear do less damage than this."

"That's what I thought. Dragons?"

Ethan nodded and ran a hand over the dry granite slab on the adjacent wall. "It looks like they were after the waterfall crystals, too." When its portals were powered, a thin sheet of water—

originating on an icy planetoid—would have flowed over another slab in Seattle, passed through draining wormholes, then trickled down this wall with a calming white noise.

Deep scratches marred the stone, and Davis pointed to a trough at the foot of the slab. "But not the ones Priya wanted."

"You're right." The marks were near the bottom of the feature. Unless the water was pumped from there, its crystals should have been at the top. Ethan set his backpack down and pulled out a screwdriver, then removed a damaged stainless-steel grate to expose the plumbing underneath.

"There's an opening here." He poked a finger inside. "No, it's just a regular drain." Then he spotted two red plastic plugs at either end of the trough and pried one out. The exposed slot was too small for his finger, so he dipped a screwdriver into it, and the tool dropped several inches before clinking against metal. "I found a smaller hole, but it's empty." He checked the second one. "Same. If these were for portal crystals, they're gone now."

"Why would a dragon come up here looking for crystals?"

"They're obsessed with them. It's something to do with how they were designed to hunt only one type of prey." But Davis had a point. Why *would* a dragon climb all this way? And why claw at the grate when they couldn't sense a crystal underneath? *Unless* …

Feeling around the edges of the plumbing compartment, which the stone trough overlapped, he dug out a two-inch long pencil-thick tube. "Got it." One end was threaded, and the other was slotted for a screwdriver. He lifted it to the light and peered through. "If that's a crystal in there, it's tiny." Then he placed the tube into one of the smaller holes beside the drain and threaded it partway in. "It fits. Definitely a portal crystal."

"Where's the other one?" Davis asked.

Ethan unthreaded the tube, then poked around the compartment again. "Not here. Maybe the dragon got it and thought there was only one."

Davis slid a tattered chair over to the wall and checked the space above the granite slab. "There are slots for crystal holders up here, but there's no damage. That means they were taken before the dragon arrived. Let me see that tube."

Ethan passed it up and Davis tried threading it into an empty slot. "It's different. The incoming crystals must have been larger." He stepped down and spoke with a trace of excitement. "We need to get the chamber door open. If someone has modified the frame to accept the incoming crystal, then they've found a way back to Earth."

"I can handle that." After digging through his backpack, Ethan withdrew a hexagonal ceramic platter.

"What's that?"

"Jack worked out a method for storing spells in the crystals our grandfather has been growing. This one is for opening locks."

"Can't you just zap it open the way he does?"

"I can move more mass than Jack, but he uses portal energy to *see* inside things." Ethan set the hex on the floor, then leaned down and whispered at it. Nothing happened.

"What are you doing?"

"I was telling it the activation phrase. It didn't work."

"Are you supposed to whisper it?"

"No, it's just that …"

"What?"

Ethan sighed, then spoke clearly. "Open sesame." Something ticked deep inside the thick metal panel.

Davis smirked. "Open sesame?"

"*He's trying to embarrass me on purpose.* I keep telling him to use better phrases."

Davis pushed against the panel. "Did it work?"

"No. Hexes are one-shot. It'll fall apart when the spell is complete. I'll try again."

Davis chuckled. "Don't let me stop you."

Ethan stood and faced the panel. "Open sesame," he said again, louder than the first time. The internal mechanism clicked, but the hex remained whole.

Davis choked back a laugh.

"*Do* you *wanna do it?*" Ethan snapped.

"No, you're doin' fine." Davis sat and leaned back in the remains of Pieter's leather office chair.

Ethan repeated the spell, speaking slower, louder, even yelling, but nothing worked. After a dozen failed attempts, he threw his arms up and shouted, "Open sesame, dammit." The lock clunked.

"Hey." Davis perked up. "That was better. It likes the arm movement." He made a shooing motion. "Try again."

Ethan scowled, but then composed himself in front of the panel. With a grand arm gesture, he said clearly and loudly, "Open sesame." The lock clunked louder. He side-glanced at Davis. "I hate it when you're right."

"Okay." Davis stood and elbowed Ethan aside. "I got this." With outswept arms and a resonating baritone worthy of a Shakespearean, he chanted, "Open sesame." The lock clunked louder still.

Ethan rolled his eyes at the smug look on Davis' face, then copied his tone and movements but drew out the last syllables of each word. "*Ha,*" he exclaimed when the lock rang like a struck anvil.

Not to be outdone, Davis added a British accent to his next attempt and got a resounding echo.

Ethan tried again, but by that point they were just trying to outdo each other. With all the accents, vibratos, and flourishes, neither noticed the crystal had finally shattered until a small cloud of ceramic dust wafted between them. They looked at each other and said, "I did that."

Davis pushed the shielded panel aside. Despite the damage on the exterior, it slid silently, and he stepped into the cubical chamber to examine the controls mounted on one side of the ring.

His voice wilted. "The address carousel is missing." Without that mechanism, no crystal could be used to initiate the wormhole, regardless of its size. "There's no passage to Earth here."

Ethan knew Davis was aware of Holden's portal, and that he

had family on Earth. He also knew Priya had refused to allow him to use it because of the risk of exposing it. And though it was the same for virtually everyone on Cirrus, he had enormous respect for the man's sacrifice, especially since Davis' family now thought he was dead.

"We'll find another way," he said.

Davis left the chamber and stood near the window. The view would have been intimidating even if the pane wasn't missing, and he looked down on a wispy cloud blowing over the city. After a full minute of silence, he turned back to the damaged water feature with a puzzled look.

"I know the upper crystals brought water from Seattle, but what are the drain crystals for? And why were they plugged? Pieter was obviously trying for some sort of continuity. Where was he planning to build next?"

Ethan frowned. Davis' logic was flawless. The flowing water would be a chain connecting Pieter's greatest accomplishments. "What would Pieter think of as greater than … Oh, wow. I think I know." He tucked the tube into his pocket. "But I'll have to get Jack to check."

"I thought he couldn't tell where a wormhole opened to."

"He can't. He can only sense what's around it. And if I'm right, the other half of this pair is somewhere *way* different. I think it's on Dawn."

Chapter 19

Jack accepted the wand from Mai. It had been a constant presence in his life for eight months, and more an extension of his will than a tool, but now it was a cold rod of crystal wrapped in a wooden sleeve. But the girl's smile was so innocent and full of hope that he could only say, "Thank you."

"Jack?" Sarah called. "Where are you?"

"In here." He tucked the wand under his shirt out of habit.

Sarah entered the yurt, followed by the old woman and Jada, who was listening carefully as she repeated single words in Chinese.

"Uh, this is Mai." Jack stepped aside so Sarah could see the boy. "And this is … I don't know."

"He is Ben," Mai said. "He does not speak."

Sarah waved a greeting. "Hello, Mai. Hello, Ben." Ben didn't look up. "What is this place? Why is it so dark in here?"

"I can only understand a few words," Jada said. "She says it's where the children live."

Mai and the older woman conversed rapidly in Chinese, leaving Jada looking lost, while Sarah moved around the yurt inspecting drawings tacked to the walls. Jack crouched at the table. "Hello, Ben. What are you writing?"

Ben dunked a short stick into a pot of watery black ink, then skated it across the curled paper, twisting its tip to vary the thickness of his line. He was drawing, not writing, and he was *really* good. Jack watched a scene based on the compound develop from simple yet bold and expressive lines.

"*Jack.*" Sarah's voice was urgent. "Come here."

He crossed the floor and examined the drawing Sarah had found. "Hey, that's me." With only a few lines, Ben had captured him and Marten. They were on the road with a cart and shovels. "And I'm … *Oh.*"

"You're talking to Hugo." Sarah's tone was incredulous.

Jack drew a finger across the paint. "It's dry." Ben had previously drawn—who knew when—an incident that had happened only minutes ago. "Someone on the work crew must have already seen this and talked about it. That's why they reacted the way they did." And though he couldn't imagine how it had happened, the conclusion was obvious. "Ben is a Traveller."

He scanned the other drawings and recognized himself again. And Sarah. And Jada and Marten, too. The images seemed to tell a story, though Jack couldn't interpret them. There was one of him and Sarah on the roof of a building, another with Marten and Jada driving an ATV. In another scene, Mai was holding a wand below a floating box.

The elderly woman spoke again before shuffling for the door, and Mai translated. "Grandmother says you cannot stay long."

"She's right," Sarah said. "There was a lot of confusion when everybody came back running. The guards will want another headcount."

Mai spoke softly to Ben, then brought over his latest drawing. Jack uncurled it so Sarah could see it at the same time.

In this one, the compound was in turmoil. Black smoke billowed from a yurt, and the compound guards—Jack even recognized Ferret—ran about with rifles. And there were dogs everywhere, more than there could possibly be given how much barking he'd heard. "He draws people well." Jack squinted at the figures. "But the dogs are strange." Ben had elongated their profiles to express speed as they streaked through the compound.

"Look again," Sarah said.

Jack tilted the paper into the light. The dogs' tails were too long and very thick, and Ben was a better artist than that. "*Oh.* Those are dragons."

"A *lot* of dragons."

"You will teach me magic?" Mai asked. She stared up at Jack with a hopeful smile.

She'd said the same thing earlier, and he realized she had been asking then, too. That's why she'd found his wand. From Ben's drawings, she must have believed he could show her how to use it.

"I'm sorry. I …" How could he explain that what she thought of as magic depended on an energy field derived from wormholes, and that it had stopped working for an unknown reason? "I can't. My wand is broken." He took it out and flicked it uselessly.

"No." Mai snatched the wand and waved it with a theatrical flourish, and the papers on the yurt's walls rustled as if there were a breeze. "See."

Jack was speechless. He'd sensed energy swirling through the room like eddies from a passing truck. Mai returned his wand.

"How did she do that?" Sarah's voice contained as much surprise as Jack felt.

"I don't know." He concentrated, but to him the wand was lifeless. "It's … there's nothing there." Mai was still smiling up at him, a ray of sunshine in an otherwise dismal corner of the world. He couldn't bear disappointing her. And though he had no idea how he would do it, he agreed. "Yes, I will teach you magic."

Ben got up from his table and crossed the room. With his gaze fixed on the floor, he wrapped his arms around Jack's waist, hugging him for barely a second before returning to his seat.

• • • •

Jack hardly noticed his aching muscles or the light rain when he resumed loading gravel. He was too preoccupied with the mystery of how Mai was able to use portal energy. Then the clouds lowered, it started pouring, and the grain became too wet to harvest. The men returned early from the fields and he was happy to join them. For their part, the workers avoided him as they had since seeing him talk to Hugo.

With the rain on the tent masking her voice as she washed the tables before dinner, Sarah told Jack what she'd learned about Mai's family: Ben was her brother; the older woman wasn't their grandmother—that was just a term of respect; and Mai's mother, a lawyer and human rights advocate, had been arrested the day before they came to Cirrus.

"They were supposed to travel together with a group of refugees," Sarah said, "but the men her mother paid for passage put them in separate vehicles. Then the police arrived. They let Mai's truck go but stopped the one her mother was in."

Jack was wiping down chairs on the opposite side of the table. "So, whoever took their money sold them out to the government?"

"Looks that way. Mai's group drove through the night and stayed in a village with the woman she calls Grandmother. A lot of the people in this compound were already there, though they came from other villages. Over the next few days, everyone walked to a river near the village and swam through the portal. Ben and Mai were the last ones through."

"Huh." Jack considered for a moment, then asked, "Was that at midnight? Midnight *our* time, I mean?"

"Maybe. She says the only light they had was from the firepit. Does it matter?"

"It does if this happened on Newton. Didn't they have power?"

"Not for a few days, apparently. The women in the kitchen talked about having to cook on the fire."

"That had to have been Newton, then." Jack lowered his voice to contain his excitement. "Look, Mai can use portal energy, and Ben is clearly a Traveller. If, like us, they were among the last people to pass through a wormhole, it means Grandpa's portal didn't cause our talents; it was *travelling* when their crystals were synchronized."

"So it's safe for other people to use?" Sarah's face brightened.

"Well, don't be too optimistic. We have to get out of here yet, and we still couldn't make it public because it would be a powerful weapon in the wrong hands. But … yeah, we can let others return to Earth without having to worry about what they would do with magic."

Sarah washed another table before she spoke. "You know, if you're right, it also means that Paul is a Traveller."

"Not only him. With all those crystals he smuggled, Danny

may have been filling *hundreds* of compounds like this one." The implications only hit Jack as he said it. He'd never thought he, Sarah, and Ethan were unique, but he hadn't considered just how many others there might be, or what they were doing with their talents. "There could be *thousands* of Travellers out there. And with Danny looking to start a war, whose side are they on?"

Chapter 20

The sky was overcast as Ethan motored out of Caerton. Without the feeble rays of the setting sun at his back, it was completely dark under the forest canopy, and the road seemed more twisty than it had when he'd followed Davis into the city that morning. Then, he'd been looking forward to challenging the winding road alone on the return trip, but he hadn't expected the tower climb to take all day.

Did Pieter go to Dawn? he wondered. That was possible considering nobody had seen the man in months, and the missing crystal fit the pattern of connecting one world to the next. He would give the tube to his grandfather for an opinion when he got home, but they'd eventually need Jack to confirm his theory. For now, he had to focus on driving.

He was on the westbound gravel roads once used for hauling grain. The paved highway to the south would have been smoother and quieter, but the bumpy grain road was shorter. Also, Davis had called Ethan's parents and told them he would be home by eleven.

He spelled a bug shield from one of his ring crystals and an invisible light from another. The bike's headlight would have allowed him to see farther, but two seconds was all he really needed to avoid deer and other hazards. Besides, no one would see him coming. If there were bandits on the road—something his mother worried about constantly despite the lack of evidence—he could avoid a roadblock without anyone even knowing he'd seen it.

As he rounded a corner, an animal slammed into him from the side and knocked him off the motorcycle. At least, that's what one aspect of his mind perceived. Instead, he hit the brakes, locking both wheels as the creature he'd imagined two seconds before blurred past at chest level.

In passing, its tail caught the edge of his shield and yanked his ring hand from the handlebars, tipping the bike into an uncontrolled slide. Then it flipped and tumbled into the undergrowth as Ethan smacked onto the packed gravel. One of the bike's canvas panniers cushioned his fall, but he felt his radio smash painfully under his hip. Though his riding leathers and helmet saved him from further injury, he was helpless to do anything except slide behind the bike for another thirty yards.

That wasn't a deer, he thought as he rolled and sprang to his feet. Swapping the invisible beam for a spotlight, he pointed it into the forest. Not a sound reached him. Even the birds and crickets were silent. He toned down the light, which lit the front line of trees but made it impossible to see beyond, and the forest became a wall of dense shadows.

Ethan backed toward the bike. His rings and two-second foresight offered decent protection, but what he really needed was his staff. While fumbling with its straps, he heard footfalls and his AI-enhanced imagination conjured a thousand variations of the imminent clash: the beast overpowering his shield; the shield holding while inertia bowled him over; the beast darting around his shield with their superior speed. However, when faced with a jaw full of razor-sharp teeth and dagger-like claws, his instincts took over the instant the dragon leaped. He ducked and rolled, and they missed him by inches.

The dragon landed cat-like and spun to face Ethan as his own momentum carried him to his feet. They were larger than any he'd encountered last year, and their coloring was different: the red splotches along their spine resembled bloodstains. Also, this one had a smooth black cowl that wrapped around its neck like armor.

"Back off!" He spelled a flare from a crystal mounted in the tip of his staff. The six-inch flame, intense as a blowtorch, would do serious damage if it connected, but he really only meant to scare the dragon away.

The dragon screeched, and a glowing orange ball blossomed from *their* crystal.

Oh, yeah. Forgot about that. With his free hand, Ethan slapped his helmet's visor down.

The dragon's fireball curved up from under their jaw and erupted into a huge gout of flame that curled around the edges of Ethan's shield. He'd seen dragons attacking Pieter with fire, and this one seemed to have mastered the spell.

"What do you want?" he shouted. If Jack was right, all dragons now had the equivalent of an AI translator app running in their minds. Regardless, he didn't need a computer to interpret the reply. Another jet of white-hot flame erupted from their pendant. *How long can my shield hold?*

As he had foreseen, the dragon leaped again, and he planted one end of his staff into the ground and crouched while tracking the creature's torso with the other. At the same time, he spelled a bracing force to make the staff as strong as steel.

The dragon hit and folded over the point. Ethan could have remained upright as he guided the beast through an arc over his head, except his talent presented countless variations of claws raking through his protective gear. Allowing himself to be knocked over instead, the dragon's jaws snapped only inches from his helmeted face.

They both landed in a roll. As the dragon twisted around and dug their claws into the hard gravel, Ethan got to his feet and feinted left. The dragon lunged and he sprang to the right while spinning the staff for an overhand strike. But even with his foresight, the beast moved too quickly for him to land a disabling blow, and his staff only nicked the creature's tail as they passed. Still, with the added force of the bracing spell, the impact was clearly painful. The beast writhed and yowled, then faced Ethan in a crouching posture.

"What do you want?" he shouted again. As far as he knew, dragons would starve before hunting prey other than what they were designed for. That meant this one had attacked for a different reason. "I'm no threat to you."

The dragon responded with a growl and began circling. Ethan

held his staff in a defensive pose as he backed toward the motorbike. As he neared the fallen machine, his talent warned of another assault: they would come in low and fast under his shield, aiming for his abdomen. He also saw his own countermoves, which weren't good enough. In every scenario, he deflected their claws but was caught by their whiplike tail. Nearly two full seconds passed before a singular vision offered an escape.

"*Bright light,*" he shouted. It was a spell he'd used accidentally before; one Jack had been experimenting with. And it wasn't just a light spell; it was *insanely* bright. And as before, he didn't close his eyes in time.

The dragon screamed, blinded by the flash, and Ethan wasn't doing much better. Through the dark blotches obscuring his vision, he saw an afterimage of a dragon at the start of their leap. He hit the ground expecting the beast to fly overhead, but the thrashing noises that filled the air were coming from his left.

Another dragon. The blotches still swamped his vision, but he saw that one was the silhouette of a second dragon coming in from his right. They had intercepted the first mid-flight, and both now tumbled in a raging ball of claws and teeth.

He didn't know why two dragons were fighting, and wasn't keen to hang around in case they were arguing over who got to eat him. Crawling to where he thought the bike was, he felt one of its wheels. With no way to see if it was damaged, he seated himself, flipped switches by memory, and heard a familiar beep. The scrabbling noises behind him abruptly stopped, and he tucked his body low, wedged the staff under his arm, and twisted the throttle.

"Night vision," Ethan gasped as the bike surged ahead. Mercifully, he'd started off in the right direction and wasn't heading towards the nearest ditch.

He drove as fast as he dared while his eyesight recovered, and had gone only half a mile when branches snapped in the forest to his left. He swerved to the opposite side to give himself more time should the dragons' fight return to the road, but heard the same noises from the right.

They're chasing me*!* He'd hoped the dragons were engaged in their own conflict and had mistakenly attacked him in the heat of battle. Now that they were flanking him, and closing in, it was clear that he was their target.

He pressed his body against the handlebars, wishing he had Sarah's field-shaping talent—a streamlined cowling would improve the bike's performance—and after a few minutes the crashing noises in the woods trailed off. He considered raising himself to a more comfortable position, but noticed a rhythmic, pulsing sound. *Flat tire?* Given the tumble the bike had taken; he could have a bent rim. *There's no way I'm stopping now.* He drifted to a smoother section of road where he might sense a telltale vibration. Nothing. Though the bike was operating well, the beat continued.

It can't be. He glanced over his shoulder into complete darkness.

The trouble with the night vision spell was that it acted through his memory, not his eyes. Working in tandem with his two-second precognition, the spell showed, in perfect detail, anything he could reach on a multitude of two-second paths. At his current speed, the road ahead was as bright as daylight for sixty yards. Even the edge of the forest was clear—crashing into it was also an option—but everything else was behind an impenetrable curtain of darkness.

He canceled the spell with a thought. His normal vision had mostly recovered, the clouds had thinned, and he could see well enough to navigate by moonlight. Fearing what he might see, he squeezed the brake lever and glanced behind.

Dragon! And really, *really* close.

He spun back and cursed. The bike's power limiter, which was supposed to keep him safe, was now the greatest threat to his survival. And the only thing that kept him from descending into full-blown panic was a tiny bit of logic: *They're just following.*

Ethan's prescience was sometimes hard to interpret. He might not always choose the best option, but the sense was always there, and the dragon would not attack in the next two seconds. As more seconds passed, it became clear they wouldn't strike in the next interval, or the next. *What are they doing?*

The road curved ahead: a broad S-turn along a meandering creek, and he tensed. If the dragon could only match his speed, they'd overtake him as he drifted from the shortest path to avoid potholes. He leaned into the corner and foresaw … nothing.

Instead of taking advantage of the turn, the dragon trailed at the same distance. He squeezed the handbrake again and risked another glance. The second dragon had joined the first.

His heart raced. They were sprinting side-by-side, not fighting. He searched desperately for a spell he could use without taking his hands off the controls. *Maybe something to remove their collars?* Without crystals, they'd be unable to coordinate their actions.

Wait, collars? He flashed the brakes again to confirm. Both dragons were wearing webbed collars. *The one that attacked me had a cowl.* What did that mean? Unfortunately, he didn't have time to ponder why there was a *third* dragon. His first turn was coming up on the right.

Still at the bike's top speed, Ethan drifted to the road's left shoulder so he could lean into the turn without slowing. But as he did, dragon-number-three came up on his right, proving they could have pounced on him at any time.

"What are you doing?" he asked, though he didn't expect an answer. He flipped on the bike's headlight for a long-distance view and saw twin points of light reflecting the beam. *Eyes.*

He slowed, knowing a two-second warning was hopeless when he was surrounded. But as he neared the intersection, dragon-number-two suddenly sprinted ahead and joined the one blocking the junction.

Guess I'm not going that way. As if to underscore his thought, the newest dragon raced to catch up after he passed, leaving the other to guard the road.

Was there danger in that direction? he wondered. Were they

helping him or leading him to a worse fate? Now that they'd left the forest, the major grain roads were laid out in a grid, meaning he only had to continue south and take the next one back to his original course. But the same thing happened there: a new dragon blocked him, then changed places with another. He'd become the baton in a draconian relay.

After hours of bypassing roads to Icarus, they reached the highway at the foot of the Spine, and there was no dragon waiting there. Ethan slowed to a jogging pace in case there was sand or gravel on the paved surface, and both his chaperones leaped into a line on his right.

He jammed on the brakes and slid to a stop, then flipped up his faceplate and shouted, "This is the last turn. What do you want from me?"

The dragons screeched and slunk closer.

"I have to go home."

One of them lowered their head and produced an ominous fluttering growl. A tiny flame glowed from the second's crystal, lighting the ground below and accentuating their claws.

Ethan raised his hands in surrender. "Or somewhere else. Whatever. I'm easy." He twisted the throttle and turned east, towards the sector wall and the high-elevation pass through the Spine.

Chapter 21

As Ethan climbed, heading south, the same pattern repeated every few miles: a new dragon turned up on the side of the road, matched his pace, and replaced the former.

He wondered what his parents were thinking. They'd know something was wrong because he hadn't called, but they'd also know he was still moving because the bike was drawing power through its remote cell. That was one of the first things they'd checked with Marten and Jada.

Of the local passes over the Spine, this was the highest: nearly two miles. Patches of snow appeared on the road's shoulders as he reached the summit, and he cast a spell to warm the bike's handlebars. How were the dragons coping, he wondered, and glanced over his shoulder.

They're gone. He pulled over and removed his helmet. *When did that happen?*

The air was cold and still, and he was utterly alone, the only human for miles in any direction, and certainly the only one on the highway. It occurred to Ethan that he'd never been so far from another person, and he felt a chill that wasn't due to the temperature.

The Spine towered on his right, and a sector wall—one of twelve four-mile-tall berms that divided the ring into sectors—dominated the horizon on his left. The Spine, of course, was desolate: too rocky and unforgiving to support anything other than mountain goats. And the sector walls were even worse. Not even grass grew on their gravelly shells.

I could go home, he thought, then dismissed the notion immediately. There would be a long queue of fully rested dragons waiting to intercept him. And he felt certain they were still watching him, anyway

As if in response, a fleeting shadow passed over the road and he turned his gaze to the sky. The Eye—Cirrus' moon—was directly overhead, meaning it was close to midnight. What had cast the shadow?

Can dragons fly? The idea seemed ridiculous until he recalled how the station's artificial gravity decayed with elevation. Even here the bike was noticeably lighter than it had been at the start of his trip. And at six miles, Cirrus's roof floated weightless on the pressure of the air below. A bird at that altitude, or a dragon, could hover with no effort at all.

Regardless, he couldn't stay where he was; a dragon would soon show up to hurry him along. But there might still be a chance for escape. Rolling onto the Spine's southern slope, he shifted the bike into neutral and tucked his body tight to its frame.

If I can get ahead of them, I might be able to reach Port Anand. He spelled a series of shields, positioning them one in front of the other in an extended cone, and the speedometer ticked higher. *Seventy-five. Eighty.* The highway ahead was perfectly straight to the reach of his headlight, and shiny patches of ice flared into view. He swooped around them, testing the limits of his two-second precognition. *Eighty-five.*

The bike had not been designed for that speed, and its rear mudguard, already damaged, flew off when the speedo verged on ninety. Then the slope tapered and the bike slowed. *Seventy. Sixty. Fifty.* The motor kicked in and propelled him on a serene glide through the foothills and onto the plain. Had it been enough? A sign warned of an upcoming intersection.

This time, two dragons blocked the road, and Ethan, resigned to his fate, turned west. He was now heading towards Fairview. Was that where they were leading him? He estimated it was another four hours to Jack's hometown, but he'd need to rest if they expected him to go much farther. *Do dragons even sleep?*

One of them darted ahead, slowed, and trotted onto an unpaved, single-lane road that curved into the trees. Then they stopped and stared at him.

Ethan looked for a sign but the road was unmarked. "You want me to follow?" The dragon turned and continued into the forest. "I guess that's a *yes*." He dimmed his headlight and cast a night-vision spell.

The narrow road wound through fifteen miles of forests and orchards, and they'd gained a thousand feet of elevation and passed through an untended vineyard when they came upon a locked barrier: a swing gate made of eight-inch steel tubes.

Where am I? The unmarked gate was very much out of place in a rural setting, and looked as if it could easily stop a speeding truck. But the dragon skittered underneath it and waited, so Ethan drove through the weeds to skirt its concrete posts.

After a few more miles, the road ended at a twelve-foot-tall chainlink fence next to an empty guardhouse, and a weathered sign warned visitors to stop and have their identification ready. Nothing suggested the purpose of the complex beyond.

The dragon trotted through the open gate and into a lane between a pair of featureless, steel-clad buildings, each about three stories tall. They had no visible doors or windows, and no company name or logo, only a large number 17 painted in bold yellow font. Ethan, already committed, followed the dragon into the complex.

Movement on a rooftop caught his eye but he turned too late to see what had been there. Checking the opposite side, he glimpsed a sinuous tail whipping the air, and when he looked down again, the dragon he'd been following had disappeared.

He flipped up his visor and slowed to a crawl as he rolled into an empty parking lot where stalls had been painted for forty cars. Those nearest the doors—the buildings' only entrances—were marked as reserved, with their owners' names stenciled in bold letters, except for one that should have read 'Doctor Ahmadi'. Someone had scratched away the title 'Doctor' and replaced it with a rude word.

The place looked abandoned except—*I hear music.*

The tune, a classical piano piece, was coming from behind a line of oak trees at the far end of the lot. He canceled the night vision spell, and moonlight revealed buildings beyond a small park and playground complete with swings and a climbing structure. A footpath led through the park, and since that was the only direction the dragon could have gone, that's where he went.

"What the—?" Ethan couldn't help speaking aloud. The buildings were the strangest thing he'd seen that night. Not because they were unusual structures, but because they were so … normal.

The path followed a gentle slope between two cottages that might have been uprooted from an American heritage town. They had manicured lawns, white picket fences, flower boxes, and—as far as he knew—shouldn't exist on Cirrus. They were definitely out of place in an industrial park hundreds of miles from the nearest city.

Eight cottages faced the park, and there appeared to be at least five rows of them upslope. Apart from the occasional dragon sleeping on their verandas, they seemed empty, and the only electric light was shining on the path at the very top of the hill. That's where the music was coming from, too.

Ethan removed his helmet and considered his options. The dragons obviously wanted him there, so it was unlikely they'd let him leave. He needed a place to sleep, but even if the cottages weren't abandoned, nobody wanted a stranger knocking on their door after midnight. He really only had one choice.

A few of the dragons raised their heads as he passed, but most either didn't notice or didn't care, and his original guide was waiting at the gate of the final house, which was sheltered under a walnut tree. Warm yellow light glowed through gauzy curtains covering its living room window, and a second light shone from a dormer overlooking the front yard. And on the porch, three dragons lay curled on the mat, the two-person swing, and the steps, like so many cats resting before their nightly hunt.

Ethan's skin prickled. "You want me to go in, don't you?"

The dragon who'd led him there nosed the gate open and joined the others, leaving just enough room for him to reach the door. And though it seemed a spectacularly bad idea, he climbed the steps and knocked on the glass.

The music ended abruptly. After a few seconds, a figure approached the door, reached for the knob, and … did nothing. Ethan couldn't see them clearly because the glass was etched with a floral pattern, but he knew they were still there. Another ten seconds passed and he considered knocking again. He was about to raise his hand when the door opened a crack.

"Yes?" The woman peering through the opening was in her late forties, of slight build, and wearing a shabby rust-colored sweater over white scrubs.

"Hi. I … I'm Ethan." And then he was lost for words. What could he say? He hadn't come there of his own accord, and she clearly wasn't expecting him. "Your, uh, dragons brought me here."

"Did they?" The woman eyed them curiously. "I suppose you'd better come in, then." She stepped back and held the door open for him.

Ethan entered and noticed two pairs of identical flat-soled white shoes neatly lined up in front of a closet. He slipped off his sneakers and toed them into line next to the others.

The woman was already walking away. "Would you like something to drink? I just made tea."

"Uh, yes. Thank you." He could see into the living room as he followed her into the kitchen. A teacup was resting on a side table beside a fabric-covered chair with a matching ottoman.

While she looked for another cup, Ethan examined the house, which had a certain quality he couldn't define. It was tastefully furnished, with many antiques arranged on shelves and in alcoves, and framed paintings hung on most of the walls. It even had a fireplace. The heated floor, made of real tiles, warmed his feet, and the countertops were slabs of granite, which were impossible to get on Cirrus but common enough on Earth. Except for the outdated styling, it was homey.

And that's the feeling he finally identified. This was a home, not just a house. The cottage hadn't been designed for showing off. Its vases, figurines, paintings, and so on weren't flashy, but they weren't the generic printed items found everywhere on Cirrus. It must have cost a fortune to bring them from Earth and create the character of a dwelling that had been owned by generations of the same family.

The woman had poured his tea and was smiling at him pleasantly, though she hadn't spoken. Ethan sipped, then realized he'd had nothing to drink in six hours, and downed it in a few gulps. And still the woman didn't speak. Finally, the awkward silence forced him into small talk.

"Uh, have you lived here long?"

"About twenty years."

"You've been here from the start?" Construction of Cirrus had begun over forty years ago. Some workers had lived in sealed habitats in the walls as far back as thirty, but they'd only completed the station's roof twenty years ago.

"Oh, not the entire time. I used to spend two months a year in Ohio."

Her casual attitude only confused him more. Almost no one who came to Cirrus returned to Earth, and certainly not yearly. The woman's home didn't have the uber-rich aesthetic of those who could afford to travel back and forth. So, if she wasn't wealthy, she must be incredibly important. And she seemed very nice, too.

"I'm sorry," he said. "I don't know your name."

"Nour."

"Pleased to meet you." He lifted his cup. "Could I have another?"

"One should be enough."

"Huh?"

"You should probably sit. I don't think I can catch you."

Ethan felt suddenly very strange, and the last thing he saw was her satisfied smile as he slumped to the floor.

Chapter 22

"This is so unfair," Jada said when she sat next to Sarah with a plate of breakfast she'd helped cook. "The guys get a day off when it rains, but we still have to work."

Marten gave her a weary look and indicated the barracks on the hill. "We're prisoners in a labor camp. None of this is *fair*. And it doesn't look like we get a break. Look who's coming."

Jack would have appreciated a day off. Aside from an escape they still had to plan, he'd promised to teach Mai magic. Unfortunately, Ferret—having failed to catch him and Marten plotting while shoveling gravel—had given up pretending he couldn't speak English. He strode to their table and gave them one minute to finish their meal, then report to the north gate.

"What would happen if we refused?" Jack wondered aloud.

"They'll punish everyone else," Jada said. "That's how they've been keeping the workers in line. They tell them they'll cut off grain shipments to their hometowns if anyone complains."

"But they're probably not delivering it, anyway."

"There's no way to check," Sarah said. "Apparently, no one who's arrived since the first group is from the original villages."

Marten sneered. "We have to stop this."

"I agree," Jack said. "And we will. But we still need to get into the bathing pool without being seen."

"Jada and I will work on it." Sarah glanced at Jada for confirmation. "You two should go before the guards start trouble."

With a second guard, Ferret led Jack and Marten outside the compound along the perimeter fence. They stopped above the pool, where the channel was clogged with debris from an earlier storm. "Clean this up." He gestured broadly at the entire area.

Marten handled the heavier logs while Jack dragged away as many of the waterlogged branches as he could while keeping his feet dry. Eventually, they were down to a dozen pieces jammed in the fence below the waterline, and they didn't have to ask to know Ferret expected one of them to go in. Silently, Marten placed a fist on his palm, and Jack did the same. "Rock, paper, scissors," they chanted. Marten threw rock against Jack's scissors, and Jack cursed, then took off his shoes and rolled up his pant legs.

Outside the enclosure the water was only eight inches deep, except right at the fence, where the channel sloped into the pool. He waded in up to his knees and braced his feet against submerged stones.

"Do you need help?" Marten asked.

Jack leaned back. "No, I got it." Suddenly, the thick branch he was struggling with loosened, and he tumbled backwards into the freezing water amid laughter from the guards. Annoyingly, the branch was still stuck.

"Here, I'll do it," Marten said.

"It's okay. I'm already wet." Jack stretched out his arm and probed along the length of the branch. "There's a metal grate under this part of the fence, and the branches are jammed in that."

As he levered the branch against the grate, the ground shifted unexpectedly. It wasn't more than a fraction of an inch, but there was definitely something wrong. Sliding his hand along the narrow gap under the grate, he expected to feel more stones, but there was nothing there. The current had excavated a huge cavity under the flat stone he was sitting on.

"Hurry up," Ferret snarled. "It's raining again."

"Almost." Now sitting chest-deep, Jack twisted the wood with both hands to wedge its end at another spot. Then, pretending to pull it free, he shifted the stone a little more, and repeated those moves with the remaining branches until it was so loose it would eventually collapse on its own and create an opening large enough to swim through. That's when he realized he had a problem: he was sitting on the back of the stone. As soon as he stood up, it would tilt and tumble with the current. He'd be caught, and probably end up in the punishment pit.

"C'mon, Jack," Marten snapped. "You're useless."

"Huh?" Jack had never heard his friend speak that way to anyone. "Hey, I'm trying—"

"You're wasting time." Marten tossed his hands up angrily and started walking upstream. He had the guards' full attention when he 'accidentally' tripped and fell into the creek.

With the guards distracted, Jack quickly stood up and hauled the last branch out. The stone created a large wave as it flipped over, but by the time Ferret looked his way, the water was smooth again.

Marten, sitting in the creek, asked, "Are you done?"

Jack gave him a knowing smile. "All good here." Now, assuming they could all get out of the compound at the same time, they only needed to charge the portal. Its capacitors were in a fenced-off area behind the barracks with the compound's generator, but he had a plan for that, too.

• • • •

After drying off and changing into another set of ill-fitting work clothes, Jack returned to the children's yurt where Sarah was waiting. "How come Ben doesn't talk?" he asked.

"He's autistic. And Mai says they keep the lights dim because he gets overwhelmed easily."

Jack could appreciate that. For most of his life he'd suffered from demophobia: a fear of crowds. Luckily, that condition was caused by the constant intrusion of other people's thoughts from the emo-detectors in their phones. For him, Newton had been both a blessing and a curse.

They checked for guards and then hurried into the yurt. As before, it was lit by a single lantern hanging from the apex of its conical ceiling. Ben, at his table, was a shadowy figure, making so little noise that he could be missed if one didn't know where to look.

"Hello, Ben." Jack kept his voice calm to match the environment. He wasn't surprised that Ben didn't answer.

Mai reached behind a pillow for the wand, which they'd left

with Ben because Jack's own yurt was subject to random inspection. Here, it would be overlooked as a child's toy. "You will teach me now?"

Sarah waved Jack away. "He will, but we need to check something first. I want you to show me some magic without using his wand."

Mai's face fell. She looked exactly as if she'd been caught with her hand in the cookie jar.

"No? Why not?"

Mai lowered her gaze to the floor. "Grandmother told me not to."

Astonished, Jack asked, "You've done it before?"

Tears formed in Mai's eyes, and she sat abruptly and buried her face in a pillow.

"What did I say?" Jack asked.

Sarah shushed him. "I think I understand. If Mai uses your wand, then it's not her doing it; it's the wand." She knelt by Mai and spoke softly. "Mai, are the people here scared of magic?"

Mai nodded, which was the worst response Jack could have expected. His own talents were viewed with suspicion in Icarus, but if the workers here feared magic, it meant they'd seen it used.

"But magic isn't bad," Sarah said. "Is it?"

Mai lifted her head a little. "It makes Ben laugh."

She smiled. "And that's the best use for magic. Can you show us? Without the wand?"

Mai wiped her face, picked up a sheet of paper, and folded it in half. Then she pulled it apart and held the sheet in an open hand with the crease down so it resembled a pair of wings. She blew a soft breath, and it lifted into the air.

Jack sensed a moving energy field. And with it, a feeling of lightness. But the energy wasn't flowing from his wand; it was already there, filling the room. Mai had merely set it in motion. "She's using the portal zone. How did you know?"

"Yesterday, when I was in the garden with Jada, I heard a lute playing. I thought somebody was sneaking around, but they weren't, were they?"

Mai shook her head, then guided the flying sheet over Ben's head as he silently giggled.

"You made the lute play a tune whenever the guards were near."

Mai nodded.

"And you dropped pine needles into the fire," Jack said, "so you could raid the kitchen for snacks."

A mischievous smile crossed Mai's face.

He laughed. That was exactly the sort of thing his cousin would do. "That was a great trick. But the lute ... that's incredible."

"How is it different?" Sarah asked.

"She made a magical early-warning system. You heard it the night we arrived, too. That means the AI has a sense of where everyone is inside a zone." He was surprised that, after so many months of working with magic and its AI, there was still much to learn.

"It also explains the changing mood on the Vault, and the stubborn feeling I sensed outside the garden."

Sarah was right. It hadn't occurred to him that a portal zone's mood was a direct effect of its energy field because it was so much weaker than what he sensed from his own crystals. He glanced at Ben, whose face was lit up with a huge smile that matched the zone's current vibe: an air of childhood joy.

Jack watched the paper glide around the yurt, flapping in a perfect simulation of wings. Mai's talent was extraordinary, and her control was superb. He could almost hear a seagull's cry as the paper circled to the ceiling in an imaginary thermal.

"That's amazing, Mai." Sarah held out her hand and the sheet swooped down to land on her palm. "But if you can already do magic, why do you want Jack to teach you?"

Mai's smile vanished. "The man will come back. He will hurt us."

Goosebumps rose on Jack's arm as the zone's vibe changed again. Sarah stiffened — she'd felt it, too — and Ben hid his face and clenched his stylus in a fist.

"What man?" Jack asked, dreading the answer.

Mai leafed through a stack of Ben's drawings and passed one to Sarah, who carried it to the window for better light. Jack, fearing the worst, looked over her shoulder.

The drawing was dark and moody: a scene from the compound's early days. The platforms that would eventually support the yurts were in place, but their panels were stacked in neat piles, and dozens of workers, stick figures in the background, worked on an uncompleted fence. In the foreground, a kneeling worker was pleading before another man holding a short staff. Rays that could only represent portal energy streamed from it, assailing the cowering worker.

"Who is that?" Sarah asked.

Jack leaned closer. There was a familiar intensity in the way Ben drew the man's eyes. "I think that's Danny."

"Did Ben see this man use magic?" Sarah asked.

Mai nodded.

And of course the workers had seen it too, Jack thought, or been victims of it. That explained their reaction to him speaking to Hugo and why they'd been avoiding him ever since.

Mai knelt next to Ben, wrapped her arms around his shoulders, and he returned to his drawing.

"He must have been terrified," Sarah whispered as the tension in the yurt faded away. "I actually *felt* his fear." Then she seemed lost in thought for a moment. "What if Ben's not just disturbing the energy? What if he can shut it down?"

"That doesn't make sense. Mai is still using it. And how could he do it, anyway?"

"You've disabled portals before."

"Yeah, one at a time. But a portal zone has *millions* of crystals. It would take forever."

"For *you.* What about dragons? I don't remember turning off my shield on the Vault."

"You think Blue did that?"

"I still think they believe the Vault belongs to you." She made a sweeping gesture towards the window. "What if *this* zone belongs to Ben?"

Jack considered everything they'd learned about dragons. They communicated through portals as easily as he would use a phone, and didn't seem to perceive time as he did, either. In that regard, they were more like the AI itself than a human Traveller. "Wouldn't that mean there's a dragon in this zone?"

"Who says there isn't?" Sarah flipped through Ben's drawings and found the one with all the dragons. She crouched and placed it on Ben's table. "Ben, have you seen a dragon for real?"

Ben stopped drawing and seemed somehow quieter than before. Then Jack realized he'd sensed another change in the portal zone. Even the birds outside had stopped singing, and the only sound was a soft scratching under Ben's blanket. Sarah backed away from the table as he reached over, pulled gently on the blanket, and held out his hand.

A spindly leg with spiky claws jutted up and gripped his finger. Then a spiked head appeared, followed by a second leg. Sarah took another step back as a fist-sized dragon crawled into Ben's hand. Jack might have done the same if he weren't already backed against the wall; the creature was *ugly*.

They had a body structure similar to their larger cousins, except their limbs were strangely jointed, with undulating frills, like a leaf mimic insect. And their coloring was mottled shades of brown and green that would be perfect camouflage on a forest floor.

Ben set the little dragon on his table and wrote two Chinese characters on a sheet. Mai stepped forward and translated.

"His name is Puppy."

Chapter 23

Priya had not slept well. She'd gone to bed planning to make a final decision after a good night's sleep, but had been unable to push her thoughts aside. In truth, though, she had already made up her mind, and the last two days of weighing pros and cons had been an attempt to rationalize her choice: *I'm going to Dawn.*

Pieter was dead or permanently disabled, she was certain of that, and Danny was no longer a threat. She'd learned that he'd been purchasing Greek antiquities and rare artworks, construction equipment and building supplies; things that suggested he was building a resort on Cirrus. *If he wants to play host to a community of entitled millionaires; he's welcome to it.* After all, they'd want privacy and exclusivity, and be forced to keep his secrets in isolation. As long as the people she cared about were safe, it wasn't her problem.

The sun had barely risen when she slipped into the hallway and strode confidently to the square mirror. A tap on the disguised switch opened the portal and she stepped back to listen. Her caution wasn't just for hotel guests. Blue could be in the antechamber.

She couldn't hear anything on the other side of the thick glass, but that didn't necessarily mean the dragon wasn't there. They were known to enter the cave and activate the portal. She could only guess at their motivation, and an involuntary shudder rocked her shoulders as she imagined someone admiring their own reflection, unaware of the slitted pupils staring back.

Priya waited another twenty seconds to give Blue time to seal the pressure door or, ideally, leave. She really didn't want to share the cramped space with them. Again. Then, hearing only the distant clatter of pots in the kitchen, she ducked into the empty chamber and closed the wormhole.

They should connect the lights to the portal switch, she thought as she groped blindly for the lamp. However, considering this would be her last trip, it was no longer her concern.

She wasn't surprised to find animal tracks in the snow outside the cave. Although they'd never discovered what Blue's preferred prey was, she'd learned that Earth's fauna lacked an evolved instinct to avoid genetically engineered creatures, which was part of the reason they were Cirrus' ultimate predator. However, she found it strange that there were no dragon prints. Blue had not been there since the last snowfall.

Priya sighed as she gazed into the clear blue sky, knowing she could put off the call no longer. Though she would explain her decision to Sarah in person, letting the village know she was on her way felt like crossing a point of no return. She lifted the radio and pressed the button.

"Icarus, this is Priya."

• • • •

Why am I still dressed? Ethan thought as he pushed away the blanket and felt the rough material of his jeans. He rubbed his eyes, forcing them open. *Where am I?* The room was unfamiliar and bigger than his tiny bedroom in Icarus. It was more like the large one he used when staying at his grandfather's mid-thirties house in Newcastle. It had a very Earth-like aesthetic, which prompted his memory: *Nour drugged me!*

Ethan tried to stand but his head also had an Earth-like feel: full of mud. Instead, he sat on the edge of the mattress and forced his gaze to the window where the streaming sunlight was painfully bright, and its angle suggested mid-morning. Slowly, he tipped himself forward and anchored his feet on the carpeted floor.

Standing was an effort but he felt better for it, and he spent the next minute working on his balance while checking out the room. From the colors and the personal items on the dresser, he guessed it belonged to a young girl. When he was certain he wouldn't fall, he wobbled to the door and inched it open.

The house was silent, so he crept slowly downstairs. The living room was empty, and he found a note on the kitchen counter telling him to eat breakfast and then come to the workshop in the east wing. His stomach grumbled, reminding him that he'd missed dinner last night.

Given the character of the home, Ethan half-expected to find store-bought packaged foods in the pantry. But as in Icarus, Nour relied on canning to preserve her harvest, although that wasn't immediately obvious. Her shelves were stocked with industrial containers that bore dire warnings under handwritten paper labels. *I really hope she cleaned these properly.* He decided to go with a jam-filled flask from the fridge and a couple slices of homemade bread from a biohazard bag.

While eating, he checked out the cupboards. *Coffee! Real coffee.* He opened the tin and inhaled deeply. *I haven't had coffee in months.* There was barely any left, enough maybe for two cups, so he put the container back, then thought, *She* did *drug me. A little caffeine will help me recover.* He found a kettle and a French press.

After his second cup, Ethan stepped onto the porch. *Where is everybody?* He'd arrived after midnight, so it wasn't unusual that the cottages had been dark then. But the yards and lanes were still empty, and he heard nothing but birds in the surrounding trees. Assuming couples and children, the population of the secluded community should have been about two hundred. People, that is.

A rattling yawn surprised him. He hadn't noticed the dragon sleeping in the corner. The dragon, however, noticed him, and they arched their back, stretched their limbs and splayed their claws like a cat's, then slithered over to sniff his leg.

Ethan backed away. "Uh, that's close enough. *Nice dragon. Good dragon.* I ... I'm looking for Nour."

The dragon shook themselves, then turned and plodded down the stairs. He had no way of knowing if they'd understood or had just grown bored with him, so he followed them down the hill and spotted his bike in the parking lot. Briefly, he thought about leaving, but there were twice as many dragons lounging on the porches as there had been last night, and some of them looked familiar.

The dragon headed for the building on the east side of the complex and went directly to the glass doors, which opened at their approach. Not knowing if anyone could enter freely or if the sensors were keyed to the dragon's crystal, Ethan scurried into the lobby before they closed.

The lobby gleamed. Chrome and glass, tile and aluminum, all polished by a swarm of bots that moved silently out of his way. And every light in the place was on despite skylights that lit not only the entry hall, but the glass-fronted offices on the second floor. Clearly, this building had a functioning fusion reactor and a working AI to manage its maintenance drones.

Two doors flanked the security desk in the center of the space. Neither was labeled, but the dragon was waiting by the one on the left, so that's where Ethan went. He entered a short hallway and spotted a door marked 'Doctor Nour Ahmadi'. *That explains a lot.* Hers had been the defaced parking spot.

He found Nour at a workstation, peering through a microscope. She'd traded her scruffy sweater for a lab coat but was still wearing scrubs. And judging by the wrinkles, possibly the same ones from last night. She didn't look up to acknowledge him, though she had to have heard him enter.

"Do you always drug your guests?" Ethan asked as the dragon settled beside her desk.

"I didn't invite you."

Fair point. "Your dragons brought me here."

"Unlikely." She leaned over and cooed at the dragon while vigorously rubbing the scales behind their brow ridge, and they curled up on the floor like a monstrous tabby.

Ethan saw the contents of his panniers spread out on an adjacent table. Every item was arranged in neat rows and columns, as if she'd cataloged them for further study, and his staff was leaning against the wall by the door. He picked up the radio. Its case was cracked, but Nour had reassembled it. He pressed the power button. Nothing.

"Looking for this?" Nour held up the radio's coin cell. "There's a very irate woman wondering where you are."

"What did she say?"

"It didn't sound like a conversation I'd enjoy." She dropped the coin onto her worktable. "Who sent you?"

"I told you. Your dragons brought me."

Nour scoffed. "They avoid people."

"I'm not fond of them either. And one of them tried to kill me last night." He held out the radio. "Here. That was Detective Singh. She'll tell you; I'm just looking for my friends."

"Why would they be *here*?"

"I wasn't looking for them here. I was driving home from Caerton when I was attacked by a dragon with a black cowl. And then *your* dragons forced me here."

"That's not possible. They're torpid right now."

"Torpid?"

"It's like hibernation. They only wake when they sense the population density of their prey is too high. They can remain in torpor for months, and these ones haven't moved in days."

Ethan pointed out scuffed scales on the shoulder of the dragon who had led him to Nour's office. "I'm positive that's the one who attacked the red dragon last night."

"A red dragon?" Nour tapped an icon on her computer screen, scrolled through a menu, and an image of a red and gold dragon appeared. "Like that?"

The beast on the screen was straight out of a nightmare, with a spiked frill and sharp ridges along their back. "*Yikes.* Not that one."

"Hmm, too bad."

"Why is that?

"Oh, not too bad for *you*. Too bad for *me*. I was hoping you knew where it was." She turned back to her microscope. "You wouldn't be here if that one were chasing you."

"*Wh-What?* You don't know where—"

"Never mind." Nour glowered. "Tell me about the incident."

Ethan recovered his composure and described how the dragons had passed him off from one to another, and also their cooperation during last year's battle with Pieter.

Nour's expression softened as he spoke. "They *will* work together, but what you're describing takes more planning than we've ever observed."

"But they communicate through their crystals, don't they?"

"No, they communicate with each other directly. The crystals used to allow *us* to work with them remotely."

"Used to?" He glanced nervously at the dragon.

"I turned that AI off when … Never mind, it was only a conditioning tool."

Ethan understood the concept of conditioning. In Seattle, he'd used a dog collar equipped with an emo-detector and motivator for training Dusty to be safe on the streets. "How could you tell what they were doing in the wild?"

"There are millions of cameras and drones around Cirrus. They're used for monitoring everything from the weather to migration patterns. I integrated our networks so we could remove any recordings of dragons."

That was another computer system Ethan recognized. Sarah had used it when she interned at the aviary. And Nour was surprisingly candid about her work. She seemed to take the most pride in its technical aspects as she continued her explanation, and Ethan would have respectfully described her as a geek.

"I also developed a method for correlating emo and environmental data to push a positive feedback signal when a dragon was in the right area or feeding on the correct prey."

He began to see similarities with another, far more widely spread network. "*You* created emoji selectors for phones?"

"No. *I* developed an adaptive system for analyzing electrical frequencies in dragons' brains. Someone else stole my design and used it for *games* and *phones*." Her contempt for those devices was evident in her tone. "They were part of the same group that developed Little Brother. So when they embedded *my* software in their camera network"—a self-satisfied smirk replaced her disdain—"I simply dumped our visual data into their servers and accessed it through a backdoor."

"They stole the software from you, and you used it to hijack their hardware." Ethan suppressed the urge to offer Nour a high-five. He'd have done the same thing in her shoes.

"Seems fair to me. We didn't have the budget for the high-end computers they were using."

"Weren't you worried about someone seeing dragons on Little Brother?"

"The data wasn't actual video. We sampled the dragon's visual cortex and uploaded that for the AI to parse. We could extract what we needed from it, but it wasn't something you could watch on a screen.

"What if the visual data got pushed to a human through a motivator circuit? They'd see it then."

"Not possible. We had control over the output ports. The data only ever came back to the server in my lab."

"What about Newton?"

"The scientist?"

"No. Well, yes. But not really." Ethan realized that Nour, who probably hadn't left the camp since the last time she visited Earth, knew nothing of Newton. "Pieter Reynard built a machine that merged all portal crystals. He intended to destroy them, but now they're linked in a way that makes it possible for any crystal to connect to any other." When Nour shook her head, he added, "I've seen it work."

She turned back to her microscope. "I don't believe you."

Ethan raised a fist and shot a plume of white fog at the ceiling. "That's C-O-2 from a fire extinguisher factory somewhere on Earth. I can tap into the cylinder filling nozzle, and it's even easier to communicate between portals." He gestured at the crystal on the dragon's collar. "I think your system is still running."

There's nothing better than empirical evidence to convince a scientist. Nour not only accepted the premise, she started working with it. Her fingers flashed over her keyboard.

"That would explain a lot." A complex graph popped up on her monitor, and she traced a series of rising lines. "This is the average comm data from insectivores in zone 12-D last month. They were showing stress, indicating prey levels exceeding what they could cope with." She indicated a mid-month spike on the second graph. "This is a cohort in 11-D. They were torpid for the first two weeks, then abruptly migrated into the neighboring zone. But the prevailing winds were wrong. That shouldn't have happened."

"Unless your software is still running and they're communicating through the AI."

Nour seemed to forget about Ethan as she scoured the data, so he scanned the lab, which was separated from her office by a glass wall. He noted the many idle workstations and dozens of empty cages.

"Where is everybody?"

"What?" Nour glanced up, looking surprised that Ethan was still there. "Oh." She shrugged. "Gone."

"But you stayed?"

"I still have work to do. These dragons aren't fully conditioned yet."

Ethan recalled the room he'd woken up in. Nour must have a daughter. "And everyone else just left?"

She sighed. "We had a disagreement. They wanted me to shut the program down and euthanize the dragons."

"I see." Though Ethan wasn't fond of dragons, he didn't like the idea of killing them. "That's hardly a reason for them to move away. You've got power here. Water. Gardens. It can't be better anywhere else in the sector."

"They told me to kill *all* dragons, not just these."

"What do you mean, *all* dragons? How could you kill every dragon?" And then it all came together: dragons can't breed, meaning their numbers wouldn't grow; Nour could track every dragon on Cirrus; and maybe— "They're immortal, aren't they?"

"They won't live forever. Hundreds of years, certainly. Maybe thousands."

The idea of creating an intelligent creature only to kill it when it was no longer useful was more disturbing to Ethan than the animals themselves. "That's probably not ethical, is it?"

"No, it's not," she said, though she didn't seem much bothered.

"And the others didn't want their research to become public."

"They did not." Nour said this in a way that suggested that was their problem, not hers.

"So you …?" He made a very tentative gesture of a knife across his neck as he stepped back.

"What? *No!* I never hurt anyone. I just released the dragons we had here."

"Untrained dragons."

"They won't harm people. But they haven't been conditioned to avoid them yet, so they stick around the camp where they get fed. Apparently that's"—she made air quotes—"unsettling."

Ethan thought Nour had far too much faith in her dragons. "Well, the one that attacked me might not have intended to *eat* me, but they'd have torn me apart if my pannier hadn't saved—" The memory suddenly came back to him, crystal clear: the way the dragon intersected his path, and how his two-second warning hadn't kicked in until it was almost too late. The dragon had targeted the bike's panniers, not him. If he hadn't braked, they'd have passed behind, not in front of him.

He recalled Sarah's confusion about a case she thought was supposed to be on the bike's cargo rack. *That was a Traveller-memory.* And she must not have been the only one to recall it; whoever sent the dragons thought he had the case, too.

"How are you able to kill every dragon at once?" Ethan picked up his pannier. "Is it something that would fit in here?"

"No, it's—"

An alarm sounded and they both turned to a security monitor on the wall. It showed a vehicle behind the barrier gate in the forest, and two men trying to force the lock with a crowbar.

Ethan's heart raced when he recognized one of them.
Danny Kou was at the gate.

Chapter 24

"That's Danny Kou."

"Who?" Nour asked.

Jack was right, Ethan thought. *Danny is alive. What's he doing* here? But asking himself the question was all he needed to prompt the answer: *Danny wants whatever is in the case, and if he came* here *for it, that means he sent the dragons, and*—"Danny wants the device."

"What device?"

"The one that kills dragons. Where do you keep it?"

Nour's eyes flicked briefly to the lab window. "It's locked up."

Ethan followed her gaze to a metal cabinet with a biohazard symbol on its door. "He'll burn this place to the ground to get it. Nothing can stop him."

"Why?" A note of panic rose in Nour's voice. "How does he even know it exists?"

"One of your colleagues?"

"No. They may not have agreed with my decision, but they'd never talk about our research with an outsider."

Ethan scanned Nour's desk, looking for a spy camera, and noticed a familiar object: a baseball-sized, multifaceted sphere. "Where did you get that orb?"

"It's a diffusion crystal. They're buried all over Cirrus. We dug this one up in the garden behind the cottages."

"I know what they are. My grandfather had a set. Remember what I said about communicating through crystals? With a decent image processor, you could put together a video of what's on the other side of that one." He moved it into shadow. "That sparkle isn't a reflection. That's light coming from a facet on another orb. How long have you been using it as a paperweight?"

Nour's anxious gaze swung to the image of the red and gold dragon on her computer. "Long enough." She slapped the power button and the screen went dark.

"Can you destroy the … whatever's in the case?" Ethan asked.

"Not without putting the dragons at risk."

"Huh?"

"It's not easy to explain."

An intense light flashed on the security monitor, temporarily blinding the camera. "Well, we don't have time, anyway." When the image returned, the gate was warped and hanging open. "How did—"

"They blew up the gate," Nour exclaimed as Danny walked away from it.

"No." Ethan felt a sense of dread. Something was *very* wrong. "That wasn't an explosive. Danny was standing far too close."

"Then what hit the camera?"

As Danny got into the vehicle, Ethan realized the item he was carrying wasn't a crowbar. It was a *tonfa*, a T-shaped baton used in martial arts and also carried by some police forces, but a weapon that was totally useless for breaking a lock. "We have to leave. *Now.*"

"What about—"

He moved to the door and grabbed his staff. "We've got five minutes. Is there another road out of here?"

"There's a trail past the gardens that leads to a cistern."

"Grab the device. I'll block the front gate to give us more time."

He dashed from the building and used a ring crystal to drag lengths of razor-wire from the top of the fence bordering the gate. It wasn't much, but it would be more effective than locking the gate. Somehow, Danny had destroyed a massive steel barrier in only seconds.

Nour was outside the main entrance when he returned, holding a silver case that was too large for a pannier, but would fit perfectly on his cargo rack.

Ethan handed his helmet to her. "Do you ride?"

"I haven't been on a motorcycle in years."

"Hop on. I'll take it easy."

Nour mounted the bike behind him after he strapped the case onto its rack, and they sped onto a service lane that circled the cottages, then continued through ten acres of gardens and greenhouses to another locked gate.

"Where are the dragons?" Ethan hadn't seen a single one as they passed.

"I was wondering the same thing."

He paused briefly at the gate, forced the lock with his ring, and pushed it open. Beyond, the dirt road was much rougher than the lane, and he'd have to go slower for Nour's sake. He was preparing to pull down more razor wire when the howl of a powerful gas-powered engine startled a pair of deer into the adjacent woods.

"They're coming around." Nour pointed to another road outside the fence that allowed access to the cistern without entering the complex.

Ethan swore. *The razor wire.* His plan had backfired. Danny would have understood it had been put there to slow him down and made the sensible decision to scout the area first. "Hang on." He twisted the throttle and bounced the bike up the hill.

Nour wrapped her arms tighter around his waist. "The road ends half a mile ahead."

He considered the forest. Though it wasn't dense, the ground was far too rough to carry Nour cross-country, and they'd be better off on foot. Soon, a circular tank came into view as the roar of Danny's engine overwhelmed the electric bike's whine.

Ethan swung around the tank's left side, hoping to find another path, but Danny went the other way. He spun his car—a two-seat ATV—into a sideways drift, and a thick cloud of dust surged towards Ethan and blocked his path.

"*Run,*" Ethan shouted.

Nour jumped off, grabbed the case, and dashed into the bush while he pulled his staff from its holster. At the same time, the man riding with Danny jumped out of the car and said, "I'll get her."

Moving without urgency, Danny stepped from the car while holding the tonfa in a manner that suggested years of experience with the weapon. Ethan let the bike fall and spelled a shield.

Priya had described Danny as a *Hopper*, the common name for those whose Traveller-memories were only a very short jump into the future. Technically, Ethan was also a Hopper, but he had an advantage: Danny's foresight was just half of one second. And he didn't know about Ethan's talent at all.

They circled each other, positioning themselves for the first strike. When it came—from Danny—Ethan easily stepped aside. But instead of showing anger or surprise at how effortlessly Ethan avoided his attack, Danny grinned.

"How long?" he asked. "One second? Two? More?"

Ethan cursed silently. He'd hoped to hide his talent until he could counter with a strike that would end the fight quickly. He moved again when he sensed Danny's next lunge. And his next. And his next. And his next!

Danny hurled himself into battle at astonishing speed. Though Ethan dodged every assault, and saw more coming, he was rapidly running out of options. Danny was expertly confining him against the cistern's waist-high wall, limiting his room to maneuver. Ethan knew which strike was finally going to land, and willed his shield to fortify that side.

When the blow landed, it was far stronger than he expected. His shield rang like a bell, and he felt a percussive resonance in his chest, as from the beat of a giant drum. It pushed him back against the cistern.

Mass-shifting. Danny was using the trick Ethan thought *he'd* invented, and he was doing it much better. The baton's metal tip struck with the force of a ten-pound sledgehammer, one that moved as fast as if it were made of balsa wood.

Danny didn't let up after that first hit. If anything, he moved even faster. The string of blows that hammered Ethan's shield weren't as strong as the first, but his ring warmed alarmingly as its crystals absorbed the impacts.

Ethan parried the next few strikes with his staff, borrowing and displacing mass to match Danny's speed, if not his strength. That would save his ring crystal from overloading, but it wouldn't be enough. He steeled his nerves and fought back, timing his strikes for the narrow window between Danny's.

Bo smashed baton over and over, making a thunderous noise but never quite breaking through Danny's defenses to sweep a leg or hook an arm. And on the few occasions when he landed a hit on the tonfa's handle, which should have knocked it from Danny's grasp, the shockwave that travelled up the staff numbed his own hands.

"Got it," a voice shouted from the forest. The man who'd chased Nour appeared with the case, and jumped into the ATV's passenger seat.

But Danny didn't relent. Stronger and quicker, he kept Ethan pinned against the low wall with an unending barrage. Ethan didn't need long-term Traveller-memories to see how the fight would end. He was making mistakes, confusing the order in which the blows would land. He had to escape.

His two-second precognition warned him that Nour was about to call for help, a momentary distraction, and he imagined a broom-like extension on the tip of his bo. As Nour cried out, he pretended to stumble, then gathered and flung dusty soil from the road in a sweeping arc. Danny blocked the staff but the dirt carried on, forcing him to protect his eyes and give Ethan the extra half second he needed.

Swinging his bo two-handed over his head, Ethan borrowed every ounce of mass the staff's crystal could muster. Its momentum pulled him upwards into a backflip worthy of a martial arts film star on a wire, and he landed on the cistern's lid with the high-ground advantage. But controlling the portal energy was exhausting, and he struggled to catch his breath.

Danny, barely winded, chose not to pursue. Without a word, he walked calmly to the ATV and drove away.

Before Danny had even rounded the cistern, Ethan hurried to

find Nour. She hadn't gone far, and the thug hadn't even touched her. Instead, she'd twisted her ankle while scrambling up the sandy hill and fallen onto a cactus. At least a dozen barbs still pinned her scrubs to her calf. Ethan helped her hobble to the bike, which they rode at a walking pace back to her lab for antiseptic and a sturdy pair of pliers.

"What was in the case?" Ethan asked as he pulled barbs from Nour's leg.

A look of shame crossed her face, but her tone was defiant when she finally spoke. "It's impossible to create a balanced ecosystem in one step. There are far too many variables. But we desperately needed a way to control various animal populations while Cirrus found its own equilibrium. So, my team explored chemical and biological options, but we couldn't eliminate the possibility of contamination." She winced as Ethan yanked out another barb. "Culling larger mammals with drones would have been easy, but that wouldn't work with insects. They're too small and too widespread. And we had to respond quickly to unexpected population shifts, even though history teaches us that introducing one species to manage another always ends poorly. What we—*Ow*. What we needed was something we could program, like a drone."

"A living drone."

"One we could remove from the environment when it was no longer needed."

"Or if it got out of control."

"There was never any danger of that with the dragons. On a conventional scale, they're more intelligent than any bird and more social than—"

"What do you mean by *conventional*?"

"They don't think the same way any other animal does. We can't even properly define their thought processes, much less quantify them. That's one of the reasons I created the AI."

Ethan was starting to understand. "You also built in a kill switch."

Nour nodded as she wiped her leg with an alcohol swab. "A crystal that grows near the base of the skull. While the dragons are still embryos, we split it and extract one half—"

Ethan had been fitting the coin portal back into the radio. He let his hands drop. "You grow crystals inside their skulls?"

"There are natural crystals in humans, too. In some of your glands, in your ears, even nanoscale crystals in your bones. They're not gemstone quality, but any crystal can be entangled if it's small enough. And we engineered ours to deliver a toxin directly into the dragons' brainstems." Her voice trailed off at the end.

"So …" Ethan glanced at the dragon who'd followed them into the lab, the only one in the entire complex that hadn't vanished. "The case contains entangled crystals. And after Newton, your colleagues wanted to use them to wipe out the dragons. And they—" Nour suddenly pitched forward and hid her face in her hands. "Sorry, I didn't mean to upset you." For all her rancor, Ethan could tell she'd devoted much of her life to the dragons and cared deeply for them. "That must have been hard."

"You don't understand." Nour was sobbing. "It was me. *I* used it."

"You've already activated it? How long does it take?"

"Not these dragons. There was a class of insectivores, modeled after a shrew, but faster and more voracious. They were critical in controlling insects for the first decade, but they've been in torpor for the last few years. When we lost communication with Earth, we …" She hung her head again. "No, it was my decision. I decided there was too much risk of their devastating the environment."

"So you wiped out the bug-eaters. What about the rest?"

"I couldn't do it. But I'd made it too easy for my colleagues. They never felt the guilt I did, and they wouldn't until after they'd done it, when it was too late. So I locked up the crystals and released the remaining dragons."

"And—surprisingly—your colleagues didn't like that."

She sat up abruptly. "Yeah, I don't get it either."

No, I don't think you do. Apparently, Nour's brain was wired differently too, and she completely lacked empathy with her coworkers. "Hold on. If Danny wanted to kill the dragons, he'd have done it here. There'd have been no way to stop him."

"No, he could just drop the crystals in acid, burn them, crush them in a—"

"That's not what I meant." Ethan shuddered at the callous indifference with which Nour listed the many ways to kill her dragons, but knew she didn't feel any malice; it was just her way. "He must not intend to kill them. He has something else in mind."

"Ethan?" The repaired radio lit up. Priya was calling. "Are you there?"

Ethan raised the radio. "I'm here."

"Where *are* you? Your parents are frantic."

"I'm okay. My radio was … I saw Danny. He's alive."

"Danny?"

He heard the alarm in her voice. "Yeah, what's wrong?"

"Nothing … I hope. Where did you see him?"

"Here, at the, uh, I don't know where I am. Some sort of genetics lab south of the Spine. I'm heading for Fairview."

"No, you're heading home. I'll—"

"I know where Jack and the others are. Well, not *exactly* where they are, but I know how to find them."

"What do you mean?"

"Danny was looking for a device that can kill all the dragons. But he didn't use it. He just took it with him. Whatever he's up to must be a continuation of his plan from before Newton. And Jack found a spot west of Fairview last year where he was building a tent city."

"I remember. He called it Horseshoe Hills. You think that's where they are?"

Ethan couldn't prove that, but he knew his reasoning was sound. Jack had discovered a cache of weapons there and a meteor-safe: a container that could survive a fall through Cirrus' flexible, self-sealing roof. Sarah had found an identical one in Caerton before destroying the hundreds of addressing crystals it contained. It was Priya herself who worked out that Danny intended to use them for smuggling people.

"They have to be," he said. "It can't be a coincidence that Danny showed up here."

"It's a long way to go on a hunch. I'll ask Suresh to check it out."

"No, wait. There's more. They, uh … They also met a dragon who warned them about Danny."

"They spoke to a *dragon*?"

"Well, you know Jack … Anyway, the dragon asked them to get the device."

"Why didn't you tell me that first?"

"I was kind of hoping I wouldn't have to."

Priya muttered something Ethan couldn't understand. "Fine. Do you know where the Horseshoe Hills are?"

"No, but DAVe does. His server will still be at Jack's workshop in Fairview."

"Fine, go back to Icarus. I'll go to Fairview and find the server."

"But you're on the Vault. You can't come down this side because the road is damaged, so you've got to go back to the highway on the north side and then over the central pass. I'll be there hours ahead of you. I'll pick up his server and wait for you there."

"No way. If Danny is back, there's too much—"

"Sorr… Pri…" Ethan mimicked a broken connection. "…ear you. Radio…"

"Stop jerking around, Ethan. I know you can hear me. Get your a—"

He switched off the radio and smiled at Nour. "Got any food? I have a four-hour ride ahead of me."

Chapter 25

A dragon named Puppy? Sarah couldn't think of a less appropriate name for the creature that had been hiding in Ben's yurt. She whispered to Jack, "It's not just me, is it? That is one *ugly* dragon."

"You're right." He grimaced and shivered. "They're—"

Mai crouched at Ben's table and reached out to pet the dragon. "He is so cute."

Sarah and Jack exchanged a look.

Mai spoke excitedly to Ben in Chinese, and his face lit up. Sarah didn't need to understand their words to recognize their shared joy as Puppy crawled onto Mai's shoulder. And their smiles quelled her own creeped-out feelings, though she expected to see those extra-large eyes and needle-like claws in her nightmares someday.

But they had work to do. "We should try again." Sarah found the drawing of Mai levitating a box and knelt by Ben's table. "I know you saw Danny using magic to hurt people, but it can be used for good, too. Mai would never harm anyone with it. Is it okay if she uses the wand?"

She could feel Ben's uncertainty magnified in the zone's mood. The boy was still scared, but a sense of trust was growing. When he nodded, she moved one of his pillows to the center of the room and gestured to Mai. "Try to lift it."

Mai pointed and flicked the wand, but the pillow merely wobbled. She tried again with the same result.

"I'm sorry, Mai," Jack said. "That's still the zone's energy."

Mai clenched the wand so tightly that her hands shook, but still the pillow refused to move, and tears ran down her cheeks again.

"It's okay, it's okay." Sarah embraced Mai and stroked her hair. "You can't stop Danny, anyway. He's far too strong."

Through her tears, Mai insisted, "I will beat him. I will win."

Sarah pulled Mai's arms away and met her eyes. "You can't fight these people. They have guns. Jack and I will escape and send help. Right, Jack?"

"Yeah." He forced a smile that she knew was meant to hide his disappointment. "I had hoped Mai could flip the switch to charge the portal, but … we'll find another way."

"I can do that," Mai said.

Jack shook his head. "It's much harder than moving a piece of paper or a pillow."

"I will learn." Her voice grew stronger. "We will escape, too. Ben needs Mother." Her arm trembled and a faint glow appeared at the tip of the wand.

Ben was no longer smiling, but watching his sister with an expression that matched her determination. Then, with unexpected speed, Puppy leaped from her shoulder and landed on his table.

"*Mai. Look.*" Sarah said. The wand's crystal was shining. "Try it again."

Mai drew a surprised breath when she spotted the glow. Then she swept her arm at the cushions scattered by Ben's table, and they immediately rose into a spiraling dance around the hanging lantern.

Jack started laughing. "You were right." He waved a hand through the invisible energy field. "Dragons *can* control crystals in a portal zone. Puppy must have re-enabled my wand for Ben."

Sarah laughed too as the pillows swirled over Mai's head: the magic was back! And she sensed another shift in the zone's mood. It was light, energetic, and hopeful. With the wand working again, Jack could make a shield big enough for all of them to walk out of the compound whenever they wanted.

And it was the right thing to do. Ben's smile proved that. Since they'd been captured, today was the first time she'd seen one of the compound's residents experience something other than fear or misery. Whatever else Danny had planned for Cirrus, he had to be stopped if only so children like Ben and Mai could have a normal life.

Then an alarm sounded: a wailing klaxon that blasted from every direction. Ben curled into a ball and covered his ears, and Puppy darted under a blanket.

"What's that?" Sarah asked.

The cushions fell and Mai panicked. "We must line up now." She quickly hid the wand under Puppy's blanket. "Fast." She coaxed Ben to stand and ushered him to the door.

Outside, terrified workers were streaming from their yurts while the guards shouted. Sarah started for their assigned place, but Jack turned back to the yurt.

"Leave it, Jack." She knew he was thinking of going back for the wand. "We don't know where Jada and Marten are. There'll be a better time."

He nodded and hurried to the clearing while she, Mai, and Ben headed for the dining tent. They were among the last to arrive, and Ben ran straight to Grandmother and buried his face in her side.

Finally, the alarm shut off and Sarah could hear dogs barking near the south gate. The barracks officer was walking down the hill with Ferret, who was carrying something small and glowing in his hands.

Jada threaded her way over to Sarah. "What's happening?"

"Oh, no," Sarah whispered when she recognized the object Ferret was carrying. "It's our radio." It hadn't occurred to her that it would start working, but its crystals, their cars' power cells, her earrings—every portal from Icarus shared the same source as Jack's wand. And when that started working, so did they.

Ferret tugged on the crystal's wires as he described the radio to the officer. Though the device was in pieces, a green light shone from its display panel, meaning the power had to come remotely through a wormhole. The officer seemed to understand and signaled a newly arrived guard to bring over his dog: a huge German Shepherd. The dog sniffed the radio, then sat down.

"It must be sensitive to portals," Jada murmured.

Sarah didn't know that was even possible. But then, strange things happened to humans who used them, so why not dogs? After all, they had to have come to Cirrus through a portal too.

The guard doing the head count reported to the officer, who appeared satisfied that everyone was present. Then, with a smug grin, Ferret pointed out Jack and Marten's yurt, and the officer ordered two guards into it with the dog.

They wouldn't stop there, Sarah knew. They'd call Danny back. And because he could use magic, he'd eventually figure out the same thing she had: the portals hadn't revived spontaneously; Ben had somehow turned them on. *He'll know that Ben is a Traveller.* She searched for Jack in the men's group, saw him looking agitated, and guessed what he was thinking. *He's going to go after the wand.*

A loud thump drew everyone's attention: the guards were hauling out mattresses and bedding, and dumping them on the wet ground. With that distraction, Jack started inching towards the back of his group, but Sarah knew he couldn't possibly outrun the guards. She had to act fast.

Fortunately, their actions meant no one was watching her, either. She ducked low and weaved through the ranks to find Ben.

"Ben," she whispered. "Our radio works through magic, too. Can you turn it off?" Did Ben and Puppy have a strong enough connection for that, she wondered as Mai translated.

When Sarah stood, Jack was still inching away and she had no way to warn him. *Please, Jack. Look at the radio.*

He seemed about to run when he glanced her direction, and she immediately jerked her head to the side to indicate he should watch the radio. Then she looked back herself just in time to see its green light wink out.

Neither Ferret nor the officer had caught the change because the officer was still watching the guards emptying the yurt, and Ferret was watching Jack. And he'd seen *him* watching her.

Then Ferret noticed the radio was dead again. He frowned and shook it, and the officer—seeing the younger man's frustration— glared. Ferret bowed apologetically as the officer marched uphill, forcing him to hurry to catch up while casting an angry scowl at Jack.

The inspection continued until the evening. Sarah had a tense moment when the dog handler led the Shepherd through the ranks of workers, but it didn't alert to her or anyone else. And the other guards found nothing in any of the yurts, not even Puppy. So, the only bad thing to happen was the guards turned off power in the kitchen and the workers had a cold dinner.

"We got lucky," Sarah said as she munched raw vegetables.

"Yeah. And not only with keeping the wand hidden." Jack slumped a little. "I wouldn't have made it. I'd have just made things worse."

"So, what do we do now?" Marten asked. "You guys can't go back to Ben's. The guards will be watching more closely now."

"While you two were playing outside," Jada said, "they had workers—"

"We weren't *playing*. Jack found another way into the bathing pool."

"Whatever. They were carrying blankets to the other side of the compound. I think they're getting ready to bring more people in."

"How many?" Sarah asked.

"The setup over there is the same as it is here," Jack said. "That means maybe another two hundred workers."

Sarah shook her head. "The portal could be busy for weeks."

"We can't wait that long." Jada had real concern written across her face, which was unusual for her. "Daddy will be going insane." She reached over and squeezed Marten's hand.

Sarah knew what they had to do, but Jack said it first. "We have to go tonight."

Chapter 26

Ethan reached Fairview mid-afternoon without seeing a single dragon. Not that he'd expected to; Danny had what he wanted now. And there was no way he could know whose side the dragons were on, or where they had gone. The one that attacked him had to be working for Danny. The others? He wasn't sure. They seemed to have an agenda that even Nour didn't understand.

From a distance, Fairview appeared as he remembered it: an orderly grouping of towers rising towards the center of a square, exactly one mile on each side. There were only four roads into it, and he was approaching from the east on the imaginatively named East Road. Jack's family's workshop was on South Road.

I'll just go downtown and make a left at the turning circle, he thought. *I'll have the server before Priya gets here.*

As he drew closer, he encountered the same post-apocalyptic suburban spread that every city had suffered: miles of shantytown cobbled together from scavenged building materials. The *new* mainstreet, a paved, two-lane highway, was clean and mostly free of obstructions, and Ethan rolled along at a moderate jogging pace. Residents stared as he passed, and he returned their curiosity with a friendly wave.

He'd gone about half a mile when he became aware of a growing din, and glanced in his rearview mirror. He saw people streaming into the street behind him, and as their voices grew, they attracted the attention of those ahead.

Very quickly, he found himself pressed to the center of the road as more people were drawn to the street by the calls of their neighbors. *What's happening? These people act like they've never seen—Oh, of course.* They *hadn't* seen an electric bike in months. Maybe never.

Fairview wasn't a conventional farming town. Before Newton,

very few people actually worked in the fields. They managed their crops remotely from the comfort of their apartments, took their breaks in one of the dozens of coffee shops, and either walked or used free public transport.

The commotion brought a burly man out of his hovel, who reacted to Ethan's approach by grabbing a plastic pole that supported the awning over his front door. The awning collapsed as he jumped onto the road, holding the pole like a weapon.

Ethan could have criticized the man's stance, but even a poor strike would knock him off the bike. He swerved to the right and the man lunged, stretching the pole to block the path. Held that way, it was only harmful if Ethan ran into it, which he didn't intend to. He leaned hard to the left, throwing the bike into a savage turn that bypassed his opponent on his unguarded side.

Unfortunately, that maneuver only worsened the crowd's displeasure and their shouts carried much farther than their complaints had. The street quickly filled with curious residents. Ethan kept accelerating, but no matter how fast he went, the crowd's reaction spread faster.

I can't believe people are turning to violence for a little electricity. Even if they thought it was portal, not battery-powered, how long did they think it would last? *I wish this thing was gas-powered. No one wants to bother with fuel.* Then he remembered he had the next best thing and thumbed the bike's control nub to select a pedestrian safety mode.

The bike purred, emulating an internal combustion engine through a front-mounted speaker. That was fine for city traffic, but this situation called for more desperate measures. He held down the nub for three seconds to access a hidden menu, selected racing mode, and set the volume to eleven.

The bike screamed. People screamed, and the street cleared as he twisted the throttle. The false engine noise was synchronized to the bike's increasing speed, and residents poked their heads from their shelters a mile ahead. Taking full advantage of his two-second warning, Ethan swerved and dodged the few remaining pedestrians.

He soon reached the town's original boundary, where permanent structures mingled with hastily constructed ones, shops where residents could get food and water, and he was forced to slow down. The engine noise diminished with his speed and was no longer offensive enough to clear a path, so he tapped the horn button.

A squeal of locked-up tires on pavement spiked his already racing pulse, and he nearly fell off the bike. He'd expected a pitiful *meep-meep*, but the bike's horn reproduced the furious juddering slide of an out-of-control eighteen-wheeler, which had an immediate and visceral effect on the crowd.

"Aargh, Jack." Ethan swore as panicked pedestrians dove from the street. He'd seen Jack near the bike last week, and suspected his cousin of tinkering with—but not reprogramming—the horn. Eventually, he'd have to retaliate with a prank of similar caliber, but for now the road was clear again.

Finally, he saw a traffic light. It was dead, but still marked the town's boundary. He held his speed until the last moment, then jammed on the brakes and slid around a corner. Instead of going downtown, he'd take the outermost of the concentric roads.

Fairview's street layout was the ultimate in boring, and it was impossible to get lost. Ethan sped into a neighborhood of two-story townhouses and spotted Jack's place. He slowed down for a look—another family was living there now—and changed the bike's ambience setting to a two-stroke motor before making the next turn.

Like its eastern counterpart, South Road had devolved into a shantytown surrounding a dozen workshops and warehouses. Slowly, Ethan puttered past the makeshift homes until he reached the Scatter's shop. He briefly considered running in and grabbing the server, but people were already eyeing his bike despite it sounding like a clapped-out tuk-tuk.

Releasing the brake, he rolled on and generated enough sputtering noises to keep pedestrians wary as he followed the curving road through four more miles of slum. And it was a further two miles before he felt confident enough to turn off the road and hide the bike in the trees.

On that cool August night when he and Jack fled Fairview, they'd driven beside a lake for a time, and Ethan was certain that it was just on the other side of the woods. Soon, he'd find a smooth road on which he could walk back to town. But the stand of trees turned out to be more than a grove, and he lost even more time trudging over the uneven ground.

Scratched and bug-bitten, he finally staggered back into the sunlight. But at least he was—*Wait, where's the lake?*

Ethan spun around, then tipped his head back. *"Aargh."* Not only had he missed the shortest path through the trees, he'd been going in the wrong direction and added another mile to the journey. He'd have to hurry if he was to recover the server before Priya arrived.

Two hours passed before Ethan returned to the industrial section, approaching through what used to be a canola field but was now a trampled campground. The Scatter's workshop was easy to find, and its rolling bay door was open. Inside, steel shelves that once held their stock of drone parts had been converted into nano-suites, essentially bunk beds stacked to the twenty-foot ceiling. With barely enough height to sit up, and only a few square feet for personal effects, the compartments were unlikely to be comfortable. But a light glowed in the fixture between the rows, so the building had power, and possibly plumbing.

"No room tonight," a curt voice said. "Move on."

A woman wearing an apron emerged from a room behind the workbench, which now bore knives and vegetables instead of tools and drone parts. The room itself was filled with sacks of flour and more vegetables on shelves.

She must have thought Ethan was checking out the pantry. "If you haven't any money, you can trade for food. There's still half a field of squash twenty miles south, but we'll give you more for corn. There's five hundred acres ripening forty miles to the east."

Ethan had seen enough. Jack's workshop had become what passed for an inn. "Maybe later. Thanks." If the server were still on the premises, it would have been in that back room.

He walked around the shop and considered the burned-out warehouse across the street. Its front door was chained shut, its walls looked solid, and from this angle the only signs of a fire were the black scorches along the roofline.

"Took you long enough," Priya said. She'd parked her ATV in the shade under the Scatter's awning, and draped her blue UN Police jacket over the steering wheel. "Get in."

Ethan shouldn't have been surprised to see her. He'd lost the lead he started with. "How did you find me?"

"A thousand people saw a motorcycle gang rampaging through the streets."

"Gang?"

"There are reasons I expect you to follow my instructions, you know." She waited until he was in the passenger seat, then looped around the warehouse through an alley and stopped by a gap where a roll shutter door once stood. "We could have found it by now."

The building's entire roof was missing except for a few slabs of insulation hanging from blackened steel beams. Its front wall and the one against the alley were intact, but the others had buckled. Whatever had been inside during the fire was now a layer of soot on the floor, but there were piles of recently added junk everywhere. And the warehouse covered ten-thousand square feet, so it was a lot of junk.

"I already asked." Priya said. "This is where everyone dumps old electronics."

Ethan stepped out of the car and pushed against the bay door's steel frame. It groaned a little.

Priya walked past him. "I'll start on this side. Stay away from the walls."

He stepped gingerly through the scattered debris: tractor parts, tires, anything the squatters had found in the workshops that wasn't useful to them. He saw a familiar shape and used his ring to shift a slab of insulation off it. "It's a portal frame."

"The owner had a licensed import business."

"Jack told me there was a smuggler in Fairview. Was this his?"

"We had no proof. But, yes, he had a connection to Danny Kou." She kicked at a pile of junk. "I think I found it. Come help me with this."

There were definitely drone rotors sticking out of the mess. "That's got to be theirs."

A mezzanine that once covered offices at the front of the building had partially collapsed sometime after the Scatter's equipment had been dumped. Priya leaned against its metal railing. "It feels solid, but I don't know what'll happen if I dig into the pile."

Ethan pointed his ring. "I can hold it steady."

"You're sure?"

He made a fist, as if he held the railing from a distance. "I got this."

Crouching, she yanked at a bundle of cables, causing the railing to creak. A trickle of coarse dust rained down from the point where the upper floor was anchored to the wall, and she scuttled back.

Ethan tightened his fist. "It barely moved."

Cautiously, Priya returned to the trash pile, and each time she pulled an item free, the railing groaned. Eventually, she'd removed enough that there was a gap below the sagging floor. "This could be it." She pulled a book-sized box from the heap. It resembled a standard personal computer except that it was twice as thick and had a multi-port adapter on the back.

"That's it," Ethan said. "The ports will be for their testing equipment. Grab one of those data cables and we can wire it directly into your car."

Priya stood with her salvage and examined the damaged wall. When Ethan released the mezzanine, it would tug on the anchors, which would pull everything down. "How far can you get while still holding it?"

"Well … that's a problem." Jack had described to Priya how he could control the raw energy from wormholes, so she knew its strengths and limitations. "I can't sense the energy field the way Jack can. I'm just holding my hand steady."

"So if you walk away, the railing follows?"

"And the wall comes down, and … yeah, you know the rest."

"*When were you going to tell me this?*"

"Honestly, I was just gonna run."

Priya groaned and shook her head. "Fine. Be careful." She turned and strode back to the car, moving aside items that might trip him on his way out.

When she was clear, Ethan faced the exit. Though he tried holding his hand steady, more crushed concrete poured from the mezzanine anchor while he checked his footing. When he felt sure he could get away, he dispelled the field and sprinted for the door.

The mezzanine immediately drooped, and the anchor bolts tore out with gunshot-like pops. The pile compressed under the sudden weight, the wall split all the way to the top, and Ethan was ten steps from the exit when the warehouse folded in on itself. Concrete blocks cascaded across the floor, and he leaped from the building in a cloud of obscuring dust, then sprang into the ATV's passenger seat.

"See? No prob—" He stopped when he saw Priya's face. The detective didn't speak, only glowered at him for a moment before speeding around the neighboring shop to return to the street.

DAVe's server normally plugged into a wall outlet, but it could also accept a standard power cell. So after recovering the bike, Ethan borrowed its cell and connected the salvaged cable to Priya's navigation system. Except for the lack of robotics, her car was now DAVe, and its dashboard console lit up to identify itself as belonging to the Scatters.

"It wants a password," Ethan said.

Priya reached for the radio. "I'll call Icarus."

"Hold on." He tapped the password field to bring up an on-screen keyboard. "Jack would have his own personal login."

"He shared his password?"

"No, but this is Jack. It won't be that hard." He typed S, A, R, A, H, and moved his finger to the enter key. He didn't press it, though. His talent warned him the attempt would fail. *Oh, well. It was worth a try.* Then he wondered if the rest of Jack's password was numbers. Unbidden, millions of combinations streamed through Ethan's thoughts: a quantum storm of two-second possibilities, and he began to feel that familiar rhythm of the dojo where some moves just flowed with a natural grace. He typed three digits that seemed random, then pressed Enter. DAVe's menu opened.

Priya leaned forward to read the screen. "You'll have to tell Jack to make his passwords harder."

"Yeah." Ethan was still wondering where those numbers had come from. Apparently, he had more to learn about the AI that controlled magic. However, given Priya's views on his performance today, he decided not to tell her he'd guessed.

She tapped a map icon and the screen filled with errors. "This isn't working."

"It's fine. They're communication warnings. We want to see …" He activated DAVe's history feature. "I know he was there the day before I landed on Cirrus." Ethan scrolled to last August and selected the date. There was only a single DAVe-track, fifty miles to the west. "Got it." He tapped the directions icon, and new-DAVe plotted the shortest route.

"That's mostly off-road," Priya said. "It'll be dark by the time we get there."

"I've got a spell that's better than headlights. Can I drive?"

She gave him a withering glare as shifted the car into gear, and he decided he'd pushed his luck far enough for one day.

Chapter 27

Where are you, Mai? Sarah silently asked.

The girl had crawled under the barracks nearly fifteen minutes ago, and Sarah was fighting the urge to climb the hill and see if she had gotten stuck.

Why did I agree to this? It was true that they needed to charge the portal's capacitors, but Mai shouldn't be the one flipping breakers on the generator. That plan had made sense when they thought she could use Jack's wand, but not now when simply enabling it risked alerting the guards.

And though Mai and Ben were the only two who could go anywhere in the compound without the guards hassling them, the portal zone's ambient energy field wasn't strong enough for her to rotate the heavy switch from a distance. Instead, Mai had offered to crawl into the generator cage behind the barracks and turn it by hand.

From the kitchen, Sarah had a good view of the barracks. That's because, though the compound was densely treed, its builders had cleared a wide corridor that allowed anyone at the barracks to see all the yurts at a glance.

Finally, Mai reappeared on the far side of the building, and Sarah breathed a huge sigh of relief.

"It is working," Mai said when she rejoined Sarah. "You can go home now."

"Thank you, Mai. But we're not going home." That was truer than Sarah cared to admit. They didn't know where the river portal came out, or if anyone in the area would speak English or one of the languages Jada knew. "We're going to find your mother and send someone back for you."

Mai only stared at the ground as they walked to the firepit.

"I want you and Ben to stay out of sight. We'll be leaving at the same time they transport the grain. If we're lucky, no one will notice the second portal running, and they won't even know we're gone until morning. But if they *do* see us, we don't want them to think you were involved. Okay?"

Mai nodded.

Sarah wrapped her arms around the girl's shoulders. "I'm going to miss you. But we'll meet again."

"I know. Ben showed me."

Sarah desperately wanted to know what Ben had drawn, but couldn't risk returning to his yurt. She said one last goodbye and walked away in the fading light.

• • • •

For Jack, the worst part of their scheme was the waiting. He'd spoken with Sarah before lights-out at nine o'clock, and knew Mai had energized the capacitors, but now they'd be out of contact until the guards called the night workers away.

The first step of their plan was easy: they'd found a tree and overhanging branch that would get them out of the compound, but he lay on his cot worrying about things he had no control over. Where was the other end of the portal? Would it be guarded? How would they find help?

It was getting close to ten, and he was listening for guards when a shrieking alarm sounded. Marten sat up immediately, fully dressed, and they both ran to the door as the other men in their yurt scrambled for their shoes.

An acrid cloud of smoke was drifting between the yurts, and a dull orange glow lit up the forest canopy from the west side of the compound. Sarah and Jada rushed over as he and Marten entered the clearing, which was now illuminated by a searchlight on top of the barracks.

Marten rounded on Jada, saying exactly what Jack was thinking. "You set the yurts on fire?"

"*Why does everyone assume that was me?*" Jada asked.

"It doesn't matter who started it," Sarah said. "This is our chance."

The guards were shouting in Korean, and the workers who

could understand them were rushing towards the fire, which left a lot of people milling around in confusion.

Instead of heading for the tree they'd planned to climb, Sarah started up the hill, keeping out of sight by moving through the forest beside the corridor. As the fastest runner in their group, she'd already checked for guards by the time Jack caught up. "Let's go." She dashed across the open corridor to the bathing pool's gate.

As expected, it was locked. But it took only seconds for them to scale the fence, which was far less than it would have taken to go around and swim through the gap. And the time Jack had spent studying the portal paid off too. They had the deck plate off and the gangway in place in less time than it had taken the guards.

"Hurry up," Jada said as she and Marten lined up behind the frame. "The water is *freezing*."

Flicking switches in the order he remembered, Jack opened the wormhole and was surprised to see no turbulence at the interface of the two rivers. Whoever designed the setup had balanced the flows perfectly, and the only sign that the passage was open was the brighter water on the other side. Too bright, actually; he'd forgotten the time zone difference. It was daytime in most of China, and the sunlight streaming from the portal was like a beacon. Worse, the smoke was thinning and the fire's fearsome glow had disappeared.

"We're running out of time," Sarah said.

"Don't worry," Jack said. Though the water provided a substantial safety margin, it was crucial to avoid a sudden change in mass, and he didn't want them to rush. "Take at least ten seconds."

Jada ducked her head into the water and stretched an arm through the portal. Despite having traveled through a water-buffered portal himself, Jack was relieved to see her hand still in one piece.

"Three, four, five," Marten counted, loud enough for Jada to hear, and she allowed the gentle current to pull her through.

Then Marten took two deep breaths, lowered himself, and Jack checked the indicators as he drifted through. The capacitors still had two-thirds of their initial charge, more than enough for himself and Sarah. *We're going to make it,* he thought. *Nothing can stop up now.*

"Your turn," Jack said.

Sarah climbed down, positioned herself behind the ring, and Jack got ready to follow. She was inches from freedom when the circle of light disappeared, and she jerked back to prevent herself from being taken through.

"What happened?" Jack rapped on the panel. Its lights were out. Then someone shouted, and he looked up and saw Ferret in the generator cage.

Sarah lunged out of the water, gasping, and saw Ferret calling for help. *"What do we do?"*

Razor wire topped the outside fence, and the gate back into the compound was not only locked, it would soon be swarming with guards. "Under the fence." He pushed aside the perforated panel at the end of the channel and pointed to the spot where the creek joined the pool.

Not waiting for an explanation, Sarah dove and swam underwater to the fence. When Jack reached her, she'd already discovered the loose stone, still partially blocking the gap. Working together, they pulled it free and jumped back to avoid an avalanche of smaller stones, which didn't matter because they were both out of breath.

Jack resurfaced just as Ferret ran onto the bridge. Then Sarah rose from the water, drew a deep breath, and dove again. The last thing he saw before diving himself was Ferret throwing off his jacket.

There were no lights around the pool, and the searchlight was still pointing towards the yurts, but better lighting wouldn't have made a difference because the water was murky with loose silt. Jack felt Sarah's legs slide past as she pulled herself through the gap, and a muffled splash told him Ferret was coming. He spun around, thinking it was better to go through on his back, and had only gone halfway when Ferret grabbed his legs.

He kicked ferociously but Ferret had the advantage of solid footing and tried to stand up. Jack countered by dragging himself up the fence, which yanked Ferret down, and they quickly reached an impasse with both of them stuck inches below the surface.

Sarah briefly grabbed Jack's wrist, but must have realized he was already pulling harder than she could, and splashed out of the creek. Struggling to raise himself another few inches, Jack realized his only hope was to outlast Ferret.

Then Ferret screamed underwater and Jack's legs were free. He hauled himself to the surface, drew a huge breath, and saw Ferret groping blindly for the bridge while clutching the top of his head. A splash erupted from the water behind him as a stone, apparently the second one Sarah had thrown, just missed him.

She helped Jack stand. "Let's go."

"Where?"

"It doesn't matter. We just need a place to hide until Jada sends help."

She sprinted past the barracks on the perimeter path, which crossed the road at the north gate, then continued downhill on the east side. Jack caught up with her when she stopped before the T-intersection at the southeast corner.

"Now what?" The road ran west along the compound's south fence, so heading east to the gardens seemed the obvious choice, except that Jack heard dogs in that direction. "We can go south, to the fields, or—"

"*Ben,*" Sarah shouted.

Of course. The children's yurt was near enough to the fence that they could call him. "You're right. He can enable my wand and we—"

"No. *That's* Ben."

The boy was standing outside the south gate, a hundred yards away. Sarah started running, and Jack followed, but they'd gone only halfway when he bolted across the road and disappeared.

"Wait." Jack pulled Sarah off the path as two guards sprinted out of the compound, apparently chasing Ben. "He might have gone to the portal chamber. We can cut through the forest without being seen."

"Why did he even leave the compound?" Sarah asked as Jack led her through the woods.

"Because he's a Traveller and he knows something we don't. Remember the picture he drew of us on a roof? I thought it was a yurt, but now I think it's the grain silo."

It didn't take long to reach the back of the transport chamber, which had no windows or features other than a set of steel rungs on the silo.

"That's it," Jack said. "He must know it's a safe place to hide."

"I don't know, Jack. I don't see a way to get there."

Sarah was right. The rungs could only be reached from the chamber's roof, which was way over their heads, and the barking was growing louder.

"There must be a ladder inside. *Hurry*." Jack dashed around the building without checking for guards. There was no point: either they'd be caught on their way in, or caught by the dogs outside. He ran straight to the door and pulled it open.

Inside, the chamber was brightly lit, and warning lights flashed around the rim of the transport ring, which was six feet across and set flat into the floor above an overflow pit. The grain chute was in position over the ring, but there was no one manning the computer terminal.

"They'd have normally started by now." The flashing lights meant that the device was fully charged and ready to create a wormhole.

Sarah crossed the room and found a stepladder leaning against the wall. She moved it under the hatchway, climbed, and pushed it open. Outside, flashlight beams played across the silo, and Jack nearly panicked when she raised herself onto the roof. Fortunately, Sarah had realized the hatch couldn't be seen from the road, and he hurried up the ladder after her and closed the flap moments before a guard opened the front door.

Angry voices and barking resonated through the chamber's metal roof, and Sarah froze on the silo's first rung. Jack felt his foot slide and reached out to steady himself, causing the roof to make a sharp popping noise. He held his breath.

Luckily, the guards hadn't heard, and they slammed the door on their way out. One of them spoke tersely, and Jack heard keys rattling. *They're locking the door.*

Neither Jack nor Sarah moved until they were certain the guards had gone, then finished their climb. Jack shuffled slowly on the silo's cone-shaped roof, noting how its metal panels bowed and rumbled like a drum. It had been designed to shed water and ice, but wasn't so steep that they were in danger of sliding off, so they laid on their backs to reduce the chances of being seen from below.

"This is wrong," Sarah said.

"I know. But Jada will send help, and then the police will—"

"No, I mean *this roof.* Traveller-memories are normally about significant events. Memorable events. Where did Ben go? He wouldn't have drawn us up here if all we're doing is waiting for someone to rescue us. And did you know that Jada followed a dragon here?"

"Yeah, Marten thought it was a dog because it was small and brown. What does that have to do with anything?"

"Doesn't it feel like we're being manipulated? If it hadn't been for that dragon, Jada and Marten wouldn't have come here, and we wouldn't be on this silo."

"Uh …" was all Jack had time to say. Without warning, a roof panel folded under them, dropping them into the silo. Jack struck his shoulder painfully on a supporting girder, then plunged into a surprisingly hard pile of wheat kernels. Sarah landed beside him, then rolled down the other side of the mound.

"*Owww.* Are you all right?" She sounded like she'd had the wind knocked out of her.

Jack coughed. "I don't think I broke anything." He scanned the ceiling in the near total darkness. The crossbars he'd struck on the way down were too high to reach. "How do we get out of here?"

If Sarah answered, her voice was drowned out by the klaxon that blared without warning. And then he felt the enveloping pressure of an energy field; the wormhole was open.

"Jack," she cried. *"Do something."*

Looking across, he could suddenly see her silhouetted against the silo's reflective walls. A shallow pit had formed in the heap that separated them. They both scrambled at the walls on opposite sides as the pit grew, but Jack felt only rounded rivet heads. His feet sank into the shifting grain.

"Help." Sarah's voice was panicky. She was buried up to the waist in a deepening hole.

He reached out. "Grab my hand." Terrible thoughts of the wormhole collapsing leaped into his mind, along with pointless questions: What's the density of wheat compared to a human body? How fast is the grain flowing?

Sarah was in it up to her neck now. Setting his feet apart, Jack dug them into the sides of the growing funnel in an attempt to gain leverage. *"I got you."* But he didn't, really. The infalling grain buried Sarah and tumbled him face-first right after.

"No," he tried to scream as Sarah's hand clamped his, and his unerring portal-sense warned him that the wormhole was less than ten feet away. Then five. Then two. A blinding white light pierced the falling grain.

"Sarah," Jack screamed as her fingers were torn from his grasp. *I wish I'd told you —* And then the world went dark.

Chapter 28

As Jack drifted lazily on his back on a calm, warm river, he heard a gentle voice calling his name.

"Sarah?" He rolled his head to either side but didn't see her on the banks.

She called again and he tried to shield his eyes from the sun, but the water was strangely thick and held his arms against his sides. He tipped his head back, scanning the river's rippling yellow surface. *Wait. Yellow?*

I'm dreaming.

Jack was a lucid dreamer, meaning he knew when he was dreaming and could wake himself at will or change the course of the dream. Sometimes, especially when the imagined surroundings were familiar, he found it entertaining to explore his level of control. He briefly considered evaporating the river to go look for Sarah, but that seemed unnecessary now that her voice was getting louder. She was coming to him. And though he looked forward to that, something niggled at the edge of his awareness. *I was doing something important.*

Careful not to wake himself by moving too quickly, he reached past his head to do a backstroke. But as he drew his arm back, it tangled in a vine. He raised his other arm and it got trapped, too. The vines tightened, constricting his wrists, and then there was pain. Everywhere.

Sarah hovered over him, calling his name, but her insistent tone didn't match up with her smile. And now she was loud. *Really loud.* The pressure on his wrists grew.

"Jack," she shouted. "*Wake up.* You've got to wake up."

His vision cleared and Sarah wasn't smiling at all; she was terrified.

"Get up. You're going to be buried alive!"

Jack gasped, inhaling grain dust. He wasn't floating in a river.

Instead, Sarah was trying to drag him from a growing mountain of wheat. Already, the weight on his chest made it hard to breathe. He twisted his body to get one arm under himself, and with Sarah pulling on the other, they freed his legs, which triggered an avalanche.

"*Run.*" Sarah yanked his arm, and they slid and staggered to the base of the pile. "There's a door this way." She guided him between dozens of similar piles.

They were indoors, under a steel roof that had to be a hundred feet above the concrete floor. At the far side of the building, a huge front-end loader thrust its bucket into another mountain of wheat, spun around with its load held high, and drove outside through an open bay door.

In his confused state, Jack struggled to make sense of what he saw: columns of grain were streaming from holes in the ceiling. Some poured continuously, others for only a few seconds, and bright sunlight shone through some openings while others were dark or lit by artificial lights.

"We came through a cargo portal," Jack said.

Sarah, who'd been peeking through a narrow gap in a door to the outside, glanced at him with a worried expression. "Yeah, we did."

"We shouldn't have done that. *It's dangerous.*" He waved his hands in front of his face. "My fingers are numb. Did we do it on purpose?"

"Sort of."

"Are we stupid or something?" He mouthed numbers as he counted his fingers.

"Uh … we might be."

"Huh?" Jack realized he was still staring at his hands. "What comes after eleven?"

"How did you count eleven?"

"I … don't remember. Should we be here?"

"We're trying not to be." Sarah checked the door again. "Come on. It's clear."

Jack followed her drunkenly across a paved lot to a group of rusty shipping containers, and she dragged him into a gap next to a fence topped with barbed wire.

"Are you okay?" Sarah asked as she supported him against a wall of corrugated steel.

"I'm great." He grinned. "How are you?" He tried to stand up straight, wobbled, then flopped back again.

"You're not great. You're not even … What do you remember?"

He took a long time to answer. "We were supposed to meet Marten and Jada?"

"Not quite. We were supposed to go with them through the river portal to China, but we got separated. They're in a remote village somewhere, and I think we're in whatever the closest city is. They must distribute it to the villages from here."

"Well, they might be in China, but we're in Seattle."

"You can't even count to ten. What makes you think we're in Seattle?"

"Oh, *ten*." He snorted. "Of course."

"Jack. *Focus*."

"Right, right. Uh, we're not in China." He pointed to the logo painted on a nearby railcar. "BN stands for Burlington Northern. And the man waiting beside the train is Paul."

Sarah had been focused on the building they'd fled and not looked beyond the fence. But Jack was right. The text on the train was in English, and she'd seen historic photos of the giant silos that stood next to the newer portal building: *Pier 86*, which was once used to transfer grain onto waiting ships, but had more recently become a tourist attraction. And the man walking across the rails was indeed the one Priya had been chasing for months.

"I'm gonna have a nap now," Jack said, and slumped to the ground.

• • • •

"What do you want?" Sarah shouted. Paul was jogging towards her and Jack was asleep, or more likely unconscious.

Paul stopped and raised his palms to show he meant no harm.

"I'm just here to offer you a ride."

"*What?*" If she'd had to guess, that would have been well down the list.

"I've been asked to give you a ride."

"Where?"

"Wherever you need to go. But I'm guessing you want to find Priya in Olympia."

"Who sent you?"

"That's complicated."

"Uncomplicate it."

Paul sighed. "Look, your friend is suffering from portal-shock. He'll be fine in an hour, but he'll be more comfortable in my car than lying on the cold ground. We can discuss it on the drive."

Sarah looked the man over. He was perhaps in his late twenties, dressed in jeans and a gray leather jacket that was decades out of fashion, and the thinness of his Balbo beard was more likely due to nature than careful trimming. But she didn't have a lot of choices, and a light rain had started. "Fine. Where's your car?"

"On the street. I'll help you carry him." He reached into his back pocket and Sarah tensed. "It's okay. Just a pair of wire cutters." He brought them out slowly to show her.

"You always carry wire cutters?"

"I like to be prepared."

He snipped a vertical line in the fence with practiced speed, then cut a shorter horizontal line and peeled back the chainlink. Sarah had already propped Jack up and was trying to support his head when Paul suggested it would be easier if she carried his feet.

Though not much bigger than Jack, Paul had no difficulty carrying him over the uneven ground, and they shuffled to his car: an ancient four-wheel drive with a removable canvas roof.

Reaching back with one hand, he unlatched the driver's door and kicked it wide open. The vehicle bore signs of rough use, and its green paint had been touched up with colors that didn't quite match. He hefted Jack higher. "The other side's unlocked. Go around and help me lift him."

Sarah set Jack's feet down and hurried around the vehicle. The door there was indeed unlocked—it didn't have a handle. Or a window. And when she pulled the top of the door panel, it resisted only briefly, as if held in place by magnets.

Working together, she and Paul maneuvered Jack into a semi-flat pose across the back seats before covering him with a blanket. He'd be sore when he woke, but at least he'd be dry. Paul turned the Jeep's ignition key and its engine rumbled to life.

"This thing runs on gas?"

"Synthetic. I have a friend with a bioreactor. Put on your seatbelt."

Sarah pulled her door closed, then leaned against it. As expected, it popped open, and she gave him a dubious look.

"I don't get many passengers."

"You said someone sent you."

"A friend." Paul steered the noisy SUV onto the street. "Well, maybe not a friend. But someone I trust."

"How did he know where we were?" Then Sarah realized that Paul had to have been waiting for them, and added, "Where we'd be?"

"Ah," Paul smoothed his beard with one hand. "That's complicated."

"What about our friends?"

He seemed to be listening to someone, though Sarah hadn't noticed earbuds. "They're fine. They're in a safe place. We'll send someone to—"

"Who are you talking to?"

"That's comp—"

"I don't care that it's complicated. Who sent you?"

Paul raised a calming hand. "His name is Coyote."

"*Coyote?* And he asked you to come to Seattle to find us somewhere we didn't even know we'd be?"

"I told you, it's complicated."

Sarah checked on Jack. He appeared comfortable, and she wasn't really in a mood for talking anyway, so she covered herself with a second blanket and settled in for the drive to Olympia.

An hour passed in silence except for the Jeep's distinctive rumble and frequent rattles, but Sarah couldn't relax as they drove past the few landmarks she recognized. She felt she was missing something important.

"I know you were one of the last people to use a portal before Newton," she said. "Which means you're probably a Traveller."

"Me? No. I'm a Finder."

"What's a *Finder*?

He raised an eyebrow. "I find things."

"Like what?"

"Like you and Jack."

"Or crystals that belong to his grandfather?"

Paul didn't respond to the implied accusation. "Jack was part of that deal." He reached into a cupholder for the twenty-sided crystal Jack had trained to open locks. "As I understand it, connecting those servers helped him, too."

"I don't know about that. All it's done so far is lead us to—" Sarah caught herself. She'd almost mentioned Asterion.

"Dragon," Jack mumbled.

"Right," Paul said. "DAIGON. I figured out afterwards that those were DAIGON hubs. And reconnecting them helps people on Cirrus."

"Not everyone. Most of us don't even have power. Wait, you know Cirrus wasn't destroyed?"

"Of course." Paul gave her a look as if this was something everybody knew. "That's where Coyote is."

"What did Coyote ask you to do?"

"Just give you a ride."

"You mentioned Priya." Sarah turned her body to face Paul. "What *exactly* did Coyote ask you to do?"

"He asked me to make sure you got to Priya's safely. That's all." Paul turned off the main highway.

"Stop the car."

"What? We're in the middle of—"

"Stop the—"

Paul didn't touch the pedals, but the vehicle suddenly lurched and its wheels locked. Fortunately, they'd only been moving at a jogging pace along the wet and twisting road, so the Jeep spun lazily and ground to a halt as soon as it hit gravel.

"She said; *Stop the car.*" Jack was sitting up in the back seat, holding the gaming crystal Paul had returned to the cup holder. It hummed with power.

"What *is* that?" Paul waved a hand through the invisible lines of force between the die and the car's wheels, proving he was sensitive to the field.

"Let's go, Jack." Sarah shouldered her door open.

Jack gestured at Paul's keychain and it flew into his hand. "Not without these coins."

"Hey, I need those," Paul cried.

Sarah hadn't even noticed the pair of Third-Eye coins hanging from the chain before Jack pitched them into the tall grass on the side of the road.

He clambered out of the Jeep. "And don't follow us." Then he tossed the die into the air and made it hover for a moment before shooting it into the sky. "I'll be tracking you."

As Paul stormed into the weeds to find his keys, Sarah and Jack continued on foot. "Can you really track him like that?" she asked when they were out of hearing range.

"No." Jack showed her the die he'd secretly retrieved. "But he doesn't know that."

"Shouldn't you have destroyed his other crystals? Someone could be controlling him."

"If that's true, they might help us figure out who that person is. And I don't know that Paul is a bad guy, anyway."

"He was trying to find the inn. *And* your grandfather's portal."

"Are you sure?"

"I didn't tell him to come down this road. He already knew how to get here." Sarah pointed to a security camera mounted on a house across the street, part of DAIGON's network. "That's the camera Priya told us about. The only reason he'd have turned onto this street is that his information comes from Little Brother. And the only way he could have known where we would end up is if Coyote got it from a Traveller, or a dragon."

Jack walked beside her in silence, putting together the same puzzle pieces she'd already worked through. This neighborhood was a red herring: Priya always drove through it to be recorded, but parked her car out of sight in an empty lot and hiked the last mile to the inn through the forest.

"Little Brother is set up to block any sort of tracking," Jack said. "Paul couldn't watch Priya over multiple cameras without the AI figuring it out."

"He doesn't have to. Remember what Asterion said about trading memories? The dragons have internet access through their crystals, and they can communicate with each other. Think about it. Someone wants your grandfather's portal, so they hire Paul, who gets information from Coyote, who gets it from the dragons on Cirrus, who are watching Little Brother on Earth. Paul won't trigger an alert because the dragons would have accessed those videos at different times."

"So ..." Jack's thoughts were still a little fuzzy, but he felt he was on the cusp of something important. "DAIGON is ... dragons?"

"Sort of. Asterion's mind works in a way ours never could. There's no difference to them between two conversations at the same time, and two conversations at different times."

Jack realized there might be even more. "And Ben's dragon can turn off an entire portal zone. So, if they're the source of Traveller-memories, then maybe they're responsible for magic, too." He levitated the die again, wondering how much power dragons really had.

Chapter 29

They found Priya's car in its usual hiding spot and finished the walk to the hotel in silence. Jack was still on the lookout for portals that might power a camera set up to track Priya, but his mind was mostly on magic. He'd never thought his ability to manipulate a wormhole's energy field was something within himself; it had always seemed like just another tool. To have it confirmed through Ben and Mai was both liberating and disappointing.

"Finally," Sarah said when they reached the inn's back lawn. "This whole thing will be over soon. Priya can track down Jada and Marten in China, and she can deal with Danny and the labor camps however she wants. She won't even have to reveal your grandfather's portal. Even better, everyone will know Cirrus is safe and things can get back to normal."

They hurried across the damp lawn to the servant's entrance, which was below Priya's window. Her curtains were drawn, and Jack couldn't tell whether there was a light on in the room. Of course, it was close to midnight, so she might be sleeping.

He flipped the cover off the peephole at the top of the staircase. "All clear."

Sarah knocked lightly on Priya's door, number thirteen, while Jack listened for other guests. It would be difficult to explain why they were lurking in the hallway, soaking wet, dressed entirely in white.

"She's not here," Sarah said.

"She must be on Cirrus." Jack had already checked the die for external links and knew it was safe, so he used it to unlock her door.

"I'm freezing." Sarah opened Priya's wardrobe. "I hope she has something that will fit me."

Jack had spent most of the evening under a blanket, so he was fine, but hardly recognized himself when he glimpsed his reflection in the mirror. *I look like a ghoul.* His baggy work trousers were stained almost black at the cuffs, then faded upwards to his waist through layers of dirt. In dim light, he would appear to be floating. And his hair was matted and scraggly, making him look like a drowning victim.

"It's a good thing there's a back entrance," he said. "They'd never have let us in the front door."

Sarah came out of the bathroom wearing light gray sweatpants and a matching hoodie. Her hair was a mess, too. "I think I'll just hide it." She flipped her hood up to cover her head.

Jack checked the hallway again, then crept across the carpeted floor to examine the frame's charge indicator. "Five bars. If she went to Cirrus, it was more than an hour ago." He tapped the hidden button and opened the wormhole.

The amount of energy available from the open portal was immense, and so pervasive it overwhelmed his portal-sense. Sarah had already put a leg through and was straddling the frame when he detected a crystal in the adjoining hall.

"Someone's coming," he whispered. The crystal was small. "With a phone."

"Quick, open a connection for me."

"Are you—?" Jack was about to ask if Sarah was sure, but she was already concentrating. The phone was rounding the corner as he created the link, though he was uncertain what she meant to do with it. He held his breath.

A well-dressed couple came into view and stopped at the first door—number ten. The woman glanced briefly in their direction, then swiped her card through the door's reader. The man looked them over suspiciously before saying, "Good evening."

Jack stiffened, afraid to move. *What happened?* The woman had looked right through him, but her partner hadn't. Then he realized both what Sarah had done and his mistake. *They only had one phone between them.* He'd suggested invisibility as workable, but didn't think it was practical. And when had she had time to work out the details, anyway? Regardless, she wouldn't have tried the spell if he'd told her there was more than one person.

"Who are you talking to, Dear?" the woman asked from inside the suite.

"There are two odd-looking—" The door closed, cutting off his words.

"Go," Jack said, though Sarah reacted as soon as the latch clicked. She dove through the opening and rolled silently on the foam padding they'd placed for that purpose. He was about to step through himself when the suite's door opened again.

"See?" The man pointed at Jack for the benefit of his unseen partner. He craned his neck to look down the hall. "Where did the other one go?"

Jack was standing with his back to the wall, blocking as much of the portal's frame as possible. "Uh …" he started. In a difficult situation, he habitually answered questions honestly, and Sarah knew this. He was about to speak when she squeezed his hand painfully, changing his words to a mournful "Oooh."

The man was taken aback until his partner spoke. He wagged a finger at Jack, said, "Don't move," then turned to face the room. "Call the front desk, there's a—"

Sarah suddenly grabbed Jack around the waist and hauled him backwards, tumbling him into the foam blocks, then closed the portal.

"I think he may have seen my foot on the way out," Jack said, but he was laughing now that they were safe.

"Well, nothing we can do about that now."

"But you actually pulled it off. The woman didn't see us."

"You were right that invisibility is like an illusion." Sarah got up and reached for the hidden shelf above the portal frame. "But instead of pushing a memory, I imagined us being so uninteresting that—The radios are gone."

"Why would she take both?" Jack asked, then figured out the answer for himself. If Priya had both radios, which were each paired to others in Caerton and Icarus, she'd be able to use them at the same time. He groped around the back of the shelf and found the notepad and pen. "She didn't leave a message, either."

Sarah twisted the door's relief valve and pushed impatiently while the air pressure equalized. The moment the door was free, she shoved it open and ran all the way to the parking spot near the cliff's edge. Jack was out of breath by the time he caught up. As expected, there was no vehicle for them to use, and though there was plenty of moonlight, he couldn't tell from the tire tracks whether they'd missed Priya by hours or days.

"What do we do now?" Sarah was on the verge of tears.

For her sake, Jack spoke more calmly than he felt. "Just give me a minute to think." But it didn't take that long to see they had no options. They had no radios, no wands, or even a spare crystal. He'd left the gaming die in a planter by Priya's door so it wouldn't disentangle by passing through another wormhole.

"How long will it take to get home?" Sarah asked.

"It's sixty miles. And we'd be crazy to hike down the mountain in the dark. We'd have to wait until morning." Jack turned towards Icarus, though its lights couldn't be seen from so far away. His head drooped. "I can't walk that far in a day anyway, so it could be two days at the earliest. And then we'd be stuck there. There's no way our parents will let us leave."

"We *have to* find another way to the compound."

"Why?" he asked, still staring at the ground. "What can we do there? None of our crystals work. We'd just be captured again."

Sarah reached for his hand. "We can't leave Ben and Mai. Danny will know we escaped soon, and he'll move them somewhere else. We have to do *something*."

Jack had serious doubts. Yes, Danny would learn that they'd escaped, and even figure out where they went. And though Jada and Marten were in China, Priya and the police would be able to find them through diplomatic channels. Would Danny move the workers to another compound? Maybe. But even if they could block him today, the man had hundreds of compounds, hundreds of Bens and Mais. It was a problem far greater than he and Sarah could tackle. And there was more.

"It was Asterion who led Jada and Marten to the compound," he finally said. "The dragon they saw must have been the ally Asterion mentioned."

Sarah didn't answer right away. "Probably."

"Which means Asterion has been manipulating us all along."

She squeezed his hand. "Maybe, but they only want the same things we do. To live in peace and not have people like Pieter or Danny ruining our world for money and power."

"I never agreed to fight Asterion's war."

"We don't have to."

"If we go back, we might have no choice." He turned around and found her still watching him pleadingly. She wasn't asking because of anything Asterion said. Her concern for Ben and Mai, and for Cirrus' future, was pure Sarah.

He sighed. *I can refuse a dragon, but never Sarah.* "Okay. We'll find another portal."

Chapter 30

Danny returned to the enclave after obtaining the case: Mentor's *key*. But he didn't take time to investigate it. He had to reflect on his battle with Ethan.

He sat on a low-backed wooden chair, the only furniture in his spartan apartment other than a bed and a writing desk, and began his breathing exercises while visualizing the morning's fight. *Parry, dodge, strike.*

The adjacent wall was a showcase of the weapons he'd mastered: nunchaku, tonfa, polearms, and a variety of swords and daggers. But the whitewashed one over his mattress was bare, and made a perfect canvas for his memories. He believed the austere décor not only helped him concentrate; it was the only appropriate setting for a true leader.

Block, block, block. Ethan's talent was remarkable. *He has to have at least a full second of prescience to outmaneuver me.* Danny recalled each move in order, fixing them in his memory, as he would the next time he met, and defeated, him.

Picturing Ethan trapped against the cistern, he saw the boy start to sweep his staff, an easily blocked move, then stumble as the woman called out. *Was that real, or a poorly played ruse?* Regardless, Danny swung—

'Am I disturbing?'

"*Aargh!*" Danny bellowed as he pitched forward and hurled his chair in a single movement. "*How dare you interrupt me?*"

The small brown dragon on his desk darted to the side, narrowly avoiding the wooden missile as an image of … *flying dust?* … faded from Danny's mind.

'I can come back.' The dragon canted its head in a gesture Danny had never seen, which only made him angrier. Worse, the creature's voice was even more distinct than before: jaunty and melodic.

"What do you want?" It was too late to recapture the serenity he needed for cementing memories.

'I have the information you asked for.'

Danny was still furious, but this was important. He calmed himself with only a few breaths and picked up the case he'd left by his door.

"How did you get in here?"

Another head tilt. 'The door was open.'

It wasn't. Had the creature been under his bed the entire time? It didn't matter. He set the silver case on the desk, flipped its latches—*weren't those locked?*—and opened its lid.

Inside the top cover was a display panel with an integrated keyboard. The lower compartment was divided into two sections: a thermos-sized gas cylinder and three palm-sized cartridges occupied the smaller portion, and the remainder was a sealed unit with labels warning not to expose the contents to heat, shock, or even air. Each of the cartridges had a red plunger, making them look like metallic syringes.

"Give me the code."

The dragon began scratching lines on the surface of Danny's desk with its claws.

"*What are you doing?*" Danny thundered.

The dragon's projected voice was annoyingly cheerful and full of childlike innocence. 'I cannot read.' It continued as if they were having a friendly chat. 'I will draw the shapes I saw. I have an *excellent* memory.'

Danny unclenched his fists and reminded himself that the information was important, and tried to ignore the dragon's mocking grin as it trashed his desk. He knew that it lacked the muscles to form a smile, but he'd have preferred the permanent snarl that most dragon's jawlines produced.

As it worked, he read the gas cylinder's label. It was a name he recognized: a nerve toxin. On the skin, a single drop was lethal. Injected? The amount was almost too small to measure. He inspected the cartridges and found one of them was locked in an airtight receptacle. The others were loose. *Spares?*

"Are you finished yet?"

'I am done.'

The dragon sat back on its haunches and blew slivers off the four alphanumeric characters it had scratched into Danny's desk. Not only were they legible, the beast had recreated their original font. Danny quietly seethed.

"This had better work." He powered on the machine, entered the code on its keyboard, and a photo of a red and gold dragon appeared on the screen along with a group of icons: Load, Charge, Discharge, Unload. He pressed Load.

A red light lit beside the screwed-in cartridge, and hidden machinery whirred. After thirty seconds of vibration, the status light turned yellow and the screen flashed the word *Loaded*. Danny pressed Charge.

The unmistakable chatter of a compressor rose in pitch and frequency until the light turned green. The machine went silent, and *Loaded* was replaced by *Charged*. A new icon appeared: Eject.

Danny ejected the cartridge, which fit comfortably in his hand with the plunger in easy reach of his thumb.

'I will go now,' the dragon said.

"Yes. You will." Danny tried to swat the dragon off his desk, but it leaped away, caught the door's handle, and pulled it open just wide enough to slip through.

He kicked the door closed and returned to the machine, which was simple in principle. He understood that the sealed unit contained many crystals, each paired with another in dragon's bodies, and that he could enter a code to load one into a cartridge. That handheld cartridge could then be charged with toxin, which would permeate the remote crystal through a wormhole.

Danny brushed his thumb over the plunger as he pondered the image on the device's screen. *So easy. One push; one dragon.* He considered the code he'd entered: four characters, one of over a million possible combinations, and it occurred to him that he didn't know how many dragons there really were. Maybe the machine could tell him.

He cleared the screen and pressed a random combination. The first letter filtered the list to around six thousand codes, the second to just four hundred nineteen. Using those values, he estimated there would be over a hundred thousand valid codes.

The number was staggering. *I had no idea there were so many. What is Mentor's true plan?* The screen also displayed a map of their territories. *Heol! They live even in the seas!*

He tapped two more keys to complete the code, and the machine displayed a green-hued dragon much smaller than the last. It also lacked the spikes and bony plates of the red and gold one.

Intrigued by the variety, Danny entered another code, but the machine didn't respond when he pressed C. He tried again with the same result but that key was apparently dead. Leaning forward for a closer look, he noticed scratches around the edge of the keypad.

Danny had other things to do, but he was certain the case had been locked earlier. He plucked a dagger from the wall rack, pried the keypad from its slot, and flipped it upside-down. There were four gouges in the exposed circuit board. Four disabled keys.

It can *read.*

Danny was livid; the creature had been toying with him. Many combinations were possible using the four characters, and he knew instinctively that the brown dragon's ID would be one of them. He clutched the dagger tightly. He wouldn't need a code to deal with *this* problem.

A knock on the door interrupted his murderous thoughts and he covered the scratched-in code with his dagger, then slipped the loaded cartridge into his pocket. "Enter."

One of Mentor's robed acolytes stood at the door. "Shifu requests the key." He glanced at the keypad and frowned.

"It needs repairs. Send a technician over."

Normally, the man wouldn't take orders from Danny. This time, the request was reasonable, and he started to back out of

Danny's apartment.

"Wait." Danny brought up a photo on his phone. "Do you recognize this dragon?"

The man nodded. "I have seen them recently."

"It's a traitor. It was involved in an attack on Detective Singh." Danny closed the case's lid. "Tell Mentor I want to test the key. And find this dragon."

The man withdrew, leaving Danny to wonder if he knew Mentor had arranged that attack. Regardless, by placing the blame on the brown dragon, Mentor would have to let him keep the key until after his *test*.

Chapter 31

DAVe—technically, new-DAVe—guided Ethan and Priya off the highway and into a swamp. Fortunately, it wasn't a big swamp, and DAVe's navigation history included a terrain map, which they used to find higher, drier ground.

As Priya piloted the car along the suggested route, Ethan stared at the small dot that represented DAVe crawling across the map. He was trying to avoid dwelling on the fight.

Over the past year, his two-second foresight had helped him avoid numerous pitfalls, but Danny had outmaneuvered him today. *I should have had the advantage. He has only half a second, and I have two. Instead, he nearly—* Well, that was the part he didn't want to think about.

"Oops," Priya said as DAVe bounced through a pothole. "I didn't see that one."

Ethan rubbed the side of his head where it had bumped the padding on DAVe's roll bar. It was yet another reminder that his foresight had limitations, and he really should have been watching the road.

The Eye was well above the eastern horizon and casting plenty of light, so they were driving without headlights in case there were drones watching from above. Still, he was surprised when a hard-packed gravel road crossed their meandering dirt track.

"This is new." Ethan recalled Jack's description of his trip into this part of the sector as being cross-country.

Priya checked the map again and saw that they were at the southeastern corner of the hills. "I agree. If that road had been here last year, DAVe would have used it instead."

According to the map, the entrance to the basin was to the left, so Ethan was wondering why she wasn't moving, and gave her another ten seconds before suggesting, "We could be there in a few minutes."

"No, this isn't right." She shifted into reverse.

"Hey, wrong way."

"That road was put down after Newton, meaning someone built it for access to a place that shouldn't exist."

"So, what do we do?"

"We wait." Priya backed into the woods, parked where they could still see the road, and shut off DAVe's power. "Turn your radio off, too. We don't need accidental noise."

"You think there are patrols?"

"I don't know what to think yet. But I'm not taking any chances."

Still questioning his talent, Ethan said, "Remember what I told you about Danny's ATV? They're not limited to Cirrus-tech."

Priya grimaced. "You're right, they might have military-grade sensors. We'll move farther—"

"Too late." Two points of light were bouncing towards them through the trees. Ethan grabbed his staff from the back seat and grounded its tip in the soil beside the car.

"What are you doing?"

"Jack told me he couldn't locate Pieter when he was shielded. That should work for sensors, too." *I hope.* He spelled a shield large enough to encompass DAVe. "And it just occurred to me that they might have heat sensors." He made it slightly opaque.

Except for its huge tires and tall suspension, the approaching vehicle looked more like a communications tower. It was studded with antennae, cameras, and devices Ethan couldn't identify, but was otherwise the same, more powerful ATV that Danny drove. When it slowed directly in front of them, Priya reached for DAVe's start button.

Ethan quickly blocked her and mouthed, "Two seconds."

Priya relaxed a little, but kept her hand near the button until the ATV continued along the track, its internal combustion engine rumbling at a slow idle.

"Now what?" Ethan asked.

"We wait." She tapped the timer function on DAVe's nav

console.

Studying the map, Ethan estimated that a vehicle would take eight minutes to circumnavigate the hills if the rest of the road was like this section. "We can get to the entrance and be inside before they come around again. And even if it's blocked, we can make it back here safely."

But Priya just stared resolutely through the windshield. "We. Wait."

Shortly after the timer passed four minutes, another set of headlights appeared, and a second patrol vehicle passed without stopping.

"See." Priya gestured at the receding taillights. "That's why I'm cautious. There isn't enough time to do this." She shifted DAVe into gear.

"Then where are we going?"

"I'm taking you back to Fairview. I'll go in with Davis in the morning."

"But it could be too late by then."

"I'm not putting you in danger."

"You don't have to." Ethan scrolled the map. "Look. DAVe *did* go into the basin last year, but Jack told me he climbed the hill first." He double-tapped the screen. Under magnification, a twinned line broke off from the main one, proving that DAVe had gone up the hill and backtracked before skirting around to the gap. "We can reach that spot in about a minute, which gives us at least two to get out of sight."

"It's too risky."

"Jack told me it was an easy climb. We'll be above their sensors in no time." Ethan's stomach clenched as he told the lie. Jack had actually said that DAVe didn't do well on steep slopes.

Priya was silent as she studied the map. Then she switched DAVe off and said, "I'll think about it."

A few minutes later, the first patrol vehicle returned, and she whispered, "Fine. We'll go to the top. But if I see anything I don't like, I'm turning around and I don't expect an argument from you."

Ethan made a lip-zipping gesture, and Priya had DAVe set a four-minute timer. Then she drove onto the gravel road after the patrol car's lights faded, turned off where DAVe told her to, bumped through tall grass for ten yards, and sank into a muddy hole.

Ethan swore. Loudly. Not only had he lied to Priya, he'd been so worried about it that he missed his own two-second warning. "We're too close to the road." No matter how well he shielded DAVe from sensors, its rear body panel would be a flag waving in a hurricane. He faced her in a panic, but she looked at him like he was an idiot.

"*Push*." She said it like it was obvious while waggling a fist.

"Oh, right." He chuckled. "I was just gonna do that." Then he flipped his hand up beside his head, and without looking back shoved DAVe forward with a steady field pressure. His rings warmed with the amount of energy required, but DAVe was soon back on solid ground.

Priya tried following Jack's path, but it was slow going and DAVe kept slipping sideways, and they'd gained only fifty feet of elevation when the timer went off. She shut down the power and Ethan recreated his shield.

After the patrol passed, she tried again, and gained only forty feet. "At this rate, we'll be all night."

Sheepishly, Ethan said, "It must have rained."

For the next two hours, they wrestled DAVe up the hill on a two-minute-driving, two-minute-hiding cycle. Ethan helped as much as he could, but Priya was sweating and visibly frustrated by the time they reached the summit. She grabbed a pair of binoculars from the door panel and stormed to the edge of the clearing for a look at the basin while Ethan focused on the surrounding plain.

Through patchy clouds, the Eye illuminated an area half the size of North Dakota, but more productive through genetic engineering. Ethan knew that the crops growing between here and the sea had been feeding millions on Earth for nearly twenty years, and that there would normally be a fleet of harvest machinery running through the night. Now, the only sound was the wind in the nearby trees. Even Priya was silent.

"Priya?" Ethan looked back. She was standing motionless with the binoculars hanging by her side, and he wandered over to see what she was looking at.

"That is *not* what I expected," he said. "Jack only mentioned a few tents and some construction equipment." Hundreds of feet below, the empty meadows where Jack found the guns had grown into a small town.

From their vantage at its southwest tip, Horseshoe Hills curved east, north, and west again to form a backward C, and encompassed a basin as large as New York's Central Park. Inside, hundreds of structures, arranged in a grid, covered the southern half, but their lights there were too dim to reveal details. The northern side was more brightly lit, and its buildings were taller and broader, and centered on a temple-like structure fronted by slender white columns. An empty area in front of the ornate building could have been a baseball field except the part of the diamond where home plate would be was a broad half-circle of steps leading up to the portico.

"Wow," Ethan said. "What's our plan?"

Priya surveyed the town silently for another minute before she spoke. "I need to recon before I go in." She passed him the binoculars and pointed to a forty-acre patch of darkness to the right of the temple. "What's that?"

In the moonlight, all he could see were trees. "A park?" No, he knew that was wrong as soon as he suggested it. There was no pattern or theme to the dark zone, whereas the rest of the basin was rigidly organized, and laid out like an ancient Roman marketplace. "I can get us closer. My two second —"

"It can wait. Davis won't be here until morning, anyway." She took the binoculars back. "There's a tarp and blankets in the car. Set up a shelter where it can't be seen if they have drones."

Ethan paused before returning to DAVe. There was something ominous about the town, especially that dark zone. And, not for the first time, he wondered if two seconds would be enough.

Chapter 32

The sky above the Vault was clear, and the stars were brighter than they'd be anywhere on Earth, but Jack was unaware of those things as he slumped on a log with his head in his hands. He still didn't feel quite right from his trip through the grain portal, and now he was contemplating making another. His headache wouldn't have been as bad had they gone through a water-portal like Jada and Marten, and he'd be feeling no pain at all if they'd used one rated for people instead of cargo.

He sat up abruptly. "Danny would never travel by cargo portal. He'd have one designed for humans. I know where it is. At least, I know how to find it."

Sarah, who'd been pacing the road beside the creek to stay warm, spun to face him. "Where?"

"You remember Horseshoe Hills, right? Where we found those guns? Well, Danny called on a *radio* two hours before he arrived at the compound, which is about how long it would take to drive from there. But before that, the barracks officer called him on a *blue phone*, which means he was on Earth. He must have a portal directly to Horseshoe."

"How does that help us? His portal could be in China for all we know."

Jack shook his head. "According to Priya, Washington has the most reliable power in the country. Danny would need that for a large cargo frame. And with all that grain coming into Seattle, he must have a base nearby. Also, Paul used to work for him and probably knows where it is."

Sarah was quiet, and Jack knew she was weighing the facts. Going back to Earth was a gamble. If they went down the mountain, they'd definitely be able to send help in forty-eight hours, but they could cut that in half if things worked out the other way.

"All right," she said. "Let's risk it."

Retracing their footsteps in the snow, Jack was wondering where Blue was when a dark shape swooped over their heads. "*Arven*," he shouted. "It's Arven. Grab the notepad. We can send a message about Jada and Marten."

While Sarah continued to the cave, Jack called the raven down. "I need you to take something to Icarus." He cleared his thoughts and pictured the one person there he was certain Arven would recognize: Natalya. Hugo and Arven had once raided her kitchen, and she hadn't taken it well. Admittedly, it was partially Jack's fault because he'd asked them to check what she was cooking. He hadn't anticipated that they'd bring it back. Regardless, the birds had learned she wasn't a human to mess with. He pushed an image of dropping the note at her feet, and Arven responded with a croak.

Sarah returned. "I wrote that they're safe, but I didn't say where they are. Suresh and Hélène would freak out." She held out the slip of paper for Jack, then snatched it back. "Should we tell them where *we* are? They'll come get us, and that might be the fastest way to the compound."

Now it was Jack's turn to consider the odds. "There's no guarantee Natalya will get the message even if she sees Arven. She's as likely to chase him off. We could be sitting here for nothing."

Sarah agreed, and they rushed into the cave and opened the wormhole. With the one-way glass in place, Jack could see the entire corridor in the reflection of the assorted mirrors, and even partway down the adjoining hallway.

"I can't see anyone, but I hear angry voices. And the door to number ten is open. It sounds like they're having an argument."

"We can't wait," Sarah said. "Paul will eventually find his keys."

"Okay, I'll go first." Jack pulled the glass panel aside and stepped into the hall. The arguing couple's voices weren't very clear, but he picked out the word 'haunted'. And their luggage was parked by their door.

Sarah retrieved the die from the planter and headed for the servant's passage. "Let's go."

"Just a second." Once the portal was closed, he'd have no access to the energy field. He waved his hand at the luggage, tipping one suitcase so it balanced diagonally, then set the other two on top in a precarious stack.

"*Jack.* We don't have time."

"Hey, I'm just boosting the inn's reputation. A ghost story will be good for business."

Paul was exactly where they'd last seen him: wading through the weeds, poking a flashlight around the ditch where Jack had thrown his keys.

"It's a bit to your left," Jack called.

Paul spun and aimed the light at them.

"Three steps." Jack pointed where Paul needed to go. "One more. Now move your hand eight inches towards that post."

Paul snatched the keychain, wiped it clean, and stomped back to his car.

"We need a ride," Sarah said.

Paul's shoes squelched on the pavement. "Too bad."

"I'm sorry," Jack said. "Honestly. I assumed you could sense the crystals the way you sensed their energy. I only meant to delay you a few minutes so you couldn't follow us."

"I already knew where you were going. I've been to the inn before." He turned the ignition key and the Jeep's headlights dimmed, but its engine didn't start. He tried again with the same result, then scowled at Jack.

Sarah walked up to the driver's door. "If you knew where we were going, why did you act like you didn't?"

"I sell information. It's a habit."

"Okay, we need information. What do you want?"

Paul sighed. "Depends on the question."

"Tell us where Danny's portal is."

"I don't know." He glared over her shoulder at Jack. "Can't

sense crystals, remember?"

"But you used to work for him."

"That doesn't mean he invites me over for a beer."

"Look," Jack said, "you've probably been there without knowing it. It'll be someplace out of the way, possibly underground for shielding, like the DAIGON hub. And there would have been a few nasty-looking guys there who spoke Russian or Korean." He sensed the diffusion orb in the Jeep's console, and Paul appeared to be listening to someone, as if through a hidden earpiece.

"Too dangerous," Paul finally said, and tried the ignition again. Nothing. He pounded the steering wheel. "This is you, isn't it?"

Sarah held her hands in a pleading gesture. "It's important. Our friends are in danger. We'll pay. How much?"

"For this." Paul shook his head. "Not money. I want another spell."

Jack furrowed his brow. "What kind of spell?"

"A high-level one. Not like the lockpick. That's like a level two."

"That spell will open anything, even a safe. It's gotta be level four, maybe higher."

"*This isn't a game,*" Sarah shouted, causing Jack and Paul to flinch. "*There are no levels.*" They both waited until she calmed herself and huffed. "Teach him to walk silently." Then she went around to sit in the back seat.

"Fine." Jack held out his hand for Paul's keyring. "I'll store a spell in one of your coins that lets you pick the quietest path through any room. That's got to be level nine."

Paul considered it for a moment. "All right, get in. Coyote says we need to go to Everett."

Jack piled into the back of the Jeep with Sarah and covered himself with the blanket. Then he slouched in his seat and grumbled, "I put a lot of work into that lockpick. It's at least level five."

Chapter 33

As the sun rose, Ethan wished he still had some of Nour's coffee; he could have used a hit of caffeine. He and Priya had taken turns watching the basin through the night as regular patrols crossed the gap at the open end of the C-shaped hills, and another car rolled randomly through the town's narrow streets. They'd determined that the darkened zone by the temple was forest, but learned nothing else. No vehicles ever drove near it.

"We're an hour away," Davis said. "You want us to join you?"

Priya, wrapped up to protect against the morning chill, dug the radio from the folds of her dull gray blanket. "You wouldn't get past the patrols. But we know there's another road into this place north of the swamp. See if you can find it. We may need to move fast."

"Roger."

"Who else is coming?" Ethan asked. He'd slept through Priya's earlier conversation.

"Tomas."

Ethan remembered Tomas, an army veteran who'd helped them defeat Pieter last year. He unwrapped a stale cereal bar Priya had brought from Earth. "Is this what a stakeout is like?"

"This isn't a stakeout." She handed him the binoculars and muttered, "I don't know *what* this is."

Ethan surveyed the tents. They were much larger than they'd seemed at night: big enough for forty or fifty people each. And the open-sided one with the chimney had to be a cafeteria with at least four hundred seats. A steady flow of people entered it, but as many were leaving and returning to the smaller tents.

"There must be a thousand people living there." He panned to the road that led out of the basin. Dozens of combine harvesters sat idle there, along with an equal number of trailers. "Shouldn't they be working by now?"

"I checked out the fields on the other side before the sun came up. They're picked clean for as far as I can see. And it doesn't look like they're planting new crops."

Another structure stood alone on the plain, a mile west of the gap. "That's a transport chamber, isn't it?" It was far enough from the basin that the nauseating effects of its large wormhole couldn't affect those living there. "And those six-wheeled vehicles beside it are …" Ethan lowered the binoculars. "Are those … tanks?"

Priya shook her head. "Armored personnel carriers."

"*What?* APCs on Cirrus? That's just as bad. Why?"

"It's an invasion." And then more quietly, she said, "I was wrong." She gloomily told him about the report she'd seen on Katherine's desk. "North Korea doesn't produce enough power to open that many wormholes to Dawn. But they'll reach Cirrus. Danny's not going to be *selling* passage. He already has millions of migrants waiting."

Ethan couldn't understand why Priya wasn't rushing back to Earth to warn them, except that her tone was despondent, suggesting she was feeling overwhelmed. "Surely someone will do something when they see millions of North Koreans on the move, even if they are just civilians."

"No one's even going to be looking." She described how she suspected Danny was involved in the railway attack in Spokane, and similar events that were still happening across the country. "This was all timed to coincide with the portals reaching Dawn. He doesn't want to risk anyone learning about Cirrus, and a civil war on Earth will convince more people to leave."

"I guess that makes sense, but how does Pieter figure into this? None of it would have been possible without his mind-control technology. What are we missing?"

"I don't know." She drooped under her blanket.

Ethan considered the implications of an invasion of North Korean farmers. "Maybe the UN should have just given them immigration privileges for Dawn. Or maybe *we* should go." He told Priya about the crystal he'd found in Pieter's office and how he suspected another one was used to create a wormhole from Cirrus to Dawn.

"Damn it." Priya sat up straight. "*That's* why Angel wanted to go to Dawn. Pieter's crystals would have been collected along with the others, but he'd need someone he trusted on Dawn to set up a frame for him. He's probably hiding in another sector until that happens."

"That's good, isn't it? Then we only have to worry about Danny. All we have to do is expose this"—Ethan swept his arm across the hills—"to prove Cirrus is still here. Right?"

Before Priya could answer, an alarm blared and he turned his attention to the north end of the basin. Even before raising the binoculars, he caught movement around the mysterious patch of forest. He focused on a torrent of figures crossing the street and congregating on the diamond in front of the temple, then zoomed in for a better look.

"What do you see?" Priya asked.

It took Ethan a moment to find his voice. "Dragons. *Hundreds of dragons.*"

• • • •

Jack didn't know when he'd fallen asleep, and couldn't tell what time it was when he woke because it was still dark. The Jeep was parked in a wooded area, Sarah was sleeping beside him, and Paul was nowhere in sight.

"Sarah." Jack shook her shoulder. "Wake up."

She startled awake with a jolt. "Huh? Where are we?"

"I'm not sure. Paul's gone."

Sarah squirmed out of the back seat and peered into the fog. "There's a river down there."

Jack stretched his cramped muscles after climbing out of the Jeep, then spun around, trying to work out where they were. The evenly spaced lights at the top of the hill were definitely streetlights, and the vague yellowish glow beyond suggested a small town.

"Someone's coming." Sarah reached for the pocket where she

normally kept her wand.

A figure was passing in front of a distant light, and their backlit shadow produced an inhumanly tall silhouette in the fog.

"It's okay." Jack recognized the approaching crystal and the familiar sensation of one of his own spells. "It's just Paul."

Like a wraith, Paul drifted fluidly through the mist, moving silently among the trees with only an occasional pause to find the best footing. His progress was impressive considering he'd only practiced Jack's *Silent Walking* spell for five minutes when they'd stopped for food.

"Satisfied?" Jack asked just before Paul stepped out of the woods.

His triumphant expression wilted. "I was. Until you heard me coming."

Jack shook his head and tapped his temple. "Portal-sense."

"Can you teach me that?"

"I don't think that's even possible. And I can't create a spell for it, either."

"Where are we?" Sarah asked. The Jeep didn't appear to be on a proper road.

"Good morning to you, too." Paul indicated a cluster of lights that were just barely visible in the mist. "That's where you'll find Danny."

"How do you know?"

"Coyote is near a portal on Cirrus, and the number of people coming and going corresponds with what I've seen here. He says Danny arrived last night."

"He's with Danny? Is that safe?"

Paul grinned. "Coyote has an odd sense of humor. He thinks this sort of thing is fun."

Jack scoffed. *What kind of person thinks spying on Danny Kou is fun?* Then he focused on the lights, which outlined the shape of a large building. "There's definitely a portal in there, a big one." His awareness was sensitive enough to tell, despite the shielding, that it was in the basement. "And they're transferring something, or someone, right now."

"Where does the wormhole come out?" Sarah asked.

"Coyote doesn't know the name of the place. He says it's surrounded by hills on three sides."

"That sounds like Horseshoe," Jack said. "Can you ask him if the building is guarded?"

Paul was silent for a moment, then looked confused. "He says it's a ... *temple?*"

"That doesn't sound right. But remember, you're not actually hearing Coyote's voice. It's the AI interpreting his thoughts and pushing an image to you as a memory. He may be saying train station, for all we know."

Paul didn't seem to hear Jack's explanation. His expression changed from confused to alarmed. *"I gotta go."*

"What's wrong?" Sarah asked.

"Coyote's in trouble."

"What sort of trouble?"

"He says Mentor's army is taking over Cirrus."

"What? Who's Mentor?"

"I don't know. He says to meet at the wheat terminal in Seattle."

"He's coming to Earth?" Jack asked.

"It doesn't sound like he has a choice." Paul jumped into his Jeep.

"Hey, wait—"

"Sorry, you're on your own from here. I only agreed to find Danny, not get you to Cirrus." Paul jabbed a finger at the lights. "There he is."

Jack leaped out of the way as Paul spun the Jeep's tires on the wet grass and drove off. "Great." He kicked a stone after the receding taillights. "We don't know anything about the building or who's in it. We're going in blind."

"And it sounds like Coyote's not having fun anymore. But ..." Sarah pulled the gaming crystal from her pocket. "It doesn't matter if we're blind. We're also going to be invisible."

Chapter 34

As Sarah followed Jack out of the woods, she thought about her invisibility spell. The technique had come to her in a flash at the inn, and she had been so confident it would work that she'd done it perfectly with no practice. *Well, nearly perfect. I only expected one person.*

She suppressed a shiver as she contemplated making both of them invisible to many people at once. It wasn't just the difficulty of the trick that bothered her, but the similarity to Pieter's efforts at widespread mind control. That wasn't a comparison she was comfortable with.

Their destination was at the edge of an industrial zone, and the only thing that set Danny's building apart from its neighbors was the extensive lighting over its sidewalk and parking lot that left no blind spots to approach from.

"There's a coin crystal in there," Jack said as they crossed to the adjacent sidewalk. "Near the front door."

"I got it." Sarah flinched when he opened a connection for her. "She's already watching us." The feedback from the crystal guided her eyes to a camera mounted above the main entrance.

"It's okay. We're on a public street. This must happen all the time."

"Yeah, but now she's *really* watching."

"Because we're stopped in front of her camera. The way you described the spell, we have to do something so ordinary that she won't notice us. Let's just go in." He moved towards the door.

"Not that way. She's thinking of meeting us."

"Right." He turned towards the parking lot. "Employees wouldn't go in the front."

"She's still suspicious" —Jack was approaching the gate—"but she's not moving anymore."

"I have to take control of the crystal for a moment. Anyone

who's allowed to be here would know the gate code." He spelled the lock open and reestablished a link to the woman's coin. "Got it?"

"She's still watching." Sarah concentrated. "And she's still curious."

He paused at the side door. "Let me know when it's safe."

Sarah took a deep breath. The woman's curiosity would be the starting point, an emotion to use as a feedback loop. She countered a flicker of interest with a sense of boredom, then nodded for Jack to move when the woman split her attention to another camera.

Jack opened the door and stepped into the front office as if he belonged there. Following, Sarah saw the uniformed guard sitting at a desk behind a security monitor, which held her attention fully—until Sarah noticed she was armed.

The guard's hand drifted to the holster on her hip.

"It goes both ways," Jack whispered.

"Right." When she'd practiced with Ethan, he got a partial sense of her thoughts whenever she tried to discover what he was thinking. Now, her fear of the guard's weapon was breaking the spell. She breathed deeply and closed her eyes. *Watch the video. There was something interesting there. Don't look away. It'll come back.*

The woman leaned forward in her chair and thumbed the camera control while Sarah repeated her mantra of watchfulness. Then, with her eyes closed, she found Jack's shoulder and squeezed it. He guided her into a hallway, paused to listen at a set of swinging doors, and pulled her into a vacant warehouse.

Sarah opened her eyes. "That was *so* much harder than the first time at the inn."

"Maybe because this one's job is to pay attention. That shouldn't be a problem for anyone else here. Are you okay to continue?"

"Yeah, but I'll have to keep my eyes closed during the spell. Anything I see could be a distraction."

Jack held her hand and smiled. "You can do this. I know you can."

Sarah returned the smile though she didn't feel as confident as he seemed. "I really *will* be going in blind."

"Don't worry. I'll be there for you." He led her through the warehouse and into a stairwell with a thick door. "That's shielded, so this will be sort of an airlock for portal energy." He trotted down three flights of stairs and stopped by another door at the bottom. "Can you feel it yet?"

"No."

He held his thumb over a glowing red button on the wall. "You will when I open the door." The button turned green.

Of course, Jack was right. As soon as he cracked open the shielded door, an energy field enveloped her like humid air in a swamp. It was no wonder he had detected it from so far away. Danny's cargo portal was far bigger than any wormhole she'd previously encountered.

"There are crystals around the corner," Jack whispered. "I'll open a connection to the nearest one."

Sarah got a keen sense of the man on the other side. "That must be a phone crystal. He has a strong bond with it." She concentrated on his intent. "He's counting something." That was fortunate: a repetitive task was relatively easy to focus on. "Let's try another."

"Here you go."

"That one's on a computer, searching for … something to do with food." Another monotonous task.

Somewhere distant, a phone rang, but Jack said, "There's only one more crystal in this section. If you can make us invisible to all three, we can go to the next room."

Still focused on the first two, Sarah guessed what the third was doing. It was a physical job, with a lot of movement. *Stacking boxes?* She tried to increase the worker's attention to the task, felt an immediate pushback, and lost her connection with the one counting inventory. Then she dropped the third link when she tried restoring the first. A loud crash sounded from across the room, and the man moving boxes swore.

"What happened?" Jack asked.

"I think I made him stumble. I can't focus on all those tasks at the same time."

Jack appeared disappointed but determined. "Then we'll have to do it by force. If we can get close enough to the cargo portal—"

"It's too dangerous. There has to be a better way."

"Well … you weren't trying to prevent the woman at the inn from looking at us, were you?"

"I just wanted her not to care about what she saw."

"Then try that. It'll be the same thing no matter who looks our way. I'll open connections to every crystal and let the AI handle the rest."

Sarah agreed. Jack's idea was so simple it might actually work. And their only other option was to fight their way through.

She shut her eyes and imagined how they would appear to an observer: they were unarmed, their clothing was dirty but plain, and they weren't touching anything important, or even interested in the cargo being shipped. In short, they were just passing through and their presence made no difference. "I'm ready." She held his shoulder as he shuffled into the next room.

Ripples of interest touched Sarah's mind when they rounded a corner. *They see us!* But Jack must have sensed her panic and laid his hand on top of hers. She could almost hear his voice: *I'll be there for you.*

Whether that was real or imagined, his presence calmed her and she sensed distinct connections, like hearing the minor differences between every violin in an orchestra. Jack had said to let the AI handle it, so she ignored the variations and pictured herself blending into the background. The worker's awareness faded and he advanced in a straight line for fifteen paces, then turned ninety-degrees to the right. After another ten paces, he turned left.

Abruptly, a wave of attention swept over Sarah; there were at least a dozen people in this room. Jack's shoulder stiffened as he braced for action, and her own alarm spread to the observers, though they weren't yet aware of what troubled them.

"What was that?" A man with an Eastern-European accent asked.

"I heard it, too," a woman replied.

"Check the generator," another ordered.

Rapid footfalls echoed around the room, and Sarah pulled Jack close. Leaning her forehead against his back, she imagined the two of them as shadows on a cloudy day.

"Everything's okay here," a voice called from across the room.

"An earthquake maybe?"

"Whatever. It's over. Let's get those pallets loaded."

Jack's shoulder relaxed under Sarah's grip, and she nudged him to start him walking again. She felt a draft on her back. *We're close.* But the open portal didn't just cause a breeze to flow to Horseshoe's lower air pressure; it provided more energy for her spell, and the worker's emotions grew more detailed and she couldn't help but wonder: *How did I know the upstairs guard was watching us, not whatever else was on her monitor?* That wasn't only mood, but memory.

It suddenly made sense. *Traveller-memories.* She recalled something Jack's grandfather had said after her first trip through a portal: the part of the brain that interprets Traveller-memories also conjures the images we see in our imagination. The same must apply to emotions, and the human brain is exceptional with those. Often, Sarah had sensed when Jada was having a bad day from the briefest glance, and even correctly guessed the problem from other subconscious clues.

This is what Jack feels. He doesn't just sense a mood; he actually hears *what people are thinking. All of them.*

She became aware of conflicts among the warehouse workers: most everyone here despised their supervisor; several were thinking of quitting except the money was too good; others had nowhere else to go; and one had a sick parent. Jack was in there too, determined and focused. But there was another side to him: he was scared and uncertain. He was doing this for Ben and Mai, but mostly for her.

She'd always known of his discomfort in crowds, but that understanding had been academic: he had a phobia; it was difficult for him; but he coped. Now she understood it viscerally. The weight of those voices was oppressive, overwhelming, alien and confusing. And they were getting stronger.

Sarah felt the urge to run and hide, except that would break her spell and they'd be exposed. Instead, she pictured a fog filling the room, one that obscured her completely. She imagined evaporating into that fog, becoming so insubstantial she could pass through walls. *I'm not here*, she thought. *Forget me. Forget me.*

Her own awareness melted away as the spell grew and the voices diminished. The draft faded, and even the firmness of Jack's shoulder disappeared. Then her hand fell to her side and startled her back into a mindful state.

"*Jack?*" she whispered. She reached for him without opening her eyes and found only empty space. *He's gone. My spell made him forget me.*

Sarah's control wavered, and she felt the breeze again and heard the worker's voices. Their thoughts rushed into her awareness and devolved into raw, powerful emotions. Her heart raced, her knees wobbled, and she found it difficult to breathe. She was standing in a room full of people who were about to notice a stranger appear from nowhere. In the back of her mind she understood she was having her first-ever panic attack, but had no idea how to stop it. She opened her eyes—

The room was completely dark except for a circle of light. Then someone grabbed her hand and people started yelling as she was dragged through the wormhole.

"Shhh," Jack hissed as he pulled her out of view.

Trembling, Sarah wrapped her arms around him. "I thought you forgot me."

"Forget you?" He held her tight. "Never. I knew your spell would break when we stepped through the portal, so I turned off the lights to add some confusion."

"I heard everything they were thinking. It was horrible."

His expression turned somber. "Oh. Yeah. It's pretty intense, isn't it?"

The lights were back on Earth-side and the excitement there was fading, but they were safely out of sight, so Sarah refused to release Jack until her knees stopped shaking. "I'm okay now. We'd better go."

The space surrounding the portal frame was another warehouse. Fortunately, it was vacant, and they found a door marked with an exit sign. Jack pushed it open and they rushed into the cool air and early morning light.

They found themselves in an alley facing a tall building built from large blocks of white marble. Or at least it looked that way. If they really were on Cirrus, then it was almost certainly a printed composite finished to resemble polished stone. And the red tiles on the roof … well, those might actually be fired clay. From their position, Sarah could see a slender column supporting an overhanging portico.

"What's that?" Jack asked. An unearthly growl echoed from every direction.

Sarah had heard the noise, but the frieze running around the top of the building's wall held her attention. It depicted dragons and men in a style reminiscent of ancient Greece. She stepped back to take in a wider view of the structure, which was strangely out of place next to the pre-fab warehouse. There was no better word for it than what Paul had used.

"It's a temple."

• • • •

"Give me the binoculars," Priya said. "Quick."

Ethan, still too stunned to speak, let go and she focused them on an alley beyond the throng of dragons.

"Is that Jack and Sarah?"

Chapter 35

"It *is* a temple." Jack scanned the surrounding hills. They'd definitely landed in Horseshoe, but not as he remembered it. "What's it doing *here?*"

"I'm more concerned about that noise." Sarah turned towards the front of the temple.

Jack was also disturbed by the strange rumbling, but couldn't see its source because the alley dead-ended in a low wall, which was topped by rose bushes. "We'd better check it out."

"I don't think we should. I've got a really bad feeling about it."

"We should at least know what we're running from."

With the south end of the alley blocked, they could only go north. He studied the neighboring buildings, looking for escape routes, then ducked and hurried over to the wall of roses. If he couldn't see beyond them, nobody would be able to see him.

There were exits at each end of the wall. The one on the left, the warehouse side, was a ground-level passage to a sidewalk. On the right, a narrow set of stairs climbed to the portico's raised floor.

While Sarah stayed low, Jack stood and parted rose branches to make an opening. Then he swore, and the color drained from his face.

"What is it?" she asked.

"Dragons. *Lots* of dragons."

Sarah raised her head and created her own small gap in the leaves. The neatly trimmed field of grass below the portico's step was slightly lower than the alley, meaning she was looking down on it. "There must be *hundreds* of them."

And it wasn't just their numbers; the creatures' diversity was astounding. Like Asterion, who had been designed for controlling the deer population, the field of dragons came in a variety of purpose-built body plans and colors. Some were ferret-like, with sleek bodies for chasing burrowing rodents. Others moved ungainly on long front legs with membranes stretching from wrist to abdomen, like bats. Many resembled Blue, who shared traits with dogs and crocodiles, and ranged in size from a housecat to a mountain lion. They had two things in common, though: their cowls were wide and black, like armor, and appeared to be molded from carbon fiber; and each had a Third-Eye coin mounted on a matching collar.

Encircling the field, Jack had also seen armed men holding assault rifles with their muzzles pointed to the ground. They seemed quietly confident as they monitored the crowd. Unlike the compound guards, these were professional soldiers.

"Danny's here," Sarah said. "And he's got the case I remember thinking Ethan had on his bike."

Danny stepped onto a raised dais at the front of the portico, flanked by two of his thugs. Besides a silver case, he also carried a T-handled martial arts baton that, curiously, had a red button on the tip of its handle.

"There's a crystal in that weapon he's carrying." Instinctively, Jack knew it served the same purpose as the one in Ethan's staff.

Suddenly, Sarah pulled him closer to the wall and whispered, "Don't move."

Being careful to avoid the thorns, he slowly turned his head to watch another pair of men, dressed in robes, stride from the temple bearing an elegantly carved curtained box on long wooden rails. Had they looked to their left, they might have seen him and Sarah in the bushes at the bottom of the stairs, but they were straining under its weight.

"That box is full of Third-Eye coins," Jack said.

"It's a palanquin. There must be a person inside, too." As the men set the ornate litter on a platform behind and higher than the dais, she added. "And see where they placed it. Whoever is inside outranks Danny."

The robed men then rounded the dais and lifted a steel cage that had been hidden from Jack's view. Inside was a small dragon with brown and tan scales. Like the carved litter, the dragon's cage was supported by two rails, which dropped from their brackets when the men lowered it onto the dais. They stepped back and swung the rails across their bodies in a familiar pose. *Fighting staffs*, Jack realized, *with metal tips to add damage*. Now, everybody under the portico was facing away from the temple and the alley.

Danny approached the cage. "The traitor …" His shout was swamped by the din of the restless dragons, but they settled immediately as another voice repeated his words.

"I can *hear* them," Sarah said, astonished. "I can hear the person in the palanquin. They're … *broadcasting* is the only word I can think of." Even the dragons all the way across the clearing seemed to have heard the voice that echoed Danny's.

He started again. "The traitor has exposed our secrets, revealed our location, and"—he swept a hand towards the palanquin—"disclosed Mentor's true identity."

The crowd responded with lashing tails and agitated growls, and Jack was nearly overwhelmed by the force of will that flooded from the palanquin. He'd once felt a similar compulsion from Pieter, but this was much stronger. If he hadn't already known that whatever Danny had to say would be a lie, he'd have believed and acted on every word.

Dragons and soldiers alike reacted to Danny's speech, and Jack knew that the one he called Mentor, hidden behind the curtain, would be a natural leader with such a talent. And if Paul had understood correctly, they already had an army.

Another thing he picked up in the torrent was that Mentor hadn't known their identity was compromised.

"The penalty for treason is death," Danny shouted. Then he faced the litter with his thumb hovering over the red button on his baton, and without averting his eyes inclined his head to one of his thugs. "Open the case."

"Did you catch that?" Sarah asked.

"Yeah." Whether through the broadcast emotions or Danny's smug expression, Jack understood that there had just been a shift in power. "That was a direct threat. Danny's running the show now, not Mentor, and it has something to do with his baton."

"The creature's name?" Danny asked.

A robed sentinel shoved his staff into the cage, pinning the Dachshund-sized dragon to the floor. The other drew a serrated knife from within his robe and slipped the blade between the dragon's throat and its neck armor. With a quick jerk, he severed the cowl to expose a tattoo behind their jaw. Leaning forward, he read, "C, Y, T, 3."

A chorus of snarls and anxious yipping rose from the dragons.

"They did not like *that*." Jack could feel the stamping and scratching of their feet resonating through the ground. "Why?"

The thug with the case entered the four characters on a keypad in its lid, and an image of a brown and tan dragon, the one in the cage, appeared on the adjacent screen.

"*Coyote*," Jack said.

"Where?" Sarah asked.

"In the cage." He finally understood what was happening. "The AI misinterpreted Asterion's description. The case isn't a *key*; it's an *index* that contains crystals for *every* dragon. And the caged one is Paul's friend, the one he's expecting to come to Earth. Their real name is C, Y, T, 3: *Coyote*."

The thug tapped the screen, and the case whirred. He tapped again, ejecting a stubby metal cylinder that resembled a syringe with a red plunger that was identical to the one on Danny's baton.

"I get it," Sarah said. "If you know a dragon's *name*, you have power over them through an embedded crystal. That's why Asterion turned away before you could read their tattoo. And that's why these dragons have cowls. They're hiding their names."

Danny's thug handed him the cylinder with an arrogant smile. "C, Y, T, 3."

Though Jack didn't know how it worked, it was obvious that Danny intended to use the cylinder to carry out Coyote's death sentence.

"We need that case," Sarah said. "If we throw it through the warehouse portal, the crystals will be useless."

"How?" Danny was watching his thug close up the case. The clearing was entirely filled with dragons. And there were armed guards around its perimeter.

Sarah turned her attention to the palanquin. "I think I know. Whoever Mentor is, they don't want to be seen."

"I wouldn't like being watched by an army of dragons, either."

"If we expose them, the distraction should give us time to swipe the case."

"But—" Jack stammered; exposing Mentor meant confronting Danny.

"Coyote will die if we don't stop Danny. And we wouldn't have even got back to Cirrus without their help. We have to do something." Sarah ducked and headed for the steps.

"Wait." Jack grabbed her hand, but the moment they locked eyes he knew she would go without him. "Okay. This is insane but … okay."

He gauged the distance from the dais to the warehouse. If they could pull off a five-second lead, they had a good chance of making it to the door before any human pursuers. But what about the dragons?

"You're faster," he said. "You go for the case. I'll go for the curtain. Once I'm in range of those coins, I'll blast Danny's cylinder and create a shield."

He crept up the narrow stairs and crouched at the top, where he was still hidden behind the roses. "Ready? Three, two, one—"

As he leaped onto the platform, Danny raised the cylinder over his head, pushed its plunger, and shouted, "It is done!"

Poison! The syringe, the paired crystals: one in the skull and the other in the case. It made sense now, but it was too late. If Jack had had his wand, he'd have thrown Danny to the dragons, whose sudden cries were so loud they echoed from the hills.

He was almost within range of the coins when Sarah overtook him, and he lunged onto the dais, tore the curtain, and tumbled to the floor. The fabric had only been held up by delicate silver rings, and he landed with it covering his face, then struggled to free himself before Danny's thugs attacked.

But they didn't attack. And the loudest sounds were his own shoes scraping the marbled dais. The dragons had gone silent.

Jack had ended up right behind Danny, who was gawking at him with a shocked expression. The thugs weren't looking at him, though. They, and everybody else, were staring past. He looked over his shoulder as a red and gold dragon the size of a cheetah screeched, spraying him with foul-smelling saliva.

Mentor is a dragon.

In hindsight, Jack should have known. Mentor's broadcast voice was just like Asterion's. And of course there were the coins, which spilled from the palanquin as Mentor thrashed their tail.

Danny's thugs quailed and backed away, and the guards around the clearing fled. Apparently, Jack wasn't the only one who'd been fooled. And even if they had known, Mentor was terrifying in the flesh.

Sarah, case in hand, sprinted past. *"Run, Jack!"*

It was too late for Coyote, so he gathered the portal energy he'd intended for the cylinder and prepared to slam it into Danny. But as he shaped the field, he glimpsed movement in the cage.

Coyote is alive.

He targeted the cage instead, ripping its door off. Coyote leaped out and bolted across the portico as Mentor shrieked. That finally spurred the dragons into action, and some climbed the steps while others chased Coyote.

Jack instinctively tried to form a shield, but the portal energy abruptly died, and he understood why: Horseshoe Hills was another portal zone, and Mentor was its master.

Rolling away from Danny, Jack gathered handfuls of coins. They were useless to him now, but highly prized by dragons. He hurled them into the clearing before racing after Sarah.

"Stop him." Danny reached for his baton.

But if he'd been commanding his soldiers, they had escaped when they saw Mentor and understood Danny's betrayal. And if he'd shouted an order to the dragons, most of them were fighting over the coins. Jack jumped from the portico and landed in the alley.

And then the alarms started.

Sarah was seconds away from the warehouse's door when Danny, barely audible over the brawling dragons, shouted, "Secure the portal."

"*Sarah—*" Jack shouted, but she'd heard the order and changed course. As he passed the door himself, the energy field faded; she would have reached the frame too late and been trapped inside with the case.

Scores of dragons poured over the rose wall as Jack turned a corner at the back of the temple to follow Sarah. She turned north into a lane that led to the wooded hill behind the complex, but he knew it was too far away. *She's not going to make it.*

He ran as far as the lane, then slid in the gravel and picked up a stone. He couldn't possibly hold off even one dragon, but he might delay them long enough for Sarah to climb a tree. The first dragons rounded the corner, and he drew his arm back for the pitch.

With a deafening roar, a barrage of rocks and sod leaped up in front of Jack, and fireballs whipped past his head. He threw himself to the ground as balls of plasma weaved erratic paths through the lane and splashed off the temple's back wall. Some of the dragons were caught in the tide of soil and flung backwards, and those who hadn't been burned, zapped, or struck by invisible forces bolted or limped back to the alley.

The lane was eerily silent as the dust settled and Jack staggered to his feet, and he turned to find Ethan standing on the road at the end of the lane, beside Priya's car. The large crystal in the center of his staff glowed ominously, and tendrils of smoke drifted from his ring.

"What … what spell did you use?" Jack asked.

Ethan chuckled nervously through a lopsided grin. "All of them."

"*Move,*" Priya shouted.

On shaky legs, Jack ran and jumped into the ATV's cargo bed while Ethan backed away, taking occasional shots at dragons who ventured into the lane. Sarah had already taken the passenger seat beside Priya and had the case in her lap.

"Where are Jada and Marten?" Priya asked.

"China," Sarah said. "We think."

"What—"

"*Duck.*" Ethan pointed his fist and directed another blast of raw field energy at a dragon who had climbed onto the roof of the nearest building. Then he grabbed the ATV's cargo rack and hauled himself into a standing position beside Jack.

Priya hit the accelerator and sped towards the basin's only exit, but they hadn't gone far when the car suddenly lost power.

"Not again." Priya smacked the dashboard. "This happened on the way in."

"It's not the car," Jack said. "It's—" The dashboard lights flickered and its motor surged. "Later." This wasn't the time to explain a portal zone, which they seemed to be skirting the edge of.

Sarah pointed at a small brown dragon running parallel to the road. "It's Coyote."

"That's a dragon," Ethan said.

"No, *Coyote* is their name. They helped us get here. We have to help them."

Priya swerved around a bend in the road, which took them farther from the chase. "I don't think we can."

Three larger dragons trailed Coyote as they weaved among the tents and prefab buildings. They were faster than the small one, but Coyote slipped through narrow gaps between crates and other obstacles, and increased their lead.

"Wait," Jack said. "I know where they're going. Is there a grain portal here?"

"We're heading towards it," Ethan said.

"Coyote wanted Paul to go to the terminal in Seattle. They must intend to use the grain portal to get there. We have to hold off the other dragons until they escape."

"That's not—" Priya began, but Sarah interrupted. "It's important. They helped us. They helped *all* of us."

"If that portal is open," Jack said, "I'll have unlimited power."

"And if it's not?" Priya checked her rearview mirror.

So far, none of Danny's men were following, but that didn't mean there was time for planning. They'd reached the gap and the portal chamber was straight ahead, surrounded by a chainlink fence.

"Don't slow down." Ethan raised his staff. "I got the gate."

"You better have," Priya warned, and held her speed. With less range than Jack, Ethan wasn't able to force the gate open until the last second, and the car cleared the opening with only inches to spare, weaved through a space between the armored vehicles, and slid to a stop at the chamber's front door.

"I don't feel anything," Sarah said. "The portal is closed."

Jumping from the cargo bed, Jack tried to sound more hopeful than he felt. "We can fix that."

Ethan tossed his staff to Jack. "I'll hold them off." All four of his rings began to glow.

Jack directed a beam of energy and the shielded door panels swung ponderously on massive hinges. Sarah hurried inside the moment the opening was wide enough.

"Here they come," Ethan shouted.

Inside, the transport chamber had a familiar layout with its grain chute, computer terminals and electrical panels, but the portal ring itself was huge. It was currently hanging sideways over the deep pit into which grain would spill if the wormhole closed mid-transfer, and a broad ramp led to it from the floor.

"This must be how they brought the armored vehicles," Jack said.

Sarah sat at a workstation and tapped its screen. "I don't know how to work the controls."

"Just turn everything on, then," Priya said.

The three of them flipped switches, turned dials, and pressed buttons. Jack didn't know which of them had done it, but machinery in other parts of the building rumbled into life, capacitors whined, and the ring slowly tilted. It settled flat above the pit, the grain chute swung into place, and the passage opened. Through the ring, he saw bright light shining on mountains of grain fifty feet below.

"That's it," Sarah said, but then the portal closed. "What happened?" A series of lights lit the overflow pit, and air blasted through the chute to clear any dust that would have remained after a normal dump.

"*Need help out here,*" Ethan shouted.

"Don't go," Sarah pleaded as the lights in the shaft dimmed. "Coyote isn't here yet."

"*Jack!*" Ethan's voice was urgent.

"I … I'm sorry," he said, then ran to help Ethan.

As he stepped outside, Coyote staggered around his leg with an unsteady gait, and caromed off the door on their way into the chamber.

Ethan was using the four crystals in his ring to create an array of shields that spanned the gate, but that left him without a weapon. And the three large dragons that had chased Coyote were only a hundred yards from the fence. Worse, four ATVs were speeding down the road from the basin, trailing plumes of dust.

Jack lobbed a fireball. It fell short, but the dragons hesitated. And then sparks ignited against Ethan's shields. The men in the vehicles were firing at random. They had almost no chance of hitting a target at their distance, but their stray shots convinced the dragons to quit the fight.

Falling in beside Ethan, Jack raised his own shield, which allowed his cousin to overlap his set into a stronger, layered barrier. They could stop bullets now, and maybe even one speeding car, but certainly not four.

"What's our plan?" Ethan asked.

"I wish I had one." The vehicles were only ten seconds away. Nine. Eight. And then an unmistakable pressure grew at his back:

the grain portal was open. "Stand back," he shouted.

With no way of knowing how long it would last, Jack didn't waste time planning. And he was already too far away to draw on the portal's energy directly, anyway. He swung the staff around and used its smaller beam to gather the larger field. Then he thrust a massive ball of energy into the ground and scooped it into the sky.

Dirt, rocks, weeds, the gate panels, everything between him and the fence roared upwards. He spread his arms and directed the cloud into a wall that spanned hundreds of yards like a volcanic lahar. The rushing material created a vacuum, grain sucked from the transport chamber pelted his back, and a crater formed in front of him. As the soil scoured away, he stepped back to avoid falling into it.

The APCs were not so lucky, and each nosed over as the ground under their front wheels vanished like a sandcastle beneath a wave. When the energy finally faded, their back ends were pointing into the sky, and their guns were mashed into the crater wall.

Jack stooped over, panting and sweating. Controlling that much energy was a full-body exercise.

Ethan, who'd been hunkering under his shield, walked over and kicked a loose stone into the pit. "Good job, Bro. Now how do *we* get out?"

Without looking, Jack jabbed the staff at a section of fence that had been flapping like cardboard in a gale. It tipped slowly, then fell flat, creating an opening they could drive through.

Ethan nodded his approval. "That'll work."

Chapter 36

Jack didn't have enough energy to walk back to the car, so it was a good thing that Priya roared up so close beside him that he only had to flop backwards into the cargo bed. Ethan jumped in next to him, and DAVe bounced over the fallen fence panel and headed north. The dust cloud Jack had raised was settling, but was still so thick that it would be impassable for several more minutes.

"Did you destroy —" he began, then noticed the case at Sarah's feet.

"I'm sorry," she said. "The computer terminal burned out before I could get to it."

Jack saw smoke pouring from the chamber's door. "That's my fault, then. What about Coyote?"

"They're gone." Her voice was uncertain. "But they didn't seem right. They sort of … *fell* … through the portal."

"Oh, no." Jack's mechanical aptitude told him exactly what the problem was, and it wasn't good news. "That was pressurized gas in the cylinder. Danny poisoned Coyote, after all."

"No, that can't be right." Sarah seemed to be trying to convince herself. "Coyote couldn't have run—"

"Remember what I said about diffusion crystals? They're like sponges. The pressure will eventually force the poison through; it just takes a while."

"Jack's right." Ethan was uncharacteristically gloomy. "I met the woman who designed the process."

"Going through the wormhole should have broken the link," Sarah reasoned.

"It may not have been soon enough." Jack didn't add that jumping through a cargo portal while he was drawing so much energy through it was likely to be even more dangerous.

"Priya?" From the radio's tiny speaker, Davis' voice sounded both impatient and worried. "I need an update."

"I've got Jack and Sarah," she answered. "Meet us in Fairview."

"*No*," Sarah said. "We have to—" But Priya shushed her.

"What about the others?" Davis asked.

"They're … It's complicated. Tell their parents they're safe. I'll—"

Sarah grabbed Priya's arm. "We *have to* go back to the compound. Ben and Mai are in danger."

"Hold on, Davis." Priya turned to Sarah. "What compound? Who are Ben and Mai?"

Sarah relayed the events of the last week. Priya understood everything but was unyielding. "No. I'm taking you all to a safe place first."

"I don't think that exists." Jack pointed to the northernmost summit of Horseshoe Hills. Dozens of dragons, mere specks at this distance, were galloping, loping, even gliding down the hill. "We're being followed."

"They're after the case," Sarah said.

Ethan mimed tossing it out of the car. "Let 'em have it."

"No way." Though she still had to be concerned for Coyote, her voice was steady as she made her stand. "Whoever controls these crystals controls the dragons. And the dragons are controlling people on Earth." She summarized everything she and Jack had learned from Asterion and Paul, or put together themselves. "Coyote told Paul that Mentor's army was taking over Cirrus."

"And Mentor's army is dragons," Jack added.

"Right. Mentor used them to convince people that Cirrus is gone. I think they intend to keep everyone else out."

"They're not the only ones." Priya told them about the hundreds of new portals in North Korea and explained how Danny fit into that scheme. "Apparently, he has his own plans for Cirrus."

"And somehow he discovered Mentor's ID," Jack said. "So now he's controlling Mentor."

"How?" Ethan asked.

"He's got Mentor's crystal." Jack realized as he spoke how far

Danny's treachery went. "Actually, it was probably Coyote who found Mentor's ID, and Danny betrayed them, too."

"So," Ethan said, "either Danny is hoping to distract the world while he invades Cirrus, or Mentor is trying to enslave people and keep it for the dragons. Either way, *we're being chased by a murderous horde.*" He mimed tossing the case again.

"Mentor can't take over unless he controls the dragons," Sarah argued. "And Danny can't get rid of the millions of people who already live here without their help. If we destroy the crystals, *neither of them* can complete their plans. We can use the compound's grain portal."

"Did you get that, Davis?" Priya asked.

The radio was silent for a few seconds. "Well, yeah. Are you asking if I believe it?"

"Doesn't matter. We can outrun the dragons, and even beat Danny to Fairview, but we'd be putting the entire village at risk. Jack, where is the compound?"

Over the years, Jack had sent DAVe on hundreds of recovery missions within two hundred miles of Fairview. He knew the layout of the grain roads well, and told Davis where they could meet. Davis, still on the highway, would reach the spot first.

And then there was nothing left to do. The dragons had fallen behind, and they had two hours of driving during which to worry about things beyond their control: the compound guards would know they were coming; Ben's drawing predicted dragons there; and Danny was running the show.

What we really need is backup, Jack thought. *But there isn't time for that. Unless—*

He recalled Asterion's words: *Call on me and I will send aid.* He'd wondered at the time who the dragon might send. Now the answer was obvious. The pursuing dragons were loyal to Mentor, so it was safe to assume Asterion had their own followers.

He glanced at the case at Sarah's feet: the key to controlling dragons and possibly Cirrus' future. *But I never agreed to Asterion's deal, and never told them I'd find the key.* And now they were planning to destroy it. Sarah was adamant that they must.

Why does Asterion want the key? He realized the unspoken question was naïve. *They want control, or power, or whatever it is that motivates dragons. But is that what's best for us? For Cirrus?*

Without the immediate threat of dragons, Ethan seemed to have relaxed, although he still looked back occasionally while fidgeting with his ring. Regardless, Jack knew he'd ditch the case if that was the simplest option. Sarah's expression was unwavering as she gazed through the windshield; she was still determined to destroy the crystals. *Do I have the right to make another choice?* He sighed. *Good thing that's not an option.*

Except that wasn't true. What they thought of as an AI was actually the dragons themselves, and he only had to direct his thoughts properly.

They were racing towards an uncertain future, one that pitted them against Danny and an army of dragons, and Jack doubted their chances of success without help. Reluctantly, he opened a connection through the car's power cell. *'Asterion, I have the key.'*

· · · ·

"Turn there." Jack pointed out a well-worn grain road that ran eastward into the fields. "They'll be on this road."

Fifteen minutes later, he spotted Davis and Tomas standing beside another ATV. They were both armed with rifles, which did nothing to ease his mind.

"Our target," Priya said after a brief greeting, "is the grain portal south of the compound. We won't engage the guards if we don't have to. All we have to do is throw this case through the wormhole, and the dragons should leave us alone."

Tomas considered the drawing Jack had sketched on the dusty road. Approaching from the southeast, they'd be able to drive as far as the gardens. "Danny will most likely approach from the hill on the north. I'll circle around and draw the guards to that side. That should make it easier for you to reach the portal chamber."

"What about Ben and Mai?" Sarah asked.

"We're outgunned," Priya said. "There's nothing we can do for them right now."

"But—"

"*No.*" Priya's tone was sharp. "I've been far too lax with you in the past. This time, you're staying out of it."

"She's right," Jack said. "Our crystals won't work inside the portal zone." He turned to Priya. "But we can keep the cars shielded until we get there, and then protect anyone who escapes. It makes sense for us to come with you that far."

Priya agreed and decided they would stop at the edge of the zone by the gardens. But they went a bit too far, and both their vehicles, with power cells cut from the same source as Jack's wand, died as they crossed its threshold.

"This is as far as you go," Priya said. "Push the cars back and get them ready to go."

"Wait." Jack opened a tool compartment and found a pair of bolt cutters and a crowbar. "You might need these if they've locked the transport chamber."

"We'll send the workers out if we can, but don't wait for us." Priya faced Sarah and glowered. "If Danny shows up, you leave. Understood?"

Sarah nodded but didn't speak, and Jack and Ethan started pushing the cars as Priya joined her colleagues on their stealthy march.

The vehicles had been on a slope when they lost power, so it took a while to move them out of the zone. Still, Ethan had plenty of time to pace sullenly after turning them around. "How much longer?"

"They've only been gone twenty minutes," Jack said. "They'll be going slow to avoid a patrol, and Tomas has to go all the way to the other side without being spotted. It'll be—"

He didn't get a chance to finish his argument. A shrill whistle rose from the compound, followed by a loud explosion. Then colorful sparks shot high above the trees.

Sarah jumped to her feet. "That's one of my hexes." Three more explosions beat the air in quick succession, a cloud of red smoke drifted into the forest canopy, and dogs barked from their various kennels and guard posts. "Jada's back."

Chapter 37

Jack was still wondering how Jada could have returned when a shot rang out from the hill overlooking the compound's northwest corner.

Ethan ducked. "That wasn't a hex."

"That must have been Tomas," Jack said. Bursts of automatic gunfire answered from various locations in the compound. "And that'll be the guards."

Sarah had been prowling the edge of the portal zone, tracking its mood and thereby Ben's state of mind. "*Mai,*" she cried. "Ben's worried about his sister. She's in danger." Then she started running. Regardless of whether Jack and Ethan agreed, she was going to the compound.

Though he didn't know how they could help, Jack couldn't let her go alone. And the moment he crossed the threshold, he felt certain she'd made the right decision. Ben's fear was clearly reflected in the portal zone's mood.

They didn't have to worry about being spotted as they raced down the hill because various colored smokes had combined in a muddy cloud to reduce visibility to less than ten yards.

"Oh, gross." Ethan covered his nose when an acrid smell hit them. "That's a stink bomb. Why are hexes working when our crystals aren't?"

"They're not from the same source," Jack said. "Puppy must not associate them with us."

At the southeast corner, they found a large hole in the chainlink fence. "Priya must have cut it," Sarah said. "Where are they?"

Jack knew that she meant the workers, but he was worried for Priya and Davis because he hadn't sensed the grain portal opening. "Something's wrong. If Priya had been waiting for Tomas to create a distraction, she'd have entered the chamber by now."

"Let's just grab the kids and go before Danny gets here," Ethan said as he ducked through the ragged hole. Then a black shape jolted the fence near his head, and he lurched and tumbled onto his back. "*What the—*" A dragon, not much bigger than a housecat, hung from the mesh above. It hissed at him, baring inch-long fangs, then flapped away on leathery wings.

Ethan swore as he got to his feet, and Sarah sprinted for the children's yurt. In the thirty seconds it took to reach the building, dozens of dragons gathered along the fence.

"What are they waiting for?" he asked. Any of them could have easily climbed or jumped over.

That was Jack's concern, too. "They know we don't have the case, but they don't know where it is." Sporadic gunfire rattled around the compound. Still, there was no sign of Priya.

Sarah found Ben behind his table, rocking back and forth with his hands covering his ears and his eyes shut tight. Speaking gently, she asked, "Ben, where is Mai?"

Ben continued rocking silently, and Sarah checked the table for clues. She found a sketch that was still damp and brought it to Jack.

"That's Mai." He pointed to a wand-toting figure in the drawing. "And those are—"

"Hexes. She must be with Jada."

"Hey, guys." Ethan, who'd been watching the fence, backed away from the door. "They're getting bigger."

Jack leaned out of the yurt. In addition to the many small dragons, a few that were larger than dogs had arrived, and that seemed to boost the confidence of the smaller ones. They began climbing the fence, and their scales suffered only surface scratches as they pushed through the razor wire.

Sarah returned to Ben's table and kept her voice low, though she couldn't hide her unease. "I know you're scared, Ben, and I know that magic can be scary. But Mai is in trouble." She smeared a line of ink to make an X over the wand in his drawing. "Will you ask Puppy to let us use magic again?"

Ben's rocking slowed.

"Here they come," Jack said. "Close the door."

Ethan jumped inside and slammed it shut just as a large dragon landed on the yurt's roof, which creaked under their weight as they scrabbled to the peak.

Sarah folded her hands together. "Please, Ben."

The dragon on the roof started tearing at the panels around the vent, and Ethan jabbed his staff at their probing claws. "You said they knew we didn't have the case."

"They must. I don't know what they—" A movement in the blankets caught Jack's attention and he understood. "They're after Puppy." Ben's dragon companion was clearly not part of Mentor's scheme.

With the word 'Puppy', Ben's rocking stilled, and he no longer looked scared. Instead, he carefully lifted the blanket and cupped his hands for Puppy to crawl into. Jack saw his lips move and thought he heard a whisper, and then he felt the portal energy flowing.

"*Ethan—*" he began, but his cousin had already pointed his ring at the ceiling. It rang like a gong when he blasted it, and the stabbing claws vanished when the dragon went flying.

Sarah breathed a huge sigh of relief. "Thank you, Ben. You need to stay here, where you'll be safe. We'll find Mai."

Ethan knelt beside Sarah and took off his ring. "Actually, they'll be safer outside the compound." He created a weak shield and set the ring on the table. "This will protect you. All you have to do is think—"

But either Ben intuitively understood how to manage a shield, or Puppy did, and the shield grew like an inflating soap bubble. It passed over everyone around the table, leaving only Jack outside the sphere when it hardened. He rapped the translucent barrier with his knuckles. "That's a good one."

Sarah stood. "Run to the garden and wait by the cars. We'll come back with Mai."

Ben's shield shrank to enclose just himself, and Sarah and

Ethan joined Jack at the exit as another hex banged close by. Jack eased the door open and stepped outside.

While they were in the tent, dragons had poured into the compound. The one that had been on the roof was lying in the weeds next to the fence. Their tail flicked weakly, and they raised their head to snarl at Ethan.

A second dragon lay on the ground between two yurts in the inner ring, and a guard was slumped nearby. Neither of them appeared to be injured, and the man was snoring.

"The bang we heard was a stunning hex," Sarah said. Another flash colored the smoke drifting from the west, followed by a series of stars that climbed above the trees. "And that's a Roman candle."

A third sharp bang sounded from the compound's northeast corner, hundreds of yards from the last.

"How is she able to throw hexes so far?" Jack asked as he stepped onto the gravel path.

"*Wait,*" Ethan cried.

Jack felt something crunch under his foot, and the world stopped making sense. He tumbled to the ground and dug his fingers into the dirt for a handhold as his senses told him he was about to fall into the sky. *Vertigo hex,* he realized. Jada wasn't throwing hexes the length of the compound; she'd buried them like landmines.

"Grab his other arm," Sarah shouted.

Jack felt himself hoisted and tried to plant his feet, but couldn't tell what direction the ground was.

"Stop struggling, Jack," she said as they dragged him away. "It'll take a minute to wear off."

"There's another buried right there." Ethan pulled him to the side.

Jack struggled to figure out where Ethan was pointing, but words like '*there*' had little meaning at the moment, and the yurts seemed to roll and tumble past. He bumped into tables and chairs, and understood they were going through the kitchen. Hexes banged and cracked from near and far, and men and dragons screamed. And though Jack felt they were sliding downhill, Ethan navigated around buried hexes up the treeless corridor below the barracks.

"Set him down there," Sarah said.

Jack felt cool grass on his back, and the whirling sensations slowed.

"I guess you can't detect hexes like other portals," Ethan said.

"Apparently not." Jack lifted his head a little. They were across the corridor from the barracks, though it wasn't easy to see in the dense smoke. "Why did we come here?"

"Someone had to have charged the capacitors for Jada."

"Mai," Jack groaned as he sat up. With his senses hexed, he'd missed his wand's signature energy. But now that the vertigo had faded, he sensed it moving. "She's under the barracks." He started to his feet with the intent of crossing the sloping corridor, then paused when he heard a powerful engine approaching from the north gate.

An armored truck sped into the compound, slid to a stop in front of the barracks, and Danny hopped out of the driver's seat. He strode to the corridor as the cloud of dust that had trailed his vehicle settled, and four puma-sized dragons prowled into view and formed a square into which Mentor skulked. Their cowls were deep red instead of black, and Jack got the impression that they were different from other dragons. *Henchmen? Henchdragons?*

"Find that case," Danny snapped.

The four dragons didn't respond to Danny. Instead, they looked at Mentor, then three of them loped into the forest. Mentor raised their snout as if sniffing the air, turned to the bathing pool, and faced Danny.

After a second, he said, "I don't take orders from you now. I'll wait for him here." His thumb brushed the red plunger on the baton's handle. "You go look for the others."

Jack couldn't sense whatever negotiation had just taken place, but Mentor's body language changed as they stalked towards the pool with their remaining guardian.

"What was that about? Ethan asked.

"See that red button on the handle of Danny's baton? That's the gas cylinder with Mentor's crystal." Then he noticed his wand moving again. "Mai's coming. I'll circle around and—"

"Wait." Ethan grabbed his shirt.

Davis stepped out of the woods across the corridor, exactly where Jack had intended to go. Aiming his rifle at Danny, he shouted, "On the ground! Now!"

"Oh, no." Jack sensed an energy surge building in Danny's baton and leaped from his hiding spot. *"Davis—"*

Too late. An invisible beam struck Davis and sent him tumbling downhill. He hit the ground hard and only stopped rolling when he collided with a yurt, where he clutched his ribs and moaned.

Exposed and defenseless, Jack sensed energy multiplying on two sides, and froze.

Danny's blast should have crossed the space between them in a fraction of a second. It should have met Ethan's shield as his cousin leaped into the corridor, but none of that happened. Instead, both crystals dimmed.

The magic was gone. Again.

Chapter 38

Jack spared only a moment to work out that Puppy must have sensed Danny's attack and shut down every crystal in the zone. But Ethan and Danny wasted no time at all; their weapons worked regardless.

Danny tried to cut Jack off before he could cross the corridor, but Ethan blocked him with a furious spinning strike that carried his weight through to an uphill landing.

In danger of losing the higher ground, Danny abandoned his pursuit, and he and Ethan fought their way to the top of the hill trading jabs and strikes against blocks and parries.

Racing around the sparring pair, Jack couldn't sense his wand anymore, but Mai had been heading for the small parking lot on the far side of the barracks. He ran past Danny's armored truck and stopped on the road. "Mai?"

If the girl heard him, she didn't answer. *Could she have left the compound?* A pair of ATVs was parked in the corner formed by the barracks and the fence, and the gate, another fifty yards to the east, was open. Jack started in that direction, then ducked when a dark shape whizzed over his head.

"Hugo? What are you—" Then Arven swooped past and landed by one of the ATVs. He hopped and flapped several times beside its wheels while making a croaking sound.

"Go away," Mai whispered.

Jack dropped to his knees and peered under the vehicle. "Mai?" She was curled into a ball and looked terrified. She must have crawled under when Danny arrived. "C'mon, it's safe. Take my hand."

Mai shook her head and pointed. "It is not safe."

He whirled around and saw a red-cowled dragon, one of Mentor's personal guards. They were lean and powerful looking, like a scaled puma, and already in a crouched position with their claws rooted in the soil. If he'd had time to think, Jack still couldn't have imagined what sort of prey they were meant to control. He tried to stand but his foot skidded in the dirt, and he succeeded only in pushing himself back against the ATV's bumper.

Arven took off with a squawk, the dragon leaped, and Jack lunged to the side an instant before a thunderclap of scales exploded over his head. As he rolled away, he saw that the cowled dragon had been knocked off course by another: *Asterion.*

Howling and screeching, Asterion and the other crashed into the second ATV with enough force to raise two of its wheels off the ground. Mai screamed and scrambled from her shelter just as the dragons bounced into it, but their brawl then carried them into the road and cut off her escape.

With Asterion being double the other's mass, the odds should have been in their favor. But the smaller dragon was unbelievably quick, and not only did they avoid Asterion's claws, they drew first blood with a lightning-fast swipe against the larger dragon's flank. That forced Asterion to retreat, and Jack rushed in to grab Mai when the other dragon followed.

He took her hand. "Your brother's in the garden. I'll take you to him."

"Do not step there." Mai pointed at a patch of loose soil as Jack led her away.

Thinking that Mai must have helped Jada bury hexes, Jack skipped over the spot and started for the gate. He'd taken only a few steps when another dragon raced through it. Then a second. And a third. And then— *"Blue."*

In seconds, Ben's drawing came to life as Blue and dozens more dragons streamed past. They were as varied in color and shape as those at Mentor's enclave, but each wore a narrow collar instead of a cowl. These were Asterion's dragons.

The new dragons ignored Jack and Mai, and even the increasingly bloody battle between Asterion and Mentor's guardian. The sounds of dragon-on-dragon battles spread through the compound, and the automatic gunfire dwindled to single shots.

"They're fighting Mentor's followers," Jack said.

Mai pointed into the haze beyond the fence. "Who is that?"

The person hurrying past along the river was obscured by smoke, but they were carrying a silver case.

"Priya," Jack shouted. She either didn't hear or was too focused on her own goal to respond, and she faded from view. "The grain portal must be closed. She's heading for the pool."

Jack stopped outside the gate. "Priya is a police officer. I have to help her. Run to the garden and—" he began, before realizing Mai wouldn't be safe alone. And with the way she was gripping his hand; she wouldn't have left anyway. He faced an impossible decision: abandon his friends, or leave Mai.

Mai dipped her hand into a pocket and withdrew a handful of hexes. "I can help."

Jack was momentarily stunned, then almost laughed when he worked out what had happened. Jada hadn't returned, after all. It was Mai all along. She had gotten past the guards, into the barracks, retrieved the box of hexes, and buried them around the compound. And she'd done it with only the feeble ambient energy of the zone. She must have been up all night, working entirely on her own.

"You're right," Jack said. "You *can* help. Stay close to me."

Mai followed him along the fence as the sounds of Danny and Ethan's battle overwhelmed even the howls of Asterion's struggle in the parking lot. At first, the ferocity was confusing until Jack sensed the water portal's unique signature. Puppy hadn't shut that one down, and they had reinforced their wooden weapons with raw energy.

As he came into view of the bathing pool, Jack spotted Priya again. She'd just pitched the case over the fence. However, at nearly thirty pounds, it splashed down only a few feet away, disappeared, then bobbed to the surface. Immediately, he heard more splashing. Someone was swimming towards it.

A random gust of wind stirred the smoke and briefly cleared

Jack's view of the pool. The grate over the channel was open, Sarah was chasing the case, and Ethan was backing onto the bridge pursued by Danny. They were both drawing vast amounts of portal energy, and the collisions of their mass-shifted weapons created shockwaves that reverberated in his chest.

Unfortunately, Mentor's dragons had seen the case, too. They streamed through the gate and would have reached the pool in seconds if Asterion's crew hadn't arrived at the same time. Half a dozen new battles began with dragons wrestling furiously at the water's edge.

The air settled and the smoke thickened, and Jack was still too far from the portal to harness its energy, so he ran to stand with Priya. Abruptly, she drew her pistol; a black-cowled dragon was splashing towards them through the creek.

Priya fired and the beast turned aside. Though her bullet hadn't penetrated the dragon's shield, the excess force would have been a hammer blow.

"Aim for the tail." Jack had seen the contours of the dragon's shield in the spray of droplets.

The dragon was bracing for another charge when Priya took her second shot. That one struck the creature's unprotected tail, drawing blood and sending them into full retreat.

Jack risked a glance over his shoulder. Sarah was only seconds away from the case, but the battle behind her was more urgent: Ethan was tiring. He stumbled backwards as Danny forced him to the middle of the span.

"Mai," Jack crouched to look her in the eyes. "I have to help Ethan. Stay with Priya."

He tried to pull her into position behind the detective, but then three more of Mentor's dragons fanned out across the creek. Two of them wore red cowls, and flames flickered from their crystals, foreshadowing a coordinated attack.

Priya saw the flames, too. She wavered for only a moment before hardening her stance and aiming her pistol. "No, take Mai with you. I'll hold them off while you escape."

"But—" An intense flash of light burst against one of the dragon's shields, temporarily blinding them. A split second later, another hex exploded and splashed a dragon with hot glue. Jack knew instantly that Mai was responsible, but her speed was astonishing. Two more hexes detonated around the dragons as Mai thumbed them from her stack like a card dealer, and accelerated them using the ambient field.

Priya, seeing that Mai had stalled the dragons, shouted, "Go!"

Jack dove into the gap under the fence as the air filled with cayenne powder, expanding foam, mini tornadoes, and other non-lethal spells. He surfaced on the other side and heard a gunshot. He might have looked back if the shot hadn't been followed by the cry of a wounded dragon; or Ethan hadn't fallen; or if Mentor wasn't stalking onto the bridge from the opposite end.

Though the pool was only five feet deep, the case was bulky and Sarah was struggling. She was still thirty feet from the portal frame when Danny brought his baton down on Ethan's desperate, two-handed overhead block. Ethan's staff snapped in two, and Danny raised his arm for the killing strike.

Time slowed for Jack.

He had no weapon, and though he wasn't close enough for proper control of the energy field, he instinctively directed every ounce of force he could at the only object in range: the case. It rose and arced towards Danny, and looked for a moment as if it would strike him. But he and Ethan—so much closer to the wormhole—were pulling too much energy, and the case plunged as his power waned. The case would pass through the open portal, the crystals would be destroyed and the dragons saved, but Ethan—

Danny suddenly leaped from the bridge in a reckless gamble to save the case. He actually got his hands on it before colliding mid-air with Mentor, who had tried the same thing, and all three fell into the channel.

"*Jack,*" Sarah cried, "get out of the water." She was already heading for shore, having fashioned a wavering shield between her and the portal. "It's going to collapse!"

It didn't require a Traveller-memory to see what was about to happen. The mass drifting towards the wormhole was unbalanced, and a failure could be explosive.

The closest exit for Jack was the fence, and he swam to it furiously while Danny and Mentor fought and the current dragged them to the frame. Ethan, exhausted, was defenseless and half-hanging from the bridge deck with one of his arms already in the water. Jack had only just pulled himself halfway up when the wormhole collapsed.

A giant plume shot from the pool and a concussion wave hit Jack's submerged legs, knocking him off the fence. The impact—from sixty feet away—had felt like falling off a roof, and he had difficulty standing as clods of mud rained down on him.

"*Sarah!*" Jack scanned the pool frantically; she'd been closer to the blast and her shield had been weak. But even the dragons had stopped fighting, and the only thing he heard was muddy rain. He started to swim to where he'd last seen her when she burst from the water, gasping.

She spotted Jack immediately, and her expression matched the relief he felt. Then she looked at the bridge. "Where's Ethan?"

Jack turned. The bridge deck, cracked and bowed, was clear except for one half of Ethan's splintered staff. "Ethan?" There was no reply. "*Ethan!*"

After splashing through the shallower water, Sarah scrambled onto the bridge, which sagged under Jack's weight as he followed. They struggled to remove the deck plate, which had been warped by the force of the collapsing wormhole. Underneath, the ring was intact, but the perforated baffles at the ends of the channel had been blown off, and the faster current had swept the passage clear. Downstream, though, a pink froth floated on the pool's surface: blood.

"*Ethan!*" Sarah shouted.

The entire half of the pool downriver was still murky, and Jack could see nothing in the water and couldn't sense a crystal. Then a piece of wood floated to the surface: part of Ethan's staff, with a perfectly smooth end where it had been sliced by the wormhole.

Jack dove into the pool and groped blindly for the bottom. He sensed Sarah moving nearby, and together they raked the muddy riverbed but found nothing. His lungs were demanding that he draw a breath when he heard a rhythmic thumping.

Sarah surfaced beside him, gasping for air, but she'd already spotted the source of the sound: a pylon that should have been supporting the bridge's deck was slapping a regular beat against the channel wall. "He's under the bridge!"

Jack dove again and followed the sound. The water was clearing now, and he could see the shadow cast by the bridge ahead. He was still a dozen strokes away when the thumping stopped.

The final yards seemed like miles, and if Sarah hadn't been there beside him, he might have panicked. Instead, they quickly found his cousin tangled in the bridge's twisted beams. He wasn't moving.

Jack braced his feet against an intact pylon and pulled back the one Ethan had been shifting, while Sarah dragged him out of the wreckage. She slapped her fingers against his neck as Jack lifted him onto his shoulders. "He's still got a pulse."

Priya was sprinting across the bridge when they heaved Ethan onto it. "I got him," she shouted as he landed flat on his back and coughed up a mouthful of cloudy water. She rolled him over as he started gagging and helped him hang his head off the deck where he could retch into the water. One of Ethan's arms, the one Jack had seen hanging close to the wormhole, was bright red and swollen, but at least it was still there. And he had somehow kept hold of a chunk of his staff, which had been sliced only inches from his fingers.

The dragons, Mentor's and Asterion's, were filing out of the enclosure as he and Sarah reached the shore. "They must have sensed the case going through the wormhole," Jack said. "They're free."

Sadly, not all of them survived the conflict. A black-cowled dragon and another with a webbed collar lay unmoving on the hill. Many others bore grievous injuries, and tears filled Sarah's eyes. "Where's Asterion?"

Jack headed for the gate, fearing what he might find on the other side of the barracks.

"There's a lot of blood here," Sarah said as they passed Danny's truck. She reached down and picked up a torn black cowl, which was split right through where its coin would have been.

Jack pointed out a line of scratches on the ground. "One of them dragged the other's body away."

"Was it Asterion?"

Somewhere above the forest canopy, a raven cried, and Jack got an impression of the grain transport chamber. "No, they're alive. And they want me to find them." Looking over the compound at the dwindling smoke and the frightened workers staring from their yurts, he asked, "Can you take care of things here?"

Sarah wiped mud off her face. Davis was escorting a group of battered guards towards the barracks, while Tomas guided the rest of them through the north gate, followed by Mai and Priya. Her voice was shaded with sadness and relief when she finally answered. "Go. We'll be okay."

Chapter 39

How did Asterion find this place? Jack wondered as he trekked from the compound. *And how did they arrive only hours after I called them?* The answer became clear when he entered the grain transport chamber and spotted Hugo perched on a workstation next to the dragon: he'd asked the raven to send help days ago. Asterion hadn't even waited for Jack to accept the deal they'd discussed.

"Thank you," he said to both the raven and the dragon.

Hugo shook his head and made a series of clicks, but Asterion didn't look up. Their scales were badly scratched, and their wounds were deep, though no longer bleeding. Sitting quietly, they stared into the dark overflow pit in the center of the room. Jack sensed a mix of emotions from them, and also noticed he'd been mistaken about the pit. The grain chute was in its docked position against a wall, exposing an inky circle on the floor that was so black it didn't seem to exist.

"What *is* that?" Jack reached for the expected energy field and found nothing. The control panel gauges showed the portal frame was consuming power, so the opening was definitely a wormhole, but at the same time, it wasn't. It was like looking into a mirror and not seeing his own reflection. "Where does it go?"

'It does not.' Asterion's voice was strong and vivid in his mind.

"A wormhole to nowhere." Jack knelt beside it. "How is that possible?"

'When you destroyed the crystals, you freed dragons from Mentor's influence. Most of them severed the links in their domains.'

"Their domains? You mean there are compounds like this one in other portal zones?"

'Mentor's ambition was to build in *every* zone.'

"And there are dragons there, too?"

'We have always known of these places. The first of us made our homes there.'

The first of us? How old was Asterion? "You said *most* dragons cut the link. Does that mean there are still working portals back to Earth?"

'Like your people, dragons do not always agree. Though some approved of Mentor's plan to enslave the humans Danny would bring to Cirrus, others believed we could live in peace.'

Jack reeled under the imagery that accompanied Asterion's speech. Their direct-to-mind communication carried so much more information than mere words could, and he saw Mentor's scheme as Asterion knew it: millions of invading North Koreans, mostly innocent farmers, would spread across Cirrus. Backed by an army of dragons, they'd displace the Cirrans and raze their cities. Jack's family, friends, and neighbors would have no choice but to flee to Dawn. Apparently, Mentor already had a crystal Pieter used for that purpose. Then they would close the spaceports, preventing anyone from taking back their prize.

"What do *you* believe?" Jack was already worried about Asterion's motives. Though they hadn't actually *lied* about the key, they hadn't been forthcoming with their intentions, either. And their revelation that Mentor intended to enslave humans wasn't reassuring. Of course, when Jack called on Asterion, he only said he *had* the key, not that he would hand it over. So, neither of them had been completely honest.

'Humans bring both order and chaos.' Asterion said. 'Before Niels arrived and wandered the myriad pathways of Icarus' portal zone, I could only use those connections to speak to my kin. His travels strengthened the links and I found other minds, foreign minds.'

"Travellers. You shared their memories."

'And learned of Earth.'

Jack realized that Mentor had been planning for a very long time, too. They were the master of Horseshoe's portal zone, meaning they'd been *one of the first*, and had known of Travellers for decades.

He stood and faced Asterion. "You didn't really need *me* to stop Danny, did you? Mentor would have eventually dealt with him."

Asterion met his eyes. 'I need *you* to understand the danger.'

"Danger? Does that mean this isn't over? And why *me*?"

'You stand at a crossroads.'

Though Asterion's words were brief, Jack knew what they meant. Now, more than ever, he had the ability to return Cirrus to the people of Earth. "I feel like I've been there for a long time."

'You can restore Danny's frames and prove Cirrus exists.'

Jack nodded. "I could. People would definitely use them. Davis would go home in a heartbeat. Then people from Earth would—" What *would* they do? They had Dawn now. Who would migrate to Cirrus? "Dawn is open to everyone, regardless of how much money they have. But the people who built Cirrus will want it back, and they'll treat it like a resort. Only the privileged will come here." He wasn't sure what that meant for him or his friends. Would they have a secure future on a revitalized and exploited Cirrus? "Do I have the right to make that choice?"

'Who does?' Asterion's gaze returned to the wormhole.

"The people who built it? Those who have lived here for decades? Dragons?" *Dragons.* Jack realized it didn't matter who came to Cirrus; they would learn about dragons. They'd find out that their leaders had been influenced—maybe even controlled— by dragons. Even if that were no longer true, they wouldn't trust them. There would be no peace.

He circled the frame and saw the body of the dragon Asterion had fought. "What will you do with …" He paused, unsure how to refer to the other. But his attention to the dead dragon was equivalent to speaking their name, and Asterion stirred.

'Death is uncommon for our kind. We do not have rituals.' Asterion was quiet for a long time. 'And we do not kill each other. I am compelled to do something … respectful.'

Jack recalled what Ethan had learned from Nour about dragons' longevity. Asterion had used the phrase: *the first of us,* but they couldn't be older than Cirrus itself. It was possible they were his age and had never experienced the loss of a friend. He glanced at the wormhole and understood what the dragon intended. "I can help."

Asterion shook their head ponderously. 'This task is mine.'

Jack felt energy flowing from the wormhole as the deceased dragon's body rose over the frame. It hung motionless there, shielded from Cirrus' gravity, until a gentle push from Asterion caused it to descend. Its tail drooped and disappeared from view, as if sinking into a giant pot of ink that refused to ripple, and scintillating lights limned the corpse as it sank into the void.

• • • •

The workers who had fled to the garden were returning to the compound when Jack went looking for Sarah. Of course, they weren't *workers* anymore. They, and the dragons, were free. They could go home now.

He sensed energy radiating from the water portal and saw Priya standing at the top of the hill with two others; Jada and Marten had come back while he was away. That was great news. Not only were they safe, Puppy hadn't permanently cut off passage to Earth.

"I see Ethan has made a new friend," Jack said when he found Sarah in the clearing. She'd already recovered her wand and earrings.

Kneeling next to Mai at the firepit, Ethan guided her clenched fist towards it, and a torch erupted from his ring, which she was currently wearing. She squealed with delight as flames played over the logs. Ben was there too, clapping his hands and bouncing on his toes while Puppy clung to his shoulder.

"She's been calling him *Big Brother*," Sarah said.

Jack watched Ethan teaching magic for a while longer. His arm was bruised from his wrist to his elbow, but that didn't dampen his enthusiasm.

"So, what happens now?" Sarah asked.

He'd been wondering the same thing and took a moment to

answer. "Well, we already knew that Danny built hundreds of compounds. But Asterion says it was Mentor who decided where they should go, and that all of them are in natural portal zones."

"So there's going to be an invasion?"

"No. Dragons are attracted to the zones the way they are to crystals. And like Puppy, they can close any wormhole there. No one's getting to or from Cirrus without their permission. Asterion wants—" He paused. Davis was entering the clearing with Priya, and he appeared happier than Jack had ever seen him.

"Well, Jack." Davis extended his hand. "This is goodbye."

"You're leaving?" Jack suspected that *leaving* didn't mean he was going back to Caerton.

"Jada ran into Mai's mother almost immediately," Priya said. "She'll be coming through as soon as the portal recharges. Apparently, she'd received a tip about the portal's location from an American."

Jack grinned. "That had to be Paul. He said he would send someone for Jada and Marten."

"Probably," Priya grudgingly admitted. "He *is* good at finding people."

"Won't it be strange, you showing up when you're supposed to be on Cirrus?" Jack asked Davis.

"I'm going to say I was captured after following one of Danny's thugs to North Korea before Newton. That way I can claim I saw Danny, which fits with Priya's story that he returned to Earth." He smirked and said, "I only just made my heroic escape against overwhelming odds."

Sarah hugged Davis. "I'm so happy for you. Your family will be thrilled. And now that you've got a good explanation, you can come back anytime."

"Hey, that's right." He faced Priya. "You'll let me use Holden's portal now?"

"Yeah, I guess." Priya's response suggested that was just one more complication she'd have to deal with. "But you have to get yourself back to the States first."

Sarah turned to Priya. "What about you?"

"I haven't decided. It sounds like Pieter may have found his way to Dawn. I want to follow up on that."

"What about the people here?" Sarah swept her arm across the compound. "What about—"

"It's okay." Priya captured Sarah's hands and held them reassuringly. "There will be time. I promise. Many of Danny's contractors know about Cirrus. I doubt he left much solid evidence, but there'll be rumors and questions that need to be buried, so I'll be hanging around for a while yet."

Sarah calmed and let Priya walk away with Davis. "She's right," Jack said. "A lot of people know that Cirrus still exists. And not just regular people; Travellers. Sooner or later they'll figure out how to communicate with Earth."

"That's something we need to discuss." Jack took Sarah's hand and gestured for her to follow, then called to Ethan. "We're going to get the car. We'll be back soon."

Ethan gave Jack an exaggerated wink. "Okay, sure. Getting the car. *I* know what that means."

Sarah aimed a shield-enclosed bubble of water at Ethan, but he deflected it easily before it burst and expanded into an enveloping cloud of icy fog.

Mai clapped her hands in delight and tugged Ethan's arm. "Teach me that one, big brother. I want to learn clouds."

As he and Sarah walked, they passed former workers happily carrying their few belongings across the compound.

"Where are they going?" Jack wondered aloud.

"They're moving into the second set of yurts," Sarah said, then stopped abruptly. "That's the first Traveller-memory I've had since we found this place. I guess shutting down the zone interfered with them."

"That's why I couldn't tell what Arven saw when he flew over. And—" Jack realized it also explained how both Danny and Mentor had failed to foresee the wormhole collapse.

If Sarah understood the same thing, she chose not to dwell on it. "I'm not surprised they're staying. Some of the Chinese were political prisoners. And the North Koreans lived in awful conditions. Why wouldn't they make this their home?"

Without smoke, gunfire, or barking dogs, the garden path was a pleasant place for a walk. A cool breeze flowed from the Spine, the trees were full of chattering birds, and they caught glimpses of the endless fields of grain. It was a comforting sight to Jack, who had lived most of his life surrounded by the tranquility of those fields.

"Asterion wants us to decide Cirrus' fate," he said. "Most of Danny's portals were destroyed by the dragons, but they can be restored—we have plenty of Third-Eye coins. All we need is for Paul to find one of the set on Earth."

Sarah didn't answer right away, and they were within sight of the car before she finally spoke. "Do we have the right to say who can or cannot come to Cirrus?"

That had always been Jack's concern. "Asterion didn't ask us to destroy the key, you know? They only asked us to bring it to them."

"So they'd have ruled Cirrus, just like Mentor?"

"Maybe not the same as Mentor. But if they didn't, someone else would." Knowing what Asterion wanted, he added, "I'm not a leader. I can't tell anyone what to do."

"Don't count yourself short. You defeated Pieter. Twice. And you helped the dragons before any of us knew they were intelligent. There's more to leading than telling people what to do; you lead by example."

Jack sighed. "If we don't do something about Danny's portals, someone else will. There are most likely Travellers living in every zone, and—like you said—they'll eventually learn how to contact Earth. Asterion wants me to convince them not to open a passage."

"When?"

"Well, there are ten to twenty zones in each sector. To start, I can work from Icarus, but then I'll have to travel. It'll take weeks just to get to the other side of the ring, assuming there are even roads. Altogether, it's going to take years."

"Did you have other plans?"

"No, but …" Jack felt himself blush. "Did you?"

"Are you asking if I'd go with you?"

"I guess."

Sarah pulled his arm and made him face her. "Then ask."

Jack was nervous as he gazed into her eyes, but reassured by her coy smile. "I'm going on a trip soon."

"Ooh, *lucky you*. Where?"

Jack laughed, then forced himself to continue. "Far away. Places where I don't even speak the language."

"Good thing you've got access to an AI to translate for you." A mechanical voice repeated Sarah's words in Tagalog from one of her earrings.

"I've got no money for food."

She gestured at an orchard downslope from the garden. "On a world literally designed to feed a billion people."

"Or lodging."

"I've seen you sleep in a car."

"It'll be dangerous."

She sparked a flame from her wand. "Sounds like fun."

"There'll be monsters." He added in an ominous tone, "*Dragons*."

She scoffed. "Who's afraid of dragons?"

"I'll be gone for months at a time." Jack stared at the ground for a moment to remove his grin, took both her hands, and asked as seriously as he could, "Will you come with me?"

When Sarah gazed back at him, he saw years of friendship and trust reflected in her eyes. Then she shrugged. "Meh, I don't know. It sounds—"

Jack abruptly pulled her in for a kiss, and she wrapped her arms around his neck and kissed him back. He was aware of his heart racing against her chest for a few beats before that sensation merged with the rest: her warm body, silky hair, and soft but firm embrace.

After either a moment or an eternity, Sarah leaned back. "Yes. I'll go with you."

He pretended to be overwhelmingly relieved. "Good. Because if you didn't, I'd have to ask Ethan."

She slugged him playfully. "He'll probably come with us anyway."

Despite the challenges they'd face, Jack was no longer anxious about the future. He walked hand-in-hand with Sarah past the gardens and they stopped at an overlook. Beyond the idyllic fields, a plume of black smoke stained the horizon.

"Asterion spoke with dragons at Horseshoe before I left. Mentor's temple is burning." It was a sobering sight and reminded Jack that they still had work to do here.

Sarah must have been thinking the same. "Does Asterion know if Coyote survived?"

"They said we haven't heard the last of them."

"That's great." She looked perplexed. "It just occurred to me. Does Paul know Coyote is a dragon?"

Jack laughed and squeezed her hand. "I'm sure he does now."

Epilogue

Paul slewed his jeep off the road and sped into the parking lot opposite the grain terminal. Skidding on the wet pavement, he had the door open even before the vehicle completely stopped.

Coyote's voice—if that was a suitable term for what he sensed—had been urgent, and Paul was racked by guilt. He'd convinced Coyote to help, and that made him partially responsible for Coyote getting caught, and possibly injured.

He ran to the same hole he'd cut in the fence yesterday. But even before he ducked through, he noticed differences around the terminal. To begin with, it was silent.

Yesterday, there had been guards patrolling the terminal grounds, and heavy machinery loading grain onto trains. Now the conveyors were still, the loaders unmanned, and the huge bay doors into the receiving chamber stood open to the rising sun.

Paul moved quickly over the railway tracks and across the concrete loading zone, then stopped at the door to the vast terminal, where dozens of grain piles formed an undulating golden-yellow landscape. The portal frames fixed to the ceiling were just that: frames. Instead of the grain that used to pour from them twenty-four hours a day, or even the light of distant chambers, he could see ceiling girders through empty rings. He stepped inside and heard his footfalls echo from the high steel walls.

"Coyote?"

There was no reply.

Paul poked the toe of his boot into loose wheat on the floor. The adjacent chamber was filled with rice, and the one past that collected canola. He was in the right spot, but where was Coyote?

He'd always found his quarry, person or object, through a blend of logic and intuition. If Coyote had come through a portal while the terminal was active, logic wouldn't identify which grain pile he was buried in. It was time for intuition. He relaxed and brought to mind memories of his youth, when he'd first discovered his talent. He could almost smell cedar and sage, and hear the drums and the songs. And then there was the voice.

Sometimes, as it was now, the voice was wordless though its meaning was clear. He angled across the immense room and skirted one of the shorter piles, which brought him to the base of another. The voice wanted him to climb, so that's what he did, and the shushing sound of grain streaming past reinforced the voice. He was close. Digging with his hands, he pushed the wheat aside to create twin funnels that collapsed the slope and exposed an unfamiliar shape.

"What *are* you?"

Paul had assumed Coyote was a man, and it would have made no difference to him if they were a woman, but the scaly flesh before him was neither. And yet, there was the voice: beckoning, insistent. *This* was Coyote. He splashed the surrounding grain away, revealing its true form, which was like nothing he had ever seen.

About the size of a small dog, its scales were shades of brown and tan. It had no visible ears, bony ridges above its eyes, and a single row of rounded bumps that ran from the base of the skull to the tip of the tail, which was as long as its body. The mouth was partially open, exposing pointy teeth and long incisors. The curved claws were cat-like, but thicker and mostly black.

The creature's chest rose and fell as Paul slid it from its grainy tomb. *Still alive, then.* Leaning closer, he inspected the black collar around its neck and found an empty slot on the front that was exactly the size of a standard coin portal.

Months ago, when Coyote led Paul to acquire the black-market coin cells, he—it?—had told him to keep a pair for when they finally met. Paul hadn't asked why, and now he removed one from his keychain and slid it into the collar's receptacle.

The creature stirred, then blinked. It raised its head slowly, painfully, and met Paul's astonished gaze.

'Hello, Paul.'

That voice. It was the one he'd heard most of his life, the one that helped him find things, the one he'd been hearing more clearly for weeks. His intuition told him he didn't have to speak aloud. '*Coyote?*'

Coyote's mouth stretched to the dragon equivalent of a grin. 'Are you ready to have some fun?'

Paul and Coyote will return in

THE TRAVELLER EFFECT

ABOUT THE AUTHOR

John Harvey is a First Nations author from British Columbia. He trained as an Electronic Engineering Technologist and worked for decades in Information Technology and Healthcare Support Services before turning to writing and freelance editing. He writes mostly science-fiction and fantasy.

The Cirrus Chronicles

Broken Sky

Blue Spell

Scattered

Your reviews are important.

If you enjoyed this book, please take a moment to rate or review it on Goodreads, your favorite book retailer, or any social media platform.